TREE OF AGES

BOOK ONE IN THE TREE OF AGES SERIES

SARA C ROETHLE

To Jesse, because I know you've been waiting for one.

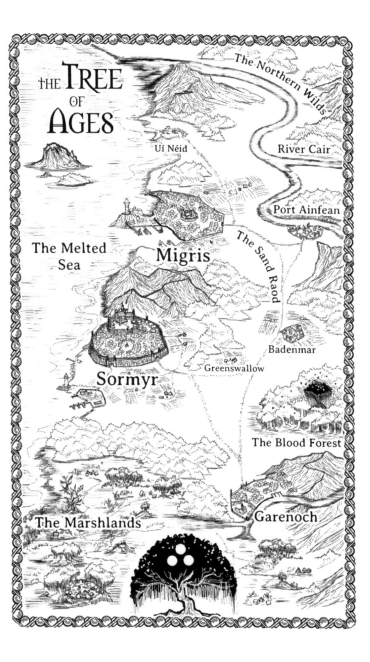

THE TREE
OF
AGES

The Northern Wilds

Uí Néid

River Cair

Port Ainfean

The Melted
Sea

Migris

The Sand Raod

Badenmar

Greenswallow

Sormyr

The Blood Forest

The Marshlands

Garenoch

CHAPTER ONE

*A*s the first hints of pinkish sunlight crept over the horizon, Finn shivered into awareness. She was glad for the sunlight. Though the solstice had long since passed, winter still hung on, making the days short and dark. She reached her branches up toward the sky, searching for a hint of warmth. What she felt was cold like she had never experienced. She searched down through her roots for the usual heat provided by the deep earth and felt . . . nothing. Then she fell over. She had never done that before. The sunlight winked out of existence.

When Finn awoke, the sun was halfway across the sky. It was at that blindingly bright point of the day that she always enjoyed the most. Yet her insides were so cold, she barely felt its heat. Insides? Her insides were usually more solid than her outsides. And why was her vision so . . . so, conical? It must have happened in the fall. Oh gods, she had fallen. So why wasn't she dead?

Feeling unstable, she tried desperately to force her roots back into the ground. She tried so desperately that suddenly her trunk spasmed. She folded right in half, and almost lost sight of the sky again at what she saw.

Those things attached to her trunk. Those were *not* roots. Those were *legs*. People legs. Finn squirmed frantically in a futile attempt to escape the people legs. She froze, then with terrified slowness moved one of her branches in front of her. She had a great deal more movement than she could ever have imagined. Normally she could only move in tiny increments in order to twitch her leaves toward the sun. Slowly her limbs came into view. It was as she suspected. Her branches were now people arms, and she only had two of them. How was she supposed to survive with only two branches?

Moisture rolled down what she supposed was now her face. She had seen such a thing happen to a person before, but she couldn't quite remember what it meant. She supposed it meant she was dying, and given what was happening, she welcomed the idea. She curled up into a little ball, tried to dig herself down into the dirt, and there Finn stayed as blackness took her again.

"Wake up lassy," a scratchy voice whispered.

Something shook her, making Finn dizzy with the movement. She opened her eyes and was once again overcome with a great sense of loss. Her vision was dim and narrow compared to before.

Her new eyes took in a gray-bearded old man. He wore a slouched grayish hat that looked suspiciously like a hempen potato sack. Its frayed ends intertwined with his dark silver hair, which melded with his gray woolen robes. The man's face was creased with kind lines, and his eyes shone a bright, cornflower blue. The eyes looked strange in contrast to the shimmering flow of his muted silver hair. She had seen the man before. Just as she had seen many men before.

"Yer bound to freeze to death lying there like that," the old man went on, consternation plain on his face. "Ye best get up and come with me."

She opened her mouth, oh gods, she had a mouth, and tried to speak. She knew the language from listening to it over the years while she watched hunters and other folk from the nearby farms of Greenswallow in her glen. Yet, she had never imagined she would have a need to speak it.

"Who-" she began, but the words felt sticky in her mouth.

"Who am I?" the old man finished for her. "Àed is me name. I live not far off. Ye best come with me so ye might warm by me fire."

Finn shook her head. "I'm lost," she lied. Her voice was much softer than the man's. It made her cringe, not because of its softness, but simply because she had a voice.

"Dinnae be silly," the old man replied. "I saw ye turn from a tree. Yer in the only place ye have ever known, at least for a very long time."

Finn blinked up at him slowly. "You saw?" she asked, the

3

words forming more smoothly. "Do you know why it happened? Can you put me back?"

Àed shook his head sorrowfully. "I've no such power. Right now I can only help ye to stay warm. Now let's try and get ye up, lass."

More moisture streamed down Finn's face, but she let the old man take hold of her arms. He slowly helped her to stand. She nearly fell several times, but finally found her balance. It felt good to be upright again, even if she was much shorter than before. She looked down at the old man and realized she could see clear over his head. At least she wasn't *that* short. With a kind smile, Àed placed her hand on his shoulder so that she might use him for balance, and they began a slow procession toward a small stone hovel in the distance.

"I've never seen that house there before," Finn commented, the words feeling slightly less strange to her.

Àed gave a slight shrug. "Been there a long time, but it was likely out of sight for ye at yer . . . previous angle."

Finn supposed that was true. She thought back to the view she had as a tree. She could see the glen. She'd watched it year after year, as its colors turned from vibrant green, to pale yellow, then back again. She could see other trees, though none of them ever communicated with her, and she could see the distant mountains. Their shape was a vivid memory for her. She had let her sight wander along their edges for so long. They were the only thing in the glen that never truly changed.

As the pair walked farther from the spot where she had taken root as a sapling, she began to look around at all of the other things she couldn't see before. This new form limited the span of her sight, but movement helped to expand it. She realized with a start that she could go see anything she wanted. She could see the distant mountains up close. She could see *past* the mountains. She wasn't sure whether or not she actually liked the idea.

They reached the small home. It wasn't as shabby as it had seemed from a distance. The front yard was enclosed in shrubbery, obscuring part of the building from view. The walls were made from good sized stones held together by mortar. She wondered how she knew what mortar was. She hadn't recalled seeing it before. How had she thought the shack shabby, when she had nothing else to compare it to? Surely this new form was causing her to lose her mind. She pushed the thoughts away as Àed opened the house's wooden door and drew her inside.

The first thing she felt was warmth. It was a different sort of warmth than what she usually felt from the sun, sort of all-encompassing. A small, dark colored, metal stove sat in the far corner of the house, with a metal pipe connected to the low ceiling. Finn could see the flames through the side of the stove's metal hatch. The flames frightened her, naturally, yet the warmth was delicious.

Finn took her hand off Àed's shoulder, and stumbled a little closer to the stove. She stumbled all the way to the floor, thoughts of falling too close to the fire racing through her mind. Instead of ending it all right there in a fiery inferno, she landed on a soft rug that covered a good deal of the dirt floor. The colors of the rug were plain, and looked suspiciously like the same material that composed Àed's raggedy, heather gray robes.

There wasn't much else to see in the small home. The

interior walls were the same stone as the outside, and a mat stuffed with straw dominated the corner opposite the stove. There were a few oaken cabinets pushed against the wall with the door, and a few small windows were scattered about the adjoining walls, letting in a decent amount of light.

While Finn was taking in her surroundings, Àed draped a deep green cloak around her shoulders. She looked back at him in question.

He cleared his throat and blushed. "Not sure if ye realized ye were bare of any clothing. Most folks might think ye mighty improper."

Finn wrapped the cloak tightly around herself appreciatively. The fabric was much softer than it looked, and felt nice on her fragile skin. At least, she thought of it as fragile. Much more fragile than her bark, at any rate.

With his back to her, Àed faced one of the cabinets and began chopping vegetables with a roughly made knife. Finn was surprised he didn't hack a finger off with the way he was haphazardly cutting into the various bulbs, potatoes, and carrots. She watched him curiously, not sure of what to do with herself.

"I dinnae know if ye eat," he began with his back still turned, "being as yer previous form was a tree, but we'll give it a shot anyhow."

Finn nodded, then realizing he couldn't see her, mumbled, "Thank you."

She wasn't sure why the man was helping her, but she truly was grateful. Without him, she would still be curled up out in the cold. Instead she was in an actual house. A house!

Who ever thought she'd have the experience of being under a roof?

Finn looked up at said roof, wondering if it was stable. It felt strange being indoors, and she wasn't sure how much she trusted it. After a short while, an eerie sense of loss began to pervade her thoughts. Though she knew that soil, grass, and other growing things were right outside the door, she couldn't *feel* them like she used to. Not appreciating this new sense of melancholy, she stood and exited the house, feeling much more steady on her feet than before. Àed did not look up from his chopping upon her departure.

Outside the air had an even greater chill to it than when Finn had first awoken. She noticed with a start that her breath fogged as she exhaled, and her fingertips hurt with the cold. She made her wobbly way around the small yard, breathing out more heavily than necessary in order to see more of her breath, while keeping the cloak wrapped tightly around her shivering frame.

When she found a fairly clear piece of soil, unmarred by large stones or sizable plants, she sat. She dug her toes into the cold hard earth, chilling them with the moisture that had sunk into the ground. Finn felt a little energy, as if she were once again connected to the living, breathing root system, but it was a dull energy. She could feel it, but not quite *touch* it. Her teeth began to chatter with the cold. The cloak, heavy as it was, was still not enough to keep the icy air away from her small, human bones.

As if on cue, Àed appeared from the house with a few articles of clothing in his hands. "These were me daughter's," he began without really looking at Finn. "I doubt she'll ever be coming back for them, so ye may as well put them to use." He held the articles out to her. "There're some boots in the house that might fit ye as well, though ye might want to clean yer feet first."

Finn looked down at her feet, which were in fact covered with moist dirt. She imagined the rest of her was probably fairly covered in dirt as well. Suddenly, she found herself wondering what she looked like. Not just the dirt, but what type of face she had. She stood and took the clothing from Àed, following him back into the house.

Àed had a large pot of warm water waiting for her inside, with a rough looking cloth draped over the rim. "For the dirt," he explained uncomfortably, then left the house for her to bathe in peace.

The soup on the wood stove smelled divine. Finn had never understood what hunger was. She had known thirst, and felt a certain lacking during the winter months when the sun was out less, but it was nothing like the pain she was feeling inside her belly right then. She wondered how humans ever got anything done with such incessant pain.

She glanced at the soup pot again, but it was obvious that Àed wanted the dirt off her before they ate, so she started scrubbing away furiously. Muddy water dripped down her legs and feet to the dirt floor. Luckily, the floor was so hard packed that it didn't seem to make any extra mud. There wasn't much she could do about the dirt underneath her finger and toenails, but the rest of her became fairly clean. She dried herself off with the green cloak, then set to the task of dressing, and quite the task it turned out to be.

The dress Àed had given her had many ties and cinches, and her fingers were already tired from figuring out the underpinnings. Roughly five minutes into the venture she considered asking the old man for help, but not wanting to ask him for more, she worked until she had the dress on straight. She did not cinch the black bodice as tight as she'd seen other women do, and the skirt, made out of a charcoal gray fabric, was far too long on her small frame, but at least she was covered.

She went to the door and peered out, looking for Àed. Her eyes found him standing off in the distance, staring at the horizon. She called out to him to get his attention. Hearing her, he hurried inside, rubbing his hands together to warm them.

He observed the job she had done on the dress and nodded, then went to fetch a pair of boots and some woolen stockings from beside the straw mattress. He handed them to Finn, and instructed her to sit down on the rug and try them on.

The boots were made of soft, pliable leather, and were far more complicated than the dress had been. Finally, with a little help from Àed, she managed to lace them up. They were a bit big on her feet, but still rather comfortable. Once she was fully dressed, Àed handed her a broken shard of mirror.

"Careful," he warned. "Them edges be sharp."

Finn handled the mirror shard delicately, lifting it up in front of her face. The glass was foggy, but she could still make out her reflection. Her eyes widened in amazement. Not because she was particularly amazing looking, but because she had a face. A human face. Well, she knew she had one, but seeing it was quite a different matter.

Her eyes were large and dark, and helped balance out a

somewhat strong nose. She had a fairly wide mouth, with her lower lip ever so slightly fuller than the upper. Her skin was pale and lightly freckled, and her head was topped with a waist-length, wavy mane of dirty blonde hair that was in need of a good brushing. She supposed she was pretty, but not in an overt type of way. Finn handed the mirror back to Àed, feeling numb and slightly giddy. Something itched at the back of her memory, but she couldn't quite place it. All she knew, was that her face was oddly familiar to her.

After placing the mirror in a cupboard drawer, Àed filled two carved wood bowls with pottage, and handed one to Finn. She took it appreciatively, wrapping her hands around the warm container. Still seated on the rug, she curled her legs to the side and placed the bowl on the floor while Àed seated himself on the straw mat and began eating. He slurped the soup noisily, and plucked hot vegetables out with his bare fingers.

"I don't remember you having a daughter," Finn observed. "I remember seeing you in the glen, but alone. Always alone."

Àed stopped eating as his expression turned solemn. He gazed in Finn's direction, but he seemed to be looking elsewhere. Seeing a different place. "I was not in agreement with her on many of her choices. I tried to change her . . . " he explained, eyes unfocused. "She left. Had a yearning for adventure, did that one. I don't imagine I'll be seein her again."

Finn gazed down into her bowl, sorry she had asked. Àed's daughter had been gone a long time. Finn had seen him trudging through the forest for many, many years, but never with a daughter. Àed set his soup aside and rose to stoke the fire. Finn ate in silence.

"I dinnae know what ye plan to do," Àed began after a time, breaking the silence as he closed the hatch on the stove. "But yer welcome here as long as ye like. I haven't much to offer, but ye'll be warm and ye'll be fed. Greenswallow ain't along any travel routes, so no one will bother ye here."

Finn nodded sadly. "Thank you, I'm not sure what I would have done if you hadn't found me. Although, I'm still not sure what I'm supposed to do now." She took another slurp of broth, then looked back up at the old man. "What-," she hesitated.

Àed smiled encouragingly. "Go on lass," he prompted, "ask anything ye like."

"Well," Finn began again, "I was just wondering what it looked like . . . when I turned into a person."

Àed's smile faltered, ever so slightly. Finn thought for a moment that he wasn't going to tell her, but eventually he spoke. "I was gathering neeps from me garden," he began, "when this Sgal arose, the strongest of winds. It smelled for the life of me like roses and rain. Like the smell of a summer storm, ye understand?

"I found meself standing and walking away from me home, guided by the wind. It pushed me along, mighty fierce. It led me to the glen where ye used to stand as a tree. There the air started to shimmer and blur, like it do on distant horizons in the middle of a hot spell. One moment ye were a tree, then I blinked, and ye were standing there in this form. There was a look on yer face like the world was crumbling around ye, and it was the most beautiful thing ye had ever seen."

Finn was not sure how to take what the old man was telling her. "I don't remember it," she commented. "I just remember falling down."

Àed smiled, but it was not a happy smile. "I left after I saw ye, and I'm sorry for that. I just left ye lyin there in the grass. I've not been around people for a very long time, and I wasn't sure I could do it again."

"But people are in the glen all of the time," she countered, not realizing that such a contradiction might seem rude. It was obvious that the old man expected her to be angry at his admission, but she was used to people paying her little to no mind. She would never have expected someone to help her.

Àed continued to smile, with perhaps a bit more warmth than before. "No one bothers an old hermit," he explained. "I saw them, and they saw me, but that was the extent of it. Talkin to ye, well this is the first time I've talked to another soul since me daughter left me."

Finn managed a small smile. "If it makes you feel less alone, this is the first conversation I've had in just as long. In fact, it's the first conversation of my life."

"Ye seem to have grasped the language quickly," Àed commented. "It takes most of us many years to learn to speak."

"I've heard countless conversations," Finn explained. "I learned from them."

Àed squinted at Finn like he didn't fully believe her. "Your speech just seems mighty fluid, is all I'm sayin."

"I don't understand what happened to me," Finn stated a

little too sharply, "and I don't know how I am able to speak to you, or why I have the lips that enable me to do so."

Àed blushed and nodded to himself. "I dinnae know either, but yer here now, so ye may as well make yerself comfortable and get some rest. We'll speak more in the mornin."

Now that Àed had pointed it out, Finn did feel a certain weariness about her. At the old man's instruction, she curled up on the lumpy straw mat. She closed her eyes, not sure what sleep would be like, and not sure if she wanted to do it at all. It took her quickly though, and she was grateful for the reprieve.

CHAPTER TWO

inn stayed with Àed for several weeks. She could have stayed in his small home forever, where she was warm and safe, but she felt like there was something she needed to do. She missed the earth, and still wasn't quite sure how to be a human. Even beyond that, something unseen pushed her forward. She somehow knew that she had a purpose, but was unsure of what that purpose might be. She'd also had memories, just brief flashes, of another life, though she hadn't told Àed about them. The scenes were only quick blurs of images, sometimes with snippets of conversation she could not make sense of.

Unsure of what these vague memories meant, she focused on remembering what it felt like to be a tree. The more she became accustomed to movement, eating, and speaking, the more she forgot what it felt like to be without such things. In an effort to remember her former life, every day she went outside and stuck her toes in the dirt, searching for some sort of connection. She could feel the distant ringing of roots and soil and life, yet she could not reach it. She would sit in the grass for hours, until her skin itched terribly and her cheeks were red with too much sun.

One particularly rainy day, Finn was stuck inside. Because she was human. Because she would get cold. She hated the cold. She'd felt it before, but never like she did as a human. It seeped into her bones in an insidious manner, leaving her shaking for several minutes even as she warmed herself by the fire.

"I think I'd like to be a tree again," she announced through chattering teeth.

Àed, who had been mending a hole in his cloak, put down his work. "I'm afraid I cannae help ye there, lassy."

Finn took a deep breath, settling her resolve. "Then I must find someone who can. Perhaps there are others who share my condition. There has to be a *reason* for what happened to me."

Àed smiled, but it was sad. "I figured ye'd want to be leaving eventually," he conceded. "Yer too young to be cooped up."

Finn offered the old man a small smile. "I'm glad that you understand."

Àed stood and stretched his back. "I've a few things to give ye first. Just wait here while I fetch them."

Finn put a hand to her chest, suddenly worried that Àed might think she expected further assistance. "But you've given me so much already. I can take nothing more from you."

Àed tugged his burlap hat firmly onto his wizened head. "I'll have none of yer arguing," he scolded. "Ye just wait here a moment."

With that, he went out into the rain. Finn opened the wooden shutter on one of the windows so she could watch as Àed walked toward the back of the house, but she soon had to shut it as the rain pelted in through the opening. The old man was gone for quite some time, causing her an increasing amount of anxiety.

Finn jumped as the door burst open, carried by the strength of the wind. Àed stood in the doorway, drenched with his hands covered in mud. He was also carrying a small, muddy chest.

"I buried this," he explained, holding up the chest, "years ago. Just in case anyone came snoopin around me home while I was away."

He placed the chest on the ground and sat down in front of it. Finn was constantly surprised at how agile he was, given his apparent age. She'd seen men as old as he in her meadow, and they wobbled around like newborn deer. He opened the chest, and peered inside with a smile. Finn scooted beside him, so that she might see as well.

Inside, was a shiny silver dagger, at least, the pommel was shiny silver. The blade of the dagger was stuck into a dark leather sheath, attached to a braided cord of similar dark leather. The dagger had an elaborate, twining pattern on the pommel that ended in a small black stone. Àed pulled out the knife to reveal a pair of soft leather gloves, a wooden comb, and what appeared to be a coin purse residing in the chest as well.

He handed the dagger to Finn, who took it by the hilt awkwardly. "I'd have no idea how to use such a thing," she admitted. "I've seen their use in the skinning of deer and rabbits, but I believe in this case, seeing and doing are quite different things."

Àed eyed her sternly. "This ain't no skinnin knife. Ye must be able to protect yerself. The road is not always a friendly place, and a weapon helps push the odds in yer favor."

Reluctantly, Finn set the dagger in her lap, and Àed turned back to his muddy chest. He removed the gloves and comb from the box next, placing them in Finn's hands without a word. At Finn's raised eyebrow, he said, "Yer hands'll get cold on the road, especially with the nasty weather we've had of late, and ye should probably brush your hair on occasion, lest people mistake ye for a wild woman."

Finally he gave her the coin purse. It was heavy; the coins clinked inside as Finn handled it. She tried to push it back at him without a word.

Àed shook his head. "I've no need for it lass. Everything I be needing is already bought."

Finn's face was once again covered in the wetness she had come to know as tears. She had not yet cried from gratitude, and found it better than crying from sadness. She gripped the coins tightly in her hand. Though she knew little of currency, she knew that coin was not given away easily.

Àed's expression turned to one of sadness. "Please don't be cryin lass."

Finn tried to stay her tears, but ended up crying even harder. She wiped at her face with the leather gloves, but it was no use.

Àed stood suddenly and set the trunk to the side. "I've a

knapsack for ye," he announced as he stood "and a bedroll-" He paused mid-speech as a worried look came across his face. After another moment he went on as if he hadn't missed a beat, "I've both for myself as well, as I've just decided that I'll be goin with ye."

"I cannot ask that of you!" Finn objected instantly.

"These old bones can carry me farther than those tree trunks ye call legs," he said firmly. "I can't very well leave ye alone on the road."

"I've no idea how far I'll have to go, or to where. There is no way you can come," she argued.

"Quit yer bickerin and get some rest," Àed ordered as he began pawing through his cupboards in search of supplies. "Providing the weather clears up, we'll be leaving first thing in the morning."

Finn was at a loss for words. She did not want to go alone, but she knew Àed would only be coming along for her sake. She would have argued further, but she had come to know the look in the old man's eyes that meant all arguments would fall on deaf ears. Her hands fell to her lap in defeat. With no other options, she obeyed the old man and curled up on the straw mat, while he continued to root through his belongings. Eventually Àed bunched up some blankets and went to sleep on the floor, just like he had every night since she'd first arrived.

"Can't ye move any faster!" Àed called from a good forty paces ahead of Finn as they walked along the next morning.

The old man was surprisingly swift, and he never really

seemed to tire. Finn on the other hand was tired all of the time. Though she currently had human legs, she had been a stationary tree for a good hundred years. All of the movement that people were expected to endure was a bit much for her.

Àed had paused to wait for her, and eyed her with impatience as she approached. "We need to make Garenoch before the sun sets," he explained. "The roads are no place to be after dark."

Finn had to stand still for a moment in order to catch her breath. "We can sleep on our bedrolls in this . . . Garenoch?" she asked.

She had never been to a burgh like Garenoch, yet she somehow knew what one would consist of. She had probably just pieced together information overheard from travelers over the years. Yet, being on the road was oddly familiar to her as well, if logically foreign at the same time.

"We'll sleep at an inn tonight lass, and as often as we can. Them coins in that pouch will more than cover it, so take a care ye don't be loosin any," Àed answered.

"There are beds at this inn?" Finn prompted.

Àed sighed impatiently. "Yes lass, and I know yer next question. We need the bedrolls, because there willnae always be an inn at hand."

Finn nodded and started walking on ahead of the old man, wanting to show him that she could walk just as well, if not better than him. Her efforts were not rewarded. Within moments, Àed had reached her side once more.

"So I never found the chance to ask ye," he began conversationally, "do ye remember when ye were first a tree?"

Finn eyed him suspiciously, but answered, "It was always so. I do not remember a beginning. Just that I always was."

"But there had to be a beginning," Àed prompted. "Whether ye rose up from a small seed, or perhaps . . . perhaps ye were something else, ye know, before ye were a tree?"

Finn did not appreciate what Àed was implying. There was nothing before her previous life. If there had been, she would remember it, just as she remembered being a tree.

"Why would you ask such a thing?" she questioned breathlessly. She was not about to admit that certain memories had seeped in. Those memories were just figments of her imagination, nothing more.

"Ye just seem awful good at being a person," he explained quickly, before she could get defensive. "Ye've managed to get hold of quite a bit in such a short time. Ye knew what an inn was, without ever having been to one." At her glare, he pointed an accusing finger back at her. "Now don't ye argue with me. I know ye knew."

"What are you implying, old man?" Finn asked with a little more heat than she'd intended.

Àed kept walking at ease, as if he hadn't heard her tone. "I'm implying that ye've done this before, even if ye don't remember it. I think ye were a human before ye became a tree, and a tree wasn't yer natural state to begin with."

"That is not possible," Finn choked out. "I will find someone who knows what he's talking about, and I'll become a tree once more. My *natural* state."

Àed shrugged. "Suit yerself. Twas only an observation."

Finn's face felt hot. Despite the cold, sweat dripped down her nose. She wiped it away and put Àed's accusations out of her mind. She was a tree, and she would be a tree again.

The sun was nearly gone by the time they reached the small burgh, Garenoch by name. Finn's feet ached, and her stomach growled. Àed had refused to stop long enough for them to pull out some of the cheese and bread they had brought. Finn didn't see what his rush was. She was the one on a mission, not him.

She was not overly stunned as the scenery transitioned from sporadic farms with grazing animals, to homes and businesses crammed side-by-side. In fact, a sickening familiarity settled into the pit of her stomach. She shoved it aside, but the feeling continued to nag at her. There was no way she had been in any place other than her meadow.

The streets still held a few people, despite the chilly air moving in as the sun lowered. The people went about their business, and did not pay Finn or Àed much mind. Shacks and larger homes which Àed referred to as *haudins* were packed closely together, making the air of the place feel claustrophobic. The houses were built upward and outward, each story protruding wider than the one below it, so that their slightly pitched roofs nearly touched. Many buildings reached three stories high, but few were larger than that, which was good, because it seemed to Finn that they might fall over if they grew anymore. The walls of most of the haudins were whitewashed, though many dreadfully needed a new coat. Àed and Finn walked on past the houses silently, searching for an inn.

The roads were muddy from the previous day's rain, and didn't have the grass of the countryside, causing Finn's boots to quickly become caked with mud as they walked. She plodded along, feeling like her feet weighed a hundred pounds as she tried to avoid large ruts in the road that would likely pull one of her boots off entirely, given that they were too large for her.

A group of travelers on horseback passed them, and Finn found herself wishing for a horse. She did not relay this wish to Àed, nor did she relay her wish for hot food and a warm room.

One of the passing riders stopped a short distance ahead, and dismounted to talk to a stableman. Finn told herself that she only knew he was a stableman by the harnesses looped over his shoulder. She did not have an answer as to how she knew that the occupation of stableman existed in the first place.

The stableman was a greasy, squirmy man with dark hair pushed back from his bony face. The corded muscles in his long arms seemed wrong on such a ferrety little man. He took several coins from the rider who had stopped to speak to him, then began to gather the reins of the party's horses as each rider dismounted.

The rider with the coin appeared to be a small woman. Finn could not see her face past the hood of her burgundy cloak, but her shape bespoke femininity. The other riders handed off their horses one by one. Three men, and perhaps one more woman.

"Are yer feet stuck in the mud lass!" Àed called from underneath the eave of the inn's door. "I'm starving over here!"

Over Àed's head hung a sign in the shape of a sheep with a garish smile carved into the wood of his face. Finn had no idea what the sign meant, but guessed it somehow related to the name of the inn. The building behind the sign was much larger than the haudins they had passed, but was built in the same style with larger stories on top.

Finn started forward with a grunt. Pushy old man. The aroma of roasting meats and fresh bannocks wafted from the inn as the riders Finn had been observing opened the door behind Àed and went inside. Àed followed them in, shaking his head at Finn's slowness as she stopped in her tracks and stood still in the mud, frozen by a strange sense of nostalgia.

The din of voices and warm light that flowed from the inn called to her in a way that they should not have. She knew she needed food and warmth to survive, but the atmosphere of the inn offered a sense of safety and belonging. She did *not* belong with those people eating and drinking in the inn.

Finn's mood brightened slightly as she imagined sitting by a nice fire with a hot meal, and a glass of wine. Wine. She had only seen humans drink it from leather bottells as they lounged beneath the shade of her limbs, yet the memory of the taste was recalled to her tongue. Feeling oddly light as she lifted her sodden feet, she started forward toward what she told herself was her first time entering an inn.

She passed through the doors to find Àed discussing something with the innkeep, a short, balding man with a gold embroidered coat that looked out of place on his less than grand physique. Àed had not taken the coin purse back from Finn while still on the road, yet he now produced four silver coins for the innkeep. Finn could not tell exactly where the coins were coming from, a sleight of hand that likely helped ward off pickpockets. She shook her head at her knowledge of pickpockets. She would simply have to stop thinking.

She walked forward swiftly, attempting to avoid eye-contact with the inn's patrons as they sat eating their suppers. Her shoulders relaxed as the room's warmth comforted her, but she instantly forced them to stiffen. She should not be comfortable here. Reaching Àed's side, she let out her held breath, then turned to acknowledge the innkeep with a tight smile. The small man's coat was almost blinding with its gold thread that reflected the lantern light as he shifted his weight back and forth. Though the innkeep was narrow of limb, the coat attempted to hide a rather full, round belly that reflected the light more than the concave areas of his body.

The innkeep grinned as he took in Finn with his eyes. "Welcome to the *Sheep's Delight,* the finest inn in all of Garenoch, burgh of Alderman Gwrtheryn."

Àed glanced up at the man from under silver bushy eyebrows. "Considering it's one of two inns in Garenoch, that ain't really sayin much."

The man's smile did not falter, but the tone of his voice was bland as he held out a key to Àed and said, "Your room is up the stairs, third on the right. Enjoy your stay."

Without a word, Àed snatched the key, then turned and ascended the wide wooden stairway beside the bar, with Finn following silently after him. She left clumps of mud as she went, and cursed herself for not wiping her feet on her way in. The feeling of eyes on her back made her think that perhaps the innkeep was cursing her as well, but she turned to find not the innkeep's eyes, but the eyes of a young man seated in the common room.

Next to him sat a young woman who looked startlingly similar to him, both in age and appearance. They each had dusky red hair, small angular faces, and large honey brown eyes. They reminded Finn of the foxes that lived in her glen. She took in the woman's burgundy cloak and concluded that they were two of the riders from earlier. Realizing with a start that she had been observing the pair for longer than was polite, Finn met the man's gaze with a glare, and he quickly averted his eyes. She may have just been a tree, but she still knew that it was rude to stare.

She ascended the stairway without looking back again, removing the hood of her green cloak and shaking out her slightly matted hair as she went. Though she was out of sight of the common room, the feeling of eyes on her back remained.

CHAPTER THREE

*A*nders had not meant to stare at the girl. His thoughts had been on the old man, actually. He knew his face, though he couldn't quite place it.

He turned to his twin sister, Branwen. She obviously had not even noticed the old man, or the girl that had accompanied him. Branwen was poring over a decrepit book on the history of their current burgh. Tomorrow there would be another book, as they would be heading toward another burgh. For the life of him, Anders could find nothing interesting about any of the little hamlets they'd passed through, but his sister acted as if each new place held great historical significance. She had loved books as a child, and now she would see the places she had read about for the very first time.

Even in the present day, Branwen was always reading one book or another. He could grudgingly admit that it made Branwen the better historian, though he'd never say so to her face. Anders, the older of the two by one hour, was at least a far superior cartographer, or so he kept telling himself. Given that their mission at present was the mapping of the lands, from Cael all the way to Migris, he thought of himself as in charge, though he'd also never voice those particular thoughts to Branwen.

He looked to their other companion, Iseult, the guard they'd enlisted before leaving the Gray City. At least Anders liked to think of him as a guard. In reality he was more of a mercenary, taking whatever job paid regardless of how lawful the job might be.

Iseult was a tall man, but not overly muscled. Anders would have doubted his abilities, if he had not seen how fast the man moved. Iseult swept a hand over his near-black hair, which hung just past his shoulders. The length was likely less of a desire for long hair, the style of the times for the gentler classes, than a lack of desire to get it cut. There was a peppering of gray at his temples, making Anders imagine that Iseult had led a trying life, as he seemed fairly young to have gray hairs. Iseult's eyes were a mixture of pale green and gray-brown. Anders realized with a shudder why the eyes had seemed so familiar to him at first. They reminded him of the eyes of a great hunting cat.

The party also traveled with Liaden, an emissary of the Gray City, and Kai, her escort. Though the latter two had already retired to their room.

Anders felt himself rolling his eyes at the thought of the travelers from the Gray City. The city's traditional name was Sormyr. Sormyr was originally built with wrought iron and basalt. It had been altogether imposing in its darkness.

The only problem was that it stood near the sea, so that over time everything became caked in salt and other minerals. The city dwellers did their best to scrub the minerals away, but most of the buildings turned to gray. Hence, the Gray City.

He could have done without the emissary, but the approval of the Alderman of the Gray City, Arthryn, granted legitimacy to any maps Anders might make, so he hadn't much choice in the matter. Without an extension of Arthryn to monitor the progress of his mapping, the maps themselves would not be worth near as much renown. Though he understood the need for witnesses under a greater authority, he did not understand why such authority belonged only to the rulers of the larger cities. He had not even been allowed to meet the Alderman of Sormyr, and was forced to deal with Liaden on all matters.

Anders turned his attention back to his present companions. Branwen was mercilessly explaining to Iseult the history of Garenoch, their current burgh. Iseult did not seem overly interested in the one-sided conversation. In Anders' opinion, the only significance that Garenoch held was as the place where he finally received a hot meal. Or he would receive a hot meal, if it ever actually reached their table. The sole barmaid of the *Sheep's Delight* (a rather questionable name for an inn, at that) was nowhere to be seen. She was very old, and continuously disappeared into the kitchen for long periods of time.

Iseult gave the hint of a nod here and there in acknowledgment of Branwen's prattling, yet he was not inclined to actually speak. Anders doubted he had heard the man speak more than three words since they had hired him. He wouldn't have trusted Iseult to protect them at all, if he hadn't come on good recommendation from a fellow scholar.

As Anders regarded the mercenary yet again, Iseult's green/gray eyes narrowed at something across the room. Anders turned to see the old man and the young girl descending the staircase.

"I know that face," Iseult muttered to himself, unaware that Branwen's expression had turned to one of contempt at the interruption.

"That's odd," Anders commented. "I thought the same thing, like I've seen his face in a portrait somewhere."

Iseult gave him such a look that Anders wished he hadn't spoken, but replied, "Not the old man. The girl."

Anders gave the girl a second look, but her face did not stand out to him. She was lovely, in a common sort of way, but he was sure he had never seen her before. The girl went to sit with her elderly companion at a table in the far corner, so that Anders had to look over his shoulder to see them. This time, the girl directed her glare at Iseult, and Anders let out a sigh of relief. The sigh caught in his throat as the mercenary turned away to look down at the tabletop, as if fully chastised. Anders had never thought to see such a look on the mercenary's face. Iseult recovered quickly, and directed a glare toward Anders, daring the smaller man to make comment.

Anders quickly looked away, only to see that the barmaid had re-emerged from the kitchen with large plates of food in hand. His mouth watered in anticipation. It had been nothing but hard bread and cheese for two days. Only the thought of a hot meal had kept him moving in the poor weather, instead of stopping to make camp in a sheltered area.

The barmaid walked toward their table, food in hand, then walked right past, setting the plates that surely should have been destined for Anders in front of the girl and the old man. The girl looked at the old man in surprise, and he rewarded her with a wink and a smile. Anders watched longingly as the pair tore into roasted grouse and potatoes the size of Anders' two fists put together. There was something about that old man, he was sure of it.

Finn was not sure why those men had been staring at her, but she knew she did not appreciate it. The red-haired man seemed harmless enough, but the other, the one with the dark hair, seemed like some sly, hunting beast. The woman with them did not stare, at least. In fact, she seemed completely oblivious to it all.

She took a bite of the piping hot potato, and had to leave her mouth open and pant on it to cool it down a bit. When it had cooled enough, and she was able to swallow, she turned to Àed.

"Those two men were watching us," she commented.

"Aye lass," he replied with his mouth full. "I saw."

"It was very rude," she prompted, frustrated that he didn't say more.

Àed shrugged. "Perhaps ye should go tell them so, lass."

Finn's face burned with an angry blush. "I was just making an observation," she muttered.

SARA C ROETHLE

Àed took a bite of potato, and had no trouble with its scalding temperature. "We are an odd pair, lass. Ye dinnae often see an old man and a young lady traveling without protection. Not lately at least. They're probably just wonderin what we're up to."

The barmaid appeared in front of their table again, carrying two pewter mugs. The woman never said a word to them, but left with a kindly smile for Àed. Finn noticed the red haired man looking after the barmaid longingly as she disappeared back into the kitchen.

"You know her," Finn commented, referring to the barmaid as she looked down into her mug to find that it was filled with dark red wine.

Àed nodded, and took a sip of his wine. "Aye lass. Sometimes being among the elderly has its benefits."

Finn lifted her mug to her lips, but hesitated. Now, not only was the red haired man looking at her, but his sister was looking too. Not directly at her though. She realized with a start that they were actually looking at Àed.

She turned her own gaze back to Àed, who didn't seem to notice the attention he was getting. "Pooks," the old man mumbled. "Who ever heard of Pooks in these parts?"

Finn waited as the old man continued muttering to himself about Pooks and magical folk. "What are you going on about?" she questioned finally.

Àed startled, and turned toward Finn with a glare. "I'm tryin to hear the news from our dining companions, if ye ˙ˉnae mind."

ˉld man had been eaves-dropping on the rest of the
ˉ. Finn was surprised that he could hear so

32

well at his age, while she herself could not pick out any individual conversations from the murmur.

"What are Pooks?" she asked, once again interrupting Àed from his listening.

"Bah," he grunted. "I'm never going to hear anything of import with all yer ramblin." He eyed her for a moment, then explained, "Pooks are night creatures. Some say they be of the Tuatha De, the faierie folk, or some say demons. They appear as twisted, small humans with goat features, horns and the like, ye know? Portents they are."

Finn nodded in understanding. "You mean Bucca. I've seen the Bucca."

She had seen them on many a night, creeping through the darkness. Small creatures walking on two legs, but more animal-like than human. Their milky yellow eyes reflected the moonlight when they were still, but they would meld into shadows a moment after coming into her line of perception.

"There are many names," Àed explained, "but the creatures remain the same. The important thing is that folk have been spottin' them. Well, they say they been spottin' them. Ye saw them as a tree ye say?"

Finn nodded. "For the past few years at least, only at night."

Àed shook his head. "Things be changin'. For good or for worse we cannae know. Pooks are a bad sign, a sign toward the latter."

"Why would seeing the Pooks be bad?" Finn pressed.

Àed took a deep swig of his wine. "The Tuatha De started dwindling off several decades ago," he explained. "There was a war, and I'll tell ye, the wars of men cannae compare to the wars of the Tuatha. No man even knew what the Faie folk were fighting over, but the fighting lasted for half a century and another half of that. Not huge battles mind ye, but the clashes were evident when they happened. Many mortals lost their lives and homes simply because they stood in the way. Forty years back the fighting stopped altogether, and the Tuatha began to disappear. There've been no sightings in decades, except for the *Travelers*. If the Tuatha De return, ye can bet the violence will return with them."

Finn had not witnessed any such fighting in her time as a tree, nor had she witnessed any Faie besides those in recent years. "I liked the Bucca," she decided, "and I think I would like to see the other Faie as well."

Àed shook his head and sulked in silence, his mood seeming to sour by the moment.

"Perhaps we should retire to our room," Finn said softly, regretting her comment on the Tuatha when she saw how it affected her companion.

Àed glanced up, once again startled out of his thoughts. "Finish yer food first. We'll have plenty of time to scamper away afterward."

Finn resumed her supper, wanting strongly to escape from the common room and the too-loud din of conversation. Whereas at first the large volume of people offered Finn comfort, now they made her nervous, especially when the ones who'd been there before kept staring in her direction. Àed surveyed their unwelcome watchers thoughtfully for a moment, shoved one last bite of potato into his mouth, then stood. Finn pushed her plate away and did the same, grateful that the meal was over.

Half-full wine glasses in hand, Finn and Àed wove through the tables and walked toward the stairs. Finn let out a breath she hadn't realized she'd been holding as they reached the threshold. No one barred their way, and they ascended while the siblings and the dark-haired man pretended to not look at them.

By the time Finn reached the top of the stairs, Àed was already unlocking the small door to their room. She caught up with him as he opened it, and he gestured for her to step inside before him.

The room was far more grand than Àed's hovel, but that wasn't hard to accomplish. Two straw mats were placed on raised bed frames with a small wooden table between their heads. There was also another small table with a washbasin and pitcher, as well as a rickety wooden chair shoved into the corner near the small fireplace.

Finn sat on the edge of one of the beds and sipped her remaining wine. "What do you think they wanted?" she asked after a time.

Àed had set himself to examining their door, then turned to the room's small window. "Not sure lass," he mumbled as he smoothed a finger along the edges of the windowsill.

Finn looked down into her cup, the small amount she had consumed had succeeded in making her feel slightly giddy. "Well then, who do you think they were?"

Àed grunted. "By the looks of it, they're wealthy. The twins are likely merchants, or something of the sort. I'd say the dark haired man is a hired sword, or sellsword as such are called. He's also a thief. Not much to worry about, I'd say."

35

"A thief?" Finn intoned. "How could you tell?"

Àed chuckled. "I've a nose for such things. I'd bet ye all of the coin in the world that the man is a thief, though I doubt his employers know it."

"Do you think he'll try to rob us?" Finn asked.

Àed shook his head. "The man would have little reason to. Not much to worry about, like I said."

Finn raised an eyebrow, but Àed didn't see. "Then why are you inspecting the room so thoroughly?" she asked skeptically.

Àed finally turned his attention to her. "I said that lot was nothing to worry yerself about. I dinnae say there weren't anything else to be worryin about."

Finn pulled the scratchy blanket off her bed and wrapped it around her shoulders. The room was absolutely freezing. On cue, Àed began making a small fire from the paltry amount of branches left in the room for that purpose.

"And what should we be worrying about?" Finn prompted. She knew better than to offer aid. The old man never took it.

Àed shrugged as he crouched on the floor. "The road is a dangerous place for all, and now talk of Pooks about. Next thing ye know we'll be hearin' of Grogochs in folk's gardens and Dullahan knockin' on doors."

With that pleasant thought simmering in her mind, Finn went to the washbasin to clean a bit of the road dirt from her skin. The water was icy cold, and chilled her fingertips until she thought they might fall off. Not quite finished, but too cold to go on, she dried her face and hands on a rough towel, then went to sit by the fire. Àed began rinsing his own face, leaving Finn to her thoughts.

Finn had felt the fates shift that night, and knew with a surety that she would see the siblings and their hired sword again. She knew it like she knew a storm was coming, back when she was a tree. She felt the pressure of it building, telling her that a downpour was on its way.

CHAPTER FOUR

Finn couldn't sleep. Àed had insisted that they go to bed early in order to get an early start, but Finn had tossed and turned for hours, unable to calm her mind. Each time she closed her eyes she would have flashes of that strange other life, a life that could not possibly be. She still could not make any sense of the scenes, yet the memories were most definitely her own. With the discomfort of the memories, that familiar aching had returned to her insides, and she was once again overcome with some need she couldn't quite describe.

Finn rose quietly from her bed, taking care to not wake her companion. She did not want to take the time to don her dress over her underpinnings, and instead went straight for her cloak, wrapping it tightly around her. She had almost reached the door when her nerves prompted her to go back and retrieve her dagger. Àed did not shift as she lifted the weapon into her hands and went back to the door. Only after she was out in the hall with the door shut and locked behind her, did she take the time to tie the dagger securely around her waist, first stringing the room key onto the leather cord.

With a final hesitant look at the door, she descended the stairway. The common room was silent and dark, except for an oil lamp that glowed dully on the bar. Finn kept an eye on the shadows that danced with the flickering of the lamp as she crept barefoot to the large front door, only to find a heavy oaken bar across it. Cursing her lack of foresight, she tip-toed to one of the nearby windows. She considered its height for a moment, wondering if she'd be able to get back in once she went out. Telling herself it was a terrible idea, and that she should just go back to bed, she climbed on a chair and pulled herself through the window and out onto the silent, dark street.

The icy ground sent pangs through Finn's feet and legs. In the shelter of the inn, she had forgotten just how cold it could be at night. With all of the moisture from the rain, many parts of the ground had become solid ice, and the mud had hardened so that her feet didn't slip on its surface. She wrapped her cloak tightly around her, but found that it was not enough to keep her warm. The deed was done, regardless. She would just have to be quick.

The hard-packed earth of the road didn't feel right to her. It felt dead. She walked around the inn, in search of an area of soil where things could actually grow.

Finn traced her fingers along the edge of the building as she circled. There were a few lanterns glowing by front doors in the street, but once between the buildings there was little light to see by.

In the new darkness, she searched more with her senses

than with her eyes. Her teeth began to chatter, but she trudged on. She told herself she would slip right back in through the window when she was done, and she would be safe in her warm bed before Àed even knew she was missing. On the other hand, if she couldn't get in she was bound to freeze. If she couldn't get in . . . she pushed the thought away as her toes found a rough patch of dry grass. She crouched to touch her fingertips to the soil. It wasn't the best area, but it would do.

Finn lowered herself to sit cross-legged, then tried to recall how it felt to be a tree. She attempted to push through that very human barrier in her mind that was now always there to block her way. The chilly air pervaded her thoughts as her human body's discomfort drowned out everything else.

"What're you doing out here all by yourself?" an oily, lilting voice questioned from her left.

Startled, Finn looked around cautiously for the source of the voice. Her eyes settled on a nearby shape, hiding deeper in the shadows. She rose slowly to her feet, hugging her cloak around her, partially to stay warm, but partially to hide the fact that she was only wearing her underpinnings beneath.

"It is not safe for young ladies to be about late at night," the voice chided.

"I was just preparing to return to my room," Finn replied as she backed away.

"Not so fast," the voice replied, quickly closing the distance. The stableman's face was briefly illuminated by moonlight as he neared her, but soon plunged back into shadow.

Finn reached numbed fingers down her side to her dagger. "I would not come any closer, if I were you," she threatened, though her insides felt like pottage.

The man edged closer, obviously not put off by her threat. A pockmarked face came more clearly into view, topped by slick black hair. Though lanky, the man was well muscled from his work, and likely outweighed Finn by a good forty pounds.

"That's a fine cloak you have there," the man commented. "I'd venture it might catch a good deal of coin. I'd venture to say you've got the coin itself as well." He took another step.

"I am but a poor traveler," she replied, trying hard to keep her voice from trembling. "Now you'd best be on your way before I report you to the guard."

The man spat into the dirt, then chuckled softly. It was a dry rasping sound, hardly a laugh at all. "The *guards* don't patrol these streets anymore. They'll all be pacing around outside Gwrtheryn's estate. The Alderman of our fair burgh is afraid of shapes in the night. Ain't no one worrying about my shape, or yours."

"Well then your employer," she countered. "I'm sure he would not be pleased to hear that you robbed one of his guests."

The man took a step closer, bringing with him the smell of too much wine. "I don't think you'll be saying much."

Finn's thoughts raced at the implied threat. She had assumed that within the burgh there would be some measure of law. It was in the Alderman's best interest to protect the burgh, wasn't it? Finn shook her head at her foolishness.

The stableman eyed her askance. "You having conversations in that pretty little head of yours?" he asked as he closed the final gap between them, reaching out to twist the ends of Finn's long hair around his fingertips.

Finn took another step back, pulling her hair out of the man's grip. The stableman followed. A flicker of movement caught Finn's attention, drawing her eyes to a second shape that loomed in the darkness behind the stableman. Her gaze turned fully to the shape in surprise, causing the stableman to turn and see what had caught her attention. Finn took the opportunity to get a better grip on her dagger, hidden in the folds of her cloak.

The stableman turned back to her, the dark shape having disappeared. "You playing games with me girl?" he asked harshly.

Finn began to raise her dagger from her cloak just as the dark shape came back into view out of the shadows. She recognized the man's face instantly. It was the sibling's hired sword, the thief, as Àed would have her believe. His short sword was partially out of its belt sheathe, his hand resting on the pommel casually.

The sellsword chuckled quietly. "I would step away from the girl, if I were you," he told the stableman calmly.

The stableman froze as he realized a new threat had approached, then turned his body partially toward the sellsword. Finn watched the stableman's expression change as he weighed his odds against the tall, armed man. "I want no trouble from you," he replied hesitantly.

The sellsword laughed again to himself. "I am not the most immediate danger in your life at the moment." He gestured with a nod at Finn.

She held her dagger steadily at the stableman's throat, her eyes focused on the tip of her blade as the man moved. He had meant to turn his attention back to Finn, but in doing so he pushed the soft skin of his throat against the dagger's tip. Finn watched in shock as a small bead of blood formed along the edge of the knife. Caught up in surprise at her own actions, she did not see as the stableman's eyes widened in shock.

"I suppose I'll be off then," he whispered, the slight quiver in his voice giving away his discomfort.

"Will you?" Finn asked, then continued, "I think you'll be off when I tell you to be off."

The man gave her the barest of nods, smearing the small amount of blood across his throat. By the gods she was freezing. What was she doing, keeping the man there?

"I wasn't really going to hurt you," he pleaded. "I was just having a bit of fun."

The stale wine on the man's breath made Finn crinkle her nose in distaste. She was grateful as the sellsword confidently walked up behind the man with his blade unsheathed. Finn thought for a moment he might slit the stableman's throat, but instead he knocked the man on the back of his head with the pommel, too quick for the stableman to react. Finn had to retract her dagger to avoid slitting the man's throat herself.

She could hear slightly labored breathing, and she realized with a start that it was her own. The entire sequence of events had happened so quickly. As her adrenaline subsided, the cold swept back in, and she began to tremble. At least, she told herself it was from the cold. She looked up at the man left standing, wondering his intent. He *had* helped her, but she kept her dagger out none-the-less.

The man re-sheathed his sword, then let his black cloak fall back over the weapon. "The stableman had a good question," he said.

Finn lifted her head defiantly. "And what, praytell, was that?"

The man raised a dark eyebrow at her, or so it appeared in the dim lighting. "The question of what you are doing out here on your own."

Finn snorted. "And I could have asked the two of you the same."

The man laughed, though Finn was not sure what was funny. "I heard someone stumbling about outside of the inn, and decided to investigate."

Finn raised her nose proudly into the air. "I was *not* stumbling. I was simply taking an evening walk, as is my right."

The man shrugged. "If that is what you say." He held out a hand toward her.

Finn took a step back. "Would you try and assault me now as well?" she asked, affronted.

The man gave her a small smile and retracted his hand. "I *was* going to offer you a hand back into the inn, seeing as you've decided to take your nighttime walk without shoes."

Finn was glad that the darkness hid her blush. "I can walk on my own, thank you."

The man nodded his assent. "Well, are you prepared to go back inside then? I've things to do, and I would not feel right leaving you out in the cold."

Finn wanted to argue, but her teeth had begun to chatter again. She nodded and turned to go back to her window.

"If you don't want to go through that window again," the man said good-naturedly, "you could always use the back door."

Finn sniffed and began walking toward the back of the inn, as if she had always intended to go that way. The man followed a short distance behind her like a rather tall shadow.

She found the door, but turned to face the sellsword once more before going through. "You were watching me all of that time, and yet you offered no aid until that man was upon me."

He raised an eyebrow at her again. "Yes, I could have helped you sooner, but my lady, you did not appear to need the aid."

Maintaining eye contact, the man reached around her, a little too close. Finn opened her mouth to speak, once again unsure of his intent. Then the door swung open behind her, and the man gestured for her to go inside.

She turned and quickly walked in, reveling in the warmth. The bar that was meant to hold the door shut was leaning against the inner wall.

The man still stood out in the cold. "Are you not coming?" Finn asked.

The man smiled. "In time."

Finn sighed loudly. "Tell me your name, at least."

"Iseult," he replied.

Finn forced a smile. "I am Finn. Goodnight."

Sighing with relief that she would live another day, she shut the door firmly behind her.

CHAPTER FIVE

*F*inn, short for Finnur. She had confirmed it. Iseult did one final circle around the inn as he went over every word she had said to him, looking for any evidence to further confirm his suspicions, though he was unsure of what he hoped to find. He had lied when he told her that he'd come outside to investigate the stumbling footsteps. It was merely a coincidence. He was as much a denizen of the night as any sword-for-hire, but that was not why he had ventured out. Finn had been on his mind since he'd first seen her in the common room. There was pressure in the air like a storm was coming, and storms always made Iseult uneasy. Growing up on the sea would do that to a man.

As a child, Iseult lived in a very different world. Or perhaps, he conceded, it was only his perspective that had changed, and not the world itself. Iseult hailed from a clan all but extinct in the present day, as far as he knew. There were very few left when he was a boy, and after his mother passed, he lost touch with his remaining kin. No, the clan of Uí Néid was gone he assured himself, but he still remembered the histories.

His mother had been very fond of the histories, and had shown him many books that she'd rescued from their homeland. The books were long since lost to him, usurped by the archives most likely, but he remembered them nearly word for word.

That was how he knew Finn. He had seen a portrait of her in the records of his clan . . . but that was impossible. She would be over a hundred years old. She didn't look a day over twenty-two. Perhaps she had been named after an ancestor, one that looked startlingly similar to her. Perhaps not. Either way, he had to know. He could not pass up an opportunity to know what his people had died for, and to right their wrongs if at all possible.

Iseult shook his head as he came back upon the still-unconscious stableman, but his thoughts were elsewhere. She didn't look a day over twenty-two, but he knew it was her. It had to be her.

Finn was back in her warm room before she paused to consider Iseult. There was something about that man that she did not like. She felt as if he hid a great deal. The shadows of night suited him. Luckily he was staying out in his shadows, and likely would not be up early to leave the inn. Given that Àed would most definitely have them up and on the road at first light, they could probably slip away before the man even woke. Finn curled up on her bed and closed her eyes, thoughts swirling. She did not think she would be able to sleep, but she was wrong.

When Finn woke, Àed was already heating water over the fire in a small, metal pot. Sensing her alertness, he stood and poured the water into the basin and turned to her. "I figured ye'd like some hot water to wash with this morning," he explained.

Finn nodded appreciatively as she sat up. The room was much warmer than it had been the previous night, and she was grateful for that fact as she climbed out of her scratchy blankets. "We'll leave as soon as we're clean?" she asked anxiously.

Àed grunted. "It'll take ye awhile to get yerself clean I imagine, given that ye were rollin around in the dirt again last night."

Finn blushed. "I couldn't sleep. It feels strange to be in a new place."

The lines softened on Àed's face as he chuckled. "Figured as much. We'll clean up then fetch some breakfast. Then we'll be on our way. There's no rush, as we'll be campin tonight no matter how far we get. Felgram is a full three days walk from here, perhaps four."

Finn nodded and rose to clean herself. She looked forward to sleeping outside, and wanted to get out of the inn as soon as possible. She did not believe that Iseult would give them any trouble, but she'd just as soon not have another encounter with him. She would only feel safe again once she and Àed had left Garenoch far behind them.

Finn did her best to scrub the dirt from her hands and feet with the warm water, then sat to run the wooden comb Àed had given her through her waist-length hair, which seemed to become matted and snarled after every night's rest. Seeing her frustration, Àed approached and took the comb from her, helped her to remove the rest of her tangles, then deftly wove her hair into a thick braid, securing the end with a piece of twine he pulled from his satchel.

When Finn gazed up at him, mildly amazed, he shrugged. "I did me daughter's braids for many years," he explained gruffly, then went to shove his few belongings back into their knapsacks.

Finn watched her companion, wishing she could know more about his daughter, but knowing it was not her place to ask. Shaking her head sadly, she donned her too big clothing and made peace with the fact that wearing the hand-me-down dress was likely the closest she would ever come to Àed's lost little girl.

As Àed finished packing his things, Finn went to wait by the door. She wore her cloak securely fastened with her knapsack over her shoulder so that she would be ready to leave quickly if need be. She wasn't sure what she was worried about, and figured that her human instincts were likely playing tricks on her. Still, she would feel rather foolish if she ignored her unease, and ended up in a bad situation because of it. Plus, she would not risk Àed falling into trouble. She knew the old man had come to protect her, but she felt the unsettling need to protect him as well.

They left their room and descended the stairs to find the common room much more full than it had been the previous night. It seemed that everyone rose with the sun in

Garenoch, from farmers and travelers, to wealthy merchants and other noble sorts. To Finn's dismay, she spotted Iseult and the rest of his company, already seated and drinking hot tea. In addition to the twins, two more had joined them, a man and a woman.

The woman held her nose up high, gazing around the room but not really focusing on anything. She had very pale skin that showed a light burn on her nose and cheeks, giving away that she had been seeing more sun than she was accustomed to. Her hair was dark, and done up in a complex series of braids that came together to fall over her shoulder. The man beside her was a little more used to the sun, as was evident by his deep tan. Wavy, deep chestnut brown hair that fell just above his shoulders was left unfettered, while most of the other men in the room wore their hair back in leather clasps. The man's golden brown eyes followed the serving maids around the room good-naturedly, if not without a touch of mischief.

Not paying the group any mind, Àed seated himself at a table near the back of the room with a few other travelers. There were no entirely free tables, and many patrons sat with others who were obviously not their companions. At one table, two farm hands sat with women in velvets, and at another a man with a billowing white shirt and a swatch of cloth knotted around the top of his head sat with three quiet men in black.

Finn followed Àed's lead and sat beside him, trying to avoid eye contact with anyone in the room. She leaned in close to the old man's shoulder and whispered, "Why are there so many people here this morning?"

Àed cast a furtive glance around the bustling room.

"Likely all the talk of Pooks and other Faie," he replied. "Folk start seeing those things in the countryside, and they're all bound to migrate to the nearest burgh. In addition, Garenoch resides along a trade road. Many travelers pass through."

Finn nodded. She supposed it was good that there were so many outsiders in the burgh. Travelers would not be a rare sight, and they would likely not be bothered much along their way. She lost herself in thought, picturing where they might end up next. Because of this, she did not notice as the red haired man rose from his table and came to sit on the opposite side of Àed, until it was too late to flee.

The old man turned to the younger one with an expectant sigh, and a less than friendly look on his aged face.

The red haired man did not seem put off in the least. In fact, his face was lit up with excitement. "Forgive me the intrusion," he began, speaking mainly to Àed, though he did spare a nod in Finn's direction. "My name is Anders Cattenach. I'm a historian of sorts, and I just realized how I know your face."

"I ain't nobody to take notice of," Àed grumbled, waving him off.

"Oh but you are," the man persisted, his honey-brown eyes staring intently. "You're Àed Deasmhumhain. Àed the Mountebank."

Àed kept his eyes on the table. "I've no idea what yer talkin about."

Not daunted in the least, the red-haired man went on. "Where have you been all of these years? Most have believed you dead."

"I am no mountebank!" Àed growled, drawing attention

from their fellow diners. He turned away from Anders, dismissing him.

"I meant no offense," Anders said hurriedly, though he was speaking to Àed's back. "I only wanted to speak with you, to have a unique viewpoint into the more recent histories. I'm sure you have a great deal of knowledge to share."

Àed grunted again, then slowly turned back to glare at Anders. "And what do ye be offerin in return, lad?" he asked almost menacingly.

Anders grew excited once more. "If you would travel with us, at least for a short way, we would provide you with horses, food, rooms. Anything you need along the way. We have a swordsman traveling with us, so we can offer you a measure of protection as well."

"Where ye traveling?" Àed asked unenthusiastically.

"This morning we are journeying toward Felgram," Anders explained hurriedly. "We plan to make the course in less than two days. Then we make for Migris, stopping in the burghs bordering the Sand Road along the way."

Àed considered for a moment. "That'll do, lad. At least for a time."

Anders nodded excitedly and stood. "I shall make the preparations, and of course, your breakfast shall be accounted for as well."

Àed paid no attention as Anders left the table to speak to the innkeep. Instead he waved down a barmaid, a younger girl this time. There were actually several barmaids that morning, carrying around large plates of eggs, bannocks, and smoked meats.

"Why would we agree to go with them?" Finn whispered

harshly as soon as the woman had taken their orders and retreated.

"Got us horses, didn't I?" Àed pointed out. "And rations and a bit of security. Road thieves will be much less likely to bother us if we're with that lot, and we can make it to Felgram in two days instead of four."

Finn shook her head in disbelief. "But we will be traveling with that man, a thief!" she replied hotly. "He was skulking around outside last night, our aim is not to travel to this . . . this Migris. Our aim is, is, well, *my* aim."

"And ye know where ye need to go lass?" At Finn's stunned expression, he went on, "I've someone that might be able to help ye, and that someone is on the road to Migris. Also ye cannae throw stones about skulking, as ye were doin the same."

Finn opened her mouth to say more, then snapped it shut. The barmaid came back with two heaping plates of food, and two mugs of hot tea.

Finn sucked her teeth in annoyance. "What was that he called you?" she prodded. "The Mountebank?"

Àed took a deep swig of his tea, despite how hot it was. "Young ones tell silly stories," he mumbled. "Ain't a single truth teller among them."

Finn smiled, pleased to have finally gotten a rise out of the old man. "What did you do?" she asked smugly.

Àed slammed his mug down suddenly, sloshing liquid onto the tabletop. "I did nothin!"

Nearby gazes turned their way again, and Àed looked down at the table in embarrassment. He took a deep breath, then continued more quietly, "It's a past havin to do with me daughter, and I won't be talkin about it."

"But you agreed to talk about it with that man. That's the only reason he's paying for our travels . . . " she began softly.

"I won't be talkin about *that* with anyone," Àed confirmed. "I'll tell the lad a few stories, most of which will be false, and we'll travel well because of it."

Finn's mood sobered instantly. Unsure of what else to say, she began eating her food. The meat was a little salty for her taste, but the eggs were wonderful. She actually began to enjoy herself as she ate, until she accidentally glanced at the table where their new traveling companions sat. None looked her way, but she had the feeling that they had only just turned away as she looked at them. Finn turned back to her food with a sour feeling in her stomach, and could not eat another bite.

CHAPTER SIX

*F*inn was not sure that her horse could be called a horse, but she liked her anyhow. The gray beast had large mule ears, and a shaggy-haired face and body. Aed's was similar, but slightly shorter and muddy brown in color.

Anders had apologized profusely for the state of the horses, apparently none better could be found in Garenoch. He even went to the extent of offering his own steed in place of her gray mare, but Finn felt it unnecessary.

The more pressing problem that Finn found, was that her skirts were not well suited for riding. There was at least enough fabric that even if it hiked up, it would billow to cover a good portion of her legs, though it would have left her ankles and calves bare if it weren't for her tall boots. Yet that wasn't the problem. The problem was found in getting up on the horse. Finn had to hike her skirts far above her knees in order to hoist one leg up in the stirrup, and the other over the saddle. Àed had warned her that showing extra skin was abnormal, but there simply was no other way to climb into the saddle. When leaving Garenoch, she'd turned the horse away from the group as much as possible, but townsfolk in the street had watched her and laughed as she fumbled her way up. The other women of the company had skirts divided for riding, and she eyed them with envy as they rode along.

After leaving Garenoch, the party plodded slowly down the dirt road in silence for several hours. In the fore, were those who Finn had learned were the emissary and her escort. They were followed by Finn and Àed, who were followed by Anders and his sister, Branwen. The two in the lead were slowly gaining more and more distance, due to Finn and Àed's slower mounts. Iseult rode ahead more often than not, but sometimes dropped back to the rear. The man had not spoken a single word to her since they'd departed, not even as they passed the spectacle of the stableman, strung up by his bootstrings from the eave of the inn. It seemed a proper place for him, swaying by the sheep sign, face bright red from being in an inverted state. It had made Finn smile, though she hid it quickly.

The road to Felgram was rocky, with deep green grasses scattered about despite the cold. The trees were shorter than they were in Finn's glen, and twisted sideways instead of up, as if the sky crushed them down. She didn't like the strange, twisted trees, but they were better than none, she supposed.

Branwen sped her horse up to ride beside Finn, forcing Àed to fall back next to Anders if he wanted to keep his horse on the path. "It's lovely having you along for our journey," Branwen commented cheerfully as the men fell back behind them.

Finn nodded, not sure what to say. The girl seemed very young to be a scholar. Her cheeks were flushed with the chilly morning air, and her red hair fluttered about freely in the wind like wisps of flame.

"I mean," Branwen went on as she leaned in to speak more quietly, "it's nice to have another *woman* along."

Finn leaned in as well and nodded in the direction of Liaden. "It would seem you already had another woman along."

"Well yes," Branwen chuckled, "but she's not a very friendly sort. Hardly says a word to us *common* folk. I'm left with just the company of my brother and our hired sword, and Kai's wandering eyes as well," she laughed again. "At least with a swordsman along, we don't have to be afraid of bandits."

"Yes," Finn replied distantly, "but aren't you afraid of the swordsman?"

Branwen only smiled. "Heaven's no. He comes highly recommended."

"I'm sure he does," Finn mumbled disconcertedly.

Branwen had to continually tug on her mount's reins to keep the horse at pace with Finn's mule-creature, but she stubbornly refused to leave Finn's side. "He never speaks though, our swordsman I mean," Branwen continued. "I've heard roughly five sentences out of him the entire time we've traveled together."

"He spoke fine last night," Finn mumbled.

"What was that?" Branwen questioned, as she had not heard Finn over the wind.

"And how long have you traveled together?" Finn asked loudly.

Finn's face was growing numb with the cold wind that threatened to pull her hair out of its braid. She tugged the hood of her green cloak up to cover her ears, but the wind pulled it right back down again, leaving her face and neck bare to the chilly air. Branwen seemed unaffected, and left her burgundy cloak flapping open around her. Why anyone would choose to travel when the air was still icy was beyond Finn's comprehension. Of course, she had chosen it, but she had good reason.

"He hired on with us in the Gray City," Branwen explained. "Many of the sellswords wait there for work. They do in all of the cities, really. Anyhow," she paused, deciding what to say, "you have a very interesting travel companion."

Finn laughed, but Branwen looked at her like she did not get the joke.

"He's not terribly interesting at all," Finn explained. "Just a grouchy old man with a good heart, who cares a little bit too much about clean feet and fast travels."

"But he's Àed the Mountebank," Branwen replied excitedly. "He must be around one hundred years old by now, maybe more. I don't know how he still gets around as well as he does-"

"Why do they call him that?" Finn interrupted. "The Mountebank?"

"Well," Branwen explained, her face taking on a studious look, "it is fabled that the Mountebank once possessed great powers. He was a conjurer, to put it quite plainly. He helped people, sure, but he also swindled them. He became well known as a trickster of sorts, talking good folk into deals that they didn't understand. He would take them for what they were worth, then point out in the end what they had actually agreed to.

"Of course, as in any good story, he eventually fell in love. The woman's name was Mira, a merchant's daughter by all accounts. Love changed the Mountebank, and he spent many years trying to live up to his wife's view of him. Eventually the wife found that she was with child, only she died in child birth. I'm sorry," Branwen smiled self deprecatingly. "I'm quite terrible at storytelling."

"Your storytelling is fine," Finn comforted. "Please continue."

Branwen nodded to herself. "Well, his wife died, and the Mountebank was left with a little girl to raise all on his own. The little girl's name was Keiren. As Keiren grew, the Mountebank tried to do well by his wife's memory, raising her to treat people with kindness. Then came the eve of Keiren's sixteenth birthday, and with that birthday came powers of her very own. Though he tried to influence her away from wrong-doing, Keiren used her power much in the way the Mountebank had. He tried to stop her, to control her in some way, but she had turned out just as powerful as he. In the end she crippled him, not physically, but magically. He had threatened her, but couldn't carry through. She was his daughter after all. She wasn't quite so sentimental."

Finn nodded, but was too deep in thought to reply further.

"I take it you didn't know any of that?" Branwen asked.

"Not quite," Finn said sadly. "What happened to Keiren?"

Branwen shrugged. "Some say she still lives, only under a different name. Some say she rules over some distant land. Others say she died alone. No one truly knows."

So that explained the old man's sadness, Finn thought to herself. She felt more sorry than before for having pushed him. She also realized he likely aided her to the extent he did, in order to somehow make up for not being able to aid his own daughter.

"And you're paying our way," Finn began, "just to have more of a chance to speak with him?"

Branwen nodded. "It's not a great expense, and when so much can be learned! Why, I could write an entire book about it. He's been missing for a good fifty years. No one has seen him. Well, there have been claims of course, but I'd wager the lot of them have little foundation in truth. How did you come to travel with him?"

It took Finn a moment to realize that Branwen had asked her a question during her deluge of words. She wished she hadn't heard it at all. She had not planned on conversing with many strangers, and therefore had not created a backstory for herself.

"Well," Finn began, frantically trying to think of a lie. Her horse snuffled as if aware of her unease. "I lived in the same glen as Àed."

"In a glen?" Branwen interrupted. "Did many people live there?"

"No," Finn explained, as a story formed in her mind, "but it was not far from Garenoch. Many people traveled that way to hunt, and there were farms not far off."

Finn's tension eased as Branwen nodded in understanding. "I'm trying to find my extended family," Finn continued more confidently. "I was planning a journey and Àed, knowing I had not seen much of the world on my own, offered to accompany me. It's not much of a story, really."

Branwen looked thoughtful. "So, he's just been living in a house in a glen all of this time?"

Finn shrugged. "I cannot account for the past fifty years," she replied, though really she could, "but he's lived there all of my lifetime."

Branwen nodded again, then looked to the front of their line. "It looks like we're stopping to eat."

Finn looked ahead of where they rode to find the emissary and her companion already dismounted. The companion was doing his best to build a fire in spite of the wind, while the emissary filled a small iron kettle with tea. Finn's stomach growled at the thought of tea, and perhaps some food as well. They'd only been traveling three hours or so, but they were a rough three hours given the cold and wind. She was more than ready for a break.

Finn and Branwen reached the others and dismounted, followed by the rest of their group. Àed had a sour expression on his face as he sat down next to Finn. It was clear that he had not enjoyed riding next to Anders. Finn was ready to give him a glare for being ungrateful, then realized she was probably wearing the same expression. She was not used to having to lie, and she found that she did not enjoy it at all.

Branwen took up a seat right next to Finn, but Anders sat next to his sister instead of on the other side of Àed. Finn imagined the old man had likely given the younger man quite a tongue lashing to have Anders acting so cowed. The emissary, Liaden, and her companion Kai were positioned across from Finn's group, while Iseult sat off to one side, clearly preferring to be apart from the gathering.

Anders opened a knapsack he had retrieved from one of the horses and began carving off hunks from a hard loaf of bread. He passed the pieces around, followed by thick slices of dry, salty cheese. When the tea was hot, Liaden poured each of them a cup. It was clear to Finn that this was the normal routine of the company, for no one spoke as the food was passed from hand to hand in an organized manner. Anders looked quite pleased as Finn and Àed took their mugs in hand, likely proud that he'd had the foresight to have extra mugs available.

As they ate, Kai eyed Finn like he wasn't quite sure what she was. The men all had obvious staring issues, Finn thought. She wondered if it was perhaps not as rude as she believed, since they all did it so blatantly. She also wondered how she knew such a thing could be rude to begin with. She must have heard it from a hunter, or one of the girls that sometimes picnicked in her glen.

Finn aimed her dark eyes right back at the man. "Is there something you would like to ask?" she said, finally breaking the silence.

Everyone stopped eating to regard her, and Kai's face cracked into a wide smile as his dark brown hair flopped about in the wind. "You are rather brazen, aren't you?" he asked mirthfully.

Finn glared and pushed at strands of her own hair as it escaped her braid to tickle her face. "Brazen would be eyeing you in return. As it is, I am simply drawing attention to the fact that you were eyeing me to begin with."

"Where do you hail from again?" he asked, ignoring her statement.

"Leave the poor girl alone," Branwen chided. "She has no need for your lascivious glances and absurd word games."

Kai chuckled and turned his attention to Branwen. "Would you rather I focused them on you?"

Finn leaned closer to Àed, who was looking increasingly irritated. "Regretting the company yet?" she whispered.

Àed grunted in reply. Finn looked past the old man to see Iseult contemplating her with a raised eyebrow, and she raised one back at him in return. He turned his attention back to his cup of tea, chuckling to himself.

"It's a good question," Liaden began, speaking over the argument that had begun between Kai and Branwen. "It has been explained to me who the old man is, but if we are to travel together, I would know where the girl is from as well."

Liaden did not appear to be much older than Finn's physical form, but she said *girl* as if she were referring to someone much younger, and of course, far less mature than herself.

"I hail from an area south of Garenoch, southeast of Greenswallow," Finn answered simply, having rehearsed the words in her head.

Liaden stared back at her, expressionless. "You do not speak or act like a country bumpkin," she stated.

Finn's pulse rose. She had not considered that she should act a certain way. "My father was a well-educated and traveled man," she lied. She had never known such a thing as a father. Or if she had, she did not remember him.

"And where was your father from?" Liaden asked, not giving Finn a moment to think.

"At what point did it become polite to interrogate guests like criminals?" Branwen interrupted, saving Finn a second time.

Liaden eyed Branwen coolly, and answered with a curt nod. Kai observed the exchange with amusement. He was likely used to his lady's attitude, and chose to find it funny instead of vexing. Finn was going with the latter herself.

"If ye all are done chattering," Àed grumbled, "we best be movin on."

"Are we in a hurry?" Liaden snapped, riled and ready for an argument.

"Storm," Iseult remarked simply.

Sure enough, a storm was brewing behind them, near Garenoch. Finn was ashamed that she had not noticed it. As a tree, a tiny shift in pressure would have been immediately evident, yet now she had to actually look at the sky to confirm Iseult's statement. Finn quickly stood and dusted herself off, frustrated that someone had seen the storm before her, and more than ready to be done with the current string of conversation. She strode to her horse, followed by the rest of the group. A storm was coming. The idea resounded with her much more than it should have.

CHAPTER SEVEN

*T*hey kept up a brisk pace, but the storm gained on them regardless. As soon as they found shelter, they would need to make an early camp. *If* they found shelter.

The landscape was still wide open, with the stunted, twisted trees here and there. The cloud-darkened sky and lack of landmarks made Finn feel like she was watching the same scene over and over again as they rode. Her half-breed horse stumbled often as it trotted across the rocky landscape, unused to the lively pace. The animal would not be able to keep up with the steady speed for as long as the others, and Finn began to fear being left behind.

Most of the party rode in grim silence, except for Branwen. She did not seem overly affected by much. Finn caught pieces of Branwen's one-sided conversation whenever the wind blew her way, but the conversation was growing more distant as the gap between the group widened.

Iseult, who was at the head of the now distant party,

suddenly veered his horse from the path without a signal to say why he was doing so. The other horses followed without question. Finn searched their surroundings through squinted eyes for an explanation, and found it in the form of a far-off rocky overhang. It was the first real shelter they'd seen that day.

Just then, the first raindrops fell. Soon the rain turned into a flurry from the wind, pelleting Finn with little drops from all directions. She was overcome with gratitude for Iseult as the first riders neared the overhang. The area appeared large enough to fit all members of the company as well as their horses. As the other riders reached shelter, Iseult left them to double back toward Finn and Àed. He did not speak as he reached them, and instead rode beside Finn silently as she urged along her less than spry mount. Finn kept her eyes forward, not acknowledging Iseult's unwarranted show of chivalry.

The rain had just soaked through Finn's cloak and was beginning to touch her clothes underneath as she reached the overhang. She dismounted, not caring how much she had to hike her skirts up to do so, to lead her horse out of the rain. Kai had already set to unsaddling the horses that had first reached shelter, while Anders built a fire from branches gathered before the rain could soak them thoroughly.

When Kai finished unsaddling his own mount, he approached Finn and reached out a hand for her reins. Finn offered them, expecting him to tease her in some manner, but he simply took the reins and winked at her from below his damp hair that looked almost black with moisture. Iseult and Àed followed and tended to their horses themselves.

Everyone gathered around the fire as it roared to life, shedding damp cloaks and hanging them wherever they could to dry. Finn, who had been late to sit down as she'd been preoccupied with watching the storm, was forced to sit close to Iseult in order to be near the fire. She felt slightly uncomfortable, but the opportunity to thaw her hands by the flames was too much to pass up. The man sat rigid as a pole, likely as uncomfortable with Finn's nearness as she was with his. To Finn's other side sat Branwen, who offered her a comforting smile, prompting Finn to relax the tension that radiated through her body. If Liaden's questions began again, she wasn't sure what she would do.

Finished with the horses, Kai wedged himself between Finn and Branwen, turning to grin at Finn while ignoring the other woman. Finn tried to make herself as small as possible, but found her shoulders pushed against both Iseult's and Kai's arms. She wasn't sure which man made her more uncomfortable, but she was leaning toward Iseult. Kai seemed harmless. Iseult did not.

"Oh for heaven's sake," Branwen scolded Kai. "Give the woman a break."

"I just don't want our guest to get cold," Kai explained, waggling his eyebrows at Finn. "You told us to be polite."

"I'm feeling mighty cold over here!" Àed exclaimed from across the fire. Liaden, who was positioned between Anders and Àed, let out an abrupt laugh.

Stunned silence fell over the rest group as they tried to figure out whether or not the Mountebank was joking. Rather than relieving the tension, Àed warmed his hands by the fire and ignored everyone's glances, though when no one else was looking, he gave Finn a sly wink.

The joke unfortunately was not enough to rattle Kai, who stayed right where he was. Though Finn was annoyed, she was also quite cold, so she settled in and took what warmth the man's shoulder against hers had to offer.

The tea kettle reappeared from the satchel strapped to Liaden's saddle, and soon Finn had the added warmth of a steaming mug in her hands. As they drank their tea, Anders eyed Àed expectantly, but was obviously too afraid to speak.

"I think," Finn began, breaking the silence, "that you ought to live up to your half of the bargain old man, before Anders bursts from anticipation."

Liaden smirked, surprising Finn with a second sign of mirth that evening. "Yes," she agreed. "Do entertain the lad, this *bursting* business sounds like a mess."

Àed grunted, but then acquiesced. "What would ye like to hear, lad? Nothing too personal mind ye."

Anders was practically bouncing with excitement as he tried to think of what to ask first. "What about your travels with Caratacus Loch'le?" he replied quickly. "So little is truly known about the man."

Àed cleared his throat as everyone turned their attention to him. "Caratacus," he began, "was a liar and a cheat . . . but so was I, so our partnership worked out quite well, as long as we didn't lie to each other. At least not too much."

As Àed continued with his story, Kai reached out and tried to put an arm casually around Finn. She glared at him and whispered, "Don't push it."

He dropped his arm, but leaned close to her ear and whispered back, "You can't blame a man for trying, eh?"

Finn smiled in spite of herself, and turned to whisper, "I

imagine you try quite a bit, and get blamed for it all the same."

Kai shrugged and pressed his shoulder back against hers. It seemed he would take what he could get. No one else noticed the exchange, all enthralled in Àed's story. All except Iseult. Finn thought that he missed very little, though at the moment he was looking out toward the sky and the worsening storm.

Àed continued his stories as the sky slowly turned to night. Finn stared out into the near-darkness, wishing for a reprieve, but the rain only increased. It was fortunate that their swatch of land rose up to meet the base of the overhang, else they would have been soaked regardless of the stone above their heads. The horses, not enjoying the rain either, stomped their hooves uneasily and searched the ground for patches of yellow grass.

Slowly, as Finn drifted off to sleep, her head came to rest upon Kai's shoulder. The last thing she heard was Anders making a joke at Kai's expense. Something about only being able to woo women when they were fast asleep. The next thing she knew was that thunder woke her, and she had somehow gotten wrapped up in her bedroll with Àed on one side of her and Branwen on the other.

She sat up slightly to see everyone else fast asleep in their bedrolls, except for Liaden, who was up to stoke the fire with twigs and branches scraped up from their dry swatch of land. Liaden noted that Finn was awake, then looked past her into the darkness.

The pale woman's dark eyes, illuminated by the fire, narrowed at something in the distance. "Did you see that?" she whispered.

Finn crawled out of the bedroll and away from her sleeping companions to look out into the darkness, but she could make out little through the fog. "See what?" she whispered back, still looking for what the woman had seen.

Liaden left the fire and walked closer to Finn. They both crept toward the edge of the overhang, but stopped out of reach of the rain. "I saw something move out there," Liaden explained quietly. "Like a tall, white figure in the dark, but when I looked again, it was gone."

Finn could smell woodsmoke and the scent of musky herbs as Laiden hovered beside her. They looked off into the darkness together, but nothing moved. They both nearly jumped out of their skins as another face appeared between them.

"Are you two well?" Kai whispered.

"I saw something," Liaden explained breathlessly.

"Probably just a muntjac or some other creature," Kai suggested.

"What's a muntjac?" Finn asked quietly.

Kai leaned his face close to hers as they gazed out into the darkness. "It's a little furry animal with horns and hooves that will nibble your toes in the night, if you're not careful."

Liaden smirked. "Only the first part of that statement is true, Finn. It was not a muntjac. It was larger."

Kai shrugged. "Well I don't see anything now." He turned to Finn. "I will gladly nibble your toes, if the muntjac fails to do so."

Liaden gave Kai a gentle shove. "Go to sleep you lascivious fool."

Kai spared a final smile for Finn, but did as his lady bid

him. Liaden took one last look out into the darkness, then did the same, crawling back into her bedroll without another word. Soon the camp eased back into the gentle sounds of slumber.

That was all good and well for them, but there was no way that Finn would be able to sleep with the idea of something out there watching them. Anything could be out there in the dark. Finn's imagination went wild with thoughts of Bucca and other Tuatha De.

When she was a tree, there were always beasts around in the night. Many of them even climbed and lived in her branches. It was a much different feeling though, when a bear would rather eat you than scratch his back against your bark, and a snake would rather bite you than curl up amongst your exposed roots. The Bucca she had enjoyed watching over the past few years now seemed fearsome to Finn, and she hoped that they were not lurking anywhere near their camp.

Finn crawled back into her bedroll, but was still awake when the sun rose, which luckily was only two hours or so from when she first awoke. She untangled herself from her bedding and rose to restoke the fire. It had burned down to just a few embers, but with some dry grass and dead branches from underneath the overhang, she was able to get it burning again.

She was startled when Àed walked up beside her to warm his wizened hands by the weak flames. There was still a light drizzle of rain outside of their shelter, painting the scenery in foggy blues and grays. His gray robes and hat matched the scenery perfectly. With the addition of his hair and beard, he would easily blend in from a distance.

Finn stood and tugged her green cloak off the large rock she had draped it over. Even with the shelter of the over-hang it had not dried entirely. The air was still cold, chilling the damp fabric, but at least the wind had let up.

"What were ye fools goin on about in the middle of the night?" Àed asked without looking up at Finn.

Finn let out a long yawn. "Liaden thought she saw some-thing in the darkness."

"Hmph," was Àed's only reply as their other companions began to rise.

They quickly ate a breakfast of honey bannocks, then returned to the road, wanting to get as far as possible before more bad weather came. The light drizzle of rain was annoying, but with any luck they would make it to the next burgh, and the warmth of an inn that night.

CHAPTER EIGHT

hey did not make it to the next burgh. Torrents
of rain had forced the party to temporarily end
their journey after only a few short hours of travel. This
time there was no crag to be found, and the party found
themselves gathered around the trunk of a great pine tree.
The tree was much larger than Finn had been, with its
lowest branches beginning well above Finn's head,
providing a fair amount of shelter from the downpour,
though there was little protection from the wind. The
horses, unimpressed with this new shelter, hung their heads
near the ground in defeat.

Liaden peered out into the mist from her post beside
Finn. "I swear I see something out there," she said for the
fourth time that hour.

"Yer jumpin at shadows lass," Àed grunted in reply.

Liaden eyed the old man sharply, her dark eyes
reminding Finn of a bird of prey . . . a wet and angry bird of

prey. Her near-black hair hung loose, dripping rivulets of water down the sides of her dark cloak.

"I am not a child to be jumping at shadows," Liaden chided. "I've plenty of experience with travels. I'm not some scared little girl."

Àed shrugged as if unaffected by the scolding. He'd hung his sack-like hat from one of the tree's lower branches to dry, leaving his silver hair to whip about around his face. "Well I ain't seen nothin," he grumbled as he wrapped his arms tightly around himself.

Finn looked out in the direction Liaden had been scanning, wishing that she felt comfortable enough to stand near the woman for added warmth. There was something . . . as quick as she saw it, it was gone. Yet she could have sworn that she'd seen white figures out in the mist, swaying with slight movement.

Finn gave Liaden a worried look, but Liaden was too distracted to see it. Finn turned her attention back to the distance, wanting to voice what she'd seen, but not wanting to be scolded as Liaden had. The white shapes came back into view. It was as if they flickered in and out of being with every blink, making Finn question whether she was really seeing them at all. The rest of their party continued to scan their surroundings, even as they brushed off Liaden's sightings as nothing more than her eyes playing tricks on her. Yet, it was clear to Finn that they did not see anything.

The rain kept on, engulfing the party in darkness long before the sun had set on the horizon. Camp was made. Cold and miserable, the party gathered around the weak, sputtering fire with solemn wishes for a clear morning.

After only an hour or so the fire was on its last limb,

metaphorically and literally. There was little dry wood to be found, and the lower branches of the pine were too green to burn. Anders had taken to scraping up dry needles to throw into the fire, but by the time he came up with another handful, the previous one had already burned to nothing. Finn pushed her hands toward the dying embers, just as her body erupted in goosebumps that had nothing to do with the cold.

At first Finn thought the figure was her imagination. Some specter her mind conjured up after her and Liaden's earlier sightings. Then he cleared his throat, and the entire company turned to face him.

No one had seen him approach, he was suddenly just there. Before Finn could blink, Iseult was on his feet with a small dagger in his hand. Finn had no idea where the blade had come from, she'd never seen it on him before.

"I mean no ill," the figure said serenely barely glancing at Iseult and his threatening blade. "I only wish to share your fire."

"Name yourself, stranger," Iseult ordered, at the same time Anders said, "There isn't much fire left to share."

The man gave Iseult a wide berth and approached the fire. As he walked, he removed the hood of his white cloak to reveal a completely bald head with skin so pale that, as the moonlight reflected off his face, blue veins could be seen flowing across his scalp. His large eyes shone in the darkness like those of a cat.

"Ceàrdaman," Àed observed.

"The craftspeople?" Branwen questioned, obviously awestricken. "*Travelers?*" she said the word like it meant more than it should.

"One and the same," the man answered amicably. "It is good to be among those who know their history."

"Tricksters and thieves," Iseult growled. "I know your people."

"And my people know you, Meirleach," the man chuckled.

Iseult glared at the man for a moment, then abruptly turned and stalked off into the rain.

"I'm afraid we don't have much to offer you," Branwen interjected, not at all put off by Iseult's departure.

"Why would you offer this man anything?" Liaden questioned. The dark haired woman had backed away from the fire toward the base of the tree, so that only the pale oval of her face could be seen in the darkness.

Finn noticed that the others had shifted positions as well. Anders stood behind Finn, as if she would shield him from harm. Kai stood near his mistress, but slightly closer to the fire, close enough that Finn could see him clearly as the flames flickered.

Finn turned back toward the fire with a start. The flames *were* flickering. The man, Ceàrdaman as Àed had called him, held his hands up to the warmth with a calm smile on his face. His fingers were unnaturally long, making it seem like each one had an extra joint.

"That's what you do with the Travelers," Branwen explained. She sat closer to the man, showing no worry about his sudden manifestation. "You offer them food and whatever else you can give, and they share with you either a craft or a secret."

Liaden sniffed. "What good is a secret to us?"

The man held up a hand with his long pointer finger

outstretched. The translucent skin of his palm stood out in the darkness, drawing Finn's attention to the Traveler's long, cracked fingernails. "Ah, but a secret is good for many a thing," the Traveler explained. "If only you knew the secrets that this group held!" He withdrew his hand and steepled his fingers together in excitement.

Finn's pulse sped. This man couldn't possibly know her secret. They had only just met him, yet her heart was in her throat none-the-less. There was something inhuman about the Traveler. Something that Finn did not trust at all.

The Traveler gave Finn a small, knowing smile. "Sadly it is not my place to tell the secrets of others," he explained, looking directly at her.

He turned back toward Branwen. "A place at your fire is the only boon I require. The gift shall be a secret, as I have been traveling a long way, and am without my crafts."

Branwen nodded excitedly as the remainder of the party crept closer. Few mortals were immune to the lure of a secret, Finn thought to herself. Iseult was still nowhere to be seen. Some already held too many secrets to have room for more.

"The seasons are changing," the man began dramatically, "and I do not mean the unseasonable rain. The lines are faltering, undoing the old and bringing life to the new. Trees will fall," with those words he looked at Finn, "and changed earth will be left in their place. A storm is coming, and once again, I do not mean the rains."

Finished, he looked down at the fire, humming as he turned his hands back and forth to warm both sides.

"What kind of a scunner-tongued secret was that?" Kai asked incredulously.

Branwen glared at Kai. "Shhh! The Traveler's secrets must be interpreted. We have just been gifted with a great wisdom."

Finn had an uneasy feeling that the Traveler's prophecy had something to do with why she was no longer a tree. *The lines are faltering.* What lines? She had to know more. She had made this journey to find answers, to find a way back to her old life. Perhaps this Traveler could help her.

"I will share your camp tonight," the Traveler announced. "Do not fear, the others of my kin will remain unseen."

"They're not unseen," Liaden snapped. "I saw them last night as well. You've been following us."

The Traveler smiled up at Liaden. The firelight reflecting off the shiny skin of his head made the light-hearted look seem menacing. "Sharing the same route is not following, Gray Lady."

Liaden glared at the Traveler, but it was obviously a cover for her unease. "How do you know where I hail from?"

The Traveler chuckled. "I do not speak of your city, my lady."

Liaden shook her head and stalked off to the other side of the great pine, followed by Kai. The rain had lessened to a drizzle, but it was still not wise to leave the sheltering circle. Iseult was still missing. The man had to be utterly soaked.

Àed had remained immobile during the entire exchange. After his naming the Traveler for what he was, he had refused to acknowledge the strange man again. Finn knew she would likely be better off following Àed's example, but the Traveler's words repeated in her head, *trees will fall*. He knew what had happened to her, she was sure of it.

Finn stood and shifted her weight from foot to foot. She wanted to speak with the Traveler of her problems, but she could not do so while Anders and Branwen were still present. She decided she would have to wait until the twins and everyone else fell asleep. Hopefully the Traveler would not mind being wakened. The Traveler acknowledged her with his strange reflective eyes, as if he read her thoughts. He further verified this with a slight inclination of his head.

Iseult was not fond of Travelers at the best of times. Not only had his people had troubles with them in the past, he had met them himself along the road on his own travels many times. He was growing less fond by the minute as he stood alone in the freezing rain, still as a statue.

The Ceàrdaman knew far too much for his liking. He did not understand why they searched for secrets, when they knew them all already. The few he had met always seemed to know everything about him, yet they pestered him about his lineage, about what he knew of his people.

They had named him Meirleach. *Thief*. It was uncomfortable to be named thief whilst among employers. The weight of what was left unsaid was more uncomfortable still.

Many saw the Ceàrdaman as mysterious, magical beings. They were what remained of the Tuatha De, or at least they were the only ones to not hide themselves from the realm of mortals. To most, a meeting with a Traveler was a treat.

Iseult knew better. He knew them for what they were, tricksters and thieves. If you did not satisfy their *payment*, they took what they pleased, not discriminating between objects and people. They viewed both much the same.

Now there was one sharing their fire. Iseult couldn't help but wonder what the Ceàrdaman saw when he looked at Finn. Surely they knew more at least than he, and he was fairly certain that he knew quite a lot. Still, knowing what was in Finn's mind could likely save him a great deal of trouble. He knew he had to know more about her the first time he saw her. He had been the one who had encouraged Anders to invite the Mountebank along on their journey, an idea that Anders had eagerly lapped up. Had Anders refused, he would have parted ways with his company in order to follow Finn.

Leaving to follow Finn on his own would have been a contradiction to his duty, as he had agreed to escort the twins all the way to Migris, but he would have done it. It would have bothered him had he needed to break his contract, but leaving Finn anywhere near the Traveler irked him far more than anything. Still, he was not ready for his secrets to come out, secrets about who he was, and what he planned, at least not to everyone.

For a time, Branwen tried to wheedle more information out of the Traveler, but he made it clear that he had said what he had to say, and would say no more. When she prompted him about what he had said in regards to Iseult and Liaden, he simply pretended not to know what she was talking about. Eventually Branwen gave up and thanked the Traveler for his visit, then excused herself from the gathering with a yawn.

Almost immediately after Branwen retired, Àed and Anders excused themselves shortly thereafter. It had been too easy to get the Traveler alone, really. Finn looked at the bald man and he once again acknowledged her with a nod. Finn suspected that he had influenced the others in some way to leave them, though she did not understand how that was possible.

The Traveler arose and reseated himself near Finn, so that they might speak quietly. "Ask your questions, Dair Child," he whispered.

Being near the man made Finn uneasy. His presence gave her a feeling like touching her body to ice. He had called her Dair Child, Child of the Oak. It was true, she had been an oak, but the Traveler made it seem as if the term meant *more*.

"Why would you answer my questions, and not Branwen's?" Finn replied softly. "I've nothing to give you in return."

The Traveler shrugged, lifting his white cloak to pool around his skinny neck. "She is not of the old clans, she would have no use for the secrets I possess, except to write them in one of her little books. The Gray Lady might have use for me, if she had bothered to be polite."

"Gray Lady?" Finn asked, though she knew it was not her business.

"Of Clan Liath," the Traveler explained conversationally, "those who see the *Gray,* the inbetween places. She did not see my people first by happenstance. The others stood no chance of seeing us."

"Liaden didn't seem to understand why the others could not see you," Finn commented.

"Liaden?" the Traveler chuckled. "What an ironic name for her to choose. Liaden of Clan Liath. More ironic still that she doesn't even know what blood flows through her veins."

Finn shook her head, unsure of what the Traveler was going on about. "I think her parents probably chose her name, but that's beside the point. I saw you. Not last night, but tonight, before you approached. Does that mean that I hail from this Clan Liath as well?"

The Traveler shook his head. "The old bloods run strong, and you are not simply of the blood. You are of the Dair, and you must tell me how you came to be here." He eyed her intensely, as if daring her to lie.

Finn stumbled over her words, not sure what to say. "I-I was hoping you could tell *me* how I came to be this way. You see," she swallowed the lump in her throat before going on, "for as long as I can remember, I was a tree."

The Traveler tsked at her. "I can see it in your eyes, the other memories. You have them, yet you deny them. What are you running from?"

Finn shook her head sharply. "I have bits and pieces. It's just my imagination. I remember nothing."

"The Dair," the Traveler began, his voice taking on a lecturing tone, "are among the oldest of the people, the old clans. Where they came from, no one is sure, not even I. My people, the Ceàrdaman, existed before the appearance of the Dair, though that is not to say that the Dair did not exist in

84

some way before us. There was no creation that my people could see, the Dair just suddenly *were*. We called them the Children of the Oak, for their command over nature. Well," he clarified, "not command really, oneness. There existed one prominent clan, the Cavari, who became more involved with the world of the common folk while their kin were content to live on the periphery."

Finn listened intently. She knew all of this, somehow. It lingered in the corners of her mind.

"The Dair lived in peace for a time, until the conflict with Uí Néid. No man knows the reason for the conflict, the people of Uí Néid and the Cavari both held their secrets closely. They took those secrets to the grave, as both clans are extinct . . . mostly." The Traveler waited for Finn to process what he'd said.

Her thoughts swirled like an angry ocean. She wondered how she knew what an ocean was. Uí Néid was near the sea. A picture of a great city formed in her mind, with rows upon rows of small ships bordering the harbors, and tall people dressed in grays and black. Finn shook her head rapidly, willing the images away. It was like all of the other scenes she had recalled. Sometimes it was a place, or sometimes it was just a feeling, swimming through her mind and eventually leaving without an explanation.

The Traveler smiled warmly. "I have given you many secrets, Dair Child. Now you must tell me why the Cavari went to war, and why they disappeared. Those are secrets known to very few, and I would have them."

"I do not know," Finn muttered, her misery apparent. "I had hoped you could make me a tree again."

Sudden anger flashed over the Traveler's pallid face.

"You know very well that a tree is not your natural state. A tree is a tree, and a girl is a girl. *You* are a girl. I have given you a great boon, and I would have it repaid."

Finn stood and took a step back, desiring distance between the Traveler and herself. "You gave your information willingly," Finn whispered harshly. "I informed you that I had nothing to trade, and we made no deal of an exchange."

"It is what we do, who we are," he rasped as he stood and took a step forward to close the small amount of distance between them. "We give our secrets, and our crafts, in exchange for boons. I have given you a very great secret, and the payment must be high." The Traveler's face was no longer serene, his reflective eyes frightening in their fury.

Finn began to tremble, ever so slightly. "I have nothing to give you. I have nothing in this world. No people. No home. No memories."

The Traveler pressed close enough to Finn that the edges of his white robe brushed the hem of her skirts. "I *will* have my payment," he growled.

Finn stumbled away, with the Traveler matching her step for step. She reached the edge of the great pine's shelter, and took another step out into the rain. Her back knocked into something hard and damp.

"You are not welcome at this camp any longer, Ceàrdaman," Iseult stated coldly.

Finn's body flooded with relief as she turned to the side so that she could have both Iseult and the Traveler in her sights.

The Traveler laughed bitterly, then sneered up at Iseult. "This is no business of yours, Meirleach. If only you knew how tragic it is, you coming to the rescue of one of the Dair."

Iseult chuckled. "I know the histories of my people, Traveler. I know secrets much greater than yours." Iseult stood perfectly still, but there was a tension to him like a bow-string strung too tightly. Where the Traveler emanated cold, Iseult was thrumming with controlled energy.

The Traveler's sneer deepened. "You cannot know such things, Meirleach. You are a mere man; a shadow of what your people once were. Your blood means nothing in this time."

A smile curved the edges of Iseult's mouth as water dripped steadily down his face. "Then why, Traveler, are you so very angry?"

The Traveler turned and spat into the fire. The flames went out suddenly with a loud hiss, as the Traveler glided away into the darkness. The Traveler's actions were muddled in Finn's thoughts, as if at one moment the Traveler was there, and at the next, he was a vague white shape in the distance.

Finn reached numb fingertips up to push damp strands of hair away from her face. "Why did he call you Meirleach?" she asked shakily as she looked up into Iseult's shadowed face. "Who are you?"

"It means thief," he stated plainly "My people were the best thieves in all of history."

"Who are your people?" Finn asked nervously, though she had a good idea she already knew.

"The people of Uí Néid," Iseult answered without emotion.

Iseult ushered Finn back into the shelter of the tree

87

while she processed his answer. He removed his sodden black cloak and gave it a few shakes before hanging it from a low branch. His only visible weapon was the short-sword at his belt, but Finn knew there must be more. It was common knowledge that true thieves kept their most deadly weapons hidden. She had no doubt that there would at least be a *Sgian Dubh*, a killing dagger, hidden in his boot or up a sleeve. She had seen it before when the Traveler had first approached them.

Finn looked in the direction that the Traveler had gone. She saw none of his people in the distance, though she would not be surprised if they yet lurked in the periphery. "Do you know who I am?" she asked, not wanting to see Iseult's face while he answered.

"I have known," he stated quietly, drawing Finn's attention to his face whether she wanted to look or not. "I have seen your portrait. My mother made sure I knew the histories. It is important to remember what my people did, what we took."

Finn tried to conjure some saliva to wet her throat, but her mouth had gone bone dry. "And what did your people take?"

Iseult shook his head, seeming almost angry at Finn's ignorance.

Finn raised her eyes defensively. First the Traveler, and now Iseult. Would no one believe that she knew nothing of her past? "I need to know what happened to me," she snapped. "*Why* it happened. You said that you saw my portrait, that I was part of history. I must know *why*."

Iseult raised his eyebrow at her sudden burst of anger. "So you truly have no memories?"

Finn refused to drop her gaze. "How much did you hear of my conversation with the Traveler?"

It was Iseult who dropped his eyes instead. "Most of it. His people cannot be trusted, but they do not lie."

Finn crossed her arms. "So once again, you waited in the dark, only to give aid at the last possible moment. Why even give aid at all?"

Iseult began to speak and stopped several times as he rethought his words. Finally he explained, "I aided you because I owe you a debt, and that debt could not be served if you were stolen away by a Traveler. Still, I had assumed that your ignorance was a bluff. I had to be sure you truly did not know your own identity."

Finn snorted. "You owe me nothing. You don't even know me. You only know stories your mother told you."

Iseult's face settled into rigid lines. Finn thought if she touched his cheek, it might feel just like stone. She instantly regretted what she had said.

"I am all that is left of my people," he whispered. "I am all that is left to fix the mistake that they made. The mistake that destroyed them. I am the only one who can bring honor to their graves."

Finn's face felt hot. She felt like she might cry, but instead she laughed, an abrupt bark of sound. Surprised at herself, Finn glanced over to where their companions slept on the opposite side of the great pine, hoping she had not woken them. Iseult looked at her in question, and she cleared her throat nervously as she turned back to him. "I'm sorry, but I do not think I am the one you are searching for. Perhaps the portrait you saw was of an ancestor of mine. I cannot help you."

Iseult shook his head in frustration. "The portrait was of Finnur, the first of the Dair to become known to the mortal realm, and High Priestess of Clan Cavari. The portrait was of *you*."

Finn shivered as she gazed out into the darkness, still expecting to see the forms of the Traveler's at any moment. "I am not who you claim," she said again.

Iseult's expression softened as he placed a hand gently along Finn's jaw to bring her gaze back up to his. "Then who are you?"

Finn shrugged. Tears began to steadily drip down her face as she stepped back out of Iseult's reach.

Iseult nodded to himself. "I will help you find the answers you seek. I swear it."

"But why?" Finn asked, barely loud enough to be audible.

Iseult smiled softly. "Because if you are who I believe, then finding answers about your past will lead me to answers about mine."

"But you are indebted to the twins," Finn whispered, slowly accepting what Iseult was saying.

He glanced in the direction of their sleeping companions. "I will return their coin. There will be no debt."

Finn shook her head. "We cannot abandon them. At least, not until we reach another burgh where they might hire a new sellsword. I would not feel right if something happened to them."

Iseult slowly shifted his weight from foot to foot while he considered Finn's terms. "If that is what you wish, then we shall depart together after we reach Felgram."

"If I am to agree to this, you must tell me everything," Finn demanded, shocked by how quickly plans were being made. Had she really just agreed to travel with a thief she had met only three nights before?

Iseult gave her a searching look, as if weighing his options. "Many years before the Faie War," he began hesitantly, "my people stole a shroud. The shroud that covered the Queen of the Tuatha De in death, to be more precise. I do not know why we took it, or why your people took it first. I do not even know what it looks like. What I do know, is that its theft started the bloodshed of the war that ended with the disappearance of the Tuatha De. My people were responsible for thousands of innocent deaths."

Finn's pulse sped with thoughts of war. Flashes of bloodshed and carrion-eating creatures dotted her memory. She swallowed a sickly lump in her throat and fought the urge to gag. "What do you mean, took it first?"

Iseult smiled down at her sadly. "My people were great thieves, and we stole the shroud from the Cavari, but we didn't steal it first. We were responsible for our own undoing, and responsible for the Faie War, but we were not the only ones guilty of such crimes."

Finn did not enjoy that little revelation at all. She thought of herself as above thievery. It could not be that her people were known for it. "So together our people started the Faie War. What does that have to do with why I'm here now?"

Iseult shook his head and wrapped his arms tightly around himself. If they did not retire to their bedrolls soon, they would both suffer hypothermia.

"I do not know," he conceded, "but things are changing. The Tuatha, who have not been seen in forty years, are now being spotted across the countryside. The Travelers are out in droves, and while I have no love for their race, they do not lie. The words the Traveler spoke tonight were prophecy. I fear another war is upon us, and I do not think you came back to the realm of mortals on accident. We cannot sit idly by when the signs are all in front of us."

"You were eavesdropping the entire time?" Finn asked, confused because Iseult had not been present to hear the Traveler's prophecy.

"Not the entire time," Iseult answered, offering no further explanation.

Finn shook her head and edged nearer to the trunk of the pine, hoping for a reprieve from the chilly wind. "How do you propose we find answers when both of our clans are gone? I have no idea *why* I'm here."

Iseult smiled as he stepped closer to her. "Have you ever heard of the Archtree?"

Finn shook her head in confusion. She knew that the Archtree was a great tree of legend. It existed in two worlds at once. Its trunk and branches grew toward the sky in the mortal realm, while its roots reached down into the shadow world where the creators and spirits of nature resided. It was said that to drink a tea made from its leaves would provide that person with answers. Answers to what, no one knew. The tree was a myth.

"The Archtree is a legend," Finn said finally. "I will not waste my time searching for a tree that does not exist."

"It does exist," Iseult assured. "My people might have been great thieves, but we were also great sailors. We found the tree on an island, and made a map so that we would always be able to find it in times of need."

Finn's heart began to race as she absorbed what he'd said. If they could find the Archtree, she could ask it how to become a tree again herself. "A map?" she questioned weakly.

Iseult had a wry look on his face that Finn did not trust. He took a step forward to block more of the cold from Finn's shivering form. "You did not think a thief would travel with cartographers by chance, did you? They have access to archives that most of us can only dream of. One such archive is in Cael, the burgh we passed through three nights before reaching Garenoch."

Finn couldn't help her smile as the first real hope she'd felt since beginning her quest fluttered in her stomach. "You stole a map?"

Iseult nodded. "We must travel to Migris, and from there we will sail to the Archtree."

"You were on this quest all along," Finn accused softly, feeling small and vulnerable between the massive tree and Iseult's tall form. "What answers do you seek from the Archtree?"

"I seek the location of the Fae Queen's shroud," he answered plainly. "To right my people's wrongs, I must return the shroud to one of the Cavari. I must return it to *you*."

Finn was not sure what to say about his mission. She wanted nothing to do with a shroud that had caused such a bloody war. "What I seek are answers," she said, "and as you say, the Archtree may give me those. I will accompany you as far as that, but I make no promises in searching for the shroud."

Iseult grabbed Finn's hands in his, startling her, though

she did not pull away. "I know that it is the reason why our clans are gone. Is that not reason enough to find it?"

"Or reason enough to leave it lost," Finn countered.

Iseult gripped her hands more tightly and looked at her pleadingly, but offered no further argument.

Finn looked up at him sadly. He seemed so young to her, at that moment. It was a stark contrast to his usual appearance. "I just want to be a tree again," she explained.

Iseult's expression softened. "So you truly were a tree all this time?"

Finn felt a single tear slip down her face. "Until very recently, and all I want is to return to how things were."

A long silence ensued. Eventually, as if making up his mind, Iseult shook his head. "My mother believed that the shroud enabled its keeper to speak with the dead," he said softly.

Finn stepped away from him once more and peered at him suspiciously. "Why did you not say that before?" she questioned. "What use do you have for the dead?"

"My people are dead, as are yours," he replied. "Would you not speak to them if given the chance? Would you not ask them what caused such bloodshed, if only to prevent it from happening again?"

"You say my clan," Finn began, "but I do not know them. If I had a family once, they are long since lost to me. Either I became a tree out of a need to be alone, or my people transformed me and left me without any knowledge of who I was. Either way, I do not hope to find them."

"You were a leader among the Cavari, their Priestess," Iseult argued. "Someone important enough to be preserved in the histories."

"That is what you say," Finn pressed, "yet you do not know what happened to me. Why should I believe you?"

Iseult closed his eyes in frustration for a moment. Just when Finn thought he was done speaking, he opened his eyes once more. "I swear to you, all that I have told you is what I know to be true."

Finn's shivering was becoming unbearable. "I will think on this tonight. For now, it is time for sleep."

Iseult nodded somberly. Those already asleep had taken their bedrolls to the other side of the pine, but Iseult's and Finn's still remained rolled and leaning against the trunk of the tree.

The two grabbed their rolls and circled the tree in search of a dry place to sleep. Their group slept close together with their individual forms barely distinguishable, due to the lack of a fire. Upon closer observation, Finn found that Liaden slept on one end, and Anders on the other. Preferring to sleep next to a woman, Finn unrolled her bedding next to the slumbering Liaden and climbed in, still shivering. She had expected Iseult to place his roll near Anders, but instead he set up next to Finn.

She looked a question at him as he laid down and turned toward her. "I do not trust the Travelers," he explained. "I would not forgive myself if you were spirited away while I slept."

Accepting his answer, Finn closed her eyes. She did not find much warmth, but still she slept, oblivious to the swaying white forms that still bordered their camp.

inn woke before everyone else the next morning. The rain had finally subsided, though the sky was still gray. She sat up slowly in her bedroll, regretting her actions as her small amount of built-up warmth left her. She almost snuggled back down, but then she noticed Liaden's empty bedroll beside her. Perhaps she wasn't the first one up after all.

She reached across Liaden's vacant spot and poked Kai's shoulder repeatedly. The first few times he didn't move, then finally with one particularly forceful poke, he sat up with a start. "What are you off your head about?" he grumbled, squinting in Finn's direction.

"Where's Liaden?" she asked, paying no mind to his testiness.

Kai waved her off. "She's probably off in the woods doing . . . lady things."

Finn shook her head. She sensed Iseult rising from his bedroll behind her, but her gaze remained on Kai. "I never heard her leave," Finn explained. "I think she's been gone for a while."

Kai rubbed his eyes and looked at Finn more steadily. "And you can hear people move when you yourself are sleeping?"

Finn sighed loudly as she got up. "I'm a very light sleeper."

She stalked off toward the nearest thicket of trees while the rest of the party began to rise from their bedrolls. The grass in front of her was littered with chunks of old, carved stone, some still forming partial walls of structures. She had failed to notice them the previous night, as they had been obscured by fog.

"Liaden!" she called out, needing to assure herself that the woman was okay.

There was no reply. She walked farther, weaving her way amongst the stones, to a rise of land where she could better survey the area.

Anders reached Finn's side, slightly out of breath. "The others are looking in different directions," he explained.

"Kai did not seem worried," Finn replied, looking toward the horizon.

"Her horse and belongings are gone," Anders explained as his eyes scanned their surroundings. "Yet there were no hoof prints leading away in the mud."

They walked farther, side by side. Anders had his hair pulled back in a leather clasp to keep the wind from toying with it, and his cloak wrapped tightly around him against the cold. The hair clasp was unnecessary as the wind had finally let up, though the air was still uncomfortably crisp.

"Do you think . . . " Finn began.

Anders stopped and faced her. "Do I think what?"

"The Travelers . . . " Finn trailed off with a sick feeling in her gut, letting her gaze drop to the ground.

Anders placed a hand on the side of her arm, drawing her attention back up. "What about the Travelers? Why would they have reason to lead her away?"

Finn forced herself to meet his eyes. "I had a . . . discussion last night, with the Traveler. When he left, he was rather angry, and felt I owed him a payment."

Anders' gaze intensified at her admission. "A payment for what, exactly?"

Finn sighed and looked back down. "He gave me information. I did not ask it of him, not really. He was upset that I did not have information for him in return. He felt he'd been cheated of a payment."

"And you were planning on telling us this, when?" he practically yelled.

"You were all asleep!" Finn exclaimed more loudly than she had intended.

Anders patted his hands at the air in a soothing gesture, though his expression gave away his own unease. "I'm sorry, I'm sorry. Do you really think that they would take her as some sort of payment?"

Finn managed a small shrug, though she felt very much like running away. "That, or she tired of our company and decided to strike out on her own."

"I wouldn't doubt that," Anders joked, though he had no smile to back it up.

After a moment of silence Anders began to pace back and forth, crushing deep green grass underfoot. Suddenly he stopped and whirled on Finn with a finger in the air. "We *have* to get her back. We need to go now before they get too far."

Finn glared at him and crossed her arms. "Of course we have to get her back, but we don't even know for sure that they took her, or where they would take her if they did."

Anders held his hands open in front of him, then closed and lowered them, as if he was trying to grasp at a way to explain. "You don't understand. Liaden is a noble of the Gray City. She can't just go missing. If we don't find her, my sister and I will have to answer for it."

Finn scoffed. "Well I'm glad to see you're so concerned with her well-being."

Anders looked at Finn like she was being silly. "The woman is a terror. I would be more worried about my sister's well being than hers if Liaden stood on the edge of the pit of doom, and Branwen was safe on a feather bed."

Finn turned as Kai trotted toward them. "She's gone," he said as he reached them, stating what they already knew. "Iseult seems to think that the Travelers took her." He looked down at Finn. "Care to explain why he is under such an impression?"

Finn raised her hands in the air and stormed back toward camp. "It wasn't my fault!" she shouted as she left them.

Branwen was rolling everyone's bedding as Finn approached. "À Choille Fala," she was mumbling to herself. "Ye gods."

Finn reached Branwen's side and stood in place to catch her breath. "À Choille Fala?"

Branwen startled, then turned to look up at Finn. "À Choille Fala. The Blood Forest, the haven of the Ceàrdaman. Where we must go to find Liaden. If we cannot find her . . . " she trailed off.

Finn held up her hands. "I know, I know, you and Anders will have to answer for it."

"You don't understand," Branwen said softly. "The Gray City will have our heads for this."

Finn shook her head in disbelief. "Why would they let someone so apparently important leave on a journey with only four companions to protect her?"

Branwen stood and dusted off her divided skirts. "It is not a matter of her import. If we were all killed by bandits, it would be one thing. Yet, if she were the only one to die . . . "

Finn raised a hand to stop her. "I think I understand. We will try and retrieve her, but if we cannot, you and your brother will simply have to run away."

Branwen shook her head. "The City would find us, I'm sure of it. Not that it matters, we will all likely die in the Blood Forest regardless."

Finn waited for the woman to say more, but she did not. Kai and Anders returned from their searching and began saddling the horses. Iseult and Àed returned to the group a short while later, empty handed. Finn was surprised that the two had chosen to search together, but she did not take the time to question it. She met Iseult's eyes for a moment, and offered him a small nod. She had not decided one way or another on traveling with him, but she was not willing to abandon Liaden when her kidnapping could have very well been her own fault. Anders ushered Finn toward her horse, wanting to start their search as soon as possible.

The party mounted and rode in silence, except for Branwen. She was no longer talking to everyone else, but she would murmur something to herself from time to time.

Àed rode beside Finn as their slower mounts naturally fell behind the others. The old man was the only one seemingly not overcome by the gravity of the situation, but he did not seem terribly happy either. He hadn't argued about derailing their journey for a woman they'd just met, and Finn found that fact increasingly suspicious.

Finn cleared her throat to get his attention. He glanced at her, then turned his attention back to the rough-hewn road. "I imagine ye be wantin' to know about the Blood Forest?" he asked irritably.

Finn nodded her head encouragingly. She had no desire to see the Travelers again, but the Blood Forest still seemed an exciting prospect to her, regardless of the circumstances.

"The Blood Forest, À Choille Fala, is a place of the Faie. One of the few remaining places where mortals may still venture, though few do," he explained.

Finn shook her head in confusion. "I thought the Tuatha De disappeared after the war, all but the Ceàrdaman."

Àed spat on the ground at the mention of the Travelers. "They disappeared from the world of mortals, but À Choille Fala is not of our world. Ye willnae see the Faie right out, but trust me, ye will feel the effects of their presence."

Finn felt a flare of excitement intermingled with fear in her chest at the idea of encountering the Faie. Hopefully they would not all be like the Ceàrdaman. "Have you been there before?" she asked, interrupting Àed as he began to mutter on about the Tuatha De.

Àed gave her a quick glare for the interruption, but answered, "Aye lass, in my youth. I had not hoped to return."

When he did not continue, she asked, "Did something bad happen?"

"Bah," Àed replied with a wave of his hand. "More of an annoyance than anything. Trow and Boobrie waitin about to trick ye as if they ain't got nothin better to do. I'm supposin they don't, really."

Finn knew a bit of Tuatha lore, whether from her time as a tree, or from her previous life, she could not quite place. She knew that the Trow were large Faie, rumored to steal children. Boobrie were human-sized, birdlike Faie who spent their time luring travelers off their paths, and tricking them into becoming so lost that they often never found their way again.

Àed rolled his eyes at her silence. "I know yer excited lass, ye don't have to hide it."

Finn's face broke into a grin, which she instantly reined in, given the reason they were going where they were going. She couldn't help but be a little excited though. She would have never been able to see such things as a tree, at least not in her glen. She had begun to develop a taste for adventure, and she ruefully admitted, if only to herself, that she wanted more of it.

"How far to the forest?" she asked, trying to sound as somber as possible.

Àed sucked his teeth in contemplation. "I'm thinkin roughly four days, three if the weather permits."

"Do you think we'll be able to find Liaden?" she asked, truly afraid of the answer.

Àed's face was grim. "There's no telling, lass. The Travelers are a community. Many of them will know of Liaden's fate. The problem is, many of them willnae be willing to say, not without a price."

Finn nodded. "I'm surprised you're even willing to derail our journey," she commented, unable to rein in her earlier suspicions.

Àed spat on the ground again. "Ye think I couldn't hear yer late night conversation with that Iseult? I knew ye wouldn't be leavin him when he had so many answers for ye, and I'm not about to let you two run off without me. Ye'd likely be dead within a week, and I told him as much this morning."

Finn scowled. So that was why Àed and Iseult had searched for Liaden together. She did not appreciate the two of them talking behind her back, but was grateful for the sentiment none the less. If she chose to find the Archtree, she would have two friends on her journey . . . though she was not sure if she'd call Iseult friend. She would have two companions, at the very least.

Kai could think of nothing beyond his cold bones and empty stomach as night finally fell. They had not stopped for lunch that day, and instead rode on until the gray sky turned black, and the horses could no longer see well enough for proper footing.

A fire was made, and all sat around it eating bread with dried venison. The meal was far from hearty enough to fill Kai's belly. He would have loved a mug of tea to take away the chill, but the kettle had been stolen along with Liaden and her horse.

Kai looked at each of his somber companions in turn. He

could have cut the silence around the campfire that night with the knife he had used to slice the bread. Having had enough of it, he cleared his throat loudly. "Could someone please tell me what this Bleeding Forest is, and how we will find Liaden once we get there."

"Blood Forest," Branwen replied morosely.

If he'd been asked the day before, Kai would have never guessed that Branwen could even have such an attitude. She was perpetually sunny. He also never would have guessed that she was capable of remaining silent for as long as she had. He knew that her sober demeanor was not out of concern for their lost companion. It was out of concern for herself and her brother. People didn't help each other if they had nothing to gain from it. Growing up in the Gray City had taught him that.

The Gray City was a merciless place where the weak rarely survived for long. He knew that being blamed for the disappearance of a noble never ended pretty for the accused, so he understood the twins' concern. Yet, he wasn't concerned with what the Gray City might do to him, unlike Branwen and Anders. That cursed city had already done all it ever would to Kai. It was the reason he owed his so-called *gray lady* a great deal, and finding her would pay off part of that debt. If he could not find her, well, he had no intention of returning to Sormyr regardless.

Kai prodded at the fire with a stick, nudging the flames to give off more warmth. "And why is it called the Blood Forest? Has much blood been spilled there?"

Branwen shrugged. "It is an old name. À Choille Fala is a forest of the Tuatha De. We've much more to fear than the spilling of blood."

Kai shook his head. "The Faie disappeared ages ago, except for the Travelers, and they are more akin to man than to Faie."

Branwen shrugged again. "There are many stories. I suppose that a few may have been embellished, but I've found that most stories have at least some basis in truth."

Finn and Iseult were whispering amongst themselves across the fire. Kai would have liked to know what they were saying, especially since he'd not seen the sellsword say more than two words to anyone else.

Kai turned his attention away from the pair and stared into the fire. "So we tread through this treacherous forest, find some of the Travelers, and then what? How do we get her back?"

"The Travelers will want a bargain," Iseult interrupted, startling everyone. "They always do."

Branwen perked up. "Do you think they will take money? We don't have much else to offer."

Àed snorted. "Some might, though most will be more interested in things not freely given."

"Secrets," Finn mumbled distantly, as if she wasn't paying full attention to the conversation.

Kai looked to Finn. He imagined the woman had more secrets than most. "It seemed the Traveler we met already knew much about us, without us willingly divulging any secrets," he countered.

Àed laughed bitterly, drawing Kai's attention away from Finn once again. "They know who we are, and where we come from, yet they do not know our *reasons*. They can tell if you are searching for something, but not always what you are searching for. There is always a loophole to Faie magic. Always."

"So we tell them the things they don't know," Kai decided.

Àed laughed again. "We'll see lad, we'll see."

Silence engulfed the group once again as Kai went back to poking the fire. That night, not all would sleep at once. Two would remain awake at all times to keep watch. As no one wanted to stay awake and chat, it was not long until Kai and Anders were left on their own to watch over the sleeping forms of their companions.

Kai glanced at his company. He wondered what secrets Anders had, and if he'd be willing to share them with the Travelers. If they would be enough.

Anders sighed loudly and turned toward Kai. "I hope you have a worthwhile secret. I doubt any of mine would be worth much."

Kai allowed himself a small smile. "Our secrets are always much more interesting to others than they are to us. I'm sure you have a few that are worthwhile in their own right."

Anders laughed quietly. "Mine and Branwen's parents are both archive scholars. We grew up among some of the most extensive collections of history available. I know a great deal of little known history, but my life has been less than . . . history making. I could tell the Travelers about how I broke my arm when I was eleven, and it never quite healed correctly, or I could tell them about the time I put live ants in Branwen's pottage, but my list of interesting stories ends there."

Kai snickered. "Live ants in your sister's pottage? I'll have to remember that one."

Anders nodded. "Just make sure the pottage has cooled enough first. Dead ants don't have quite the same effect as live ones."

As their quiet laughter died off, silence ensued until Anders asked, "What secret will you share?"

Kai paused in contemplation, then shook his head ruefully. "Now if I told you, then it wouldn't be a secret."

In truth, Kai was not sure what secret he could share that would be of any value to the Travelers. He had been a slave of a sort, more of an indentured servant, and now he was not. He had found his way out, and that's all there was to it. He had a few secrets that might be of interest to his party, but he would not be sharing those any time soon, not if he wanted their help in retrieving his companion. No, he did not know what secret he would share. Regardless, he did not look forward to any of his secrets being known, even the ones that he imagined the Travelers would know to begin with.

While Anders' eyes scanned the darkness, Kai looked over their sleeping companions once more. Iseult slept on the far left, followed by the smaller forms of Àed, then Finn, and then Branwen. His eyes looked across the group, then came back to rest on Finn. While the twins remained intrigued with the old man, it was his brazen young companion who piqued Kai's interest. She was clever, which he appreciated in a woman, but she was dishonest. It was obvious to him that she had lied about her past. He couldn't really hold it against her, it wasn't like he was shouting the details of his past, or even his present, from the mountain-tops, but still . . . he would very much have liked to know the truth about her.

The rest of their watch was spent in silence, both men too deep in their own thoughts to speak to one another. When their time was up, they went together to wake Branwen and Finn, who had volunteered for the second watch. Kai knelt above Finn's head while Anders knelt beside his sister, each gently waking their respective women.

Kai could see clearly by the firelight as Finn's eyes slowly opened. Her dark eyes looked black in the dim lighting as she regarded him sleepily.

"Is there something I can help you with?" she whispered up at him.

With a start he realized he had hovered over her much longer than was necessary. Branwen was already rising out of her bedroll and he was just kneeling there, looming over Finn like an idiot. He quickly stood and brushed the dirt from his knees while Finn pulled her legs out of her bedding.

Once the women were both up and to work on stoking the fire, Kai and Anders took their turns at sleep. Kai watched the shapes of the two women huddled near the fire for a long while, until sleep finally took him.

"I'm sorry," Finn eventually said to Branwen, breaking the drawn out silence. Their shift was nearly over, and she needed to get her apology out while they were alone.

Branwen jumped in her seat at the sound. "Whatever for?" she asked breathlessly.

Finn looked down at the fire. "It's my fault, I think. The Travelers took Liaden because I couldn't pay for the secrets he told me."

Branwen's forehead wrinkled in confusion. Finn thought she looked quite tired. "You spoke to the Traveler after we had all retired?" Branwen asked.

Finn nodded. "I assumed Anders had told you. I did not realize what would happen. The Traveler was very upset. If Iseult had not intervened . . . "

"Well, there was quite a bit of drama while we slept then," Branwen observed. "Never-the-less, the Traveler would not have been at our camp at all if not for me. I invited him in. I should have been more cautious. If anyone is to blame, it is I."

Finn moved a little closer to the patch of grass Branwen had chosen to sit on. "Let's both be to blame then, and let's just focus on getting her back."

Branwen nodded happily in agreement. "And as soon as we have our sharp-tongued lady back, we'll help you and Àed get to wherever you need to go. If you're willing to enter the Blood Forest with us, it's the least we can do."

Finn looked down at her lap, feeling guilty that she had planned on leaving Branwen at the next burgh. In fact, she still planned on it.

Taking Finn's silence as gratitude, Branwen offered Finn a small smile. "Come on," she said, giving Finn's shoulder a nudge. "Let's wake our replacements a bit early."

Branwen hurried over to Àed, leaving Finn to wake Iseult, who rose without complaint. Finn suspected that he had already been awake for some time when she gently nudged his shoulder. He gave Finn an almost cheerful nod, then strolled over to where she and Branwen had sat.

Àed was not quite so gracious. As Finn snuggled back into her bedroll, she could hear the old man mumbling something about, "scunner-tongued, moss-brained, black-livered women."

Finn ignored the insults. With the knowledge that Branwen did not blame her, a great weight had been lifted from her shoulders, even if she still had to break the news that their party would be disbanding after Liaden was retrieved. She fell back to sleep quickly.

CHAPTER TEN

They did not take the time to make tea the next morning, and instead just ate small chunks of bread on the road. The party had planned on a short journey to the next burgh, and so had only provisioned enough for a few days. Rations would likely run low before they even reached the Blood Forest, but there were few places to provision in between, and they could not lose the time it would take to return to Garenoch.

There were likely to be small settlements along the road to the Blood Forest, but they might not be of much help. Clans kept close together in the wild areas, and weren't overly fond of strangers. Though sightings had all but ceased in recent years, there was still always worry of Trow wandering in from the reaches of the forest to spirit away children and steal livestock.

The first settlement the party reached early that afternoon was composed of but a few houses, all with shutters and doors tightly sealed. Small flocks of sheep were kept close to the buildings, surrounded by high fences built more to keep things out, than to keep sheep in. Finn wondered why anyone would settle in the area at all if they were forced to live so cautiously.

Branwen cleared her throat softly as the party rode close together through the quiet village. "Where are all of the people?" she whispered.

Finn smiled to herself. Even in dire times, Branwen simply could not resist the urge to speak.

"Likely sealed up in their homes," Kai answered from Finn's other side. "I'd venture they saw us coming from a mile off. These seem like unfriendly parts."

"It must be because of the Blood Forest" Branwen stated morosely.

Kai shrugged with an easy air, giving Finn the sense that he was not worried in the slightest, though she suspected it was simply an act. "I don't know anything about the forest, but borderlands are never hospitable. Reivers will be about this far East, robbing travelers then crossing back into the wilds to avoid retribution."

Branwen's eyes widened in panic. "So now we have to not only worry about the Faie, and about finding food, but we have to worry about Reivers?"

Kai shrugged again. "Worrying about it won't do much good."

"That won't stop me from doing it," Branwen mumbled to herself.

The scent of a cookfire wafted over Finn, making her salivate. She lifted her head and took a deep whiff of the flavorful air. The small amount of food she'd been given that morning seemed a distant memory.

"There'll be nothing to be had from this lot," Àed commented, reading her hungry expression.

Finn's stomach growled in reply.

"We'll eat when we make camp," Anders assured as he rode up behind Finn and Àed. "If we stick to only eating in the morning and at night, we won't starve for at least four more days."

"That is not terribly reassuring," Finn groaned. "It cannot hurt to at least talk to the townspeople. Perhaps they would be willing to sell us a few things."

Anders looked at the silent buildings thoughtfully. "Perhaps it couldn't hurt . . . " he trailed off.

"Or perhaps we could end up robbed of the little we have," Àed barked.

Anders' face lost a bit of its color at Àed's statement. Finn was glad she was not the only one out of her depth in the current situation. She was also grateful that Kai, Iseult, and Àed seemed to know what they were doing, even if she and Anders did not.

Branwen cleared her throat again. "How will we eat if we cannot trade with anyone along the way? We'll be starved by the time we reach the forest."

Kai laughed, startling Finn so that she nearly jumped out of her saddle.

"What's so funny?" Branwen asked hotly.

Kai shook his head and smiled. "Nothing, just remember that not all of us were raised in the safety of an archive. We may get a little hungry, but we will not starve as long as game is available."

Branwen blushed. "I did not think of it that way."

Finn had not thought of it that way either, but didn't

volunteer that information. She was glad that they likely wouldn't starve, but hoped they would stop and catch something to eat soon, before the empty pit in her stomach became unbearable. It was shocking how often humans had to eat in order to survive, and to compete with this need while riding a horse for long hours was simply torture. She had managed the first two days of riding without much discomfort, but the lack of breaks now made her entire body ache.

Unfortunately, several more uncomfortable hours passed before Finn was finally allowed to stretch her legs, far from the silent town. She had done an awkward dance as she dismounted, her too-long skirts and sore limbs making the simple task difficult. The land where they stopped was densely forested, so that Finn could no longer see what might await them in the distance.

Iseult came to stand beside her as she tried to see further down the primitive path they followed. His silent presence soothed her worries, as she felt infinitely safer with him around. She shook her head to rid herself of the feeling. She barely even knew the tall man standing beside her like a stalwart oak, unmoved by his surroundings no matter what dangers they might hide.

"I hear water," Branwen observed from behind them, breaking the silence. Finn had heard it too, but hadn't paid the sound much mind. She turned to join the rest of the group with Iseult following close behind her.

The party went silent once more as they listened, all but Finn thinking the same thing; fish could be found in water.

"I don't hear anything," Anders said after a moment.

"Nor do I," agreed Kai.

"I hear it," Branwen argued, "as clear as day. It's not far from us."

Àed shook his head. "Tuatha tricks."

"But we're not in the forest yet!" Branwen exclaimed. "We were still supposed to have another two days!" She looked around frantically, as if the Faie might descend upon them at any moment.

Àed sternly surveyed their surroundings. "The border of the Blood Forest *is* two days away, but we be in Faie lands already, don't ye be mistakin'."

"How is that possible?" Iseult asked, obviously not sharing in Branwen's alarm.

Branwen's horse began to prance about, unsettled by the nervous energy of the woman holding its reins. Branwen paid no mind to her horse as she turned her attention to Àed. "The Traveler said the lines are faltering. Is this what he meant? Changing borders?"

Àed grunted in annoyance. "Did ye remember that fool's words verbatim?"

Branwen did not catch the old man's sarcasm. "Of course. The seasons are changing. The lines are faltering, undoing the old and bringing life to the new. Trees will fall, and changed earth will be left in their place. A storm is coming." She looked at Àed matter of factly.

Àed let out an irritated breath. "I'm not thinkin' that's what the man meant, but there's no use dwelling on it regardless. We are in Faie lands now, it doesn't matter the reason. What matters is that we tread lightly, and don't be believin' everything ye see. Really, we should be countin' ourselves among the lucky. Perhaps our journey will be shorter than planned, and our rations will not be an issue."

Branwen's gulp was audible. Not wanting to tarry, the party mounted once more and rode on, if more slowly this time. Finn could still hear the running water as clear as if it was actually there. She wondered if maybe the trick was on those who couldn't hear it, and they were all passing up a good opportunity in listening to the old man. She shook her head again, wondering if all humans had such little control of their thoughts as she.

Within minutes of riding, much of the sun's light was blotted out by the rising trees. The air was chilled and smelled of growing things with the underlying scent of rot. Finn's nose crinkled in affront, though no one else seemed affected. She wondered if they smelled the foul stench as well, but decided to keep her thoughts to herself as they rode on.

Branwen did not enjoy being in Faie lands, not in the least. The only positive aspect of the situation was the smell. Something smelled absolutely delicious, like lavender tea and fresh baked honey bannocks. If she wasn't mistaken, they were nearing the smell as they rode.

Still, she regretted the journey. Perhaps if they had gone back to the Gray City and explained, they would not have been blamed for Liaden's disappearance. Surely they were powerless against the will of the Travelers?

The smell thickened still. Branwen glanced over at Finn, who was cringing like she smelled something foul. The woman was obviously falling prey to Tuatha tricks. It would make sense that the Faie would want to disguise such a wonderful smell, in order to keep travelers from seeking out its source.

Branwen looked down at her horse's hooves. Perhaps it was a plant breaking under their steps making the smell. Her eyes darted around for a source until they settled on a plant unlike any she had ever seen. Its stems were long and thick, deep purple in color, with wide green and purple speckled leaves and pale purple flowers. Her horse had stopped right next to one of the plants. Had she pulled the reins? She couldn't remember. The flowers looked slick with some sort of sap or pollen. She tried to observe the flowers so closely that she nearly fell out of her saddle.

Her brother grabbed onto her burgundy cloak from the opposite side and pulled her back into place. "What are you doing?" he asked breathlessly.

"I was trying to look at the flowers," she stated, as if it were quite obvious.

The rest of the party looked at her like she had lost her mind, except for Finn, who looked at the flowers in disgust. Branwen wasn't sure why the entire party had come to a standstill, just to stare at her in disapproval.

The old man stared at her harder than the others, and Branwen tried to remember why they had invited him along at all. "Them flowers are as poisonous as deathroot," he grumbled. "Even smellin' them too close would make ye lose yer breakfast."

"But, they smell lovely . . . " Branwen argued.

Finn gave her an appalled look, but still did not speak. The party moved on without another word, though everyone seemed to be riding closer to Finn than to her. Was it her imagination? Surely not, Branwen may have been hoodwinked by the flowers, but she could still judge distance.

With both of the women acting odd, Iseult felt uneasy. He had been in the areas around the Blood Forest before, and so knew a bit of what was in store. Yet, things should not have been happening so soon. His memories told him that they were still many miles from the Blood Forest, but it felt like they were already in it. Could the forest have eaten up that much land in the few years since he'd been in the area? It did not seem possible, yet many things of the Tuatha did not seem possible.

Beyond his worries about the forest, he did not like taking time to search for a woman that was most likely lost. He had heard of the Ceàrdaman kidnapping people, but he had never heard of any of those people returning to their normal lives. Venturing into Faie lands was an unnecessary risk. Branwen had nearly fallen face first into poisonous plants, and they'd only been in the lands for an hour or so. He glanced at Finn as she looked at the ground with distaste. He would not lose her to the Tuatha, not when he'd only just found her.

"We should probably stop and rest soon," Anders said, almost more to himself than to the party.

"We've still got a ways to go before we make camp, lad," Àed countered. The old man seemed to be the only one keeping his wits about him, besides Iseult of course. Iseult would be cursed before he would fall prey to Faie trickery ever again. The first time was still too clear in his mind, though he'd been but a child of twelve.

His earliest encounter with the Tuatha occurred shortly after the majority of the Faie had disappeared, oddly enough. Fighting with the Cavari, followed by the effects the Faie War had on the countryside had left Iseult's people homeless and poor. The proud men and women of Uí Néid were reduced to lowly sailors, working under various Aldermen and fish merchants far from their ruined home. Most of Iseult's people, including himself and his mother, had migrated south to the great city of Migris to find work.

The brother of Iseult's father had taken it upon himself to teach Iseult to sail the coasts of Migris, as Iseult's own father could not do so from the grave. Iseult learned quickly, and soon went to work on various crews with his uncle. One such job landed them on a small fishing ship, with only a few men in the crew. They had been trawling the coastline when they fell afoul of Sirens. No one had questioned the appearance of the large school of fish, their scales glimmering like silver. The Faie were long gone by that time, or so Iseult had been told. It had been a rude awakening when the crew followed the school of fish into a desolate cove.

Iseult could still picture the calm waters beneath the ship, and he could still hear the singing. The men of the crew had jumped into the water and drowned themselves one by one, all but Iseult. He had wrestled with his uncle, and begged him not to go, but in the end had chosen not to drown along with him.

Eventually the singing subsided and Iseult was left alone on the ship. He could not man it himself, and so jumped into the water. He would either swim to the shore of the cove, or die like the rest, and after the horrors he had witnessed, he didn't really care which way it went.

When he made it, shivering and soaked through, to the home he shared with his mother, she'd sent him away. He could not very well tell the Lady of Migris that the ship had been overtaken by Sirens, leaving him as the only survivor. He would be marked as a liar and a coward, an offense punishable by death. His mother was supposed to meet him on the road, but she never came. Later Iseult discovered that she had died for his alleged crime. Someone had seen him run.

"I don't think I slept enough during the night," Anders argued, startling Iseult back into the present. "It wouldn't hurt to rest, just for a short while."

The man did look awful. Deep bags were prominent under his golden brown eyes. He'd taken off his cloak as if he was hot, though the air was cold enough to warrant full winter clothing. Iseult observed the rest of their party for similar signs. None seemed affected in the same way as Anders, though Finn continuously tried to put distance between herself and the other riders. Each time she fell back, either Iseult, Kai, or Àed would discreetly drop behind to usher her on. She never seemed to notice.

Àed looked to Anders. "Did ye touch anything since we entered the forest?"

"Is he under a Faie spell?" Branwen squeaked worriedly.

"I did no such thing!" Anders argued.

Àed spat on the ground. "Calm down, the both of ye. I've never felt the forest like this before. Perhaps we should turn back."

"We cannot abandon Liaden," Kai argued before anyone else could jump to agree.

Their horses had come to a standstill once again. Iseult noticed that Kai now held the reins of Finn's horse while the woman looked longingly off toward something he could not see. Taking Finn's reins was a good precaution, as long as Kai did not fall prey to the same Faierie fancy.

"We move on," Iseult agreed, though he did not like it. The memory of icy water struck him, and he swallowed the lump in his throat, pushing down the fear and hatred that had plagued him most of his life.

Kai held tightly onto Finn's reins. He had been herding her forward for thirty minutes or so, when he finally just took her reins from her. She did not seem to notice either way. Half of the time her expression was one of great distaste, and the rest of the time it was as if she saw the most beautiful thing in the world and wanted nothing more than to hurry toward it. During the latter times, she would veer her mule-horse away from the group, only to be reined back in by Àed, Iseult, or himself.

The twins were both obviously Tuatha-stricken as well, making for uncertain odds. Anders looked plagued with fever, while Branwen was jumping at every sound, and sometimes when there were no sounds to jump at as well.

If the two unaffected men held out with him, they might be able to find the Travelers safely enough, but if one more succumbed to flights of fancy, it might become difficult to keep everyone together. He was beginning to think perhaps they should have left Finn, Anders, and Branwen at the outskirts, yet there had been no way of knowing they would be so strongly affected. They *should* not have been so strongly affected. From what Àed had previously explained to him, as long as they stayed on the paths and did not eat anything, they would be fine. Yet Kai could already see that things were not as he'd been told. Something must have changed the forest.

He stifled a shiver. The ground underneath their horses' hooves was crunchy with frost. It was far too late in the season for frost, even with the unseasonable weather. He watched uneasily as his breath fogged the air in steady torrents. His breath caught in his throat and he was nearly dismounted as Finn's horse jerked violently to the side, then went crashing off through the trees, taking its rider willingly with it. Kai's hand burned where the reins had slid across his palm. He stared in shock for a moment before galloping off after her, his mind racing with thoughts of the woman becoming lost in the cursed forest forever. There was also the possibility of getting lost himself, but he could not focus on it as he avoided the branches and tall brambles that were attempting to poke his eyes out. Kai felt only slight relief when he heard the hooves of other horses following behind him.

The terrain was uneven and slick, making the quick pace difficult for Kai's mount. He saw the gray rump of Finn's mule horse fleeing ahead of him, moving impossibly fast for the half-lame creature. As he kept his eyes on Finn, he realized he could no longer hear the sound of hoof-beats behind him. He glanced behind for just a moment, then had to come to a sudden halt in order to not run directly into

Finn's horse. Finn sat perfectly still in her saddle, staring off into the distance.

"Are you bladdered woman?" he asked as he dismounted and grabbed Finn's reins from where they hung below her horse's foaming mouth.

Finn did not look at him, but instead continued to gaze into the forest. "Don't you see it?" she whispered without looking back. What Kai could see of her face had grown startlingly pale, so that she looked like a ghost, or some sort of icy goddess.

Kai looked in the direction of her gaze, but saw only trees and darkness. "May the horned one take you woman, there is nothing there."

He pulled Finn's horse around and began to lead her in the direction they'd come from. Hopefully the others would be near where they had left them.

Finn looked back over her shoulder so far that she almost fell out of her saddle. "We're going the wrong way! I saw my family back there!"

Kai stopped and glared up at her. "Your family is not in this forest. We can go looking for them *after* we get out of this cursed place."

Finn crossed her arms as a petulant look took over her face. "How would you know? You don't know my family. I haven't seen them in over one-hundred years, and now you would just drag me away from them."

Kai sighed. "Finn, you have not been alive one-hundred years. You have not even been alive thirty."

"You don't know!" she shouted. "Just because I was a tree, doesn't mean I wasn't alive!"

The woman had completely lost it, Kai thought. He

began to worry that once out of the forest, she might not go right again. Before he could stop her, Finn hopped off her horse and started walking back in the other direction. Kai quickly went after her, pulling both horses behind him.

Holding both sets of reins in one hand, he grabbed her arm with his other and turned her to face him. She had a wild look in her dark eyes, and the effect was only increased by her snarled, pale brown hair whipping about in the breeze. A small bit of color had returned to her lightly-freckled cheeks, but her mouth and the rest of her face remained bloodless. Kai considered undoing his cloak to put around her, but realized with a start that the ground was no longer icy in this area. In fact, it felt as if heat was radiating from the earth itself. That same heat radiated from Finn, despite her pallor.

His hand itched with a feeling of bugs crawling over his skin, but Kai held tight to Finn's arm until she gave him her full attention. "Remember where we are," he told her shakily. "What you see is not real, it is a Faie trick."

Some measure of light went out of her eyes with that, and her brow creased in confusion. "But I saw . . . " she paused as the crazed expression melted from her face. "I'm not really sure what I saw."

Kai let out a breath of relief. "We need to find the others."

Finn raised a gloved hand to her mouth in sudden worry. "I can't believe I ran off like that!" she gasped. "Let us be off."

Kai nodded. Thank the creators, the woman was back to her senses. He looked in the direction where they had left the rest of the group . . . at least he thought it was the right direction. Everything looked the same in the eerie, Faie woods. They remounted their horses, but Kai kept hold of Finn's reins, just in case.

Damned fools, the lot of them, Àed thought to himself. He would have thought it out loud, if there had been anyone around to hear. As soon as Finn went riding off, Kai and Iseult went running after her, while the twins went running off in the opposite direction. Àed had tried to keep up with the two men following Finn, but his mount could not match their pace, though he should have been able to pace Finn's horse easily. They were gone before he knew it.

He was alone, but did not worry about himself. He was more worried about those dust-brained fools under Tuatha compulsion. They had succumbed far too easily. He had traveled the Blood Forest safely many times before. The most recent, which wasn't really recent at all, had been with three companions. The trio had hired him to find a missing child, assuming he had been stolen by one of the Faie. One fool had eaten a toadstool and saw visions for a week, but they had all still emerged with their lives. There was something new here now, or something old reawakened. Either way, it was not good. He thought back again to his last venture into the Blood Forest. The child had been found several days later, drowned in the river Cair, not taken by the Faie after all.

Àed plodded along in no direction in particular. He tried with all of his might to sense where Finn had gone, but it was one of the abilities he had lost when his daughter

Keiren had crippled him oh so many years before. Where he'd failed at finding Keiren after she left, though he searched for many years, he assured himself that he would not fail at finding Finn.

After a short time he came upon a clearing. In the clearing was a spring, and beside the spring sat the twins. He might have missed them if it wasn't for their dusky red hair standing out in contrast against their green surroundings. As he drew near, the twins raised invisible cups in *slàinte*, clicking the invisible rims against each other.

Àed hopped down from his horse and ran to them, then swatted the invisible cups out of their hands. The old man did not feel a thing, but the twins looked up at him as if they had been stung.

"What did you go and do that for!" Anders demanded.

"Get up ye fools. Yer Faierie-bladdered all the way," Àed replied. He could hear laughter that sounded like rasping leaves coming from the trees around the spring. "Merrows," he mumbled.

"What about Merrows?" Branwen said petulantly. "You've interrupted our afternoon tea."

Àed felt an overwhelming urge to haul Branwen and Anders to their feet by their ears, but resisted. "Merrows ye fools. Cursed water sprite tricksters. Likely tryin' to get ye drunk to make drownin' ye nice and easy."

Branwen paused in contemplation, then looked at her brother. "What were we doing here again?"

Anders appeared quite dumb-stricken, and offered only a shrug in reply.

Àed shook his head in annoyance. "Where are yer horses ye fools?"

The twins stood and brushed themselves off. "I'm not quite sure," Branwen answered, embarrassed.

Àed tried to contain his wrath. The Blood Forest was not a place to let yourself be overcome by anger or other emotions, especially not under the circumstances.

"Where are the others?" Anders asked suddenly, as if he had just then realized they weren't with Àed.

"Bah." Àed waved them off. "We'll find them eventually. Hopefully they have a bit more sense than the two of ye."

Àed began walking with his shaggy horse's reins in hand, giving the twins no choice but to follow him back in the direction he had come, or stay and be drowned by Merrows. At that moment, he did not particularly care which choice they made.

"*How* will we find them?" Anders asked, catching up to Àed's side.

"Like I said," Àed replied. "hopefully they have sense. If they have *sense*, they will backtrack, then they'll get out of this tainted forest the way we came in. The forest may have changed, but there are still paths, if yer not too blind to see 'em."

The cursed forest had no paths at all, Iseult thought as he slowly walked along. Luckily the ground was at least soft enough to show him hoof-prints in the soil. He had chased after Finn and Kai, only to lose sight of them, and sight of the rest of the party behind him as well. One moment he was gaining on Kai and Finn, and the next they had simply disappeared.

He had been walking slowly, keeping a close eye on the ground for a good hour or so, using tracks and broken branches to guide his way. He should have watched Finn more closely. It was obvious how much she was affected by the forest, but he had not expected her to gallop off so suddenly.

He stopped and listened. For a moment he thought he had heard voices, but those voices were soon drowned out by the sound of the ocean. Yet, there was no ocean to be found anywhere near the Blood Forest. He strained to hear over the sound of the crashing tide, but the voices eluded him.

With a deep breath of frustration, Iseult continued his tracking. As long as he did not lose the trail, he would find them eventually. He ignored the sound of the sea, but never-the-less he was assaulted by memories of the only place he ever thought of as home. Memories he had not allowed himself to dwell on for many years.

Kai could tell it was getting dark, though with the thickness of the trees, it wasn't a drastic change. Regardless, it was becoming difficult to see, and he thought they might have to stop and make camp soon. He was grateful that a portion of their party's food was in his and Finn's saddlebags, and he always carried a flint and other small tools with him. He considered setting a rabbit snare, but was fearful of what they might catch.

Finn had fallen silent a long while back, and he hoped she was not bespelled once more. Being lost in the forest was bad enough without having to worry about his only companion running off on him. Kai glanced over at Finn in an attempt to calm his nerves, but she only gazed down at the back of her horse's neck with a dejected expression on her face.

He pulled his horse to a stop as they came upon a clearing, at least as much of a clearing as could be found in the dense woods

Finn gave a questioning look as Kai tightened his grip on her mule's reins, bringing her to a stop beside him.

He observed her for a moment, and she seemed clear-headed enough. "We should stop for the night. It won't do us any good to walk over a hole in the ground and break one of the horses' legs."

After a moment of consideration Finn nodded and dismounted. Kai did the same, then tied his horse and her mule-creature to a nearby tree so he could unpack the few things they would need. It was probably unwise to make a fire, but the temperature of the forest had shifted back to freezing, so he planned on making a fire despite his better judgment, though he didn't unsaddle the horses. It would be his fault if they ended up with saddle sores, but if he unsaddled them, then it would be his fault that they weren't able to make a quick getaway in the event of an attack. He wasn't sure what type of creatures might mean them harm within the Blood Forest, but he had no desire to find out.

Finn followed his lead as he set to gathering kindling and some small dead logs, then sat across from him while he built it all into a proper stack for a fire. As he was striking his flint, she cleared her throat.

Kai paused what he was doing and looked up at her.

SARA C ROETHLE

"I was just wondering," she began, not meeting his gaze. "What did I say while I was ... entranced?"

Kai went back to his flint until he got a few sparks going. He blew on the tiny embers as the kindling caught, then looked back up at her. "You said you saw your family, and that you hadn't seen them in one-hundred years. You also said you were a tree," he laughed. "A load of midden obviously, unless you're not a real girl after all."

The color drained from Finn's face. "Yes, a load of midden, obviously."

Kai stood and backed away from the fire to dig into his saddlebag for something to eat, pondering Finn's reaction. He should have been thinking about rationing their food, but his stomach was so empty and cramped that he didn't care. If it came to it, he would set a snare, and they would eat whatever he caught. With his hands full of most of his portion of the provisions, he walked around the fire and handed Finn a strip of dried rabbit and a piece of crumbly bannock. She raised an eyebrow at the food.

"My secret stash," he explained. "Hard bread and cheese every day wears on a man's soul."

Finn laughed softly, then looked at the fire. "Do you think perhaps the others will see our light?"

Kai stuffed a piece of bannock in his mouth and shrugged. "Perhaps. Though anything else in these woods might see it as well. I wouldn't have made a fire at all if this forest kept to normal temperatures."

It was a sobering thought. They had not even come into actual physical contact with any of the Tuatha, and they had already been led astray and separated from the rest of their party. Hopefully they were still near the outskirts, and would be able to get out. Then they could regroup and come up with a new plan.

Kai shook his head, the only problem was telling which way *out* was. He could have sworn they were walking back in the direction they had come. He'd even seen their hoof-prints, but they never reached the edge. He did not express his fears to Finn though, for it would do little good.

"Did you see anything?" Finn asked suddenly.

It took Kai a moment to figure out that she was still wondering about her Faie-influenced actions. "You mean earlier, when you ran off?"

Finn nodded as if afraid of the answer.

Kai considered questioning why she thought he might have seen anything, but decided the woman had probably been through enough. "I saw only you and that fool horse of yours standing alone in the woods."

"You didn't hear anything either?" she pressed anxiously.

Kai narrowed his eyes suspiciously. "No . . . " he trailed off.

Finn nodded, not catching his suspicious gaze as she stared down at the fire with a distant expression on her face. "Good. That's good."

Kai watched Finn for several minutes as her face wrinkled in confusion, then smoothed out into contemplation. The woman had so many secrets that they were coming out of her ears, he thought. With a quick nod of his head, Kai decided he would take the time to find out every single one. Knowing the secrets of others was always useful in one way or another.

"We should get some rest," he suggested. "Tomorrow will likely prove to be a *very* long day."

Finn nodded, still deep in thought. Kai fetched their bedrolls and unrolled them near the fire. He insisted that Finn sleep closer to the warmth, but really he just wanted to trap her in between the fire and himself as much as possible. He did not fancy the idea of waking up alone.

The sound of the ocean crashed all around him, nearly deafening Iseult to any other noise. He held his hands to his ears with his horse's reins looped around his elbow. What he could see of the sky had grown dark, and he kept a very slow pace in order to not lead his horse over any burrows or other holes in the ground.

He squinted his eyes in the darkness, trying to see more than three feet in the distance. Where just a moment before was solid black, he saw a distant light, like the light of a campfire, and hope blossomed inside of him. Perhaps he had found some of his companions at long last. Hopefully he had been the only one separated, and he could convince Finn to leave the Blood Forest at once. Only a fool would argue with him now. Iseult shook his head. There would be arguments, he had no doubt.

Iseult made his way toward the light, and found that he was making remarkable progress as the luminescence grew closer and closer. Then he realized that he was standing still, and the light was still coming toward him at a steady pace. His horse wickered nervously and tried to tug backwards on the reins. Iseult backed up and hoisted himself into his saddle, steadying the nervous beast. The light had picked up its pace and was less than ten feet away. He knew running would risk injury for his horse, but he had no choice.

He turned his horse to escape the way he had come, but was confronted with lights coming at him from all directions in perfect unison. From a distance the light had seemed like the light of a fire, but closer he could see that the flames were far too white to be from any normal campfire.

His horse stomped its feet and skirted from side to side, unsure of where to run. He hardly noticed as the sound of the ocean crashed louder and louder still, seeming to intensify as the lights neared. Soon all Iseult could see were the lights, blindingly bright, and he could hear the sound of his mother's voice welcoming him home.

CHAPTER ELEVEN

When Anders woke, he was glad to see that the old man had not left them in the night. The trio had made camp shortly after dark, then took turns resting. As an added precaution, only one person slept while the other two remained awake . . . just in case. He had first stood watch with Àed, followed by a shift with his sister, making him the last to sleep.

He and his sister had lost their belongings along with their horses, so they each had taken turns crawling in and out of Àed's bedroll. Anders could replace his bedding and clothing once they reached another burgh, as his coin pouch was still on his belt, but other things were not so easily replaced. Along with several one of a kind texts, they'd lost all of their cartography research, making the trip they'd taken thus far useless. He had detailed everything, from the smallest stream to the barest rise of hills, in order to make the most detailed traveler's map the Gray City had ever seen. It was all lost.

"Quit lollin' about and put up me bedroll ye lout!" Àed barked, seeming wide awake despite lack of sleep.

Anders sighed and rose from the bedroll. Àed was waiting by his horse, with its reins looped around his right hand. It was just their luck that the only horse left was Àed's mule-creature. Anders eyed the mule-horse skeptically. It would probably keel over well before they reached the edge of the forest.

"Where is Branwen?" Anders grumbled as he rolled up the bedding.

The old man glared back at him. "She's right here ye blind fool."

Anders looked past Àed, but his sister was nowhere to be seen. As panic took him, Anders asked again, "Where. Is. Branwen?"

Àed looked over his shoulder to find that the woman was indeed missing. "Faierie-bladdered fools! She was right here a moment ago. Get things packed up already before she gets herself caught in another Faie net!"

Anders scrambled to hastily gather up their few belongings, though he felt compelled to just leave them. As soon as everything was strapped to the mule-horse's saddle, they began their search. Àed kept a pace that Anders could barely match, though both men were on foot. Anders wanted to ask how they would find his sister, but did not want to interrupt the aged conjurer as he scanned their surroundings through barely open eyelids. As he followed Àed numbly, Anders found it a wonder that the old man did not trip himself up with the way he was going about things. He appreciated the urgency Àed had placed upon the situation, though his heart had wedged itself up into his throat, making it hard to breathe as they hurried forward.

Suddenly the old man darted away from the path, like a hound with the fresh scent of a rabbit. Anders sincerely hoped that the rabbit they were chasing was Branwen.

Neither Finn nor Kai slept much, and it was not only out of fear of lurking Faie. They had heard a man shouting for much of the night, calling out for someone in the dark. They would have liked to pass it off as more Tuatha tricks, but both Finn and Kai had heard it quite clearly and couldn't help but wonder if it was one of their companions.

They had searched for the source of the shouts, but wherever they walked, the sound never got any closer. Eventually they had given up, though the yells continued.

It was with heavy hearts and eyelids that they began their travels that morning. They kept a slow pace, searching for signs of a path, or more importantly of their friends. They went on that way for quite some time, recognizing some areas as they passed through them, while others looked completely foreign.

Finn's thoughts continuously returned to her encounter the previous day, after she'd ridden away from the group. She hadn't meant to take off so abruptly, but she also hadn't felt in control of her own actions. She'd sensed a presence not long after entering the forest of the Faie, a presence overwhelming and all-encompassing. She knew with a surety she had never felt before that she needed to reach its source.

The presence called out to her as she escaped her companions, urging her to find it. Then she'd seen it in the near distance. Trees just like her, transforming into people. She'd tried to speak to them, but they'd disappeared as Kai found her. She'd kept her eyes on the trees of the forest ever since, hoping for another sighting.

Many of the aged, knobby trees they currently passed looked familiar to her, and she was sure that they must be nearing the edge of the forest, when they came upon an unusual sight that they had definitely not come upon previously.

The mounds rose two to three feet above the ground, covered in an even layer of vibrant green grass. There were eight in total, arranged in a circle around an empty central point.

"Barrows," Kai commented.

Finn nodded, she had thought the same thing, and was sure she had seen such barrows before, but she dismissed the thought quickly. "We should not linger here. I would not linger upon such burial places even outside the Blood Forest."

Kai shook his head, gazing off into the distance. "Nor would I, but I believe I see a person over there."

Finn looked to where Kai pointed. Indeed there was the dark shape of a distinctly feminine form. "Is . . . is she dead?" Finn asked, hoping that it was not one of their companions.

Kai shrugged. "There is only one way to find out."

The pair dismounted their horses and approached the shape cautiously. As they neared, Finn saw long, red hair fanned out around a still, pale face.

"Branwen!" Finn shouted as she rushed to the woman's

side. She grabbed Branwen's shoulder and turned her onto her back, causing her limbs to flop about bonelessly.

Kai tied their horses' reins to a nearby tree and joined Finn. He leaned over Branwen and checked the fallen woman for a pulse, looking stern and disconnected. "Her heart beats steadily, but much more slowly than is normal."

Finn laid a hand gently against Branwen's cheek, willing her to wake up. Feeling silly for even trying, Finn removed her hand, then slowly Branwen's honey-colored eyes opened. Finn gasped in excitement, then let out a sigh of disappointment as Branwen's half-open eyes looked right through her.

"Branwen?" Finn questioned, but Branwen remained unmoving, except for the occasional rise and fall of her chest. Finn leaned back on her heels against one of the mounds, and jumped off just as quickly. It had felt as if the mound was alive, like some great sleeping beast. She stifled a shiver as goosebumps erupted across her arms and legs.

Her eyes met Kai's. "We must move her from this place," she said quickly, wanting to be as far from the mounds as possible.

Kai nodded, looking just as shaken as Finn felt. "I couldn't agree more."

Together Kai and Finn helped Branwen up from the ground. Branwen was not much help, and did not respond to any orders they tried to give her. It was easy work lifting her though, as she was not a particularly large woman.

Finn and Kai managed to carry Branwen to the horses, then hoisted her onto Kai's mount. She sat up in his saddle, but made no move to take the reins. Kai ended up walking beside her to make sure she did not lose consciousness again, while Finn walked ahead with the reins of both horses.

Neither spoke until they were far out of sight of the mounds, and then a little farther still. Once the eerie feeling of the barrows had subsided, Finn stopped walking to look back at her two companions nervously. "Do you think she will come out of it?"

Kai cast a worried look at Branwen, then turned back to Finn. "Let's just get her out of the forest. Perhaps she will come out of whatever trance she is in once we're away from Tuatha magic."

Finn swallowed a lump in her throat. "What if she doesn't?"

Kai gave her a look like she was being silly, making light of a serious situation. Finn might have been appalled if she didn't suspect he did so for her benefit. "There is no use worrying about it. What will be, will be, and there's little we can do to change it," he replied.

Not wanting to revert to silence, Finn glanced back at him once more as she started walking again. "What about the Travelers and Liaden? We likely did not come close to finding her, and already we must leave the forest."

Kai's expression shifted, though Finn had turned to watch her footing so she did not see it. "I will see you out of the forest, then I will return to find her."

Finn nodded her head thoughtfully. She kept her gaze forward to watch where she was walking, but couldn't help asking another question. "Are you in love with her. Is that why you must find her?"

Kai laughed, causing Finn to jump. She cast a glare over

her shoulder at him. "Are you Faie-charmed? That wasn't a funny question."

Kai chuckled again. "If only you knew how funny it actually was. I view Liaden like a sister. Well, a very angry, older sister. She's family, at the very least. Also, she only likes women, so I wouldn't waste my time there."

Finn scoffed. "You can love someone that is like a sister to you."

Kai tsked at her. "Oh, but you did not ask if I loved her. You asked if I was *in* love with her. There is quite a difference."

"Oh shut up," Finn grumbled, embarrassed.

"Would you be jealous if I had said yes, that I did love Liaden?" Kai prodded.

It was obvious to Finn that she was being teased, though she still did not appreciate Kai's question. "I would think that a rather silly thing to be jealous of," she replied curtly as she walked a little faster.

"Oh?" Kai questioned. "Most women would argue that love is most definitely a thing to be jealous of."

Finn smirked, though Kai could not see it. "I imagine love from a man like you would only bring a woman misery. So to answer your question, no, I would not have been jealous had you admitted to loving Liaden."

Kai sighed. "Suit yourself. Feel free to let me know if you change your mind on the subject."

"I highly doubt that I will."

"You will come to love me in time," Kai joked. "You'll see."

Finn shook her head ruefully, glad that Kai could not see her small smile.

"The path forks up ahead," Kai observed.

Finn had noticed too, and observed each of the paths thoughtfully. Unsure of which way to go, she glanced back at Kai expectantly.

He shrugged. "Your guess is as good as mine."

Finn turned to the paths again. The trail on the left seemed to have a sliver more sunlight than the one on the right, so Finn led the horse and mule to the left. The day had warmed considerably, which she was glad for. She hoped it meant they had indeed gone in the correct direction, and were reaching the outskirts of the forest.

She glanced one more time at the right hand trail as they passed it by. She thought she saw a figure standing in the shadows, but as soon as she blinked, it was gone. The figure had not possessed a form that could easily be considered human. She imagined that it would have only reached her knees in height, though it had been rather rotund. She had not glimpsed it long enough to pick out any other details.

Fearing she was becoming Faie-struck once again, she stopped and turned to Kai. "Did you see that?"

"No," Kai answered, as the color drained from his face, "but I do see *that*."

Finn turned back around. The figure was now standing a good fifteen steps ahead of them on the trail. Her original judgment of the creature's shape had been correct. What she had not noticed, was that the creature had deep violet colored skin, and a nose that looked like a long, scraggly turnip. The creature's round head was mostly bald, except for a few thin tufts of black hair sticking out here and there. The creature's odd body was clothed in a tunic and breeches that nearly matched its plum colored skin.

Finn guessed the stout man had been waiting for them to come down its path, but when they changed courses, it had changed positions.

"Should we turn back?" Finn whispered, trying to move her mouth as little as possible.

"What if it knows the way out?" Kai whispered in response.

"I do know the way out!" the creature called to them. Its voice was much deeper than Finn had expected, rumbling with a deep baritone.

"Uh," Kai began, speaking normally this time, "I don't suppose you'd like to tell us which way that is."

The creature hobbled up to them excitedly. Finn expected with the way the thing moved, it would fall over any moment, but it managed to reach them all the same.

"For a price," the creature answered, grinning. The few teeth in its mouth were cracked and broken. Given that, the creature wouldn't likely bite them....at least, Finn hoped that it would not bite them.

"What price?" Finn asked.

The creature hopped from foot to foot in excitement. "You could give me that woman in the saddle. She is obviously useless to you, and her parts could catch me something of real value in trade to the right Faie."

"I think we'll manage on our own, thank you," Finn replied quickly, horrified at what the Faie had suggested.

The creature hopped around even more frantically. "Now just you wait. I'll lead you out for a lock of your hair. Some would value a lock of hair from one of the Dair Leanbh very highly."

Kai looked at Finn as if she'd just sprouted a new head. "What does that mean?"

"Nothing to you, outlander," the creature replied with a glare, though Kai had asked the question of Finn. "Tuatha business is Tuatha business. Now give me a lock of your hair, and we can all be on our way."

"We'll find the path on our own," Finn stated again, hoping to keep the creature from saying anything else. As far as she had gathered from the Traveler, she was not of the Faie. Of course, who really knew what was or wasn't Faie in origin?

Finn attempted to walk past the creature, but each move she made was mirrored by the little purple man. "I'd like to be on my way," she said firmly.

The creature grinned, showing his few, jagged teeth once again. "I'm not to let you leave, dearie. Terribly sorry."

"Yer not to be stoppin' her either," a voice called from behind them on the path.

A moment later, Àed came stomping up beside them, followed by Anders with Àed's mule-horse. The Tuatha man looked between Àed's group and Finn's, and grinned again. "I see you've brought more bargaining tools, Dair Leanbh."

"I will not trade my friends," she snapped at the little man. "Now remove yourself from our path, or I will remove you myself."

The little man's smile was sickening. "Not like any Dair child I've ever met," the purple man whined. "Suit yourself. There will be other opportunities, to be sure." With that, the man backed away into the trees and disappeared.

As soon as the purple man was gone, Finn threw herself

at Àed, engulfing him in a hug. He patted her back awkwardly, not sure what to do with the show of affection.

"How did you find us?" Finn asked as she pulled away.

Àed spat on the ground. "Dumb luck really. That fool redhead went runnin' off and we were trackin her. Tracked her to some mounds where I got a sense of ye. I'd thought it was a skill long since lost to me, yet here ye are. Them barrows were a good six furlongs from where we lost her. Don't know how she traveled that far so fast. Ye must have gotten to her not long before we came upon that place."

While Finn was greeting her friend, Anders had gone to greet Branwen. Only she did not seem to recognize her own brother. Anders pulled his sister from the horse and set her gently on her feet. She stood on her own in front of him, but made no move to do anything else.

He placed his hands on his sister's shoulders and shook her gently. "What's happened to her?"

Kai placed a hand on Anders' arm to get his attention as he stared at Branwen. "We found her by the mounds," he explained when Anders finally turned toward him. "She was unconscious at first, and her state hasn't changed much. She hasn't spoken a single word."

Anders looked close to tears as Kai helped him put his sister back in the saddle. Branwen looked forward from her place on her mount, staring into oblivion.

Anders stared up at his sister. "She was only lost to us for two hours at most. I don't understand how this could have happened."

"I do not know," Kai replied, "but I'm beginning to realize that we are no match for the Faie of these woods."

"We should leave," Anders stated solemnly. "We need to get out of this forest as soon as possible."

Finn hated to draw attention away from Branwen's predicament, but others could still be in danger. "What about Iseult?" she asked softly. "Has no one seen him? I had hoped he would be with you," she finished, forcing herself to meet Anders' gaze.

His face contorted with anger, and Finn knew immediately she should have just waited and asked Àed instead. "What about my sister!" Anders shouted. "I'm not going to risk her by going back to find some hired sword."

Finn calmly put her hands on her hips and stared down each of her companions in turn, not allowing Anders' outburst to faze her. "Then I will go back myself," she announced.

Àed moved closer to Finn. "No ye won't."

Anders gave Finn an *I told you so* kind of look. Finn turned to argue with the old man, but he interrupted her. "Because I'll be goin with ye."

Finn's jaw dropped as she tried to think of an argument to not risk her friend any further, though in all reality, Àed was much better off in the forest than she. Before Finn could argue, Kai moved to stand on her other side. "I had been planning on going back for Liaden regardless of the dangers. I will accompany you as well."

"Well what are the rest of us supposed to do!" Anders exclaimed.

"We've reached the outskirts ye fool," Àed replied gruffly. "I wouldn't bring ye two Faierie blighters back in with us even if ye begged."

Anders' face went rigid. "Finn was caught up just as much as I."

Àed waved him off. "And she'll have the only two of us not taken by fancies to watch over her. If ye have a mind to, ye can make camp and wait for us farther out. Perhaps we can even return yer precious Gray Lady to ye."

"What about my sister?" Anders asked more pleadingly this time.

Àed did not appear sympathetic, so Finn stepped forward. "If we find the Travelers, we will ask them how to cure her. I want her well again too. She may even come out of it on her own once she's completely away from the forest."

Anders nodded and managed the barest of smiles. "Thank you. You are a small beacon of light in this hell. I apologize for yelling at you before."

Finn nodded, unsure of what else to say. She handed Anders her mule's reins. Kai had already set to retrieving his things from his horse, leaving Finn to hand Anders the reins to the second horse as well.

"Branwen needs the horse, and two horses will not do three riders as much good as they'll do you, so you shall take mine as well," Finn explained as Anders looked down at the reins in his hands skeptically.

Anders gripped the reins tightly. "We will wait for you on the outskirts," he assured.

Finn nodded as Anders turned and led the horses away with his sister sitting rigidly in Kai's saddle. With a deep, settling breath, Finn turned to go back into the forest with her two companions following close behind her. Àed's poor mount was led back into the forest with them to carry the few supplies they kept for themselves. They had enough provisions for that day only, and none for the day ahead. They could perhaps have left with Anders to re-provision, but at any time their missing companions could cross the point of being lost forever. Perhaps they already were.

CHAPTER TWELVE

*I*seult rubbed at his aching skull as he sat up in the grass. His limbs were stiff and cold, which was no wonder since the ground he laid upon was covered in frost. He got to his feet, but his knees buckled, tossing him back to the ground.

Suddenly memories stabbed through his brain so fiercely that he turned to the side and expelled pure bile, as there was no food left in his stomach. As his dizziness subsided, he looked around for his horse, but the animal was gone.

The lights. That was when he had lost his horse. As the lights closed in his horse panicked, and he was too stunned to fight as he was bucked from the saddle. It was not the lights themselves that put him in such a state, but the sound of his mother's voice. His mother had spoken to him through the lights.

He shook his head. His mother was dead, and had been

dead for over twenty years. The lights had used a voice they knew he would listen to . . . but how had they known?

As he sat on the ground shaking with cold, he remembered asking his mother to help him, but his pleas had been ignored. Instead the lights spoke of Finn. She was important to them, and would need to be saved. Chaotic images of battle flashed through his mind of the Travelers fighting with other Faie. Iseult was shocked more by the different shapes and colors of the Faie than he was by the bloodshed. Once beautiful white canopies framed the scene, their edges now covered in blood. In the middle of the bloodshed was Finn, central to the action, but somehow not a part of it.

Iseult forced himself back to his feet. His body screamed with every step, but still he moved forward. Finn would soon be in danger. Time was running out.

Finn, Àed, and Kai had been walking for several hours, and were yet to see any sign of Faie trickery since leaving the purple man. The three companions stuck to the path, searching for the Travelers rather than their individual quarries. The camps would be large, as the Ceàrdaman were one of the few semi-faie races still great in number. The camps would also be deep enough into the forest to not be happened upon by random humans, but close enough to the edge to allow for easy travel into the outside world.

Finn had many voices in her head that asked how on earth she thought they would be successful, when their first attempt was such an utter disaster. She argued that the forest had taken them unawares the first time, and now they knew what they were doing. The voices argued that she had been the first to succumb to Tuatha tricks, and likely would be again. Finn told the voices to shut up.

The companions walked on as morning turned to afternoon. The going was easy on the paths, and the terrain seemed smooth enough, yet tired and hungry, Finn stumbled constantly. They walked on regardless, not wanting to take the time to rest when time for their companions could be running short. Instead they ate the remainder of their meager rations while they walked.

Finn felt as if she were walking in a dream, and worried that she was being influenced by the Faie once again. The path around her seemed blurry, and she could not keep her eye on single focal point as she stumbled along. Soon her vision blurred completely, and the utter silence of the forest was pervaded with song. Finn could pick out several common instruments accompanied by unearthly voices, rising and falling in mournful harmony.

"Please tell me you both hear that," Finn groaned as her vision slowly returned, frustrated that she was so susceptible to Faie magic.

"Aye lass," Àed answered without glancing back at her.

Finn shakily caught up to Àed as hope sprang up in her chest. "Is it the camp? I had not thought to find it so soon."

Àed nodded, but did not seem to share Finn's hopefulness. "I reckon that this time, the Travelers wanted to be found. Though what the problem was before, I am not sure."

Kai stopped walking. "Did anyone's vision just blur?" he asked nervously.

Finn nodded almost excitedly, glad that she was not the only one.

"We've passed through the Traveler's protective glamours," Àed explained.

Kai rested his hand on the pommel of his sword and looked to Àed for instruction. Àed shook his head. "Weapons will do ye no good here, lad."

"The Mountebank is correct," said a voice to their right. Where just a moment before was empty space, stood a woman draped in white robes. She looked startlingly like the Traveler they had met on the road, right down to the bald head and translucent skin. Her overly long, knobby limbs were most evident in the arm she held outstretched toward the party. The palm of her thin hand was empty, as if she was waiting for them to give her something.

Kai stepped in front of Finn with his hand still on his pommel. Affronted, Finn stepped forward to stand at Kai's side. Àed remained where he stood, grumbling to himself about dratted moon-faced whelplings.

"I will require your weapons," the Traveler said in a sing-song voice, still holding out her hand.

"I don't think so," Kai replied just as Finn was unsheathing her dagger to hand to the woman.

"If the Gray Lady is to go unharmed," the Traveler replied calmly. "I will have your weapons."

"We don't want some blighted *Gray Lady*," Kai growled. "We're looking for the woman you kidnapped from us."

"I am aware," the Traveler answered as the shadow of a smirk crossed her lips.

Kai looked to Finn, who shrugged. She had no doubt that

physical force was not the way they would retrieve Liaden. Even with their weapons, they would be at the mercy of the Travelers. She only hoped that one of them would have a "secret" that would quench the Travelers' thirst.

Kai reluctantly undid his leather sword-belt, and handed the sheathed weapon to the female Traveler. An impatient look from the woman prompted Kai to reveal and hand over several other small blades from various areas of his person. Finn relinquished the dagger from her waist, and the party began to move forward.

The Traveler did not move. "Not the Mountebank," she ordered. "He is a weapon in and of himself. He may not enter."

Àed laughed bitterly. "I'm not what I used to be, lassy."

The Traveler cocked her head as if listening to something only she could hear. "Still," she replied finally, "you are not without your tricks. You will wait here."

Àed's face reddened, and Finn could tell he was about to launch into one of his tongue-lashings. The Traveler cut him off before he began. "You have come this far unharmed on the word of the Ceàrdaman alone. It would not be wise to test your luck."

"Unharmed?" Finn questioned. "I would not call the current state of my party *unharmed*."

The Traveler cocked her head to the other side. "You yet live. That is enough."

"What about Iseult?" Finn countered. "Does he live?"

The Traveler listened again. "He lives, but he is not our concern. He will be a part of things soon enough. Now come, if you would see the lady of Clan Liath alive. Time is running out for us all." She turned to Àed and dumped the weapons into his waiting arms as if offended by them.

Finn was unsure of what the Traveler meant by *running out of time*, but had no time to question her as she turned to lead them into the camp. As they had little choice, Finn and Kai followed a safe distance behind the Traveler. Finn glanced back at Àed, who stood in place looking torn with his arms full of weapons and his mule-horse snuffling at his fraying hat.

"What is Clan Liath?" Kai whispered as they walked.

Finn shrugged, unsure if it was her place to tell Kai of Liaden's lineage. "I don't see as that's of much importance at the moment. I'm more worried about this *time is running out* business."

The scale of the camp alluded to the fact that it was a fixed meeting place, though Finn could have sworn they'd gone this deep into the forest on their first trek. Large poles were hammered into the ground to support sheer white canopies, their ends gently trailing over the earth. The canopies were large enough to cover a gathering of thirty people apiece, though the wooden chairs and tables below them were mostly vacant. Small wooden hovels were also built into the upper branches of trees, with no visible way to reach the structures other than shimmying up the tree trunks, though Finn doubted the Ceàrdaman were much for shimmying. The hovels appeared vacant, in fact, the entire camp seemed empty as they approached, but as they walked Travelers began to appear seated around the various fire pits underneath the canopies. Finn could never quite see the Ceàrdaman as they appeared, they were just suddenly there.

The music grew louder, but Finn could still not determine its source. As they walked, it began to seem as if the music was coming from above them. She looked up, and realized with horror that the music was coming from dozens of small cages. Tiny, winged Faie were trapped in the cages, singing and playing tiny instruments as if their lives depended on it. Most had wings too tattered for flight, so that if they did by chance manage to escape their cages, they would likely just plummet to their deaths. Finn glared at the back of the female Traveler, willing the woman to turn around so she could see just what Finn thought of her and her people.

When the Traveler did not turn around, Finn glanced over at Kai. He looked around worriedly as they walked. She was not used to him showing his nerves, but she supposed the situation warranted it. The Traveler had acted as if Liaden was alive, but there was no saying how close to death she might be. Finn met the passive eyes of many Travelers as they passed. Perhaps there were worse fates to be had in these woods than death.

Their guide came to a stop in front of a large white tent made of a fabric less sheer than the others. Also, unlike the canopies, this tent had four sides that were staked at each corner into the ground. The front flap was split in two and hung loose at the inner corners, forming a door. The female Traveler stood to the side and motioned for Finn and Kai to enter the tent.

"I'll go," Kai said softly. "There's no need for both of us to enter. If I do not return, run. Don't wait even a moment to see if I am alright."

The female Traveler clucked her tongue at them. "You

must both go. Both or none. I assure you, it is not a trap. At least, not the type of trap your mind has conjured."

"Why is it so important for both of us to go?" Kai questioned suspiciously.

"Would you leave her out here alone then?" the Traveler asked in reply.

Finn's eyes widened at the idea. "We'll go together," she said quickly, not wanting to ever be left alone with one of the Ceàrdaman again.

Kai considered for a moment, then nodded before entering the tent just ahead of Finn.

It was a trap, were Finn's first thoughts. The tent was completely empty. Only it wasn't. At their feet was the entrance to a great cavern. Stale, moist air wafted up from the abyss.

"It's a cave," Kai commented. "Of course it's a cave. Why wouldn't there be a cave inside of a tent?"

Finn grabbed Kai's hand in an attempt to settle the man's nerves. "Shall we?" she asked, acting much more brave than she felt.

Kai nodded, and they took their first step into the cavern. Steps carved out of dirt turned into stone a few feet down. The cavern had been very wide and flat to the earth at the entrance, but as they descended the steps a flat ceiling became barely visible above their heads. It was like walking into a cellar, where first you only see stairs going down, but it opens up into a deceivingly large space.

Glowing lights lined the walls, looking almost like fire, yet too white to be ordinary flame. They were also not held in any sconces that Finn could see. Instead they just floated in place along the walls, illuminating Kai and Finn's way.

"What is that scraping?" Kai whispered.

Finn had heard it too, though she'd been attempting to ignore it. It sounded like the click of tiny nails scurrying in places just out of sight. "Rats, maybe," Finn replied, though she highly doubted it was something as mundane as rats.

The light intensified as they reached the main chamber. High, sweeping walls made out of glistening stone composed the alcove. The walls seemed too tall for how deep into the earth they had traveled. Either the incline of the path was deceiving, or they had entered a chamber underneath a large rise of land, though Finn had seen no small mountains anywhere near the tent.

An exaggerated sigh greeted them. "Oh not you again," whined the Traveler they had met on the road, what seemed like weeks, but only days, before. His face was illuminated by the eerie lights, casting harsh shadows below his long nose and sharp chin. "Go away Dair Child, you have nothing to offer me."

The familiar Traveler was accompanied by three more of his kind, yet these three were abnormally tall, even for the Ceàrdaman. Their heads reached up into the darkness as they swayed in their white robes to an unheard rhythm, oblivious to the appearance of their visitors.

Finn noticed a dark form crumpled at their feet. The form was wrapped in a charcoal colored robe with a large hood, obscuring its face from view, though a tendril of long, dark hair trailed out from the shadowed hood. *Liaden.*

"Well we'll just take our companion and be off then," Finn replied, gesturing to the hooded form.

The Traveler's annoyed expression shifted into a wide grin, showing his disturbingly sharp teeth. "She was the payment for your information. You are wasting your time. Unless . . . well, unless you have something better to offer."

"What are you doing to her?" Kai interrupted angrily.

The Traveler cocked his head at Kai. "I was not speaking to you. You have nothing to offer."

Kai started toward the Traveler in a rush of anger. Finn barely managed to catch his arm to hold him back, but after a moment's hesitation, he obeyed her gesture.

"What do you want?" Finn asked as the lump in her throat dropped to her stomach.

"I will trade one woman for another. You may take your friend's place," he said, as if he weren't asking her to give up her life.

She had to buy time, though for what, she did not know. "What would you do with me?"

The Traveler took a step forward, making Finn's pulse quicken. It took every ounce of her self-control to not take a step back as her stomach turned to ice at the man's nearness.

The Traveler laughed, greatly amused by Finn's discomfort. "The Gray Lady sees the inbetween places. With her, I can see them too. That is quite a boon to give up, and I would not do so at all if you weren't of the Dair. You can teach us to travel the trees. That could be of great use to us, especially in the coming times."

Finn had no idea what the Traveler was talking about. "What do you mean?" she questioned. "The coming times?"

"The *changes*," the Traveler said excitedly. "I told you they were coming. It will provide great opportunities for the more . . . industrious races. You must decide quickly. We are running out of time."

Again with the *running out of time* Finn thought. "That doesn't explain anything. I would know what you would have of me before I agree to anything."

The Traveler clucked his tongue as if Finn was being very silly. "I've explained that already. We require knowledge of your gifts. Not another Dair Leanbh has been sighted in one-hundred years. You aren't exactly a prime specimen, but you'll do."

Finn began to step forward, but Kai grabbed her arm and pulled her back. "This is mad. We are not trading anyone. You kidnapped her from us, you've used her against her will, and now you will give her back."

"No," the Traveler stated simply. "I will not."

Finn allowed Kai to hold her close to his side, away from the Traveler. Had she really just attempted to trade herself for Liaden? Her mind felt as if it was covered in thick mud. "Then why not just take me as well?" she asked, confused. "Why even give us the option of a deal?"

The Traveler took a large step forward, and suddenly was just inches in front of Finn's face. He acted like Kai wasn't even there. "There is power in a proper deal, my dear," the Traveler whispered. His breath smelled like spoiled milk. Finn wrinkled her nose and wanted dreadfully to step away, but her feet felt frozen in place.

"Well we never made any deal, so I don't think you have any power," she whispered back shakily. "I think I'll take my friends and leave."

Surprise crossed the Traveler's face, but was quickly wiped away as he reached his knobby hands toward Finn's cheek. Seconds before he would touch her, Finn brought the heel of her boot down onto his toes. The Traveler looked at her in astonishment, allowing Finn the time to pull away from Kai and swing her fist, landing a club-like blow against the side of the Traveler's nose. He fell to the ground, cursing and bleeding all over the place. During Finn's distraction, Kai rushed from her side to gather Liaden. The three tall Ceàrdaman watched expressionlessly as Kai lifted Liaden into his arms like a child and carried her toward the entrance of the cavern.

Finn hurried to follow him, then stopped short as another white-robed Traveler appeared blocking their way out of the cavern. The hallway was too narrow to go around him, so they would have to go through. Kai had begun to charge the Traveler with Liaden still in his arms, when red blossomed across the belly of the Traveler's robes. An object shifted underneath the red-stained fabric, then withdrew. The Traveler dropped to the floor, dead.

In his place stood the best sight Finn could think of at that moment. Iseult, covered in blood, holding his short-sword in his right hand. His face was pale and rigid with fatigue, but Finn could see the relief in his eyes as he paused for a fleeting second to stare at her.

"Stop them!" yelled the Traveler who Finn had incapaci-tated. He clutched a bloody nose as he got to his feet. "Get them!" He ordered the tall, silent Travelers. "Leave the women alive!" he added as the large forms glided toward them.

Iseult grabbed Finn's arm and shoved her ahead of him. Next came Kai with Liaden. They ran down the stone corri-dors, with the eerie lights flickering wildly. *Time is running out,* Finn thought giddily as fear and excitement fought for control of her brain. Her sleeve was damp with blood where

Iseult had grabbed her, and she tried to not think too hard on where it came from. She reached the cavern entrance and exited the tent ahead of the others. She had expected more Travelers to bar her way, but she had not expected the utter chaos in front of her, making the blood on her sleeve seem minor in comparison.

Faie of all shapes and sizes fought with the Ceàrdaman. The white canopies that had seemed so elegant before were tattered and stained with dirt and blood where they touched the ground, and some had been set on fire.

The small cages that hung from the trees had been opened to reveal that the tiny, tattered Faie could indeed still fly. Finn witnessed this firsthand as one of the ethereal forms came to hover right before her eyes. Rage twisted the tiny creature's face as it considered Finn, then flew on. If Finn had not been mistaken, the creature had held a small twig, whittled to a needle-like point in his hand. The point had been stained crimson with blood.

Finn shuddered and started forward, seeking a way out of the chaos. She would have tripped over the bloody prostrate form of the female Traveler that had guided them to the tent, but Iseult grabbed hold of her arm and guided her around the corpse, instructing her to go around the backside of the tent instead. Kai followed with Liaden still unconscious in his arms.

The way behind the tent was less crowded with fighting, though not entirely clear. "Left!" Iseult shouted just as a quarreling pair nearly took Finn's right arm off from behind. The fighters tumbled to the ground in front of her, oblivious to her presence. As she watched, the Traveler in the fight ripped a lizard like creature the size of a small wolf off his now mutilated leg, and began stabbing at the base of the creature's neck with a small dagger. The creature attempted to rear back, but only managed to drive the dagger up underneath its reptilian skull, effectively ending its life.

With the lizard creature dead, the Traveler shoved the corpse aside and turned his attention to Finn. This attention was short-lived, however, as Iseult promptly shoved his sword through the Traveler's chest, nearly pinning the man to the ground. "Go," Iseult ordered as Finn stood frozen in shock.

When Finn did not move, Iseult withdrew his blade from the Traveler and pulled her forward. She tried to shut out the scene around her, but her eyes were inevitably drawn to the carnage. The forest had seemed so empty in their travels, yet the number of Faie attacking the Travelers far outweighed the numbers of the Travelers themselves. Where had they all come from?

"We have to do something," Finn mumbled to herself.

"This is not our fight," Iseult replied, pulling her close to his chest to avoid a slim, nymph-like creature with scales covering her slender legs. The creature went screaming past them, intent on a nearby Traveler wielding a large axe.

"Why aren't they attacking us?" Finn asked as they took a quick respite near the trunk of a tree.

"They are here for the Travelers. This is the beginning of a war," Iseult answered.

"Another war amongst the Faie?" Kai breathed heavily. Carrying Liaden was beginning to take a toll on him.

Iseult nodded, looking in far worse shape than Kai. "And it will not remain contained in this forest. We must leave this place and get as far away as possible, preferably to another continent."

An army of tiny flying men darted past and Iseult urged Finn forward once more. They neared the edge of the battlegrounds, but still had to exhibit caution as various Faie were steadily pouring in from the periphery. Most of the Travelers remained in the center of the battle, defending their camp. Eventually the sounds of battle grew distant, and the tension within the party eased.

"The Travelers will be slaughtered," Finn observed quietly as she was ushered into a relatively tranquil copse of trees. "Why?"

Iseult's face was grim. "The Ceàrdaman have kept the Faie in the Blood Forest all of this time. We believed they had left the mortal world willingly after the last war, but we were wrong. Things are changing now, and the Faie believe that to remain trapped here would mean their end. Each race wants to assure their place in the world."

They strode farther on and stopped in an area more hidden by trees. Kai took the opportunity to set Liaden down momentarily, then looked back to Iseult. "What do the Faie intend to do once outside of the forest?"

Iseult shook his head. "That is not something I intend to stay around to find out."

Finn leaned her weight against a nearby tree, still confused. "The Ceàrdaman knew this was coming, that time was running out. They stand no chance of prevailing. Why would they stay?"

"*Time is running out,*" Kai repeated, more to himself than to his companions. "You're right, they knew."

A large crunching sound from behind them drew the

party's attention. A creature greatly resembling a tree revealed itself from within the shadows. Its long trunk-like body, covered in chipping bark, was disproportionate to its short, spindly legs and arms, but that was not the most unnerving thing about the creature. On top of the trunk was one of the ugliest faces Finn had ever seen. Pieces of bark fell off the face as its crooked mouth formed a smile under a massive, knobby nose. Kind, deep green eyes peeked out from uneven, wrinkly eye-sockets to focus on Finn.

"Is that what I think it is?" Kai asked quietly.

"I think . . . " Finn began. "I think it's a Trow."

"I can hear you," the creature bellowed. "I would think you would be less astonished, Tree Sister."

Kai looked at Finn askance. "Tree sister?" he questioned skeptically.

Iseult grunted in impatience. "We must go. I do not want to be here when the Faie finish with the Travelers."

The Trow cleared his throat, making a sound like the breaking of a hundred tiny branches. "So you will not join us in our fight?" he asked, looking directly at Finn and ignoring the men.

"I fear I have nothing to fight with," Finn said quickly, not wanting to anger the creature, "and we really must be going."

The Trow waved them off with one spindly arm. "As you wish," he grumbled, then stalked past them toward the sounds of battle.

"Gather the woman," Iseult instructed Kai.

Kai did as he was told and retrieved Liaden. Iseult led them farther away from the battle, and soon the sounds of fighting could no longer be heard at all. Finn was not sure if that meant that they had gained enough distance, or if the fighting had finished. Her stomach turned at the thought of the slaughtered Travelers.

"Where are we going?" Kai demanded. "Won't we just get lost again?"

"The Faie will not hinder us this time," Iseult answered plainly.

Kai stopped walking. "And just *how* do you know that?"

Iseult sighed, his impatience clear on his face. "I had . . . an encounter. The Faie no longer desire this forest. Keeping us here would be pointless. They will not try and trick us again, though if we keep wasting time, they may grow tired of toying with the corpses of Travelers and come looking for some new entertainment."

That was enough to get Kai moving. Finn scanned the forest for signs of Àed. They had left him at the opposite side of the camp, and had not seen him at all during the fighting. She hoped he was alright.

Her prayers were answered quite suddenly as the old man in question came stomping through the forest toward them. He had Kai's numerous sheathed weapons and Finn's small dagger strapped around him, making him look like a haphazard porcupine. "What are ye fools waitin for!" he called out. "There's a war a'happenin and we need to be as far away as possible!"

Iseult gave Kai an *I told you so* kind of look as the party picked up their pace to catch up with the old man. Àed's shaggy brown mule-horse trotted behind him, matching the old man step for step. Finn noticed that Àed was not even holding the horse's reins anymore. It simply followed him of its own will.

Àed stopped long enough for Kai to place Liaden across his mule-horse's saddle, then they ventured on together, trusting that Àed was leading them in the right direction. The forest had lost some of its darkness, and the light trickling in showed them the late afternoon sun.

Finn could no longer hear the sounds of battle, and though she felt nearly too tired to walk, it seemed they had escaped the worst of the forest.

Hope blossomed within her chest. Soon they would be out of the forest, and she could continue her quest to become a tree once more. Of course, if there was an opportunity for a little more adventure before she grew new roots, she would not shirk it.

She glanced at Iseult as they walked. He had more color in his cheeks now, though he still looked ready to keel over. She opened her mouth to ask if he needed to rest, but didn't get the chance as he placed a hand against the small of her back to urge her on more quickly.

When Liaden regained consciousness, she found herself awkwardly slung across the back of a shaggy, short horse. The horse was keeping up a rather brisk, bumpy pace that was quite irritating. The last thing she remembered was a Traveler pulling her from her bedroll, then she was submerged into a world of grays.

She had walked through long halls for days, or perhaps weeks, she was not sure. She had heard voices, and felt as if there had been several consciousnesses within her skull. The extra minds had guided her through the maze-like corridors with soft coaxing. Occasionally she had seen other human forms, but they were always hazy, and did not seem to notice her.

Eventually she found what the voices were looking for. It was a great tree that appeared to be mostly dead. Yet there was life in its roots, and she somehow just knew that those roots reached into another place, and not just into the ground. The tree's name echoed in her mind, *Archtree*.

Brought back to reality again by the harsh movements of the horse, she tried to right herself in the saddle. It became apparent that someone was holding her in place, and she began to thrash about until she fell from the horse to the ground. The next sight she saw was Finn standing over her, only not looking how she was supposed to. Veins of light could be seen flowing underneath Finn's skin like wildly writhing serpents. The lights shone particularly bright where her heart should have been.

"Liaden!" Finn shouted, causing the light to intensify. She crouched closer, bringing her headache inducing brightness with her. "Are you all right?"

Liaden flinched at the sound, then waved Finn off. "I'd be fine if you'd just stop shining so brightly."

"S-shining?" Finn asked, but Kai appeared before an explanation could be offered. He lifted Liaden up into a sitting position. "Are you hurt?" he asked.

She pushed away from him to sit on her own. "The Travelers?" she asked, wondering how she had been freed from her captors.

"Dead," Kai replied as he got to his feet.

"How?"

Àed came into view. "That's not important now. What is important is that we're going to be just as dead if ye fools don't get up out of the dirt and get movin'."

She allowed Kai to help her stand, but instantly almost lost her footing again. She felt absolutely exhausted, and hungry. Very, very hungry. She noticed that Àed shone with a similar light to Finn's, only his was more muted and golden in tone.

She held on tightly to Kai's arm as he guided her back into the saddle so they could begin moving again, reveling in the feeling of being near someone she trusted. She shivered as she thought of the cold touch of the Ceàrdaman. Closing her eyes against the sharp pain in her head and the sick feeling in her stomach, she asked, "Would someone please explain to me what is going on?"

"The Faie are at war," Iseult answered blandly from somewhere behind her. "Because of this, we'd like to get out of their forest as soon as possible." Despite his words, she doubted he would be able to make it out of the forest as he leaned heavily against a nearby tree for support.

"How far do we have to go?" she asked, discarding all of her questions in favor of a more pertinent one.

"We're close," Iseult replied simply.

The conversation ended with that. She would have liked to know where Branwen and Anders were, but she could see something shining in the distance, and she felt that this thing might not be as welcome a sight as her companions had been.

"There's something up ahead," she warned.

"I see nothing," Kai replied from beside her, scanning the trees farther up the path.

While she watched, a line of bright lights journeyed in single file from within a thick copse of trees. The lights seemed almost like free-floating fires, but were too bright white to be flame.

"Those are the lights that lined the Traveler's cavern," Finn observed.

Liaden let out a sigh of relief, glad that she wasn't the only one who could see the lights.

"They're Faie," Iseult clarified, as he looked at Finn. It was a rather tender look for a mercenary to give. "They guided me to you," he explained, still looking only at Finn.

Finn turned from Iseult's gaze to stare back at the lights. "Look," she said, pointing to where the lights had come to a standstill. Open land could be seen past the lights. They seemed to be encircling the border of the forest.

"How do we get out?" Finn asked.

"Wait," Iseult instructed as he stared at the lights, shifting his weight from foot to foot uneasily.

Àed had moved closer to Finn, and to Liaden, the two of them together was almost blinding. White light mingled with gold to create a dizzying shine. She turned back to the lights at the border as they pulsed brighter and brighter, as if they were building up to something. With a final pulse, they exploded in a fiery flash. A hot wind rushed past her face, and the pressure changed, making her ears pop. She looked where the lights had been, and could find no sign of them.

Àed groaned. "They destroyed the border. The Faie are

171

free. We needed to be gone from this place a fortnight ago, a year ago!"

The party stared at the old man as if he had lost his mind. "What are ye waiting fer!" he scolded. "Get movin!"

They did not need to be told twice. Liaden set her heels into the horse's sides to urge the creature on. Everyone else ran as if there were flames licking at their heels.

CHAPTER THIRTEEN

*A*s they ran, the ground behind them began to shake steadily. The mule carrying Liaden didn't seem as worried as everyone else on foot, and kept an even pace despite the trembling. At first Finn thought that perhaps the earth was going to tear itself apart, but she soon realized that the shaking was caused by footfalls. Thousands upon thousands of footfalls.

Finn watched in horror as several Trow surpassed her on their way to the border. Another Trow reached her side. "Faster, Tree Sister!" he shouted at her. "Even with the Ceàrdaman weakened, the border will not stay down for long!"

The Trow then picked up his pace, quickly leaving Finn and her party behind. Finn stumbled, but Iseult was quick to catch her so that she did not fall completely. Liaden kept pace with them, even though she could have easily ridden ahead. Àed outpaced them all, constantly looking over his shoulder to urge his companions on. The old man scurried and hopped over the underbrush like a fox. It would almost have been an amusing sight if they weren't all running for their lives.

"Faster!" Kai urged, also looking over his shoulder. Finn stole a glance back, then indeed ran faster. All shapes and sizes of Faie followed in their wake. The tiny winged Faie that had once been in cages caught up and buzzed past Finn's ears on their way to freedom. Her lungs burned as she labored to suck in enough air. The border was so close, but her steps had begun to falter. Her pace slowed as she resigned herself to being overtaken by the stampeding Tuatha.

Just as she was ready to drop to the ground, Finn let out a yip as someone picked her up effortlessly from behind. For a moment she thought that Iseult had rescued her, but the arms around her were not human. The twig-like arms of the Trow now carrying her were much stronger than they appeared. Panicking, she tried to pry herself free as she was carried away from her party, and eventually over the border. The Trow carried her a few steps farther, then turned to look back at the other fleeing Faie .

As Finn watched, all of the various Faie crossed the border and disappeared into the scenery. Some took to the sky, others scurried over the ground and into the brush, and others simply faded from sight.

The Trow let Finn down to her feet as her party reached them. "You are safe for now, Tree Sister," the Trow rumbled, "but I would not remain near the border long. Many of the Ceàrdaman still live, some in the forest, and many others outside of it."

Kai grabbed Finn as soon as he reached her, pulling her away from the Trow's side. The Trow laughed in his strange, deep voice, then hobbled away to melt in with a copse of nearby trees.

"When that creature grabbed hold of you, I thought-" Kai began.

"He was trying to help," Finn interrupted, "and lucky that he did, my legs were ready to give out."

Come to think of it, her legs still felt like pottage. She was surprised that she was able to stand at all. With that final sprint, the long walk had caught up to her.

"We best be leavin'," Àed commented. "Not all these Faie will be as benevolent as that Trow." Àed looked Finn up and down. "Up on the horse with yer friend now," he ordered.

Finn looked skeptically at the horse with Liaden in its saddle. Despite its rickety looking body, it did not seem weary in the least. Finn turned back to Àed. "How is that horse the least tired among us?"

Àed grunted in reply. "I've a way with animals. Now up ye go."

Finn obeyed, and they made their slow way away from the forest. In the few moments they'd stood conversing, the tumult of the stampeding Faie had nearly died down completely. They were out in the world of humans now. Finn knew the day's events would have dire consequences for the world of her companions. She supposed it was her world as well, even if she preferred to live in it as a tree.

Really, they were probably more safe at that moment than they would be upon reaching the next town. They were in the last place the Faie wanted to be. The mule-horse seemed to sense that the need for great haste was over, and kept a slow, lolling pace. Àed returned Finn's dagger to her, then handed Kai his various weapons as they walked. Finn watched curiously as Kai returned each blade to its proper place, stumbling with fatigue as he did so.

Liaden, who was sitting in front of Finn in the saddle, turned to meet the eyes of her fellow rider. "Where are the twins?" she asked. "I hope nothing tragic has befallen them." Though Liaden's words were sympathetic, Finn sensed that they weren't entirely genuine, perhaps because of the way Liaden squinted at her while she said them.

Finn looked back at her sadly, ignoring her strange squinting. Liaden had been through a lot, after all. "They live. At least they were alive when we left them, but Branwen fell afoul of some unknown Tuatha spell. We found her lying among Faie barrows. Once she awoke, she behaved as if in a trance, like a sleepwalker. We left her with Anders at the border when we came back to find you."

Liaden's expression turned thoughtful. "You lacked two members of your party, yet you still came to find me?" she asked breathlessly, as if truly puzzled.

"Three actually," Finn answered. "Iseult was missing as well."

Liaden twisted her mouth in confusion. "But why? Why would you and the old man risk your lives for the life of a stranger?"

Finn's eyes narrowed, not sure if she should be offended or not by the line of questioning.

"Don't misunderstand me," Liaden said hurriedly. "I am grateful, just . . . well Kai I understand, that boy knows no fear, but you owed me no such rescue."

Finn shrugged, suddenly uncomfortable. "I suppose I just didn't feel there was another option. You and Iseult were both within the forest. If we did not find you, who would?"

Liaden shook her head, but smiled to soften the gesture. "You are a very strange woman Finn, and I am grateful for it."

"Of course no one is grateful to the *old man*," Àed piped in. "I only kept all yer fool hides safe through this whole debacle."

"Thank you Àed," Finn, Liaden, and Kai said in unison. Iseult remained quiet, but Finn was quite sure that she had seen a small smile cross his exhausted, pale face as he walked beside Àed's horse.

The party went in silence for quite some time. Whenever they passed through a copse of trees, Finn felt a certain sense of unease. Any manner of Faie could be hiding in the foliage . . . but the trees were always empty. At least they *seemed* empty.

The sky was more clear than Finn had seen it at any point that year. Clear enough that the sun beat down on their shoulders whenever they left the shade of trees. Her entire body ached, but her stomach ached the most. She worried that they might starve, but did not say so out loud.

"I'd still like to know how you found us," Kai said to Iseult, breaking the drawn-out silence.

Iseult offered the barest of nods as he walked beside Kai, but did not speak.

"Well?" Kai pushed.

Iseult ignored him completely. Surprisingly it was Liaden who cut in. "I don't think any of us really want to divulge our experiences in that cursed forest. I, for one, will not be answering any questions, so I shan't blame the sell-sword for doing the same."

Kai raised his eyebrows in tired surprise and turned his attention to Liaden. "You won't even tell *me?*" he asked, though it was clear he'd turned to teasing.

Liaden let out a snort of weak laughter, then turned her attention away from Kai. "Do we have any food left? Or more importantly, water? I feel as if I've had nothing to eat or drink for a week."

Iseult silently untied his water skin from his belt and handed it to Liaden. She took a long swill from the skin, then handed it over her shoulder to Finn, who took it appreciatively. The water ran down Finn's dry throat almost painfully, and it was an effort to stop herself from draining the waterskin entirely. As Finn handed the container back to Iseult, he held her gaze until she gave him a nod of understanding. They had many things to discuss, but not while in the presence of Kai and Liaden.

Finn very much wanted to know what had happened to Iseult in the forest, but the swig of water had brought to light more pressing concerns. They were nearly out of water, and entirely out of food. She hadn't eaten since that morning, and the portion had been so small she felt it hardly counted. She began searching through the horse's saddle bags in earnest, and to her surprise came up with two small pieces of bread, though there was no meat or cheese to go with it. Kai or Àed must have purposefully reserved the bread, knowing there was no food to find within the Blood Forest.

Finn handed one piece to Liaden, fearing that the Travelers had not bothered with feeding her at all. The other piece she handed to Kai to divide up. What she ended up with was a small fourth of a piece of bread. The men had attempted to deny their pieces, but Finn refused to eat them. Liaden gnawed at her hunk of bread like a starved wild animal.

Finn's belly protested the meager portion, letting her know that it would have rather had nothing, than just a bite to whet her appetite. Hearing the groan of her stomach, Kai looked up at her with a raised eyebrow. "We'll stop and set some traps soon. We likely won't find much, but we'll survive."

Finn knew that Kai was only trying to console her. There was always the chance that they would not be able to catch any game at all. If that was the case, starving to death became a real concern. Her stomach cramped, nearly doubling her over. Perhaps it was a concern already.

"There is another problem," Liaden added. "Even if we manage to feed ourselves until the next town, I've lost all of my belongings, and it seems most of you have as well. Do we even have any coin to purchase rations once they are available?"

The party took a moment to search their persons. Finn still had Àed's coin purse, which had remained quite full. Iseult and Kai both carried a fair amount as well. Luckily they had all kept their coin on themselves and not on their mounts.

With that settled, they walked on. It seemed to Finn that they had been walking forever, when in reality it had a few hours. They had seen no sign of the twins since leaving the forest. Finn hoped they were well, especially Branwen, yet she had to admit that a part of her was glad to delay their meeting. They'd had no chance to seek answers with the Travelers, and given the Traveler's recent lowering in numbers, possibly never would. Finn dreaded telling Anders, feeling he would blame her alone, as she was the one who had first promised answers.

~

The voices in Branwen's head told her not to wait any longer. Her brother had brought her to the outskirts of the forest, but he wasn't important. The forest had served its purpose, and now Branwen had to move on. Her heart pounded as scenes of bloodshed flashed through her mind, though the forest in front of her appeared empty.

The forest. She had found new purpose there. Some small voice in the back of her mind protested this new purpose, but its influence was negligible. The voices in the front of her mind were much more prominent, and they had given her a mission to fulfill.

"*Go*," the voices urged her.

Distant sounds from within the forest distracted her brother, and she took the opportunity to kick her horse into motion, despite the fact that her reins were looped around the pommel of her brother's saddle.

Branwen's horse reared up, unable to move forward as its rider commanded. The horse reared again and turned to the side as Anders' own mount panicked. Branwen's reins came loose from his saddle before Anders could react. As soon as her horse was freed, Branwen kicked its sides again. She clung to her saddle as her horse took off away from the forest, with her brother galloping after her and shouting her name.

As none had the energy to walk through the day, Finn and her companions stopped to make camp while the sun was still high above them. Luck was on their side, and Iseult found a nearby river to refill the few waterskins left between them. Kai set snares for rabbits, but with nothing available to attract the rabbits to said snares, he was not hopeful about the results. The best he could do was set them near the river, in an area that would be convenient for small animals to stop and drink.

While they waited for night to fall, Finn and Liaden excused themselves to bathe in the chilly river, which was really more of a stream. Finn would have forgone the icy water altogether, but Liaden claimed she needed to wash away the feeling of the Traveler's touch, and Finn did not want to make her do so alone.

Once they reached the bank, Liaden shed the charcoal gray cloak that the Traveler's had wrapped around her, dropping it in the dirt, then looking at it in disgust.

"I'll not be putting that *thing* back on," she commented tiredly. "I do not care how cold I get."

Underneath the cloak, she still wore her own garments, luckily, as Finn did not doubt that Liaden would consider going nude if she had no other option.

Finn stripped down, but did not submerge herself in the cold water, choosing instead to stand on the shore and splash water onto her skin, also taking time to rinse some of the blood from the sleeve of her dress. Liaden stripped, then crouched beside her to do the same, using her long, dark hair to obscure her face from Finn's sight.

Finn felt ill at the sight of Liaden looking so terribly broken, when before she possessed such an air of strength. She wanted to ask Liaden what had been done to her, but felt it was not her place to do so.

It was Liaden who finally said, "Do you think they're all dead, the Travelers I mean?" Liaden had not looked at Finn as she asked the question.

"Not all," Finn said honestly, "but I believe those who kidnapped you are no more."

Liaden nodded to herself. "I hope their deaths were drawn out and painful."

Finn did not know how to reply, so they finished bathing and dressed in silence. Liaden left the charcoal gray cloak where she had first dropped it, refusing to even look at it as they moved to rejoin their companions.

Liaden was grateful that Finn had chosen to bathe with her. If she'd done so alone, she likely would have been brought to tears, and crying was something she had not done in a very long time. The days when other people could make her cry were long since past, though the Traveler's had come close.

She looked at Finn as they made their way back to the camp. She still shone like a small sun, as did the old man, and Liaden wondered what it meant. Iseult and Kai did not shine in such a way. Perhaps Àed shone because he was a conjurer, but why Finn? Liaden sincerely hoped that Finn was in no way connected to the Faie. She'd had more than enough of the Tuatha to last her a lifetime.

They found the men sitting around a large, well built fire. Liaden seated herself near the soothing flames, feeling hollow and weak as Finn did the same.

Finn and Àed huddled together for warmth, and while Liaden would have appreciated the warmth of another body, she did not think she could stand being touched, even by one of her human companions. Just as she began to shiver, Kai removed his cloak to wrap around her, not questioning the disappearance of the charcoal Ceàrdaman cloak.

She wrapped his cloak tightly around herself, reveling in the lingering warmth from Kai's body. "Where do we go from here?" she asked to no one in particular as she gazed into the fire.

"Badenmar is the closest hospitable burg," Iseult volunteered. "We could resupply, and seek out any word on Anders and Branwen."

"I doubt we will find them again," Kai commented, voicing a reality Liaden couldn't help but agree with.

Liaden caught Finn's subtle nod at Iseult before he said, "If we cannot find word of them, then we will part ways."

"You would leave Finn and Àed to fend for themselves?" Kai asked, misunderstanding Iseult's meaning.

"I will be going with them," Iseult said plainly.

Finn's eyes remained downcast throughout the exchange. If Liaden didn't know any better, she'd guess that the girl felt guilty about moving on. Liaden did not really care either way. With Anders and Branwen gone, the purpose for her entire journey was lost. If they could not find them, she would just as soon return to the comfort of a larger city far away from the remnants of the Blood Forest.

A loud squeal pierced through the air, but was abruptly cut off. Kai was on his feet in an instant, running off in the direction of the river to check his snares. Everyone waited in anticipation with thoughts of roast rabbit on their minds. The sight of Kai returning with a mutjac, a small deer, instead of a rabbit in his arms was a welcome one. The animal's neck hung limply, broken by the snare. Liaden smiled at her long-time companion as he approached, feeling sickened by the sight of the dead deer, but at the same time very, very hungry. They would all sleep with full bellies for the first night since leaving Garenoch, what seemed like months ago.

PART 2

CHAPTER FOURTEEN

*A*nders' nerves felt ready to snap as he rushed through the foliage on horseback in search of his sister. In her sleep-like state, he hadn't expected her to run off like that, thought it was obvious to him now that she'd simply been waiting for the right opportunity. The only explanation he could fathom was that some insidious Faie had possessed her, but that problem could not be dealt with until he found her.

He slowed his horse and searched his surroundings wide-eyed, worried that the sky would grow dark before he picked up Branwen's trail. He replayed the scenes in his head, going back to when they'd first entered the Blood Forest, wondering if there was anything he could have done to save her. *He'd* been the one to convince their parents that he would keep his sister safe, but who was he kidding? He was a man of twenty-five who had hardly even left the safety of the archives.

He and his sister had led highly sheltered lives focused

on learning as opposed to actual experiences. It was the way of most archives. Knowledge was passed down through generations, and children were expected to eventually take on the running of the archives when their parents passed. If it were up to Anders' father, both he and Branwen would already have found other scholars to marry. Anders shook his head. He just *had* to see the world before he settled down to a life among books. Not that Branwen had argued when he proposed the idea of making a traveler's map. She had wanted to escape the archives just as badly.

Now everything was lost: his books, his research, and most importantly, his sister. All because he didn't want to grow up and do what was expected of him. His parents would never forgive him if he returned without Branwen. He would never forgive himself.

Though it wasn't entirely his fault, he reminded himself. Finn and the others had forsaken him. They left him alone with no way to fix his sister, all to go after two people who were probably already dead. Not to mention the fact that Finn was at fault for them having to venture into the Blood Forest to begin with.

He tugged his horse to a sudden halt at the sight of his sister's horse drinking from a small stream, riderless. He dismounted the shaggy horse Finn had lent to him to investigate. His squishy footsteps as he crept across the soggy earth sounded deafeningly loud in his mind, as did the snuffling of his unhappy mount. There was no sight of his sister anywhere near the stream, and he had gathered both horses with the intent of moving on when he heard her.

"I don't know where she's gone," Branwen said pleadingly.

Anders hopped over the small stream, trailing the horses behind him, in the direction of his sister's voice.

"I've never been *North*," she argued. "You'll have to show me."

Anders approached a dense, thorny thicket, curious and at the same time terrified to see who his sister was talking to, but she was the only person who came into view.

Branwen turned quickly at the sounds of her brother's approach, and clammed up at the sight of him. She looked from side to side as if she might run, but Anders was able to rush around the thicket to her side before she could act.

She shook her head over and over as he grabbed her arm and guided her back toward her horse before helping her into the saddle. This time, he climbed into the saddle behind her, and tied the riderless mule-horse to the pommel. Branwen's snarled, red hair shook with movement as she began to sob. She grew increasingly upset as Anders guided their horse back in the direction of the Blood Forest, but he could see no other choice. He held on tightly to his sister, grateful that she was small-boned and not overly strong.

As frightened as Anders was of the forest, and as displeased as he was at his other companions for abandoning him, Finn was his only possible source of answers. He had to go back to find her, if nothing else. With the tired horse traveling at a walk, and the mule-horse constantly pulling on its reins in search of a little grass, it took over an hour to get back to where they'd started. Branwen, who had settled into softly crying in defeat, grew clearly alarmed as they neared Faie lands once more. Yet, her alarm was unwarranted. The forest was no longer there.

Where the boundary had stood, now were only a few

sparse trees. Anders blinked furiously as he clung to his sister to keep her in the saddle, not believing the site before him. There was no sign of the excess trees being felled. They had simply disappeared. Further investigation revealed that the forest had been cleared out entirely. Just as there was no evidence of the Faie, there was no sign of Finn or the others. If he hadn't known for a fact that the forest was there only hours before, he would have passed right by the unremark-able area.

He waited where the forest should have been until night fell and he finally had to give in to the fact that he desper-ately needed to sleep. He made camp a short ways off, still feeling uneasy about being in the area, even though the forest was gone. He reluctantly secured the now-silent Branwen with a length of rope before helping her into what was once Kai's bedroll, but still he slept very little. Each time he woke he checked the forest for signs of movement, yet his lost companions did not reveal themselves.

The next morning he had to admit that if they stayed any longer they would starve. Since then, he had wandered with his sister in tow, intent on asking after Finn in each town they passed. If they managed to make it back to their family's archives, then he would resort to books to cure his sister.

Finn's party departed the next morning in good spirits, even though most of them had slept wrapped in their cloaks for lack of extra bedrolls. With their hunger sated, and a good night's rest under their belts, hope was renewed. They passed by the small, more hostile hamlets along the road entirely, knowing they would not find much aid within them. With any luck, the twins had done the same and would wait for them in Badenmar. It was the only burgh in those parts, unless you traveled several more days south-west to Garenoch, or north to Felgram, and so would make sense as a meeting place. From what Finn had been told, Badenmar was only a small village, but qualified as a burgh as it was ruled over by a lesser Alderman. That same Alderman was also the sole innkeep.

Iseult was the only member of their company that had been to Badenmar in recent times, but Finn trusted his judgment on the place. He deemed it their best choice to resupply, though they would likely find no horses to purchase there. Horses, Finn had been told, were mostly to be found in the larger cities, as most common villagers could not afford them.

Since they were traveling on foot, it was nightfall once again before they finally reached Badenmar. The party was greeted by the gentle thrum of music, causing Finn to have a sickening flashback to the Travelers' camp. She repeated to herself that this current music was man-made, and they had no Faie to worry about in this new place, but the prickling sensation at the back of her neck remained.

Torchlight glowed along the road into the burgh, accompanied by the scent of woodsmoke, giving a comforting air of welcome. As the first homes came into view, Finn could see that they differed a great deal from those she'd seen in Garenoch. The buildings were much lower to the ground, and spread out lengthwise rather than up. Their walls were painted in dark greens and browns, blending in with the trees surrounding the burgh. The village had been built around an open central location, which was where most of the townspeople were gathered. Finn's attention was drawn to the gathering as they approached, and she found herself pausing to watch the festivities, rather than following her companions.

Kai walked up beside Finn, his attention on the crowd. "In all of this action, I'd forgotten about the Equinox. It looks like we're just in time for the Ceilidh."

Finn knew that a Ceilidh was a type of festival, though the customs varied. She did not know for sure if she had ever been to a Ceilidh in her former life, but she had vague memories that made her think that she probably had.

The women of the town moved to the rhythm of the drumbeat in what was either a previously choreographed dance, or a longstanding tradition, as not one woman missed a step. The women in Badenmar had a unique style of dress that served to accentuate their movements as they swayed in an almost seductive manner. Heavy, layered skirts done in dark tones swirled around their legs in unison. The skirts were held in place by wide belts that covered the bottoms of rather revealing loose tops that hung off the women's shoulders artfully.

The men stood around the circle of dancers, wearing more traditional outfits composed of cloth breeches and varying colors of tunics. The men clapped in time with the music, but left the dancing to the womenfolk. The musicians, a group of five, were at the very center of the circle, playing with great fervor. Finn hesitated on the boundary of the festivities, wanting to step forward, but not sure whether outsiders were welcome.

Realizing that she had been observing the dancers for several minutes, she turned just in time to see Àed and Iseult leading the horse toward the back of what had to be the town inn.

"Do you both see that?" Liaden asked, stepping up between Kai and Finn.

"The dancers?" Finn questioned, not seeing anything else of interest.

"In the trees," Liaden said, gesturing to the distant foliage, partially obscured by the houses. "I see lights."

"I see nothing," Kai replied.

"You see what's in-between," Finn replied softly. "That is what the Travelers said. You see what most cannot."

Liaden rubbed at her eyes. She still looked tired, despite the good night's rest they had managed. "I never saw these things before. Whatever the Travelers did changed that."

"I'm sorry we did not find you sooner," Finn said, not sure what else to say.

Liaden turned to her, squinting her eyes slightly. "Don't be sorry. Just stop shining so brightly. You're blinding me." With that, Liaden walked away toward the inn with her arms wrapped tightly around herself.

Finn turned a questioning gaze at Kai. "Shining?"

Kai shrugged. "I haven't the slightest idea." Suddenly he smiled as he turned his full attention toward Finn. "Let's dance."

Before Finn could argue, Kai grabbed her hand and dragged her toward the crowd. As they approached the center of the dancing, the women dispersed themselves amongst the men, and the dancing degenerated into ruckus stomping and spinning. The music grew louder, predominated by an intense drumbeat.

Finn allowed herself to be pulled into the action as Kai put an arm around her waist and spun her in dizzying circles. The steps of this new dance were not difficult to pick up, and Finn soon found herself stomping along with the crowd. She felt a buzz of energy in her head from being surrounded by the twirling throng, making her heartbeat pick up speed until she felt slightly queasy.

As they spun, the townspeople began switching partners. A tall woman with jet black hair pulled Kai away, and Finn suddenly found herself in the arms of an older man with steel gray hair and icy eyes. The man was fit and muscled for his age, obviously either a long-time fighter or laborer. From the way he held himself, Finn guessed fighter. She did not like the way his calculating, icy eyes lingered on her face as they began to dance.

"You are not from this place," the man commented over the din of sound, holding Finn delicately in his arms.

The pace of the music had slowed, and she found herself increasingly uncomfortable with the man's attention. "No, I am not," she answered quietly.

"A traveler then," the man observed, "but from where?" He raised one gray eyebrow at her, and Finn looked down quickly, feeling like the man saw far too much.

"Garenoch," she lied, as it was the only other burgh she knew.

The man shook his head. "You do not speak like a country person. Try again."

Finn raised her gaze and an eyebrow in turn. "Would

you call me a liar?" she asked coyly, trying her best to feign confidence.

"I would never dream of it, but you do travel with interesting companions, especially as a young lady from Garenoch." His tone was mocking, but not outright rude. "And look at that," he said with mock surprise as he glanced down at her arm, "you appear to have dried blood on your sleeve."

Finn could feel a nervous blush creeping up her face. She'd done her best to scrub her sleeve where Iseult had grabbed her when he found her in the Traveler's lair, but the stain had dried on the gray fabric to an ugly dark brown. Where had Kai gone off to? Ignoring the question of the stain, she asked, "And what is so interesting about my companions?"

The man let out a sudden laugh, letting the issue of her sleeve slip. "None of them can be said to possess much moral fiber. You seem quite sweet yourself. It just seems an odd combination."

"You seem quite sure of yourself for a man who knows nothing about me," she snapped.

The man's eyes widened slightly at her tone. "I meant no offense. Forgive me if my curiosity has caused you discomfort. It is simply my nature."

"Well you should try to not let your nature get the better of you," Finn chided as she sought Kai out in her peripheral vision.

"You're as venomous as a snake," he laughed as he spun Finn out of reach of one of the village men who had hoped to steal her away. "Perhaps I misjudged you."

He opened his mouth to say more, but Kai mercifully

approached and reclaimed Finn with an uncomfortable smile and a nod to the silver-haired man.

Finn switched partners willingly, and was led away into the crowd. "That," Kai remarked as he stopped and pulled Finn close to him, "was a very dangerous man."

"You know each other?" Finn questioned, confused.

Kai shook his head. "I only know him by reputation. I doubt he knows me."

"Who was he?" Finn asked, now more curious than before.

Kai maneuvered Finn into the rhythm of another slower dance. "Óengus. He is a hunter of some renown."

"Hunter?" Finn questioned, not sure why a simple hunter would be infamous. "A hunter of what?"

Kai glanced back to where Óengus stood, now on the perimeter of the dancers. "People," he answered softly.

Finn turned her full attention to Kai, though she had the overwhelming urge to keep an eye on Óengus. "He had quite a few questions about my *amoral* companions," Finn explained. "Could it be possible that he is hunting one of you?"

Kai smirked. "That's doubtful," he assured, "and he is in no position to throw stones. I, for one, am the picture of pure goodness."

Finn cocked her head to the side. "Now why do I doubt that?"

"Because you are a naïve country girl who knows little of the world," he said tauntingly.

Finn huffed in indignation. "Would you call me a liar now as well?"

Kai lifted one shoulder in a slight shrug. "No one would

fault you for it. You could tell us the real reason you're traveling around with a notorious conjurer."

"I lived in a glen near Greenswallow for as long as I can remember," she stated plainly, daring Kai to prod her further. It was the truth, as far as she was concerned. If she had lived in other places, well, she did not truly remember them. "And I knew nothing of Àed's history until Branwen told me," she added.

Kai smiled in amusement. "Calm down. I was not aware this was such a sore subject for you."

Finn was glaring up at Kai as Liaden and Iseult returned to watch the celebrators, a good distance from where Óengus stood. Noticing them, Kai and Finn left the dancers to join them on the outskirts.

"They had no rooms at the inn," Liaden explained as their companions approached, "but the innkeep was *kind* enough to provide bedding for us in a storage room," she finished in a tone that let Finn know Liaden hadn't thought the act kind at all.

Feeling out of breath, Finn glanced around in search of their final companion, but saw no sign of him. "Where is Àed?"

Liaden snorted. "Testing every type of whiskey the inn has to offer."

Finn laughed and it eased some of the tension inside of her. She followed Liaden as she turned and led the way to the inn, with Kai and Iseult following close behind. Finn's stomach rumbled for something other than mutjac and stale bread, and she hoped the inn had a proper selection. Some wine would not be out of order either.

Finn walked underneath a hanging wooden sign

carved in the shape of a coin purse, into a simple, but clean inn. On the short walk, she had been informed that the place was called the Dealer's Den, though she could see no gambling taking place. Once inside, Finn found that she much preferred the clean, open common room of the Den to the Sheep's Delight back in Garenoch.

She scanned the tables. Sure enough, their elderly companion was seated at a table with a dram of whiskey, and several empty mugs besides. A few other patrons sat drinking whiskey or ale, but much of the common room was empty, as the townspeople were all out in the square.

Finn seated herself next to Àed with Iseult on her other side. Iseult sat rigid as a pole, obviously up in arms about something.

In complete contrast was Kai who, perfectly at ease, waved down the barmaid before seating himself across the table, next to Liaden. The barmaid approached and set several drams of whiskey on the scuffed and uneven table-top, even though no one had ordered them, then disappeared into the kitchen to fetch their suppers.

Finn reluctantly took up the dram that Kai pushed toward her, then held the small container to her nose and took a whiff. She broke out into a fit of coughing at the acrid smell, almost spilling the whiskey in the process.

"You know," Kai explained, "you are supposed to drink it, not sniff it. You'd think even a girl from Greenswallow would know that." He threw back his own dram of whiskey as if it were nothing.

Not wanting to be outdone, Finn plugged her nose with one hand, and threw back the whiskey with the other, glaring at Kai all the while. It seared her throat all the way down, but left a pleasant warmth in her belly.

Liaden sipped daintily at her glass, while Iseult ignored his entirely. Iseult was even more restrained than usual as his calm green eyes monitored their surroundings. Finn tried to catch his eye as she pondered his silence, but either he did not notice, or he was ignoring her. He looked around the room coldly, like there were dangers all around, and he was not impressed by any of them.

The silent barmaid delivered their meals, which consisted of some type of fish and roast turnips, then sauntered away, making it clear she would much rather be out enjoying the Ceilidh.

The meal was not particularly good, but Finn savored it, glad that it was not unseasoned, roast mutjac. The sounds of ongoing festivities drifted in through the open windows as they ate. Occasionally someone came stumbling in through the door for another round of ale, but they quickly went back outside. Finn was yet to see the Alderman/innkeep since they'd arrived, though she'd been watching for him. She was rather curious what type of Alderman would want to preside over a small burgh like Badenmar, and would choose to be an innkeep as well.

As the night wore on, patrons began to filter into the common room to continue their drinking where they could rest their feet. After questioning many of them as to whether or not they'd seen a pair of red-headed twins, the party retired to the stockroom. The room was not lavish by any means, but a mat and bedding were provided for each person. In the morning they would look into replacing their bedrolls and other supplies.

Since there'd been no word on Branwen and Anders, Finn wondered if Kai and Liaden really would venture off on their own the next morning. She'd grown attached to the pair, and didn't relish the thought of never seeing them again, though she knew it was necessary if she was to continue on her quest. Finn only wished she'd had more time to converse with them that evening, but the two had been deeply immersed in a private conversation.

Kai and Liaden's hushed conversation continued as they claimed the two straw mats in the far back corner of the room, away from the rest of the group. Finn grumbled as Àed guided her toward the bedroll in the middle of the room so that he and Iseult could sleep closest to the door.

As candles were extinguished Finn closed her eyes, not feeling tired despite the large amount of walking they'd done that day. After a time, the breathing of her companions slowed into the gentle rhythm of sleep, leaving Finn alone with her thoughts.

She tossed and turned on her straw mat, too filled with restless energy to leave the waking world. It was the first time since Garenoch that Finn had slept inside, and she had mixed feelings about the situation. She found that she was actually grateful for the shelter, and that thought alone worried her. What worried her even more, was that she hadn't thought about being a tree all day. She was, in fact, beginning to like life as a human. She liked being a part of what people did, beyond lending them shade, or a trunk to lean against. She liked dancing and conversing. More than the sense of community, she enjoyed adventure and having the ability to move about as she pleased, meeting new humans and creatures along the way.

It was that thought that drew her out of her bed. She still enjoyed being near the earth, but it was the promise of new people and new experiences that lured her. Much of the celebration had died down, but she could still hear soft music and the gentle hum of conversation through the walls of their room.

She quietly donned her cloak and boots, then let herself out into the common room. There remained only two pairs of people in the establishment. One pair, a man and a woman, were deeply absorbed in the act of romancing each other. The other pair, two men, were instantly deemed by Finn as less than fitting company. She guessed they would rob her and slit her throat before they would ever converse with her.

She exited the inn with a second wary glance toward the sinister pair. They watched her go, but without much interest.

Once outside, Finn discovered that many of the dancers were still present, only they danced slowly and close together. Some of the dancers hung onto their partners, half-asleep. The musicians still played, but their arms moved in a slow, jerky manner, as if they had no real control over their limbs.

"I'd appreciate if you would stop running off," a voice said behind her.

She turned to see Iseult, sullen and tired in his black cloak. He turned his gaze from her to the dancers, worry creasing his brow.

"Something strange is happening," Finn whispered. None of the dancers seemed to see them as they neared.

Finn approached a young man dancing with a woman

old enough to be his grandmother. The woman wore no cloak over her festival clothes, though the night had grown chill as the fires died down. Neither of the dancers acknowledged Finn's presence, even when she put her hand right in front of the young man's face.

"If I did not know better," Iseult began as he reached Finn's side, "I'd guess we were still in the Blood Forest."

A startling thought came to Finn. Since the denizens of the Blood Forest were now free, the rest of the land would be exposed to their magics. Of course, occurrences would not be quite so concentrated, but they would inevitably transpire.

"Why are only some of the townsfolk affected?" Finn asked warily.

Iseult shook his head, as if he did not want to believe the reality that had been placed before him. "Why were only some of us affected in the forest? It could be based on a weakness of will . . . " he glanced down at Finn, who was glaring back at him, "or the Faie could be targeting certain bloodlines," he amended. "Or perhaps different Faie choose to target different sorts of people."

A thud to the left drew their attention. One of the dancers had passed out from exhaustion. Finn went to the woman's side to make sure she had not been injured in her fall. The woman had long salt and pepper hair and wore heavy skirts and a loose shirt like the other dancers. The woman was also quite dead.

Finn pulled her hand quickly away from the woman's skin. It had felt cold, though she surely was alive just a moment before.

Iseult half drew his sword from its scabbard as he stood

over Finn. His calm hunter's eyes surveyed their surroundings, but the threat had not yet made itself visible. The next thing Finn knew, Iseult had whirled around and now held the tip of his short sword at a man's throat.

The throat in jeopardy belonged to the silver haired man that Finn had briefly danced with earlier in the night. Óengus held his hands up, showing that he was harmless, though Finn sincerely doubted the legitimacy of the gesture.

Óengus backed away from the sword's tip. "Now now boy, that is no way to treat one of your superiors."

"You are right Óengus," Iseult replied as he lowered his blade. "Should I find someone I deem superior, I shall be sure that they do not meet my blade."

Finn took a step back, surprised that Iseult knew Óengus personally, but found that it put her too close to a pair of the entranced dancers, so she placed herself back by Iseult's side. While they stood, another dancer dropped.

"We have to do something to stop this," Finn demanded. Iseult and Óengus continued to stare each other down, ignoring Finn's pleas, so she stomped off toward the treeline in search of the Faie culprits on her own. Iseult sheathed his blade with a growl and both men turned to follow Finn, though they kept a decent span of distance between each other.

Finn marched into the darkness, not sure what she was looking for. She saw a few flashes of movement as she searched, but nothing that she could quite train her eye on.

"There," Óengus said, pointing deeper into the trees as he came to stand at Finn's side.

"I don't see anything," she replied while Iseult glared at the older man from Finn's other side.

Óengus held up a pewter locket that hung from a thin chain around his neck. "Red Verbena," he explained. "It wards off Tuatha glamour."

Iseult's eyes rested on the locket. "Why would you wear a charm against glamours?" he asked suspiciously. "The Blood Forest is a long way off from this place."

Óengus tucked the locket safely back inside his shirt. "There have been whispers across the countryside of Faie sightings. Things are changing. I have experienced the Faie before, and would not go into such an encounter unprepared again."

Finn thought she heard the sound of laughter trickling down from the overhead branches.

"Geancanach," Óengus observed, looking up through the trees. "It makes sense I suppose."

"What are you talking about?" Finn snapped, her impatience outweighing the uneasy feeling the man gave her.

Óengus pointed again, and this time Finn saw what he'd been looking at. A small creature was climbing down the trunk of a nearby tree. There was enough moonlight to illuminate its diminutive form and show that it was covered in leathery gray skin devoid of hair. The creature had small, bat-like wings on its back that Finn doubted served any real purpose.

The Geancanach reached the bottom of the tree and slowly approached them. It mostly walked on all fours, but would occasionally stand on its hind feet to tip-toe across a thick fallen branch or rock. As it neared, Finn noticed that it had large, pure green eyes set in a small head that looked quite a bit like a rock. Its wide mouth opened into a grin as it looked up and regarded Finn.

The creature chirped unintelligibly in its language, but Finn recognized the word *Dair*. The creature danced from foot to foot while looking up at Finn, obviously wanting her to join in the dance.

"Stop that!" Finn shouted at it. "You're killing people!"

The creature squinted its eyes in anger, and its chirping language turned to guttural grunts.

"You should not have done that," Óengus chided.

The creature quickly scurried back up the nearest tree, disappearing into the canopy. Moments later, a loud humming emanated from above.

Óengus lifted his hands as a new sense of pressure rose in the air. "Do you feel that?"

Finn definitely felt it. Suddenly she felt uncontrollably dizzy. Óengus collapsed where he stood with a soft thud as he crumpled to the ground. Finn tried to run, but ended up falling to the side against a tree trunk. As soon as she touched the tree her mind cleared slightly, though she knew she would not be able to get to her feet.

It was all Finn could do to keep her eyes open long enough to watch Iseult as he tried to walk toward her. He almost made it, falling close enough to reach out and touch Finn's boot. An eruption of laughter came from the branches of the surrounding trees a few seconds before Finn lost consciousness.

CHAPTER FIFTEEN

Finn awoke, oddly enough, slumped over in a sitting position. Stranger still, she was moving. She opened her eyes, realizing she was on a horse, and had fallen asleep while riding, though the sun shining brightly overhead let her know it was only midday. She quickly reached for the reins, startled to discover her hands were tied to the pommel of the saddle. Her feet were similarly tied to the stirrups, tight enough to cut off her circulation. There were two people leading her horse, but they walked with the hoods of their cloaks pulled up, so she could not tell who they were.

She tried not to panic, hoping that her captor would not realize that she had awoken. Her first thought was Óengus, and some unknown companion. Perhaps he had risen before her, and had taken the opportunity to kidnap her. Kai had said that he was a hunter of people, though why he would want her, she did not know.

"Are you sure the Faie did not permanently damage her?" a woman's voice asked.

"How should I know?" the man leading the horse responded. "At least we have her alone now, and hopefully it will be a long time before Iseult awakens. I'd rather not have him on our tail."

She knew these two voices. Though now her being tied to a horse made very little sense. She waited in silence hoping to overhear a bit more.

"I most certainly hope so," the woman's voice said. "He had obviously taken a liking to her. I would not doubt that he will try and track us down. We really should have killed him."

"And lose part of the bounty?" the man questioned sarcastically. "Rumor says that none of her companions were to be harmed."

The woman chuckled. "Better than losing all of it. If Óengus is after her, you know that the bounty, even halved, will be worthwhile."

"If we can even weasel our way into the deal," the man chided. "We're stealing a job that was not ours."

"I'd just as soon not worry about that now," the woman said. "We'll have enough trouble getting her all the way to the river as it is. If they want her, they will pay."

Finn had had enough. "You deceitful, malicious, crag-headed villains!" she shouted.

"Looks like she's awake," Kai said lightheartedly, peering over his shoulder at her.

In response, Finn began screaming at the top of her lungs. Perhaps if they had not ventured too far Àed or Iseult would hear her.

Kai handed the reins to Liaden and quickly untied Finn's bindings. She tried to kick the horse into motion, but Kai was already pulling her from the saddle. She swung her hands and feet violently as he attempted to cup a hand across her mouth to stifle her screams. Finally Liaden had to pin Finn down while Kai shoved a balled up piece of cloth in her mouth, then fashioned a rough gag to hold the cloth in place. He then tied her hands behind her back and left her sitting in the dirt a few feet away from the horse.

All three listened for signs that someone near had heard Finn's screams, and was coming to the rescue, but all was silent around them. Finn cursed at her captors around her gag, but the words were too muffled for either to know just what she was saying. Although they both could have ventured a fair guess.

Liaden crouched down beside Finn and waited for her to finish her muffled tirade. Eventually Finn met Liaden's eyes. Inside she was still cursing the woman's very existence, but her gag was getting moist and uncomfortable, so she kept those thoughts to herself.

"First," Liaden said, "I apologize for the unceremonious kidnapping. We had hoped to do things a little differently. Unfortunately for you, opportunity knocked, and we took it."

Finn continued to glare in reply.

"Second," Liaden went on, "we have no intention of hurting you, and your kidnapping was not even our original intent. It was recently brought to our attention that you are the object of a rather immense bounty, so we took a chance. Third, your screaming will do no good. You were unconscious for a full day in which we walked non-stop. We also traveled several miles down a small stream, so there will be no tracking you in that manner either. Now, if you promise not to scream, we will remove the cloth from your mouth."

Finn nodded slowly. As soon as the cloth was loosened, she spit the wad out of her mouth and began screaming in earnest. She was rewarded with the replacement of the gag, which was now covered in dirt that had stuck to her saliva.

She struggled as Kai lifted her to a standing position. When he held her too tightly for her to run, she let her legs go limp so that he had to hold her up, or put her back in the dirt. He did neither, and instead slung her across the horse's saddle on her belly while Liaden kept a short rein on the creature. Her hands and feet were tied in place, and they resumed their journey in silence.

Finn seethed as they rode, still not understanding why she was taken. Even if Kai and Liaden had figured out who she was, no one else knew. The bounty they'd mentioned had to be for someone else. It was the only explanation.

Finn was forced to remain uncomfortably tied to the saddle for several hours, until darkness fell and Kai and Liaden stopped to make camp. Finn's stomach felt bruised, and her legs were so stiff that Kai had to help her to stand as he finally freed her from the saddle. He removed the gag, and this time she did not scream. Kai smiled with relief and helped her wobble over to where Liaden was building a small fire.

"Why are you doing this?" Finn asked weakly as she sat. "I thought you were my friends."

Liaden smirked as she stoked the fire. "Why does anyone do anything?" When Finn did not venture a guess, Liaden answered, "Coin."

Kai knelt in front of Finn and tied her feet together to slow any attempts she might make at running. Finn glared down at his apologetic expression, but made no move to fight him. Finished, he left her to take a seat next to Liaden.

Finn hunched down, fully prepared to sulk. "So I am assuming neither of you are really who you claimed to be. Were even your names a lie?"

"Only hers," Kai answered, gesturing to Liaden. "Pretending to be a noble requires a noble's name."

Liaden smiled warmly. "My true name is Anna."

Finn wanted nothing more than to slap that smile off Anna's face. "My next question is, who on earth do you think I am? I assure you, I do not merit a kidnapping."

"You are a girl who was once a tree," Kai answered matter-of-factly, shocking Finn, "and someone apparently has great interest in little girls with that interesting quirk. Like Anna said, kidnapping you was not our original intent. We had heard of the bounty previously, but would never have thought that it was for you, if not for the events in the forest."

Finn glared, ignoring her empty stomach as it attempted to make itself heard. "And of what events are you referring?"

"Just a few instances that revealed your identity," Kai explained. "When you were Faie-struck, you claimed to have once been a tree. I thought that perhaps you were just talking nonsense, until the Faie began referring to you as Dair Leanbh. Oak Child. "

"So really," Anna went on. "You're just as much a liar as either of us, telling us of your small village life and your traveling father. Do you even have a father?"

"I am sure that I do," Finn snapped, "and who is to say

that he is not well traveled?"

"And who is to say that I am not a noble, at least in someone's eyes?" Anna countered.

Finn had no good answer to Anna's question, and there was something plaguing her far greater than her alleged friends' betrayal. "What does this man or woman want so badly, that they would pay you scoundrels to apprehend me?"

Kai shrugged, like it did not really matter. "That question is not relevant to the job, therefore it is not for us to know. If Óengus was hunting you, which we believe he was, then the bounty is legitimate, and that's all that matters."

Anna handed Finn two slices of bread sandwiched around a piece of cured meat. She considered shunning the food out of spite, but she really was far too hungry to do so.

"How did you make the Faie attack us?" Finn asked as she gnawed on the hard bread. She did her best to keep her calm outwardly, though inside, her mind was racing with possible ways to escape.

"You sure are full of questions," Anna observed.

Finn glared at her. "And answering them is the least you can do for me."

Anna sighed. "Very well. We had nothing to do with the Faie attack. Kai followed after Iseult had left the inn, and witnessed the whole thing. It was a great opportunity, and the old man was sleeping like a stump, so we acted while we could."

"Then what about the twins?" Finn asked. "Had Anders not offered us a place in your company, we surely would not be where we are now. If I was not your original quarry, what was?"

Kai rolled his eyes as if it was quite obvious. "The maps, and maybe a few of their books, which are now all lost, unfortunately. The twins needed to add validity to their project. The *noble* lady Anna agreed to accompany them on their mission, as long as it was on the twins' funding. The twins, knowing that they had much to gain in the completion of verified maps, namely renown and a great deal of coin, agreed to her terms. Of course, their great error was in not confirming Anna's identity, so anxious were they to find accompaniment."

"That doesn't explain what you wanted with maps and some old books," Finn pressed.

Anna sighed and continued Kai's explanation. "We would have sold the maps and the books. Even unverified maps of such extent are worth a decent amount of coin, and many of the books they carried were one-of-a-kind, and far more valuable than any map could ever be. They were fools to remove the tomes from their Archives to begin with."

"You're nothing but petty, terrible thieves," Finn grumbled, feeling thoroughly disgusted and wondering how she had ever believed that such people were her friends.

Anna shrugged. "The world is a petty, terrible place. Given the lives we have led, no one can blame us for being opportunistic. The weak do not survive in this world."

Finn laughed bitterly. "You would have been left with the Travelers if not for those of us you call weak."

Anna's face shut down at the mention of the Travelers.

"And now you would sentence me to imprisonment, after I helped save you from being nothing more than a plaything," Finn continued as indignant rage boiled up inside of her.

Anna unsheathed her dagger and lunged, lightning quick, at Finn, pressing the blade to her throat as their bodies made contact. "I am no one's plaything," she growled, "and you will not mention the Travelers in my presence again."

"And to think," Finn whispered, "just a few days ago you were thanking me for going back for you. I find your sense of gratitude-" Finn's words were cut off as Anna drew a thin line with the blade across Finn's neck. Finn held perfectly still as a rivulet of blood leaked down to her chest.

"*Anna,*" Kai said sharply, "we need her in one piece."

Anna was up before Finn knew it, stalking off into the dark forest.

"Time for rest," Kai announced softly as he approached her.

Finn sat rigidly as a fine trembling took control of her limbs. Her tear ducts betrayed her as she reached a shaking hand up to dab at the blood on her throat.

With a look of sympathy, Kai crouched and lifted Finn gently into his arms. Shocked as she was from the encounter, Finn felt like she was floating as Kai carried her to a bedroll. He set her down, then to Finn's surprise he reached for the rope he had secured at his belt.

"How am I supposed to rest while tied up?" Finn asked, though it came out more like a sob.

"And how are we supposed to rest while worrying about you scurrying off all night?" he asked with a smile that did not reach his eyes.

Finn inched backwards toward the fire, prepared to fight despite the fact that she could not run, and felt shaky enough that standing was risky all on its own. She swiped at the tears on her face, frustrated that she could not make them stop flowing.

"Now, now," Kai soothed. "You're going to be tied up either way. You could cooperate, and end up in a fairly comfortable position, or you can fight and I'll tie your hands behind your back, and I'll pull back your feet and tie them to your long, long hair."

Finn only had to consider a moment before holding out her hands. Kai ended up tying her arms crisscrossed across her chest. She glared at him, wondering if he was being extra cruel.

"Trust me," he said. "You'll sleep more comfortably this way than if your hands were tied behind your back."

"You speak as if you know from experience," Finn replied, barely above a whisper.

Kai laughed. "I'll be willing to tell you about my past as soon as you tell me the truth about yours." He helped her lower herself back down to the bedroll.

She held Kai's gaze as he pulled the bedding up to her neck. "You'll both pay for this," she threatened.

Still crouched beside her, Kai wiped the last tears from her face. "I don't doubt that at all," he whispered.

With that confusing sentiment, he stood and walked out of sight. Finn shivered in her bedding and resigned herself to the fact that she would not be escaping that night. Her thoughts turned to Iseult, hoping he would find her soon since she thought escaping on her own unlikely. It was strange to think that she could entrust her rescue to a man she'd only recently met, but she knew with a surety that he would come for her.

CHAPTER SIXTEEN

*I*cy water woke Iseult as it splashed across his face, drenching his shirt and hair. His blurry vision focused on Àed, holding an empty bucket and looking like he wished the bucket had been filled with acid.

"It's about time ye bladdered fool!" Àed screeched. "The town wakes up to six of their own lyin dead in the square, and you and one other fool sleepin so heavy that we thought you were dead as well! And me girl is gone!"

Iseult sat up and tried to clear the fog from his mind. He was in the inn's stockroom with Àed and a dreary looking Óengus. As recollection hit him, he stumbled to his feet and lurched across the room at Óengus' hunched form. He grabbed the man by the collar of his shirt and jerked him to his feet roughly, all the while resisting the urge to simply stab him.

"Where is she?" Iseult snapped, inches from Óengus' unimpressed pale eyes.

Óengus eyed him coolly, making no attempt to pull away. "Your guess is as good as mine."

Iseult pushed away from Óengus and turned back to Àed. "Where are the others? We must leave at once."

Àed snorted. "Gone, and this one won't tell me a word of what happened." He gestured at Óengus.

Óengus just stared back in reply. Iseult's hands shook as he approached the man once more. "Why are you still here? Who are you hunting?"

Óengus let a small, wicked smile creep across his face. "Oddly enough, the target we both now seek is the same. I am after the girl who calls herself Finn."

Faster than any eyes could follow, Iseult had a knife at Óengus' throat. "What do you want with her?" he asked, his voice even and calm.

"I want the bounty on her head," Óengus replied just as calmly. "Though since that is likely lost to me in this late hour of the race, I imagine you would pay just as much for her return."

Iseult removed the knife and began to pace, knowing that scare tactics would not work on a man like Óengus. "And how would you return her?"

Óengus smiled even wider. "I know the ones who have her. In fact, you know them as well. They were your traveling companions for quite some time."

Iseult's jaw tightened. He knew to whom Óengus referred. He ran his fingers along the edge of his knife in contemplation. He was not a killer unless it was in defense of his life, but part of him longed to put an end to the man in front of him. "Where are they taking her?"

Óengus cast a worried eye on Iseult's knife, making

Iseult realize that he had inadvertently stepped toward the man once again.

"I believe as long as that dagger is in your hand, I will not be answering your question. In fact," Óengus continued. "I will not answer you at all except to warn you that you will want to find the girl before she gets to where she's going, and you'll not likely find her without my help."

With a growl Iseult slipped the blade into his belt, though that was not where it had come from. He would not give Óengus the advantage of knowing where he kept each of his blades. "We leave now," Iseult ordered. He eyed Óengus steadily. "You will help us to track her. If we do not find her, or if she dies, you die. If she is returned to me alive, you will have your bounty and more."

Óengus held out his hand. "Agreed."

Iseult ignored the offered hand and stormed out of the room to find horses and supplies, with Àed following closely behind him. He would find Finn, and he would kill those who had taken her. He did not delight in taking life, but for the two traitors, he would make an exception. He knew that Óengus meant Liaden and Kai when he spoke of previous companions. The twins did not possess the skill for such a scheme. Plus, they would have been dismissive of Liaden's capture by the Travelers if Finn had been their target all along.

"The townsfolk will not be letting ye go easily," Àed said, interrupting Iseult's thoughts. "They have six dead, and no explanation. Those that survived the night remember little of it."

"That is not my concern," Iseult replied coldly.

Àed wrapped a hand around Iseult's wrist, halting

Iseult's motion and surprising him with the strength of the grip. "They will make it yer concern, laddy. Yer lucky they didnae hang ye while ye were asleep. As it is, ye'll have to stand trial."

As Àed's hand dropped back to his side, Iseult slowly shifted his weight from foot to foot while he surveyed the empty common room. He could not spare the time to deal with the people of the burgh. Running would make him look guilty, but at that moment he couldn't have cared less. With Finn he had found purpose, and he would not let her go so easily.

He moved to peer through one of the small windows at the front of the inn. Many of the townsfolk had gathered in the square to listen to a tiny man, draped in an ornately embroidered blue cloak, as he stood on a roughly erected wooden podium to speak to them. The townsfolk yelled and gestured angrily as the man spoke, wanting answers about their lost loved-ones. With that sort of energy, there would be no trial. Another group of townsfolk approached the podium, several with torches in hand. The Alderman turned green as he glanced in the direction of his inn.

Iseult glanced back toward the room where they'd left Óengus, then looked down to regard Àed. "Instruct Óengus to gather his things and meet us on the road north of town. Find your way to the stables without being seen. I will meet you there shortly. Can you manage that?"

Àed glanced out the window at the increased sounds of shouting, grunted and spat on the wooden floor, then turned back to Iseult. "I can manage a lot of things, lad," he grumbled, then walked back into the stockroom to speak with Óengus.

Àed gave their new companion his instructions, then made his way to the stables, muttering all the while. Could he go undetected? Of course he could. He was the Mountebank, after all. Escaping the inn had not been difficult. Though men had been placed at both the front and back entrance to make sure the "criminals" did not escape, the inn boasted plenty of windows. He was still as spry as a man of twenty, and didn't mind a test of his long-unused skills.

In his prime, he would have been out of the town with three fresh horses and a week's worth of supplies before the sun had moved a single inch across the horizon. Of course, in his prime he would have never been fooled into trusting the untrustworthy in the first place. As it was, climbing out of a second story window was the best he could do.

Once outside, he waited in the shadows for a pair of townspeople to pass. He willed the shadows to surround him, and was pleased to find that he was at least still capable of that old trick. He was not sure how Óengus planned to escape the inn, nor did he care. He knew beyond a doubt that the man would try to take Finn as soon as they found her, and he would likely have to be killed. Àed preferred to leave the business of unnecessary deaths in his past.

He approached the stables and the two men set to guard the horses. Rummaging through his satchel as he went, he crept up behind the unsuspecting men. Before the men could even turn around, they were enveloped in a cloud of dust that promptly put them to sleep.

"Can I manage? Pfft," Àed mumbled as he began to saddle his shaggy horse.

～

Iseult approached the stable, surprised to find Àed already sitting on his shaggy horse, the old man's face scrunched in impatience. Iseult had almost considered leaving Àed behind, as he would need to move swiftly to find Finn, but perhaps the aged conjurer would be useful after all.

Iseult left his spot in the shadows and approached with several sacks of supplies slung over his shoulder. The goods had not been hard to come by, luckily, though he had only taken the time to rob the inn's storeroom of the bare minimum needed for travel.

Iseult raised an eyebrow at the fallen men. "I suppose that counts as undetected."

Àed snorted in reply, letting Iseult know that he had not been at all surprised by his sudden appearance from the shadows. It was not often that another man could detect him before he chose to show himself, and it further affirmed the choice to bring Àed along.

"Perhaps you should take a faster horse," Iseult offered as Àed gave a sharp tug to his mule's reins, halting the beast in its efforts to procure a little more hay for its breakfast.

Àed sat up straighter in his saddle, as if offended by the suggestion. "Mine will do just fine. I am no longer in the business of stealing things."

"Well then I will not tell you just how we obtained our supplies," Iseult said as he began saddling the best horse he could find.

Once finished, he climbed into his saddle and glanced around the stable yard. None of the townsfolk had seen him leave the inn, and so likely thought that he was still trapped inside, patiently awaiting a *fair* trial.

With a nod to Àed, Iseult urged his horse into action, trusting that Àed would not be far behind. The pair were spotted almost immediately as the tiny Alderman came running around the side of the inn in search of them. He waved his fist and tripped over his ornate cloak as he shouted at them, ending up face-first in the dirt as Àed and Iseult galloped past. Several men helped the Alderman to his feet as he wailed, and soon a mob had formed around him. A few saddled horses, and many ran down the main road with torches in hand, but they were too late.

Iseult and Àed's horses' hooves pounded down the North road, leaving the townsfolk to choke on the dust in their wake. Óengus was waiting for them a short distance outside of the village, just as Iseult knew he would be. He turned his horse to join in their escape, and the three left the angry yells of the townsfolk behind. They ran until their horses could run no longer, then took to the woods in case any tried to follow them.

"How did you avoid pursuit?" Iseult asked of Óengus as their horses picked their way through the dense underbrush.

"Never stable your horse at the inn," Óengus replied simply.

Iseult grunted in reply. Óengus was not his first choice in companions, but he knew he was the best choice if he wanted to find Finn alive. Óengus specialized in tracking people, and he was not choosy as to which people he tracked. Whether they were felons or scholars was of no consequence to the pragmatic man.

Iseult had traveled with Óengus once before, when he was still young and not such a good judge of character. Óengus would often hire extra swords if his quarry was likely to put up a fight. Iseult had been one of those hired swords. When the man they were hunting tried to escape, Óengus cut off his feet and cauterized the wounds with a blade he had heated in their cookfire. Óengus had justified his actions by explaining that the man was wanted for murder, and he could be hung with or without feet. Iseult had never worked on a bounty since.

"I see no tracks," Iseult observed.

"And you won't," Óengus replied. "The pair we follow will not have left any. We simply follow the route that would make the most sense for them, given their destination."

"Then it would stand to reason that they would take a different route, knowing that we would follow," Iseult countered.

"They would not care with the start they have on us. I imagine they have acquired horses by now. Following the same route, it would be impossible to catch up," Óengus answered.

"Then why in creation are we following the same route!" Àed shouted, scaring some nearby birds into flight.

Óengus smiled like he hadn't a care in the world. "Because, they will go straight to a pre-agreed upon location to wait for an intermediary to take the girl on a ship. We simply need to go to this location, and intercept the intermediary. Find the intermediary, and he will lead us to the girl."

"That still does not tell us why we follow the same route," Iseult forced out between gritted teeth.

"We follow, dear friends, because the quickest way to *their* destination, is also the quickest way to ours," Óengus answered lightheartedly. "It does not matter if we arrive first, only that we arrive before the intermediary."

Àed spat on the ground in frustration. Iseult found himself hard pressed to not mimic the gesture.

At first Anders chose their route according to his knowledge of nearby towns. They had eventually reached a small burgh called Badenmar, where the townsfolk eyed he and his sister with great suspicion. They had little news to share, only that a murderer or two were on the loose. Not wanting to add murderers to his share of troubles, he had purchased what food he could before moving on. They had enough food for a week, though Branwen would barely eat, no matter how often he tried to persuade her.

After Badenmar, Anders had done his best to reach the Sand Road, but his sister threw tantrums each time he headed West, until finally Anders decided to follow her confusing guidance instead. Whenever Branwen was pleased with a path, she would mumble excitedly. If not, she screamed until he abided her wishes.

Anders snapped out of his thoughts as Branwen's ongoing chatters turned into a high pitched keening. He supposed it probably meant they were headed toward something important . . . at least something important to his sister's Faie-addled brain.

CHAPTER SEVENTEEN

*A*nna shook Finn awake and pulled down the blankets to untie her arms. Finn's shoulders and wrists ached, but she admitted, if only to herself, that it would have been much worse had her arms been tied behind her back. Anna waited long enough for Finn to stretch out her limbs, then handed her a hot cup of tea. She did not apologize for her actions the previous night, but her inability to meet Finn's eyes said that she was at least slightly ashamed of her behavior.

Finn sipped her tea slowly, still partially in her bedroll while she observed Kai and Anna's morning interactions. It seemed to her that Anna did not share much in common with the fake persona of Liaden. She had even pulled her dark hair back from her face into a tight braid, making her look younger and less severe. Where Liaden had been cool and distant, this new person was fiery and mirthful, laughing as Kai made jokes about their situation. At times she even seemed good-natured, at least as good natured as a

227

kidnapper could be. Still, Finn did not doubt that Anna would slit her throat without a second thought if the situation called for it.

It became evident that it was time to go as Kai buried the fire pit with sand, and Anna saddled the only horse.

Finn observed the dappled mare as Anna tightened the belly strap under its saddle. She was a horse bred for speed in her prime, with a slender body and powerful legs, but now she was in her later years. Not much speed would be had with three riders and one elderly horse, and Finn was glad for that fact. The longer it took them to reach their destination, the more time Iseult and Àed would have to find her.

Finn cleared her throat to gain Anna's attention. When Anna turned to her, she asked, "Why did you only purchase one horse? You would think that you would want to be rid of me as soon as possible."

Anna tugged on the horse's reins and led it to where Finn was sitting. "We were in a hurry, and as I lost all of my coin, and we did not *purchase* her. We had no idea how long your friends would be asleep, so we took the first horse that could be easily obtained. We'll find extra horses as soon as we get the chance."

Finn inched out of her bedroll as Kai approached so he could untie her legs. At least, she hoped that was his intent. Unfortunately, he first tied her hands behind her back before removing the rope from her legs.

Finn cleared her throat as he helped her to her feet.

"Yes?" he questioned.

Finn eyed him askance. "Drinking tea," she explained, "tends to lead to other bodily functions."

Kai almost appeared embarrassed, giving Finn a great deal of satisfaction. "Anna, I believe I'll let you handle this one."

Anna handed the horse's reins to Kai, then took hold of Finn to lead her to a nearby patch of shrubs. Finn could sense none of the hostility from the previous night as they walked. In fact, Anna handled her rather gently. After untying Finn's hands, Anna even walked away to gave her a bit of privacy. Though, Finn would have enjoyed the privacy more if it had been given without the threat of cutting one of the tendons in her ankle if she tried to run. In light of this threat, Finn dutifully returned to her captors and allowed them to hoist her up on the horse before tying her in place.

Finn surveyed the camp as they left, only to find that it did not look like a camp at all. Despite their claims that no one would be able to follow them, Kai and Anna were obviously still worried.

Finn held onto that small shred of hope as they walked along. She still had no idea why someone would be looking for her, or how anyone even knew that she existed at all. She almost looked forward to meeting this person. Perhaps they might have some of the answers she was seeking. Of course, they could have just talked to her, rather than hiring thugs to take her prisoner. That fact alone meant that the meeting might not be much to Finn's liking.

The day dragged on. A few times Finn managed to convince Anna to take the saddle for an hour or two so that Finn might stretch her legs. It was nice to walk, but her hands remained tied behind her back at all times. She wasn't sure why she had to be tied at all, given there were two captors and only one prisoner, and they had confiscated her only weapon, but her arguments fell on deaf ears.

By dusk, Finn was too exhausted to even think about escaping. Kai had scouted out a secluded campsite within a copse of trees where they would rest for the night. As they unpacked, Anna watched the trees warily.

"Do you see something?" Finn asked curiously, remembering what the Traveler had said of Anna.

"Shhh," Anna warned as she crept closer to the trees.

Kai came to stand beside Finn. He had no weapons in his hands, but his stance was one of protection. Anna disappeared into the darkness. Silent moments went by, but Anna did not return.

"Should we go after her?" Finn asked. She wasn't particularly concerned for the woman. On the contrary, now that she only had one captor, it was her best chance to escape. Even if she was bone tired.

"Give her time," Kai whispered back.

Finn considered her situation. Her feet were loose so she could run, but she doubted she could outrun Kai, especially in skirts with her hands bound. She could attack Kai, but imagined that would end badly for her as well. Her slim hopes were dashed as Anna reappeared.

"There is another camp," she stated as she approached. "I'm going to acquire some more supplies, and hopefully two more horses."

"Do you think that is a wise risk?" Kai asked incredulously.

"What is life without a few risks?" Anna said with a smile, then turned to leave again.

As Anna faded from view, Kai turned to Finn. "We won't be having a fire tonight, just in case."

"Fine," Finn answered crankily. "Will you untie my hands now?"

"No," Kai answered as he began unpacking their bedrolls.

As soon as the bedding was on the ground, Finn plopped down to sulk. Kai sat beside her as he unpacked some more of the bread and cured meat and offered her a bite after he'd sandwiched them together. She lifted her nose and snubbed the food, preferring not to be hand-fed like a helpless animal. She stared Kai down as he ate his portion.

He paused mid-bite. "Oh fine," he huffed, setting his food down on his bedroll, which was directly beside Finn's, and motioning for her to turn her back to him so he could remove her ropes.

Finn obeyed, then clenched and unclenched her freed hands a few times before finally taking the offered food. The bread was stale, but given that they had not eaten all day, she gnawed it the best she could.

"How does Anna plan on acquiring new supplies from the camp? I imagine they only have whatever supplies they need for themselves," Finn questioned as she greedily scarfed down her meal.

"Well we need them a bit more," Kai replied. "Anna will decide what method to employ as soon as she is sure of what type of travelers she is dealing with."

"So she will steal?" Finn asked.

Kai shrugged. "If she has to. If they are kindly folk, she will likely be able to talk them out of some of their belongings."

Finn shook her head, wondering how on earth one woman might manage to talk a man out of his belongings. Then she blushed with realization and tried not to think about it anymore.

"Do you hear that?" Kai asked with his head cocked to the side, as if trying to catch a distant sound.

She listened for a moment. "All I hear is the creaking of branches."

"Exactly," Kai replied. "There is no wind."

Finn looked around in the dimming light nervously, but could not find the source of the noise. The horse whickered and stamped its feet, confused.

"It is good to see you again, Tree Sister," came a rumbling voice from along the line of trees. Finn watched in astonishment as the trees all began to uproot themselves and shamble toward them.

"Trow," Kai groaned. "Of course we would choose to camp right next to a copse of Trow."

Finn recognized the Trow that had spoken as the one that had carried her out of the Blood Forest. "Have you lost your other friends?" it asked as it approached.

"No," Finn began, but suddenly she had an idea. "I was actually taken from them," she finished, "by this man beside me."

Kai's eyes widened. "Not true," he argued quickly, seeing what Finn was doing. "She's just a little sore about . . . a bad joke," he lied as he looked around for a means of escape.

"Would you call Tree Sister a liar?" the Trow asked, obviously offended.

Kai got to his feet and pulled Finn up beside him. "We

must be going now," he stated as he began backing away, Finn in tow.

"What would you have us do, Tree Sister?" the lead Trow asked worriedly as Kai pulled Finn away.

Finn thought for a moment as she struggled against Kai. What she wanted was to escape, but she also wanted Kai to pay for betraying her. "I would like to take this man prisoner. If you could just hold him still while I tie him up?"

The Trow approached from all directions, blocking any chance Kai might have had to run. He didn't attempt to fight as the Trow took hold of him, wrapping their spindly hands around his arms and shoulders. There were about a dozen of them, and they could have easily crushed a man without much effort. Kai glared at Finn as he was held immobile by the Trow.

Laughing on the inside, Finn approached and tied Kai's hands behind his back with the same rope that had been used on her, looping the ends of the rope around his chest to secure his arms at his sides. She quickly searched him for weapons, hoping that Anna would not return too soon and complicate things. She found her dagger on his belt and paused to tie it around her waist. She then searched the rest of his person, throwing several other weapons to the ground as she found them.

As his weapons hit the ground, Kai began to struggle against his restraints. "Those were expensive!"

Finn threw the final dagger in her hand to the grass. It landed with a heavy clink as it hit the other discarded weaponry. "I'm sure you did not pay for them."

Finn looped the horse's reins around her arm, and drew her dagger to press against Kai's back as the Trow released him into her custody. Before departing, she turned to face the Trow that seemed to do all of the talking for its group. "Thank you. I am in your debt, but I must ask one more favor."

"Of course, Sister," the Trow replied.

Finn smiled even wider. "If a woman returns to this place, could you perhaps detain her? I do not wish her harm, mind you, but I'd rather she not catch up to us."

"As you wish, Tree Sister," the Trow said with a crooked smile.

Finn looked down at the bedrolls and the satchel that held much of their food. "Would you kindly throw those things across the horse's saddle as well?"

One of the other Trow approached and did as she asked, strapping the satchel on top of the bedrolls to secure them. He bowed without a word and retreated.

Finn bowed her head to the Trow in return, then prodded Kai out of the copse of Trow and trees with the dagger, leading the horse behind them. They walked unhindered by any Faie until they were a good distance away from the copse, as full darkness fell upon them.

"Why even take me?" Kai asked angrily as he stumbled ahead of Finn, having trouble seeing his footing in the darkness. "You know I'll escape you the moment you remove that dagger from my back."

Finn smirked, though Kai could not see it. "Then I will not remove it. Do you think you can just betray your friends and not be held accountable?"

Kai grunted as he stubbed his toe on a rock. "I thought we made it quite clear that we were never your friends."

"Well I thought you were," Finn replied petulantly, "and I don't have many friends. I don't take such lies lightly."

Kai sighed and breathed out the words, "I'm sorry."

"What was that?" Finn asked. "I couldn't quite hear you."

"I'm sorry," he said more loudly. "Now will you please let me go?"

"No," Finn answered. "I don't think you mean that apology, so I will not be accepting it."

Kai sighed again as they walked on. Finn was not sure what she intended to do with him. Though she did want him to pay for his betrayal, she had taken him more out of a desire to not be alone in the woods without any idea where to go. If he had to accompany her as a prisoner, then so be it.

After stumbling through the dark for hours in no particular direction, Kai finally asked, "Do you have any idea where we're going?"

Finn didn't answer. She didn't know where she was going, but she refused to stop, even as the first hints of sunrise peeked down through the trees. Her first instincts were to find Iseult and Àed, though she wasn't sure where to start. She hoped that the two had stuck together. At least that way if she found one, she would find both. She knew they would be looking for her, either together or apart.

If they had searched in the correct direction, it would stand to reason that she should head back in the direction she had come. Of course, they could be on one of many roads or paths, and there was no way to know which one to choose.

"Curse you for doing this," Finn grumbled.

"I believe we've already covered that yes, I'm a lowdown scoundrel," Kai replied. "We also covered the apology part. I don't know what else you want me to say."

"I want you to help me find my friends," Finn answered. "My *real* friends."

"Trust me," Kai said. "I would give you back in a heartbeat if I could."

"Where were you taking me?" Finn asked abruptly, ignoring Kai's sarcasm.

Kai glanced back at Finn, but quickly turned forward as she pushed the dagger against his back. "I suppose there is no harm in telling you now. We were taking you to Port Ainfean. There you would have boarded a small vessel to sail down the river Cair."

"And where would I have gone after that?" Finn prompted.

Kai shrugged. "Your fate would have been out of my hands at that point."

"Just like that," Finn said, almost lowering the dagger in shock. "You would have sent me off to possible death or torture?"

Kai shrugged again. "Death and torture seemed unlikely. The parameters of the bounty required that you be delivered alive and unharmed. I don't see why anyone would request that you remain unharmed, if their intention was to harm you upon delivery."

"So when Anna threatened to cut my tendon if I ran . . ." Finn began.

"Oh, she probably would have done it," Kai answered. "Even if it cut our payment in half."

Finn stumbled on a rock, and nearly stabbed the dagger into Kai's back. "Sorry," she mumbled as she regained her footing.

Kai looked over his shoulder again. "If you're tired. Feel free to ride the horse. I'd rather like to avoid getting stabbed tonight."

"And let you get away?" Finn asked, making it evident that she had no intention of doing so.

Kai rolled his eyes. "It was just a thought."

Finn began to shake her head, then turned her attention to the nearby shadowy trees instead. "What's that noise?"

Kai sighed. "That noise was me trying to reason with you."

Finn glared at the back of Kai's head, as he had turned back around. "Not that. I heard a branch break."

Kai kicked at the dirt in annoyance. "It's probably just a wild bear coming to put us out of our misery."

"Not a bear," a man said as he appeared. "But the second part is about right."

Finn could see in the hint of morning sunlight that the slender man was not overly tall, giving the impression of being quick on his feet. He wore rather ornate clothes for a person tromping through the wilderness. Gold embroidery lined the cuffs and collar of a stiff blue velvet shirt, and well-oiled mustaches completed the look.

Finn thought she sensed Kai's energy as it shifted from irritation to anxiety. "Mius. Of course you would be here," he groaned.

"Oh yes Kai," Mius replied. "Act as if you are the one who

has been wronged. I imagine that pretty young thing with the dagger fell afoul of your tricks as well."

Kai struggled against his restraints to little avail. "It was a fair game. As for the girl . . . her anger might actually be warranted."

Mius took a moment to look Finn up and down, lingering on her too large clothes then settling on her face. "If you'd like to do the honors, you could go ahead and stick that dagger in his back."

Kai grabbed at Finn's skirts with his hands in an attempt to induce her into cutting the ropes.

"He is my prisoner," Finn said bravely. "You'll have to wait your turn until I'm done with him."

Mius took a step forward. "Oh no, my dear. I'm not in the habit of waiting my turn."

Kai groaned again as two massive men came walking out of the forest to flank Mius. One had a large scar across his face, and the other had too much weight in his belly, but they otherwise looked quite similar. Kai began tugging at Finn's skirts again. Seeing no other choice, she cut the ropes from his hands, allowing him to quickly remove the one around his chest.

"How did you find me?" Kai asked, ignoring the thugs in favor of staring down Mius.

Mius chuckled. "In a strange trick of fate, your companion Anna came waltzing into my camp last night. I knew you had to be nearby."

"What did you do to her?" Kai asked sharply.

Mius shrugged. "I've no quarrel with Anna. Though I did have my men detain her."

The two large men circled Kai as Finn backed away. Kai

held his hand back to Finn for her dagger, and once again seeing no choice, she relinquished it. The thugs drew long swords of their own as they circled.

"It would seem you are outclassed, my friend," Mius observed.

It was Kai's turn to laugh. "Outclassed and outnumbered are two very different things. When I feel outclassed, I'll let you know."

Ignoring Kai, Mius turned his gaze to Finn, pulling at the edge of his mustache in contemplation. "As soon as we dispatch of this fiend, I would gladly escort you to Port Ainfean."

"W-why would I want to go to Port Ainfean?" Finn stammered, worried that Mius knew of the bounty.

Mius smiled. He didn't seem at all tired for the early morning hour. "It is only the best port burgh this side of the Melted Sea. A pretty lass like you would be well taken care of."

Finn was not sure she liked the idea of being *taken care of.* "I've other places to be. My apologies."

Mius shrugged and raised a hand in signal to the thugs. Like trained dogs they closed in on Kai in perfect unison. The scar-faced thug swung his sword in a downward motion that would have nearly cut Kai in half, but Kai ducked under the blow, narrowly missing the blade. The pot-bellied thug swung with much the same result. The men were large, but obviously not well trained. Still, it would not be long before one landed a blow. Kai's weariness from having walked all night was evident in his movements.

Finn tried to think of what she should do, but if she neared the men she would likely be cleaved in half. Kai landed a slice with the dagger across the scar-faced man's chest, causing him to back away. The uninjured thug charged only to gain a slice across his back in passing as Kai avoided the attack. Scar-face, seeing that Kai was distracted, took the opportunity to wrap his trunk-like arms around the smaller man. The muscles bulged in scar-face's arms as he squeezed tightly, immobilizing Kai.

The pot-bellied man closed in, ready to skewer Kai, and Finn could stand by no longer. Even though Kai had betrayed her, she could not simply watch him die. She charged the thug who was ready to stab Kai, and leapt on him full-force. She barely moved the man at all, but in his surprise he dropped his sword. Finn slipped back to her feet and grabbed the sword from the grass, but became entangled in her skirts and ended up on the ground.

The swordless, pot-bellied thug took his time walking over to her, all the while looking down on her with amusement. The mountain of a man had numerous small scars littering his face, emphasized by a nearly bald head. Finn held the sword up in a shaky, two-handed grip, keeping the pot-bellied man from fully reaching her. All of the men laughed, except for Kai, who seemed to be not getting enough oxygen. Finn's mind raced as she wondered how she might get out of the situation, when the ground began to shake.

Thick roots shot up from the earth like tentacles, surprising Finn enough to almost make her drop the sword. Loose dirt rained down upon her as the roots twined their way around the pot-bellied man's legs. Thin tendrils grew around his limbs as the thicker trunk inched upward. The man's laughter drained from his face to be replaced by shock, then fear. His feet were ripped out from under him and he hit the ground without so much as a thud, as the roots absorbed the impact. He swatted at the roots to no avail. Like serpents, they quickly engulfed the remainder of his body, cutting off his screams just as they started.

The roots squirmed violently, the smaller tendrils writhing like worms, until the sounds of bones cracking and being pulled from their sockets could be heard within the mass. Everyone watched in shock as the sickening popping sound seemed to drag on forever, then finally came to a silent end. When the roots were finished with their work, they retreated into the ground as if they had never been, leaving a large patch of upturned earth underneath the man's mangled corpse. The whole scene was over in a heart-beat, leaving Finn wondering if her mind was playing tricks on her.

Finn swallowed a lump in her throat. She had started sweating out of fear, and released her clammy hands from around the sword's hilt, letting it drop to the grass. The thug's crumpled corpse stared up at her.

"You Tuatha witch!" Mius cursed.

Finn did not turn to acknowledge him. She was too busy staring at the dead man in front of her. The living thug had dropped Kai and was backing away with his hands held in front of him, as if to ward off a blow. When he had gained some distance, he turned and ran.

Mius looked as if he might attack Finn, but then he turned and walked stiffly away. Moments later, the sound of horses running could be heard as Mius and the living thug fled back to their camp. Kai gave the corpse a wide berth as he walked over to offer a hand to Finn. She took his hand and stood shakily.

"What in creation was that?" Kai asked quietly as he gazed down at the corpse.

"I-I don't know," Finn stammered.

Kai looked at her, his eyes wide with fear. "I mean, was it you?"

"No," Finn answered as she shook her head too quickly, though she was not sure of her answer. "It was probably more Faie escaped from the forest."

"Oh . . ." Kai paused. He glanced down at the crumpled corpse again. "Well, thank you."

Finn's thoughts felt slow and muddy. "For what? I told you it wasn't me."

Kai managed a small smile, though he still looked green. "For not letting them kill me. I wouldn't have thought you would care."

Finn felt the heat of anger creep across her face. "And would you have let me be killed, had the situation been reversed?"

Kai smiled a little wider, and Finn almost thought he wouldn't answer. "No," he said finally. "No Finn, I would not have let them kill you."

"Good," Finn replied and she and Kai moved to put distance between themselves and the corpse. "Now what do we do?"

"Well it seems," Kai began, halting his pace to turn toward Finn, "that we are at a bit of an impasse. I am no longer your prisoner, and you are not mine."

Finn took a step away from Kai and eyed him warily. She also glanced back at the sword on the ground.

Kai held up his hands in a soothing gesture. "You just saved my life, when you could have just as easily been rid of me. My honor would not allow me to take you prisoner now."

Finn scoffed. "I wasn't aware that you possessed any honor."

Kai took the insult in stride. "Well I do, and now I believe we should leave this place before the wolves come for the corpse."

Finn's stomach turned at the thought. "What about Anna?"

"Anna . . ." Kai began, "will not be very pleased about the loss of our prisoner, so you really shouldn't be around when I tell her. I will escort you to Port Ainfean-"

Finn threw her hands up in exasperation. "I thought you said I wasn't a prisoner!"

Kai glared at her. "If you would let me finish. I will escort you to Port Ainfean. If your friends are industrious, they will learn of the bounty. You were to be delivered to any number of ports along the river Cair. As Ainfean is the closest, it would stand to reason that they will look for you there first."

Finn took another step back. "And how am I supposed to believe that you will simply not turn me over once we are there?"

Kai shrugged. "You can try and make it there on your own if you like."

Finn sighed, as she did not know the way, and there wasn't really anyone else to ask for directions. "Fine!" she took a final look at the corpse. "Let us go."

Their horse stood partially hidden in the trees, looking

at them both like they'd gone mad. Finn was surprised the mare hadn't run during all of the excitement. Then again, she looked tired enough to drop dead from exhaustion. Finn had never related to an animal more than she did in that moment.

CHAPTER EIGHTEEN

*O*engus knew that the girl would be delivered somewhere along the river Cair. There were several ports, and each hunter would have been given a different port. Most contracts worked that way. Different delivery locations cut down on hunters waiting in ambush to steal your bounty at the last moment.

The port he had been given was Port Uelli, but that was not where they were going, because he also knew that the bounty had originated somewhere northwest on the Sand Road. You could find out almost anything by placing the right amount of coin in the right pocket, though he had not managed to find the bounty's backer. Still, he knew from his sources that once the girl had made it to one of the ports, she would be given to an intermediary, who would pay off the hunter, then ship the girl to Port Ceardh. After that, Finn would be taken back up the Sand Road to where the bounty had originated. He planned on finding her before she made it to the Sand Road by bypassing the other ports and heading straight for Ceardh. He'd lied to Iseult about knowing which port the girl would be taken too, but felt it his only chance of gaining the man's trust on the matter. If Óengus' plan was successful, he might still claim the bounty. If he was not, then he would steal the girl back from those who wanted her, and he would receive payment from Iseult instead. He would win either way.

He did not voice this entire plan to his companions. Iseult had proven himself to be a rather brash man. Óengus knew he would not have the patience to accept a plan where the girl would remain captive until the most opportune moment. Iseult wanted her for some reason that Óengus could not fathom. If Iseult did not want the bounty, then he wanted this tree girl for himself.

The girl's description painted her as something clearly of the Faie. From what Óengus knew of Iseult, he was not particularly fond of the Faie. Yet, he wanted the girl. This piqued Óengus' curiosity, and his curiosity would be satisfied before he allowed Iseult or anyone else to escape with this mysterious girl. If he let them escape at all.

"There was a camp here," Iseult commented as they rode.

There had been an admirable attempt to hide the camp, but a mistake had been made. Though there was no sign of a fire, there was a large patch of dirt that had clearly been smoothed over. At one edge of the dirt, it was clear that two humans, and one horse, possibly with a third human, had left the cleared area. None but an experienced tracker would have noticed it, and even then it was hard to spot. Iseult would have done well in Óengus' line of work, had he been able to handle such work without empathy.

"Two sets of footprints, and one horse. It could very well

have been them. Especially in an area so far from the travel roads," Iseult went on.

Óengus bit his lip in frustration. If they attempted to track Kai and Anna, they would always remain one step behind. "We should not stray from my plan. It truly is our best chance of reclaiming the girl."

"We follow the tracks," Iseult demanded.

Óengus sighed but did not argue. The tracks would eventually be lost to them, especially since they belonged to those who were attempting to go undetected. Then Iseult and the old man would have no choice but to follow Óengus' lead.

Óengus watched as Àed, silent until then, dismounted his horse and looked at the tracks more closely. He placed his hand over one of the tracks and closed his eyes. Óengus wondered if the old man had access to some magic after all. He knew that he was the one who was once known as the Mountebank, as word of such a character re-emerging traveled fast, but he had assumed the Mountebank had simply been a con man. Many things seemed like magic to the untrained eye, but were really simple tricks and sleights of hand.

The old man finished what he was doing and gestured for his horse to move forward. The beast obeyed, though Àed never reached back to grab its reins. Magic indeed.

Àed followed whatever path he had found wordlessly, and Iseult followed him without question. Seeing no other choice, Óengus let out a sigh of annoyance and followed behind Iseult.

≈

Finn dragged the long sword that had once belonged to the now-deceased thug across the forest floor, even though the blade was much too large for her height and weight. She had thought that Kai would want her to have the dagger and would hence take the sword, but when she suggested it, he only laughed and kept the dagger in his belt, all the while complaining about all of his other lost weapons.

Since she did not have a weapon she could properly wield, Finn refused to let Kai walk behind her, though he did not seem to fear her being at his back in the slightest, perhaps because she had passed up two opportunities to be rid of him. She was not sure how wise either choice had been.

Yet, she assured herself that she'd really had no alternative. Despite her past memories, she did not fully know the current world of humans. She felt better having at least one world-wise person along. Even if that person was a deceitful scoundrel.

That was all of little consequence though. The decision that weighed most heavily on her mind was the decision to continue on to Port Ainfean. The choice was risky at best, but she could think of no better course. As far as Iseult and Àed might know, she was still a prisoner. At least, she hoped they knew. With her as a prisoner, they might be able to figure out some idea of where she would be taken. So, it would stand to reason that she should continue that course, and hope that they'd find her.

Of course, it could all turn out to be some grand trick on the part of Kai, and she would end up a prisoner in reality once more . . .

She shook the thoughts from her head. "How many days will it take to reach Port Ainfean?" she asked.

"Two, perhaps three," Kai answered, not bothering to turn around. "Depending on how quickly your delicate legs tire."

"My legs will do just fine," she snapped.

Their minimal conversation had bordered on argument since they'd left the scene of the attack behind. Each time one of them would start a conversation, they would receive a rude comment or chastising from the other, regardless of how much either of them actually wanted to talk.

"The horse needs to graze," Finn observed, not ready to let the conversation drop once again.

"The horse can graze when we camp," Kai argued.

Finn looked back at the tired beast, stretched to the end of its reins. It had not been a very lively horse to begin with, and was clearly not used to long travels.

"She seems about to keel over," Finn pressed.

Kai finally stopped and looked back at the horse. The annoyance on his face was replaced with concern.

"We'll have to turn her loose," Kai stated. "She won't be of any good much longer."

Finn nodded and tried to hide her small smile over finally winning an argument. They unstrapped their bedrolls and meager supplies from the horse, then strapped them across their own backs. Finn was surprised to see Kai take the heavier load without a word. With how he had been treating her, she imagined he would have given her the heavier load out of spite.

Finn removed the horse's bridle and sent her on her way. Hopefully she would make it to a farm where someone would care for her. Perhaps she would even make it home, as horses often returned to their stables when set loose. She envied the horse for a moment before they set about their way again.

"So I was thinking," Finn began.

"Of course you were," Kai said sarcastically.

Finn ignored him and continued, "Back when you first completely and utterly betrayed me by taking me prisoner, you offered a deal."

Kai trudged on, not bothering to glance back. "And what deal was that?"

Finn cleared her throat. "You told me that when I was ready to tell you the truth about my past, you would in turn tell me the truth about yours."

Kai was silent for a moment. "And what if I simply choose to lie?"

Finn hoisted the sword up over her shoulder, hoping to make it easier to carry. "Well I don't think you will. Though you've omitted many, *many* truths. You haven't really lied to me."

Kai finally looked back. "That you know of."

Finn ignored his comment and took a deep breath. "I was a tree for over a hundred years . . . "

Her explanation carried them on until the sun set behind the horizon. Though her feet dragged with exhaustion, she forced herself to tell him most everything she knew about herself; from what she had learned, to what her memories told her. She could see no reason not to be honest. He already knew the most damning things about her. The only part she left out was what Iseult had told her about his clan, and the mission they had decided to undertake together. Those things were not hers to tell.

Kai stopped at a small clearing and unstrapped their supplies from his back. He took a moment to stretch, then set about making a small fire and heating a kettle for tea. Finn watched his impassive face, waiting for him to speak.

"Do you have nothing to say?" Finn finally asked, frustrated.

Kai was silent for a moment, then looking up from the fire, met her eyes. "You stood in that field, for over a hundred years?" he asked, slightly astonished. "How did it not drive you mad?"

Finn shrugged and sat. "As far as I knew, it was what I was supposed to be. It was peaceful."

Kai nodded as he sprinkled herbs into the kettle. After a few minutes he poured Finn a cup of tea and handed it to her.

When he did not speak, she said, "It is your turn."

Kai sighed, and Finn thought he would not speak at all. Finally he began, "I was born into servitude. My family owed a great deal of coin, as many farm families do outside the Gray City. I was raised in a state of slavery, working to pay off a debt that only increased the more my family worked."

He looked into the fire. Finn could tell that he was embarrassed of his past, and almost regretted demanding his story.

"Eventually I gave up. Though in a way I was doing quite the opposite," he went on. "I refused to work any longer. A city official sent to monitor the farm whipped me with a switch of braided leather. He had hoped to scare me back into submission, but the harder he whipped, the more vehemently I refused. I cursed the Gray City and the so-called *Alderman* that had enslaved us. The guard whipped me until I passed out.

"I awoke in a field, covered in my own blood, and realized I had been left for dead. A young woman found me, and nursed me back to health. That woman was Anna."

"Anna . . . " Finn began as the pieces fell into place.

"Anna taught me a different way of life," Kai went on. "She taught me that the most important person in the world is not an Alderman or a friend, it is yourself. Sometimes we've worked with others, with each other, or alone. Yet no matter who I've worked with, the person I've worked *for* has been me, and no one else."

"That sounds lonely," Finn commented.

"And being a tree for one-hundred years was not?" he countered.

Finn shook her head. "As a tree I was connected to everything. I was never alone."

"Well you asked for my story, and now you have it," Kai said tiredly.

"What of your family?" Finn pressed.

He shrugged. "They think I am dead, and it's for the best. I deserted them that day."

Finn scrunched her face in confusion. "I hardly think being whipped nearly to death counts as desertion . . . "

"I deserted them when I refused to keep working," Kai replied. "My mother believed we would some day work our way out of debt, yet I couldn't help but see the futility of it. Tariffs were raised on a regular basis, and we could never produce enough to pay what was required. We remained in debt, because that was where the city wanted us."

"I still don't see how that counts as desertion," Finn argued.

"I knew I would be killed or jailed," Kai explained. "I knew in refusing to work, I would leave my family even worse off than they already were."

Finn looked down at her lap as understanding dawned on her. "Then why did you do it?"

Kai opened his mouth to speak, then closed it again. He stared into the fire, and Finn realized he was trying to figure out an answer he simply could not explain.

"Well thank you for your honesty," Finn said quietly, not wanting to push any further.

Kai smiled back, but it was a sad smile. "Who said it was honesty?"

Finn smirked. "And who said I was *actually* ever a tree?"

As their soft laughter died down, they sat in silence for a time, staring into the fire and thinking their own thoughts.

Eventually Kai cleared his throat to speak. "I did feel bad you know . . . about kidnapping you. It's just that Anna had her mind set on it, and after what happened to her, I was simply glad to see her acting like her old self. Then with you planning on running off with Iseult and Àed the next day. I had little time to think things through."

"Oh my," Finn said as she looked up at Kai's slightly hunched form. "That almost sounded like a genuine apology."

He let out an exaggerated sigh. "Well at least I tried," he stated ruefully.

"Yet you still would have turned me over?" Finn asked

seriously.

Kai had the grace to look embarrassed. "Well yes, but I would have felt bad about it."

"Well," Finn replied. "If you help me to find my companions again, I might consider forgiving you."

Kai shook his head. "I said I'd get you as far as Port Ainfean, then I'll be about my way. I would not want to face Iseult when the two of you are reunited."

Finn laughed. "And why is that?"

Kai shook his head again. "I've no doubt that he will try his very best to kill me, and that is a fate I'd rather like to avoid."

Finn smiled and shook her head. "I would not let him kill you, even if I've considered it myself."

Kai laughed. "As interesting as it would be to see you trying to stop him, I think I will have to pass."

After several minutes of silence, Kai asked, "Why is it that he's so set on you?"

Finn perked up out of her thoughts. "Iseult?" she questioned, not sure what Kai was asking after the pause in conversation.

Kai nodded. "You've known him as long as you've known me, and the two of you already had plans to continue traveling together. It just seems odd to trust someone so quickly."

"Not everyone is like you," Finn replied, but with little heat to her words. "Some people can be trusted."

"And you trust Iseult?" Kai pressed.

Finn nodded. "I do."

Kai shook his head like he wanted to say more, but held back.

"Mock me if you must," Finn taunted. "I can see that you would like to."

Kai held up his hands in a surrendering gesture. "I was not going to mock you. I was going to ask if you were in love with him, because I can see no other explanation for such blind trust."

Finn raised the corner of her mouth in a crooked smile. "And would you be jealous if I was?"

Kai chuckled. "Oh Finn, I imagine love from a woman like you would only bring a man misery."

Finn yawned as the day and night of walking, and lack of sleep hit her all at once. "Well then it is fortunate that I have no intention of falling in love."

Kai stood to retrieve their bedrolls, then laid them out side by side near the fire. Finn climbed into the bedding, feeling light and floaty from exhaustion.

As she closed her eyes, Kai said, "Love doesn't care about intentions."

Finn smiled softly with her face turned up toward the dark night sky. "And I do not care about love," she replied.

Later that night as Finn tried to sleep, she battled contradicting emotions. Part of her told her she should escape in the night, and take her chances backtracking. Yet, the other part was oddly content in her situation. Before she could decide either way, sleep took her.

The next day as they walked, Finn quietly let the too-heavy sword drop down into the dirt. It really didn't do her much good to carry it, as she would never be able to properly wield the monstrous thing. She didn't think she would need it regardless. She looked at Kai's back, hoping he had not noticed as she discarded the weapon. No, she did not need it. Kai might be a liar, and he might have tied her up, but she knew with a fair amount of certainty that he would not do so again.

It was difficult for Anders to sleep while his sister was in such a state. As soon as the sun had set on their travels, she started mumbling about a war, and that "they were coming". She spoke of the Cavari and other ancient tribes. Branwen of course knew of the tribes from her research, but Anders believed it was something more. Though she spoke of ancient tribes, she also spoke of recent events. She spoke of the end of the Blood Forest, and of the current Alderman of the Gray City.

Besides the names, he could not make much sense of what his sister was saying. She spoke of a great search to turn the tide of war. Yet there was no war to speak of. At least not yet.

His sister was curled up in her bedroll, still mumbling quietly to herself. Suddenly she sat up and turned directly to her brother, looking at him this time, rather that through him.

She whispered three words.

"They are coming."

Hoof-beats thundered in the distance. Branwen whipped her head in the direction of the sound. "It is too late. I have failed."

CHAPTER NINETEEN

*P*ort Ainfean was not what Finn had expected. Metal spires lined the gates, raising twenty feet over Finn's head to block out portions of the sun. The spires were topped with brightly colored banners, wafting about in the brisk wind.

Kai leaned in close to her ear. "Stay close," he ordered.

They passed through the gates unhindered, though the guards eyed them as if they would memorize every last detail of their faces. Finn turned away from their searching gazes to observe the large port town. The presence of the river Cair was evident throughout the hard-packed streets. In Garenoch, the earth surrounding the various buildings had been hard and dead, but in Port Ainfean the deep green of moss and grass could be spotted in between buildings and sometimes even on rooftops. Shirtless men carried planks of wood strung from one end to the other with fresh-caught fish, in fact, the entire town reeked of fish guts.

Many of the inns and shops had names relating to the river, fish, or both.

Kai reached behind Finn and pulled the hood of her green cloak up over her head as they walked. "Hide your hair," he ordered.

Finn pushed the loose locks of her hair back within her hood without argument. The Port town made her nervous with its bustling streets and strange architecture. Many of the houses were no more than shanties made of driftwood, though Finn could see that there were nicer parts of the town further in.

"I feel as though we are likely to lose our coin walking in these streets," Finn observed.

Kai laughed. "I would not say that too loudly."

Finn blushed and tugged on her hood to cover more of her face. "Should we not be finding an inn? I imagine that is where we'd gather news of Iseult and Àed, if there is any to be had."

Kai shook his head. "That might be so, but that is also where news of the bounty would have spread. I imagine another kidnapper would not be as kind as I have been."

Finn snorted. "Yes. Kind. I wonder what your definition of that word might be."

Kai smiled and took a turn down an alleyway. Finn had to side-step various puddles as they walked, and found herself hurrying to keep up with her companion as he strode confidently forward. The pair passed several back doors and stables before Kai found what he was looking for, though Finn could see nothing remarkable about this door compared to the others. Kai pounded his fist in a pattern of knocks on the small door, then waited patiently as he rocked back and forth on his feet. After a few moments, the door swung inward to reveal nothing but darkness.

Kai grabbed Finn's hand and pulled her into the eerie darkness before she could ask with whom they were meeting. The door shut behind them, revealing a diminutive woman with several missing teeth, half of her face cast in shadow. Her dress was a plain brown that nearly matched the color of her lackluster hair.

Finn could see the soft glow of oil lamps further into the house, though the entryway was void of any lighting of its own.

"Haven't seen you in these parts for ages," the little woman commented cheerfully, if not without a touch of disdain.

"I've been working elsewhere," Kai explained vaguely. "This is Breya," he added, gesturing to Finn.

Finn almost corrected Kai as he gave her the made-up name, but realized quickly that giving her true name was likely a bad idea. She cleared her throat as she looked down at the tiny woman, confused as to what social protocol might be necessary. Erring on the side of caution, she took the woman's hand in her own. "L-lovely to meet you."

The little woman raised an eyebrow. "Not your usual type," she said looking back to Kai.

"Now what is that supposed to mean?" Kai asked good-naturedly, yet with a hint of sarcasm.

The woman turned back to Finn as she laughed. "She looks so proper. Skinny little thing too. My name is Malida."

"I'm not his-" Finn began, but was cut off by a pleading look from Kai.

Malida's face turned suspicious as she aimed a more scrutinizing eye on Finn. "Not his what?"

Kai stepped up beside Finn. "She's not my lady friend. She's my wife."

Finn inhaled too suddenly and started choking on her own spit.

Kai smiled warmly. "She's not used to the term yet."

Malida continued to look suspicious, but after looking Finn up and down one more time, led them deeper into the building. Finn could tell that they were in the back of some sort of shop by the various crates of whiskey and other goods piled about haphazardly. The space they passed through had no windows, but still had the feeling of a small home, with candles and lanterns illuminating overstuffed chairs and wooden furniture in a flickering glow.

"Are you two waiting for passage?" Malida asked, then added, "You better not be waiting for that Anna."

Kai winked at Finn behind Malida's back. "No Anna. We have parted ways."

Malida turned around with an enormous smile on her face, showcasing the few teeth she had left to her. "Well you two lovebirds can have the room at the end of the hall. I'll fix you up something to eat. Don't you worry about a thing."

Malida hurried off down the hall while Kai ushered Finn in the opposite direction. They reached the end of the corridor and Kai held the door open for Finn, gesturing for her to enter before him. She did so quickly, and as soon as the door was shut, she turned to face him.

"Why did you tell her all of that?" Finn whispered angrily as her peripheral vision took in the sight of a sparsely furnished room with one small, wood-framed bed.

Kai grimaced. "Malida doesn't like it when I bring my work with me. She would not have let us in."

"Then why did you say I was your *wife?*" Finn pressed.

Kai sighed. "Because you were acting strangely and she was starting to get suspicious."

Finn took in a deep breath. "Then *why* did you not warn me before we faced her?"

Kai shrugged. "I assumed we would be dealing with her husband, Buerny. Malida is usually running the tavern up front during the day while her husband manages their other affairs."

"What other affairs?" Finn asked suspiciously.

Kai shrugged. "Buerny and Malida transport certain goods for . . . certain people."

"They're smugglers!" Finn gasped. "Don't we have enough trouble already?"

Kai looked at her in surprise. "Now how do you even know what smugglers are?"

Finn glared. "Just because I was a tree, doesn't mean I was born a week ago."

Kai laughed. "Very well, oh wise one. I brought you here because Malida is just as good at hiding people as she is at hiding stolen goods."

Finn sniffed. "Fine," she acquiesced. "Now how do we find my friends?"

Kai unstrapped his portion of their sparse belongings from his back and set them on the wooden floor. "You will stay here. This evening I will ask some questions, and ask a few people to keep an eye out."

"I will *not* stay here," Finn argued, tossing her hood back in frustration. "For all I know, you're still trying to turn me in."

Kai crossed his arms. "And what if someone figures out who you are? You have no idea who else might be tracking you."

"They just know that I'm a girl who once was a tree. They don't know what I look like," Finn said smartly.

"And how do you know that?" Kai countered. "Word travels fast. Anyone could have overheard something about you in any of the towns you have visited."

"I'm coming," Finn said flatly.

Kai rolled his eyes and began unpacking his belongings. "If we're lucky, Malida might fix us a bath," he said, changing the subject. "I'll even let you go first."

At the mention of a bath, Finn let the argument drop. She was pretty sure that she had won it anyhow. A knock on the door announced Malida with two heaping plates of food. Finn wolfed hers down appreciatively before allowing their hostess to lead her off to get clean.

She followed Malida's small form back through the living-area, and into a small bathing-room. The room was mostly barren, with a large tub dominating the center, and a small wooden bench to be seated on near the tub. The walls were made of the same rough wood that composed the rest of the house, boasting only a few rough towels hanging from hooks near the door. Finn mimicked her hostess as she crouched in front of the bath. At a gesture from Malida, Finn handed her kindling from a small container as Malida built a fire in the metal vessel underneath the already full tub of water.

Once the fire was stable, they sat on the small bench to

wait while the water heated. As Finn waited for the inevitable conversation that would take place while they sat, she repeated in her mind that her name was Breya, and she was Kai's wife.

Malida shifted in her seat to make herself more comfortable. "When was the marriage? It must have been recent, judging by your reaction when Kai told me."

"Oh, um, yes recent," Finn mumbled in reply.

"No need to be shy lass," Malida consoled as she nudged Finn companionably with her elbow. "I'd just like to get to know the woman that finally settled Kai down."

Finn blushed. "How do you know him?" she asked, truly interested.

Malida smiled as her eyes turned distant with memory. "Known him since he was a boy. He wasn't the only one better off away from the Gray City. I left a few years before he did, then ran into him on his travels years later with that Anna. Glad he's rid of her."

Finn went over the story of Kai's past in her mind, glad he had told her, though hopefully what he told her was the truth. "So you know about what happened to him then?"

Malida's aged face settled into indignant lines. "The Gray City is not a kind place for those of the lower classes."

So perhaps Kai had indeed told her the truth. Somehow Finn knew it had been so. She wondered why Malida would still look out for a man she had known in a town she had left a very long time ago, but she did not press the issue.

"How did the two of you meet?" Malida asked when Finn made no effort to fill the silence.

Finn cleared her throat, deciding to tell as much truth as possible so that she would not have to remember too many lies. "We met in Garenoch," she explained. "Our parties had decided to travel together, as the roads can be unsafe."

"Go on," Malida urged.

Finn glanced at the tub, secretly willing the water to heat more quickly. "We fell in love," Finn blurted, then turned to Malida as the blush returned to her face. "It's hard to explain," she finished apologetically.

Malida patted Finn's shoulder. "Calm down, lass. I had no intention of causing you embarrassment."

Malida stood slowly like it hurt her bones and went to dip her hand into the bathwater. Nodding in satisfaction, she turned back to Finn with another warm smile. Finn found that she enjoyed Malida's smiles, even with the missing teeth. "I'll take your dirty clothes and leave you to your bath," she said as she dried her hand on her skirts.

Finn stood and stripped her clothes off quickly, glad that the conversation was over, and anxious to be clean. As a tree she had never worried about the dirt that built up on her bark, but she was beginning to find that the same dirt felt far different on human skin. She slipped down into the warm water as Malida left, closing the door behind her.

While she bathed, she considered the strange events of the past several days. The events of the Blood Forest seemed like they had occurred ages ago, and her life as a tree seemed even farther back still. Though she felt less and less like a tree every day, she had not regained any more of her previous self, the self that had existed before she was a tree. In fact, the few memories of that long ago life she had acquired seemed to be fading as they were replaced by more recent events. Àed and Iseult seemed real, as did Kai and Anna. The Cavari and the past events that had been told to her all seemed like a story, interesting and meaningful, but not at all real.

She had almost drifted off to sleep in the hot water when knock on the door pulled her back into awareness. "Yes?" she called, hoping that Malida had returned with her clothes.

"Will you hurry it up?" Kai called through the door.

Without waiting for a reply, he opened the door and walked into the room, pausing to set a bundle of fabric down on the wooden bench. He came to stand in front of the tub, wearing only a towel and an annoyed expression. Road dirt was evident on his tanned chest and wrists where it had reached beyond the edges of his clothing.

"Malida already took my clothes," he explained. "So if you wouldn't mind hurrying it up, it's a bit drafty in here."

Finn quickly sunk down into the bath so that only her head could be seen above the rim. "And what am I supposed to wear if I get out?"

Kai gestured to the bundle of fabric on the bench. "She seems to think these will fit you better than your old ones. Not that she bothered getting *me* any new clothes."

Finn glanced at the bundle of clothes on the bench, the returned her gaze cautiously to Kai's irritated face. Her eyes widened as he took a step closer.

"Get back!" she demanded, almost sitting up in the water before thinking better of it. "I'll get out when I'm ready."

Kai rolled his eyes and took a step back to sit on the bench next to the clothes. "Well I'm not waiting around the house in a towel. Malida's daughter is terrifying."

"Daughter?" Finn questioned, hoping to distract Kai from standing up again.

"She's eighteen," Kai explained as he pushed his tangled dark hair out of his face. "And very, *very* forward."

Finn snorted. "She sounds like just your type."

Kai raised his eyes from the floor and smirked at her. "Oh but I already have a wife. A wife who happens to be very selfish when it comes to bath time."

"I haven't even washed my hair," she complained.

Kai sighed. "It will take hours to wash all of that mess hanging off of your head."

Finn rolled her eyes and dunked her head down into the water, ignoring the sound of Kai's foot tapping on the wooden floor. She came back up and used a hard, yellow bar of soap to clean her scalp. "You're the one who told me to go first," she commented as she scrubbed, then ducked down into the water again. She re-emerged to find Kai's eyes already resting on her. "Hand me a towel and turn around so I can get out," she demanded.

Kai stood silently and handed her a towel from one of the hooks on the wall, but failed to turn around.

Finn raised an eyebrow at him and he shrugged, finally offering her a small smile. "Can't blame me for trying."

Finn shook her head as Kai turned around so she could exit the bathtub. She was reluctant to leave the water, but also intrigued by the new clothes Malida had found for her. She was quite done with wearing too-long, dirty skirts.

She wrapped the towel tightly around her and gathered the clothes from the bench, but paused as she noticed Kai's bare back. Silvery scars crisscrossed his flesh, starting at his shoulders and trickling all the way down to the top of his towel, evidence of the whipping he'd received before escaping his past.

Realizing she'd been staring, she schooled the emotion out of her face, then stepped in front of Kai with an expectant look.

Kai just stood there with an infuriating smile.

Finn huffed. "I need to get dressed."

When Kai only looked at her, still smiling, she checked to see that her towel was firmly in place, then turned to leave. She would take her chances changing in the room Malida had given them.

"Don't leave on my account," Kai said as she walked toward the door.

Finn turned around with a witty remark on her tongue, only to find Kai had already dropped his towel and was stepping into the tub. Feeling like her face was on fire, Finn fled, slamming the door behind her.

She had hoped to make a quick dash to the room they had been given, but instead she was met by an angry eighteen year old, much taller than her mother. In fact, the girl was taller than Finn, and looked down on her with cool, dark eyes.

"Good day," Finn said hesitantly.

The girl glared at Finn, then whipped her long dark hair and skirts around as she turned and stormed off. Finn let out a breath and escaped the rest of the way to the specified room.

Once inside, she set her towel on the drab blanket that covered the bed, and dressed as quickly as possible. The bodice of the new dress was done in a deep burgundy and hugged her ribs closely. The skirts, which did not drag on the floor like those of her last dress, were a purplish red so deep they were almost black. The color of the dress would show road dirt horribly, but she was just pleased to no longer feel like she was swimming in too much fabric.

Once she was dressed, Finn searched through her belongings for the wooden comb Àed had given her before they had set out on their journey. As she pulled the comb through her damp locks she thought of her missing companion sadly. He had done so much for her, and she had only caused him trouble to the point of risking his life repeatedly.

She had begun to cry when Kai finally entered the room, dressed in his now-clean clothing. He smoothed the extra water out of his hair, looking irritated until he glanced down at Finn, then his face fell into concerned lines. "Do you not like the dress?" he asked, half-joking.

Finn sniffled and attempted to rein in her tears. "The dress is wonderful. It was very thoughtful of Malida to give it to me."

"Shall we go?" he asked as he approached where Finn was perched on the bed, making no further comment on Finn's tears.

Finn nodded as she wiped at her face and stood, feeling nervous about going out, even though she had insisted that she come along. Kai grabbed her green cloak from the wooden chair she had draped it over, and wrapped it snugly around her shoulders, giving her arms a reassuring squeeze as he did so.

"Will we be outside much of the night?" Finn asked curiously as she looked down at her cloak.

"We do not want you to be recognized," he explained. "Keep your hood pulled up. Many who pass through Ainfean don't want to be seen. No one will question it."

Finn nodded and pulled the hood up. The tattered green fabric looked out of place with her new dress, but it would have to do.

As Kai led the way out of the small home, they came across Malida's daughter once more. The girl smiled sweetly at Kai, then turned a fiery glare toward Finn as soon as he walked past.

Finn quickly averted her gaze, and walked forward pretending not to see the jealous, young girl. She inadvertently bumped into Kai's side as she reached him. He looked at her questioningly, but she simply pulled him forward and out through the door they had first entered.

Finn let out a breath as soon as they were outside, understanding fully why Kai had avoided the young girl.

They crossed the alleyway and walked back out to the main street, which had grown far more crowded since they first arrived. Every other building seemed to be a tavern, but Kai chose the one called "The Blushing Butcher", a particularly loud and colorful establishment.

Once inside, Kai purchased Finn a mug of wine and left her sitting at the long oaken bar. The wine was bitter and sweet all at the same time, nothing like the wine she'd had in Garenoch. She had to force herself to take small sips while Kai sat at a table with a few fisherman.

She darted nervous glances back at her companion, wishing she could hear what he was saying. She didn't like that she wasn't allowed to be included in the search for information, but had eventually settled in to stare into her mug of wine when a conversation caught her ear.

"It looked for the life of me like a battlefield," a man a few seats to the left at the bar said.

The bartender poured the man another drink with a stern expression on his face. "But no bodies ye say?"

Finn turned to see the first man shake his head. "No bodies, but blood, lots of blood. Kicked up dirt too, like some huge struggle."

The bartender let a huff of air out through his lips, disturbing his bristly mustache. "There's been word lately. Rumors. People are saying the Tuatha have returned."

The man shook his head in reply. "I heard them too, but this weren't no Faie trick. The blood was real. Had my hounds in a frenzy."

Finn tuned out the conversation. The Blood Forest no longer seemed distant. Perhaps the Travelers had been doing the countryside a favor in keeping the other Faie trapped. Or perhaps it had been another battle against the Travelers that the hunter had stumbled upon.

A cloaked woman approached, sat on Finn's right, and ordered two mugs of wine. Once the mugs were delivered, she sat the second one in front of Finn.

"I owe you a drink," the woman said. "It's not often that my quarry escapes me."

Finn glanced at a face partially obscured by a cloak, just as her own face was obscured, then turned to fully face the women as recognition dawned on her. "Anna! How did you get here?"

Anna snorted. "I walked, silly girl. As soon as I escaped Mius' camp, I was delayed by a group of Trow. I assumed you had something to do with that, but I honestly expected to find you back in ropes. It's not often that Kai loses a quarry either." She paused to look back at Kai, who was yet to see her. "Oh look," she said sarcastically. "He hasn't lost you after all."

"What do you want?" Finn asked sharply.

Anna's face showed mock surprise. "Now, now, you can be friends with Kai, but not with me?"

Finn glared. "I never claimed to be friends with Kai. He is simply repaying a debt to me."

"A debt, hmm?" Anna paused to take a sip of her wine. "Interesting."

When Anna did not continue speaking, Finn cleared her throat. "What do you want?"

Anna chuckled to herself. "Well now, I originally came here wanting to recapture you and get my bounty, but I believe my plans have changed. I think I'd rather like to see how this all plays out."

"How what plays out?" Finn pressed, but Anna didn't answer. Instead she stood with her cloak still pulled up to block her face, and made her way out of the tavern.

Moments later, Kai approached and took Anna's seat. "Who was that? She was speaking to you."

"Just some woman," Finn lied. "She spoke of her day then moved on."

"She bought you a drink," Kai observed.

"She said I looked like I needed it," Finn lied again.

"Well I can't argue with her," he conceded. He raised his own mug in sláinte. "Someone matching Àed's description was seen in the woods south of here, and there is likely more information to be found. It's going to be a long night."

Finn took another sip of her wine and thought that it tasted even more bitter than before.

CHAPTER TWENTY

*A*ed ran ahead like a hound with a scent, impervious to the darkness, with his mule-horse bouncing right along behind him. Iseult and Óengus pushed their horses to a trot just to keep pace. The old man moved astonishingly fast.

"Where is he going?" Óengus asked. "We lost any sign of tracks hours ago."

"I do not know how he does it," Iseult replied, "but I know he goes toward Finn."

Óengus grunted. "You still have to pay me, you know, given that I will be losing out on a large bounty."

Iseult nodded. He did not care about the money. If it would eliminate the threat from Óengus without bloodshed, then he would pay.

The distant glow of braziers in Port Ainfean came into view, raising a spark of hope within Iseult. Óengus had claimed that Finn would be taken to a Port. Perhaps they could find her before she was sent down the river, for if that happened, she could well be lost to them.

Óengus eyed the distant spires, dully illuminated by moonlight, in a calculating manner. "If she was taken to Ainfean, she may be on the river by now, or at least waiting to board a ship."

Iseult cringed as Óengus echoed his thoughts. "Then we will go directly to the pier, and search for her from there."

"It is a large port . . ." Óengus began.

"We will find her," Iseult said flatly.

Óengus did not argue, surrendering to the futility of that endeavor.

Finn scowled as Kai left her uncomfortably alone at the bar once more. She could be of better use if he would allow her to go with him to talk to people, and she didn't like sitting at the loud bar alone. Seeing Anna had made her feel unsafe, which brought to light the fact that she'd felt somewhat safe in the first place. She knew she shouldn't trust Kai. The man had wanted to stick her on a boat to some unknown fate, after all. Yet she was not on the boat, and she was not sure she would have ended up there even if the Trow had not helped her.

Then again, it was after he had gotten to know her that he was still willing to kidnap her, so perhaps the river really would have been her fate. Thinking about it, she began to get angry. The mug of wine Anna had purchased for her still sat by her elbow, so she finished her own mug and started in on that one.

Kai came to stand at her side. "It's all dead ends here. We should move on to the next establishment."

Finn downed the bitter wine in a few gulps and stood to follow him. Kai seemed like he wanted to make comment, but he held it in. His restraint was a wise choice, as Finn would not have minded a reason to lash out at him.

The next tavern was called "The Green Sea". The name was carved into an ornate wooden sign in the shape of a rolling ocean wave. A flash of memory hit Finn at the thought of the ocean. It was the first memory that had resurfaced in several days, and it drowned out all other thoughts.

She saw the sea, and her kinfolk. They gathered around a large fire, discussing what needed to be done. The war could not be won if both sides were eliminated. They would have to wait it out and preserve the clan.

"Finn!" Kai whispered harshly as he shook her.

She blinked back into reality. "Yes?" she asked, confused.

Kai eyed her warily. "Where did you go just now?"

Finn blinked again. "Nowhere. I was just thinking about the ocean."

Kai stared at her for another moment. "Are you well enough to go on? I could walk you back to Malida's . . . "

Finn snorted and walked into the tavern ahead of him. There was no room at the bar, so she took a small table in the far back corner, feeling slightly dizzy. She had not been sitting long before one of the barmaids came to see if she wanted a drink.

"I will have wine," Finn told her, "though hopefully it is not quite so bitter here."

The barmaid smiled and flipped her curly, auburn hair

over her shoulder. "Best wine in the Port," she guaranteed, "all the way from Migris."

Finn nodded. "Good, did you see the man I came in with? He will be paying for the wine."

The barmaid raised an eyebrow. "You're not the usual type on Kai's tab."

Finn glared at the man in question. "The least he can do for me is buy me a drink," she said with more heat than she had intended.

"I'll bet," the barmaid said with a wink before sauntering away.

A few moments later, Finn had a fresh mug of wine in her hand that tasted just like the wine at the previous establishment. She sipped it, thinking about how far she and Iseult could be on their journey if they hadn't taken the time to save Anna, and if Anna hadn't subsequently kidnapped her. It was all Kai's fault, she thought drunkenly.

She could have spent the time she lost on Kai searching for the Archtree, rather than risking her life repeatedly only to get nothing in return. She wanted to blame Kai for the escape of the Faie as well, but realistically she knew that it would have happened with or without his presence.

She glanced at Kai again to find him speaking closely with the barmaid that had served her drink. Finn narrowed her eyes at them and took a large gulp of her wine. The barmaid turned and caught her eye, then offered her a small smile. Finn forced a smile onto her face, but knew it did not appear pleasant. The fake smile was cut short as a large, lumbering mass came into view.

The man was clearly drunk, though not quite at the

point of belligerency. He wore the loose, sun-bleached garb of a fisherman. He also wore the smell of a fisherman, but he obviously was not overly concerned by it as he took a seat and pressed in close to Finn. His face was red from the whiskey he had been drinking, and he had two fresh drams in his large hands. His hair was concealed beneath another plain-colored swatch of cloth.

"The wine here is terrible," the man commented, pushing one of the drams toward Finn.

She took it almost fiendishly and threw it back into her throat. As she sputtered from the burning liquid, she said, "My husband would be happy to pay you back for the drink."

The man waved her off. "I don't see no husband around."

Finn nodded in Kai's direction. "He is right over there, conversing with the barmaid."

The man moved in a little closer and breathed his whiskey breath in Finn's face. "Now why is he over there talking to the pretty, young barmaid, when his wife is sitting over here all alone?"

"She's an old friend," Finn quickly lied, though it may have been the truth in Kai's case.

Finn's head spun from the wine and whiskey. She wished the man would just go away. "I'm very tired," she said as she stood to excuse herself.

"Well let me help you home," the man offered, "since your *husband* is so preoccupied."

"No thank you," Finn said politely as she began to walk away.

The man reached out, grabbed her arm, and tried to pull

her back down into her seat, surprising her so much that she almost fell in the process. She noticed Kai observing the slight commotion and heading her way, yet there was no need for an intervention. Her anger at Kai had found a new target. She righted herself and picked up her empty mug with her free hand, bringing it back intending to hit the man in the head with it. Before she could, Kai's fist punched the man square in the face. The man toppled backwards out of his seat, letting go of Finn in the process.

Kai pulled the mug from Finn's hand and urged her toward the door. "We need to get out of here. *Now.*"

Finn glanced back as the man started getting to his feet while several other fishermen came to his aid. She turned forward as she and Kai spilled out into the moonlit darkness, just as the men began to give chase.

"This way," Kai ordered as he darted down a dark alleyway.

Finn pushed her dizziness aside and ran after Kai, though it was a struggle to remain focused on his shadowy form. Shouts and heavy footfalls followed them through the maze of alleyways.

Luckily both Kai and Finn were smaller, and therefore faster than the well-muscled fishermen. The men gave chase for a while, but after a long sequence of deft turns, Kai and Finn managed to lose them.

"You're a madwoman," Kai huffed as they came to a standstill. "Do you know that?"

Finn shrugged as she waited for her breath to catch up with her, feeling quite sick after drinking so much alcohol. "I'm not the one who punched the man in the face."

Kai put his hands on his hips, still breathing heavily as

well. "Right before you were about to hit him with an empty mug."

Finn sniffed. "He had earned a smack on the head."

Kai rolled his eyes. "Only because you took his whiskey and tried to leave."

Finn looked down at her feet, suddenly embarrassed. "I did not think you were watching."

Kai glanced nervously at the shadows around them. "Well I was," he admitted. "It wouldn't do to have you snatched away before I could pay my debt."

Finn held up her nose. "I thought you said that your debt would be paid after you got me here in the first place."

Kai looked back up to meet Finn's glare. "I thought about it, and it didn't seem like an equal trade of effort." He watched her face closely for a reaction to his words.

Her glare softened, but her lips were still tight with annoyance. "I don't think you would have traded me in. I think you are a better man than I've been led to believe. You don't fool me for a second, Kai." The words poured out of her mouth like water before she could think to stop them.

Kai wrapped his hands around each of Finn's arms and looked at her steadily. "Had things gone as planned, you would have been on that ship, and I would have been a very rich man."

Finn held up her nose even higher, but did not reply.

"Perhaps I second-guessed it a time or two," Kai added. "That does not mean I wouldn't have done it."

Finn pulled away and began walking back toward Malida's. At least, she thought she was walking toward Malida's. Kai ended up having to correct her sense of direction a few times, which she accepted grudgingly.

279

By the time they were back in their room, Finn was exhausted and filled with some sort of sorrow she didn't quite understand. There had been no sign of Malida or her daughter, though it was not terribly late at night. They were likely manning a tavern just as full as the others.

Finn sprawled across the bed as soon as the door was shut, wishing very much that she had not had so much to drink.

"And what makes you think that you will be taking the bed?" Kai asked from where he stood by the door.

Finn rolled over to look at him. "You really would have done it?"

Kai rolled his eyes. "Why is that so hard for you to believe? Or is it just the mass quantity of alcohol speaking?"

Finn curled up and turned her back on him. "I just don't understand it. I could never befriend someone, just to completely betray them."

Kai came to sit on the edge of the bed near her feet. "I did not befriend you with that intent. I did not know who you were at first."

Finn curled her feet up away from him. If only her head would stop spinning. "Your intention was the same. If it had not been me, it would have been Branwen and Anders."

Kai stood abruptly. "This is what I am. This is what the world is. You must look out for yourself, because no one will do it for you."

"I look out for myself just fine," Finn said with a yawn. "It does not mean I cannot look out for others as well."

Finn did not see Kai's sad smile as she drifted off to sleep. He unfurled one of their bedrolls on the hard floor and tried to sleep as well, though it did not come easily. The woman snoring in the bed above him had muddled his thoughts far too much for his liking.

CHAPTER TWENTY-ONE

Kai had finally drifted into a deep sleep just as Finn awoke, feeling embarrassed and angry with herself for drinking so much the night before. Having acquired a new, sober perspective, she silently gathered her things and allowed herself one final glance at the slumbering Kai. She had trusted this dishonest man long enough. He had done his best to assure her that her trust was misplaced, and she would be a fool to not heed the warnings. She would find Iseult and Àed on her own.

She made her way unhindered through the silent home, and was reaching for the lock on the back door, when a small hand wrapped around her arm. Finn turned around, quickly trying to think of an explanation.

Malida shook her head before Finn could say anything. "He shouldn't have tried to hang onto a girl like you," she said softly. "Did you at least give him a reason?"

Finn's heart stopped for a moment, then she let out a breath. Malida would not try to stop her. "He knows why."

Malida nodded as she let her hand fall from Finn's arm to open the door for her. "Be careful," Malida cautioned as Finn stepped out into the early morning light.

Finn looked back to acknowledge Malida's warning, but the door had already shut behind her. Not wanting to waste another moment, she ran quickly down the alley, fearing that Kai might wake up and come looking for her, and yet, also fearing that he would not.

Her plan was to get out of the city so that she could backtrack and find her companions. She had one bedroll, a small amount of food, her cloak, and her dagger, and she assured herself that was all she would need. She was heading in the direction of the gates through a cross-section of alleyways, going over the way back to Badenmar in her head, when arms reached out and grabbed her.

After a moment of shocked stillness, she tried to struggle, but the man had one arm wrapped around her chest, and the other covered her mouth. He used his height to lift her off her feet and carried her into a dark building.

Once inside, he let her drop to the ground. She fell to her knees, and instantly scurried away on all fours. She turned to watch her kidnapper's back as he lifted a heavy bar and placed it across the door, trapping her inside. Silver hair and cold gray eyes turned to face her.

"You!" she shouted as she rose and flung herself at him.

Óengus tried to hold her off, but she managed to get a few good scratches in at his face. Suddenly another pair of strong arms gripped her from behind, prying her off Óengus.

Finn kicked the new attacker in the shin, and was

allowed to fall to the ground where she crouched defensively. She shifted around to face this new threat.

"You found me!" she exclaimed, standing straight to throw her arms around him.

Iseult accepted Finn's enthusiastic hug and patted her back awkwardly, not sure what to do with the sudden display of affection.

Àed came hobbling into the room through a door that went further into the building. His bone-tired face was the best sight Finn could have hoped for. "I found ye actually," he grumbled. "These two are worthless as trackers."

Iseult and Óengus took on similar grudging expressions as Finn went to Àed and stooped down to hug him. Finally she turned to Óengus. "I'm sorry . . . I suppose."

Óengus cleared his throat, but didn't acknowledge Finn further. Instead he turned to Iseult, who tossed him a heavy looking coin purse.

"You will find the rest with Miriam in Ousepid," Iseult explained.

With a smile and a nod, Óengus gathered his belongings, then unbarred and opened the door. As soon as the man was gone, Finn turned back to Iseult.

"Where are Kai and Liaden?" he asked her before she could speak.

"Kai and *Anna, alias Liaden,* are no longer our concern," Finn replied happily. "We must begin our search."

"*They* kidnapped you!" Iseult said with an uncharacteristic amount of emotion. "They were lying to us all from the start, and planned on selling you to the highest bidder. They must pay for what they did to you."

Finn's eyes widened as she pictured what Iseult might do

to Kai if he found him. "They are not here," she lied, "and we will not find them."

Iseult watched her face carefully as he asked, "Then how did you come to be here?"

Finn sniffed indignantly. "I have two legs," she said, gesturing to said legs. "I *walked*."

"And how did you know the way?" Iseult asked, ignoring her sarcasm.

Finn bit her lip as she tried to think of a believable explanation. She was about to open her mouth and beg Iseult not to hurt Kai when Àed cleared his throat. "Yer acting like Finn ran off on purpose," he chided. "Stop questioning the girl."

Iseult regarded Finn for a moment longer, then conceded to Àed's point with a curt nod.

Finn felt like she might pass out as relief washed through her. Though part of her still desired vengeance on Kai, she did not wish him any real harm. "Where do we go from here?" she asked, not wanting to give Iseult any reason to revert to the previous line of questioning.

"For now, we will continue down the Sand Road," he explained, though he still seemed agitated. "Àed knows of someone along the way who might possess useful information."

Àed gave Finn a knowing look. Finn supposed he knew that she had lied, and that Kai was not far away at all. She felt torn, and almost wanted to go back and let Kai know that she had found her companions. Yet, she could not very well bring Iseult to Malida's, and she did not think it likely that he or Àed would let her venture off on her own when they had only just found her. Just as well, she thought. If Kai was the man he claimed to be, he would continue living just the way he had been. He would forget all about her.

A few tears dripped down her face. Àed glanced at her again, but she quickly turned her eyes forward to follow Iseult out of the building, batting angrily at her unwelcome tears.

Àed followed behind Finn, knowing full-well what the tears were about. He'd found Finn the night before in the alleyway with Kai, while Iseult and Óengus slept. His first impulse had been to charge in and rescue her, but after listening for a moment, he hadn't had the heart to interrupt their conversation. He was glad that Finn had chosen to leave on her own. Still, he didn't appreciate the fact that someone had caused such sadness in a girl that he looked upon like a daughter, and Kai would feel the full strength of his distaste if he bothered showing his face again.

He glanced at Finn as he caught up to her side while they walked and he pondered what he could possibly say to console her. She had pulled her green hood up to cover her features, and had even tucked all of her long hair back inside of her cloak. It would have been wise for him to hide behind a cloak as well, as Anders had proven that some might still recognize him. Any that might recognize Finn also likely knew that she traveled with him.

Still, the idea of hiding did not sit well with Àed. It seemed to not sit well with Iseult either, as his black hair blew about freely in the chilly morning air. Yet, the tall man somehow managed to blend in with the crowd. Iseult had a talent for hiding in the periphery. It made sense really, given that he came from a long line of thieves.

"They could not have been planning on taking you all along," Iseult said as he hovered over Finn's shoulder, unwilling to let the subject drop after all.

Finn shook her head ruefully. "Their original targets were Branwen and Anders," she explained. "Kai and Anna intended to steal the map they were making, as well as many of the books they carried with them."

"They told you all of that?" Iseult questioned, surprise evident in his tone. "Did they actually hope to justify their actions?"

"Well Kai-" Finn began, then blushed as she cut herself off.

Iseult grunted and let the subject go once again.

Àed shook his head in disgust. Had Finn been about to defend Kai? As far as he was concerned, Kai and Anna were a lowly pair of vultures, taking opportunities as they came. Likely the thieves had discovered Finn's identity in the Blood Forest, presenting a new opportunity just as the opportunity the twins had presented slipped away. If there were no maps and books to sell, they would sell a tree girl instead.

He kept his eyes on the ground as he walked, too caught up in his own thoughts to keep an eye on the townsfolk as they passed. With as Faie-addled as Finn had become in the forest, she'd probably told Kai everything there was to tell during their time alone. It still bothered Àed that he had not watched Finn more closely. Of course, having her stolen away while he slept bothered him a great deal more. In his prime he would have seen such an act coming a mile away . .

. and Kai and Liaden/Anna would not have lived to tell the tale.

He could at least be proud that he had found her again. He had not lost her like he lost Keiren. It had been Keiren's choice to go, but it was still his fault that she'd made that choice. How could anyone have expected a man like him to raise a daughter? She'd been fated to turn out even more corrupt than he. It was in the blood, after all.

He looked at Finn as she cast a worried glance over her shoulder, as if someone might be following them. He knew Keiren's fate could just as easily befall Finn. Though she was kind, and seemed to have a firm sense of morality, she was powerful. She didn't know it yet, but she would. For any with the wherewithal to look properly, she shone like a small sun. She was shining more each and every day, making it easier for him to sense her when she was not near.

He wondered what events had occurred since she had been kidnapped, because something had brought her power to the surface, whereas before it was deeply buried. He would have very much liked to put her kidnappers to the question, but Finn protected them, and he would not go against her wishes. He would not alienate her as he had Keiren. He would also not make her aware of the power she possessed any sooner than he had to. It had done Keiren no good, and would do no good for Finn.

As they neared the gates of the port, Àed's thoughts led him to their current plan, a plan that would bring far too many answers to all. Iseult had devised a way to reach the Archtree, which was all well and good, if he actually knew how to find it. Àed knew that Iseult had a map, as he was nothing if not observant. Whether the map was correct or not . . . that was a whole other thing entirely. He hoped that the map was not correct, but he would not bar Finn from the tree's answers if they found it.

Àed shook his head. That dreaded moment was still far off. Their current task was to meet with Gilion. Gilion had been around longer than him, and likely even longer than Finn. Gilion could tell them if the map was valid. Not that he would, but he *could*. There was no need to worry, at least not yet. The map might not be the right map at all. Iseult was not aware that Àed even knew of the map, nor was he aware of why they were going to see Gilion. Àed had led him to believe that Gilion possessed information on what had happened to Finn. He might even have such information in reality, though once again, knowing information and being willing to tell it were two very different things.

Àed glanced back at Iseult. While he was grateful for Iseult's obsession with keeping Finn safe, he was also wary of his intentions. The Cavari had destroyed Uí Néid, yet Iseult seemed to genuinely care about Finn when the two should have been mortal enemies. Still, despite Iseult's affections, he highly doubted that the man's only goal regarding Finn was to right the wrongs of Uí Néid.

Àed glanced back again, and for a moment almost thought that he saw Óengus following behind them, but when he looked more closely, the man was nowhere to be seen.

Finn looked up at the ominous spires of Port Ainfean as

Iseult guided her and Àed toward a large horse stable near the gates of the port. As they approached the stable, she first noticed Àed's shaggy horse, then the two normal looking horses saddled beside it.

"I requested upon our arrival that the horses remained ready," Iseult explained as he handed her the reins to a chestnut colored horse. "I was not sure if we would have to depart quickly."

The stableman approached, then quickly retreated after Iseult placed several coins into the palm of his dirty hand. Iseult turned and helped Finn up onto her saddle so that she would not have to hike her skirts up higher than necessary, then mounted his own horse, a sleek black creature that Finn found somewhat intimidating. As Finn's horse pranced about, unhappy with the new weight on its back, she found herself missing the shaggy mule-horse she had left with Anders.

Her heart ached slightly as the three of them rode out of the stable and through the gates of Port Ainfean. She did not appreciate the aching feeling at all, and wished more than anything in that moment to be a tree again. She never ached as a tree.

Óengus had been waiting outside the small house where they had first procured Finn, as she and her companions emerged and made their hurried way out to the main road. He'd heard Iseult mention the Sand Road, which meant they were either going to Migris, or one of the small settlements along the way. He could rationalize Iseult's desire to rescue

Finn, he obviously cared for her, but he was unsure of Finn's motives. There had to be a reason for a girl who was once a tree to travel the Sand Road. Either there was somewhere Finn needed to be, or she was looking for something of great importance. People would usually pay a great deal for things of importance, and he was not limited to only procuring people.

He casually sauntered out to the main road, feeling confident as his mind set to a new endeavor. He could see Iseult's tall form, and the smaller shapes of Finn and Àed in the distance. He followed, leading his horse behind him, keeping enough distance to not be noticed, but staying close enough to never lose sight of his quarry.

Kai rolled over in his bedroll, feeling a bit of a headache from the night before. He imagined Finn would be much worse off than he.

"Are you alive up there?" he called in the direction of the bed.

There was no answer.

Kai inched his way out of his bedroll, then stood to look at the empty bed. At first he thought perhaps she had just gone in search of Malida, but then he noticed half of their supplies were missing, as well as the extra bedroll. Now fully awake, his jaw dropped in surprise with the realization that Finn had left intentionally.

His initial urge was to go after her, but why? He would not be turning her in for a bounty, so she was of little use to him. Even if he chose to be of use to *her*, it was clear that Finn wanted to be rid of him. He shook his head. She was a magical Faie-type being for earth's sake. How could he actually hope to be of any use to her? She had no place in his life, and he had no place in *anyone's* life. Not permanently at least.

He quietly gathered his things to leave, not in search of Finn, but in search of the next opportunity. He would find Anna eventually, and they would continue on much as they had before. Nothing had really changed.

Malida caught him as he was attempting to sneak out the back door, and he cringed at her sudden appearance. "First the girl, and then you, trying to sneak out without sayin' goodbye," the little woman chided.

Kai rubbed at his groggy eyes and did his best to look apologetic. "It was a very long night."

Malida clucked her tongue at him. "You shouldn't have let her go. She was good for you. I can always tell."

"I did not have much choice in the matter," Kai replied, "and she's better off without me anyhow."

Malida raised both eyebrows in mock surprise. "My Kai, thinking of someone else before thinking of himself? The girl really *was* good for you."

"I'm sure new opportunities will come along in no time," Kai replied jovially, though his smile did not quite reach his eyes.

Malida just nodded and patted Kai on the shoulder before turning away. Kai turned back to the door to make his escape, but again his way was abruptly blocked, this time by Malida's daughter as she came inside and shut the door behind her.

"Where's your *wife?*" the young girl asked coyly.

Kai sighed and looked over his shoulder to assure

himself that Malida had gone. "I'd like to know the same thing, honestly."

The girl's expression softened. "I was out at dawn, gathering eggs for making breakfast in the tavern. I saw her on the main road, with a tall man and an old man."

Kai nodded, feeling a nervous flutter in his chest. She was safe. "Good, that's good. Thank you for letting me know."

The girl's face lit up, happy to be useful. "They were also being followed by a silver-haired man. I do not know that they saw him."

Kai's expression turned to contemplation. The bounty was still available, and Óengus would want to fill it. With all of his conflicting emotions, he hadn't considered the fact that others would still be looking to fulfill the bounty. Perhaps she was not so safe after all.

He thought for a moment longer. "I need to go," he decided. "Thank you."

He patted the girl on the shoulder absentmindedly as he left, too distracted to notice her scowling after him.

He was so deep in thought that he did not notice the dark female form following him, yet always remaining hidden in the shadows, as he wove his way from alleyway to alleyway.

As they rode, Àed could tell that Finn was unsure of the task ahead of them, as if she questioned her choice to continue on. He knew it could not be so, because the girl had been positively irritating in her insistence to find answers. One would think that finding a tree that could give her any answer she sought would be her sole objective.

Yet he could see the longer she spent as a human, the more she became like one, and the more she was concerned with others. In the beginning, the girl could not have cared less about companions or the world of men in general. Now she fretted about leaving a man behind that had caused her nothing but trouble.

As they gained more distance from the port, Finn expressed her worries over the Faie, puzzling Àed, since someone who wanted to be a tree should not be overly concerned with what the Faie might do. However, he had to admit, the Faie worried him too. Talk had spread across Port Ainfean of more strange sightings, of bloody battle-fields without evidence bodies, and people disappearing into the night.

Of course, there was not much to do about it, just as there was not much to do about Finn's developing human-ity. There was no way for him to alter either event, and Àed highly doubted that any Faie they came across would be willing to explain what they planned, so it was better to not come across them at all.

"I keep getting the strange feeling of being followed," Finn stated casually.

"As do I," Iseult agreed from where he rode near her side. "We will be able to see anyone who follows once we're on the Sand Road. There will be little shelter to hide behind."

Àed had not felt the presence of someone following them, and he blamed it on being too entrenched in his own thoughts. He glanced behind him and to either side, but could only see trees. "Gilion lives only a few days' ride from here," he announced. "Once we reach the road, it should be an easy journey."

He looked around at the trees once more. Yes, it would be an easy journey to find Gilion. It was the journey after that, that occupied his thoughts. *That* portion of the journey would be anything but easy. He glanced up at the sky as dark clouds slid in to block out the sun. A storm was coming. Àed hated storms.

CHAPTER TWENTY-TWO

*A*nders recalled the thundering of hoof beats, and now his sister was gone. He stumbled back out into the area where the confrontation had taken place. If it could be called a confrontation. He had not put up much of a fight.

He had pulled Branwen into a thicket to hide just in time. The hoof beats came to a halt in the clearing. First Anders saw the horses' legs. He shifted slightly in hopes of seeing riders, but there were none. These were no horses. Where the horses heads should have been were human bodies. No, not human, Faie.

Their skin where it met with the body of a horse was gray-tinged and bloodless, like that of a corpse. The bodies otherwise seemed human, but not the faces. The creatures' faces were too angular to ever be seen as human, especially with the large pointed ears as long as Anders' outstretched hand. Large, up-tilted eyes dominated their bony faces, peeking out under unkempt silver hair. While Anders tried to remember how to breathe, one of the creatures turned those large, up-tilted eyes toward him. The eyelids came down to briefly cover pure red, pupil-less eyes, then the eyes locked on Branwen.

The creature spoke in a strange clicking voice, and pointed to the thicket. Two more of the creatures approached. Anders tried to pull his sister away so that they might try and run, but Branwen pulled against him in the direction of the creatures. Anders had a hold on one of her arms, but she reached her free arm out towards the horse-like body of the nearest creature regardless.

Ignoring Branwen's outstretched arm, the creature turned to Anders. It was the last thing he remembered, and now his sister was gone.

Now he stumbled about on foot, as both his horse and Branwen's had run when the creatures approached, taking with them all of their supplies. He could clearly see what direction the hooves of the creatures had gone in, and did his best to follow them. Perhaps he could hire some sort of militia to get his sister back. No, he thought, those creatures dropped me without an ounce of effort. He tried to remember if the creature had struck him, but he had no recollection of such an occurrence. His mind felt foggy, but he had no telltale ache of a head injury.

He began to stumble along in the direction of the tracks, unsure of what else to do.

Àed looked off toward the other side of the nearby river. The past few days of travel had been uneventful, except for the rain. He had been convinced that the rain would never stop, when finally the sun made an appearance. The sun now shone on a small stone cottage with a cloud of gray smoke drifting from the chimney. The home stood alone, and was the only building near the Sand Road for two-hundred furlongs in either direction.

"How did I only notice that place just now?" Finn asked from atop her chestnut mount. They had camped not far from the small structure the previous night, but Àed had not bothered announcing that they'd reached their destination.

"Because ye didn't have me to point it out to ye," Àed replied as he urged his mule-horse toward the riverbank.

Finn prodded her horse into motion to catch up to his side. "Is it some sort of magic?"

Àed nodded. "Of a sort, aye. Gilion prefers not to have visitors."

Iseult rode on Finn's other side, never taking an eye off her since they found her in Port Ainfean. "Explain to me again, what good will he do us?" he asked without taking his eyes off the distant house.

Àed looked past Finn at Iseult. "He's had a longer life than meself several times over. He may even be older than our Finn."

Finn glared over at him, her face a furious blush. "I'm not *that* old."

Àed chuckled. "Old enough, lass. He can tell us if Iseult's map there is the correct one."

"How did you-" Iseult began, finally turning his gaze to Àed, then held up a hand to stop any answers. "Never mind," he conceded. "Let us meet this Gilion."

Àed nodded gruffly. The party rode their horses across the River Cair, which had dwindled to little more than a shallow stream at that point, though it overflowed its banks with the extra rainfall.

As soon as they were clear of the water, they dismounted and tied the horses' reins to a nearby tree. The vibrant green hill that led up to the house was steep and muddy, and better traveled on foot. It was only when they reached the top of the hill, panting with exertion, that they could see how deteriorated the building had become. There were holes in the roof, and the mortar of the house was crumbling in several places to the point where it looked like the walls might cave in. Weeds and brambles grew up to cover the weakened walls, as well as part of the door.

Not wasting any time, Àed pounded on the rickety door. His knocks were quickly answered by a very tall man, who looked just as old as Àed had claimed. Long, pure white hair reached the man's waist. He wore white robes that were unstained, but seemed to have a fine layer of dust on them, especially heavy at the shoulders. The same dust coated the top of his head and the tip of his long nose.

The man's eyes were a pure milky white, highly evident as he looked around blindly through the vines that obscured his door. His unseeing eyes settled on Finn and widened, then he promptly slammed the door in their faces. The sound of a lock sliding into place sounded shortly after.

Àed knocked again, but the door did not open. He placed his hand flat on the door and closed his eyes. After a moment, the lock could be heard sliding back into its original position.

The door creaked open slowly and Àed led the way

inside. Finn and Iseult both had to duck in order to fit through the vines that Àed had easily passed under. The tall old man sat huddled in the corner of the room, making himself as small as possible. The entire interior of the house was covered in dust, just like Gilion. The man shook as if very afraid.

"Go away," he said, with a tremor in his voice.

"What has happened to ye Gilion?" Àed asked. "Yer cowering like a little girl."

The old man looked up with tears in his blind eyes. "The seasons are changing. The lines are faltering, undoing the old and bringing life to the new. Trees will fall, and changed earth will be left in their place. A storm is coming"

"Yer spewin' Traveler drivel now I see," Àed commented. "Ye'll need to pull yerself together for a moment. We need ye to look at a map."

"She cannot be here," the man said pointing at Finn. "*She* wants her."

Finn took a step back toward the door. "What is he talking about?"

"Trees will fall," Gilion mumbled. "Change the earth."

"Who wants her?" Iseult asked, ignoring the fact that Gilion was bordering on hysteria.

"Keiren," Gilion said, a look of clarity returning to his face. "She doesn't just want her. She *needs* her."

"What do ye know about Keiren?" Àed asked coldly. "What lies do ye tell about me daughter?"

Gilion looked nervous again. "She was here. She wants the girl. The girl is the key."

"The key to what?" Finn asked, stepping forward once more.

"What do you think you were meant for?" Gilion snapped, suddenly no longer afraid. "You are a tool. Your people put you away until they were ready to use you. Your presence here shows that the time has come. The Cavari will return."

Finn shook her head as tears began to stream down her face. "I don't understand."

"Quiet," Iseult ordered the old man. "We came here to find the location of what we seek, not to have you to speak ill of our companion."

"Companion, pfft," the old man said, suddenly angry again. "When the time comes, you won't be on the same side. None of you will." The old man's stern expression melted as if he was listening to things that only he could hear.

Àed's entire body trembled as he tried to process the information. "Where's me daughter!" he shouted suddenly.

Gilion snapped back to attention. "You won't find her. Well, you might if you stick with the Cavari wench . . . eventually."

Iseult's face was an emotionless mask. "We are wasting our time. If he cannot see, he will not be able to tell us if the map is accurate."

Gilion turned his milky gaze to Iseult. "Eyes are useless. I can see more than you could ever imagine."

Having had enough, Iseult slapped his map down on a dusty tabletop near the old man. "Tell us if the map is accurate, and we will leave you."

Gilion glanced at the map and rubbed one edge between his fingertips. He turned back to Iseult. "You'll have to betray her in the end, you know."

Iseult stood over the man menacingly as if he might strike him.

"What do you want with the Archtree?" Gilion asked, his voice sounding fearful once more.

Iseult lifted the map and began to roll it back up. "So it's accurate?"

Gilion tsked at him. "Answer my question first."

Iseult turned to go. "My answers are my own."

Gilion cackled. "You do not want to lie in front of them. You're afraid they'll find you out."

Iseult reached for the door wordlessly while Àed and Finn watched the scene play out, mere spectators to something they didn't fully understand.

Gilion's eyes lit up with recognition as he stared at Iseult's back. "Uí Néid? I thought I smelled it on you. You want the shroud of the Faie Queen."

Iseult turned to glare over his shoulder at the old man in response.

Gilion brought his palms together in front of his face and smiled. "*She* wants the shroud as well. If you find it, she will simply take it from you."

"I will not!" Finn interrupted.

Gilion gave Finn a disgusted look. "Not you. Keiren. It would be very bad if *she* were in possession of the shroud. If she had the shroud and the Cavari girl both? Utter disaster. Not that it matters anymore. She'll have what she wants in the end."

"Keiren has no need for the dead," Àed said, his voice cracking with emotion. "As I recall, she hardly had a need for the living."

Gilion tsked at Àed. "The shroud has nothing to do with

the dead. She who holds the shroud will be a uniting force of the Tuatha. She could stop what has been put into motion, or she could make it much, much worse."

Àed huddled around himself as if cold. "And which way does me daughter hope to go?"

Gilion shrugged. "Neither, would be my guess. She cares not for the tides of war, all she cares for is power."

"If she's so power hungry," Finn cut in. "Why has no one heard a thing about her since she disappeared?"

"Because you have not been listening right!" Gilion shouted, straining his willowy neck out like that of a chicken. "You think the Gray City is ruled by some Alderman? Think again. The Gray City has been under the rule of a lady for decades, and the Lady of Migris? One and the same. Countless other cities. I believe she'd quite like having the Tuatha under her control as well."

"What is she planning?" Àed asked, strain evident in his voice.

Gilion laughed again. "If she has the girl and the shroud, it will not matter. The Tuatha will follow her, and nothing will stand in her way." He paused and looked directly at Finn with his eerie white eyes. "Especially if she has the girl."

Finn backed up against the wall near the door, shaking her head frantically. "I want nothing to do with it. I do not want the shroud. I just want to find my people so they can make things right."

Gilion smiled. "Are you sure about that lass? Your people would not like the company you keep."

Àed reached up and patted Finn on the shoulder. "We

should be goin'. The old codger won't be tellin' us anything of use."

Gilion looked around nervously again. It was as if his more confident self was a possession, and the nervous man was the real Gilion shining through. "Follow the map," he whispered quickly, "and destroy the shroud."

Àed paused, sensing the return of his old friend. "What about the Tuatha? They must be stopped."

"It is not worth the risk!" Gilion hissed. "If it were to fall into *her* hands . . . " He started shaking his head over and over again, until the confident self came back. "If you bring me the shroud," he began with a sly smile.

"Let us go," Iseult said as he gently guided Finn toward the door.

Gilion lunged for the map still in Iseult's hand, but Iseult spun away from Finn and held it easily out of his reach. The walls of the small house began to tremble with some unseen force, and within moments were shaking violently. Dust covered books and pottery toppled to the ground, creating huge puffs of powder as they hit.

Àed grabbed Finn and pushed her through the door as Iseult opened it. The trio ran down the hill with the earth trembling beneath their feet, not taking the time to look back. As they reached the riverbank and their nervous horses, their attention was drawn by a series of resounding crashes. They turned back to see that the walls of Gilion's home had begun to crumble, and were falling in on themselves.

"We have to help him!" Finn panted as she turned pleading eyes toward Àed.

"He is already too far gone," he said sadly, just as the roof fell in.

The tears that had never really stopped since Gilion began speaking now flowed even harder down Finn's face. Gilion had not been particularly pleasant, but she suspected that he had been tormented by some unseen force. Even if he had destroyed his own home to get rid of them, Finn felt compelled to go back and see if he still lived. She thought of Keiren and what a terrible person she must be, but did not say so out loud.

A caravan of travelers that had been making their way down the Sand Road approached the bank to see what the commotion was. It was obvious that they could all see the rubble of the house now that whatever enchantment Gilion had placed upon it was destroyed.

"We need to go," Iseult stated as he glanced back at the gathering crowd.

Àed shook his head one last time at the sight of Gillion's crumbled house. "Aye, I fear we must be goin'."

Finn spared a final glance at the rubble, then aided her companions as they calmed their frightened horses. A few spectators looked questioningly at them, but then seemed to decide that they had simply happened upon the sight like the rest of them.

Óengus had not expected the building to come down so quickly. He had worried that Àed would sense him as he crouched beneath the back window of the house, but the old man had obviously been too distracted.

He had run in the opposite direction when the foundation began to shake, and was sure that the party had not seen him.

After the spectators had continued on their way down the Sand Road, he crept back up to the crumbled foundation. As he watched, several of the large stones that had composed the walls of the house were shifted aside. A moment later, out poked the head of Gilion, looking rather startled, but no worse for wear.

"What happened?" Gilion asked, looking up at Óengus.

Óengus stared down at him for a moment. "Your house crumbled down around you."

Gilion scowled. "It was *her*. I would never have brought my own house down." Gilion craned his neck around, looking for a means of escape.

"I might be able to help you out of this rubble," Óengus offered.

"I used to know how," Gilion said, looking quite pitiful. "I can't seem to remember things these days."

Óengus tried to hide his annoyance. "Quite alright. I'll just need a favor in return."

Gilion perked up. "A favor? Yes, anything. Just get me loose."

Óengus smiled. The Faie Queen's shroud could be worth quite a bit more coin than a silly tree girl.

CHAPTER TWENTY-THREE

She paced back and forth across the cold rock floor in a tower that rose far above the surrounding hills. The unyielding stone of the tower bore a resemblance to the expression on her face. She stopped and gazed out through a small window in the stone. Her icy blue eyes reflecting the sunlight made her look blind to the woman sitting in the corner, awaiting orders.

Bedelia had been summoned to her lady's side early that morning, but had not learned much in the hours since she arrived.

"I cannot see them," Keiren snapped as she turned away from the window. "She cannot reach it first." Keiren twined her deep red hair through her fingers in a rare show of anxiety.

"Cannot see whom?" Bedelia questioned, surprised that anyone could escape her lady's clairvoyant sight.

Keiren whirled on her, making Bedelia sit up a little more erect. Despite the light leather armor she wore,

Bedelia suddenly feared for her life. It was a gift of Keiren's, instilling fear. She'd driven many a mortal insane without lifting a finger.

The feeling of panic was suddenly dampened as Keiren approached seductively. The quick change made Bedelia light-headed. Keiren came to stand in front of her and reached a hand out to Bedelia's short, dark hair, wrapping its ends around her fingertips before letting it fall back against Bedelia's neck.

"It has been a long while since you came to me," Keiren said coyly as her icy eyes bored into Bedelia's dark brown ones.

Bedelia smiled. "I have been sailing the Summer Isles in search of the Archtree my lady, as you requested."

Keiren smiled back, and leaned down to place a gentle kiss on Bedelia's lips. "I have missed you," she said as she stood straight, pulling Bedelia up with her.

Keiren was taller than Bedelia by several inches. It did not say much about Bedelia's height, as Keiren was taller than many men as well. Keiren leaned her neck down to kiss Bedelia again. "I have a new task for you," she whispered a hair's breadth from Bedelia's mouth.

"Anything," Bedelia whispered in return, feeling the call of her lover's lips like lightning pulsing through her veins.

Keiren's lips curled into a smile, still within kissing distance. "There is a girl traveling with my father. Something hides her from my sight. Gain her trust, and bring her to me."

Bedelia smiled a predatory smile in return. "With pleasure, my lady."

∿ ·

"What is it like in Migris?" Finn asked as they rode. They had a week before they would reach the great city, and Finn wanted to know as much as possible by then.

Iseult glanced over at her before replying. "It borders the ocean. Within its walls is the largest port along the Melted Sea. Much of the trade from the distant marches runs through the port of Migris, which makes for large fluctuations of people within the city. It is also very windy there, and often very cold."

"Why is it called the Melted Sea?" she asked, thinking it was a rather strange name for an ocean.

"Sometimes large chunks of ice can be spotted in the sea, larger even than the largest of ships," Iseult explained. "There is a legend that the entire sea was once composed of ice, but that much of the ice melted, making it what it is today."

"What melted it?" Finn asked curiously.

Iseult shrugged. "It is only a legend, and as is the case in most legends, it was the Faie who melted the sea."

Finn glanced over at Àed. He had spoken very little since they'd heard news of Keiren. Gilion had claimed that Keiren was after the shroud, but Finn still felt that the shroud was better left unfound. What she wanted to find was the Archtree.

Finn knew that the tree was her only real chance for answers. The Travelers had given her some idea of who she was. Then Gilion . . . Finn did not want to believe what Gilion had said. The old man was mad, and could not be trusted.

Although, she could not call the man a liar, not for certain, as she still did not know her past. If her people had been the ones to turn her into a tree, wouldn't they have found a way for her to keep her memories? Unless her memories did not serve the Cavari's purpose. Finn shook her head in an attempt to shake the thoughts away. Soon she would have the truth.

She had not spoken to Iseult about the shroud since Gilion had revealed what the shroud was really for. Her heart hurt for Iseult. He had wanted to use the shroud to contact his family. Now he would simply have to settle for any answers the Archtree might offer him.

"Now explain to me again how to find the Archtree," Finn requested in order to distract herself.

"The map shows that it is on an island, far North in the Melted Sea," Iseult explained. "We will find a small ship in Migris, and do our best to navigate by compass in order to find it."

It seemed to Finn that it would be rather hard to navigate when all of the water looked the same. "This map has existed for over a century," she began. "Why has no one else sought to use it?"

Iseult looked off into the distance for an extended period of time, as if he were debating what to say. "My people created the map," Iseult reminded her. "After we discovered the Archtree, and we realized that it was in fact the tree of legend, we did not want others to find it. We created the map to appear as if it led to nothing of value, just the small uninhabitable islands farther North than most feel the need to sail," he finished. "It was kept in the Archives simply because it was old."

"But-" Finn hesitated, "how did your people find it in the first place?"

"As it was told to me by my mother," he explained, "A group of Uí Néid sailors had set out on an expedition to map the Summer Isles, though most of the isles are just large jagged rocks. In times of bad storms, many ships had been destroyed by them. My people wanted to map the isles so that they would not run afoul of them in times of low visibility. It was while mapping these isles that the Archtree was discovered.

"The crew had landed on one of the larger islands to seek out any resources that might be found. As the night grew chill, they made a fire from some dead branches that had fallen off of a grand tree. As some of the smoke from the fire entered the crews' lungs, they began to hallucinate. To each member, the truths he most fiercely sought were revealed. Upon waking the next morning, the crew realized what they had found and created a map."

It was quite a story, but there was one thing still unclear to Finn. "You say that the crew was given answers without asking. How do you know that the Archtree will lead you to the shroud?" she asked.

"It was my mother's greatest wish to absolve my people of what brought their end. The theft of the shroud was what brought about the war, and it should be returned to the Faie," he explained. "The location of the shroud is the answer I want more than any other."

"I thought you wanted to give the shroud back to the Cavari, not the Faie," Finn prompted.

"I believe the Cavari to be Faie, and you are Cavari. Giving you the shroud will absolve my people," Iseult said.

Àed had ridden further ahead, obviously not interested in their conversation. Finn did not blame him, he had enough on his mind.

"The Cavari stole the Faie Queen's shroud from the Travelers," Iseult went on, revealing details that Finn had not yet heard. "The Ceàrdaman were my people's allies, once. They told us of the theft of the shroud, but we were misled on what the shroud actually does, apparently. Though I do not know the histories of that particular exchange, I'm sure they did not actually lie. The Travelers have a way with words. They could, given the time, make you believe the sky is green . . . " he trailed off.

"Did the Travelers ask your people to steal the shroud back?" Finn prompted, seeing that Iseult's mind had gone elsewhere.

Iseult shook his head. "They were not even aware that we stole it at all. My people believed the shroud to be a connection to the dead, another great secret, like the Archtree. We did not want to steal it for the Travelers. We wanted it for ourselves."

Finn was silent, waiting for Iseult to go on.

"Then the Faie War started," he said finally. "My people refused to tell the Travelers why the Cavari, who had been peaceful until then, attacked us so ferociously. We could not tell them that we had stolen what had been taken from them, only to keep it for ourselves.

"Though Uí Néid possessed greater numbers, the Cavari had powers that we had not imagined. My people were nearly decimated, though they took many Cavari with them. A portion of my clan was left alive, including my great, great grandmother, who was with child at the time.

We held our histories close, never forgetting what had happened, but never sharing it with others either," he finished with a distant look on his face.

"Why did the Cavari stop? You would think they would have attacked until the shroud was returned to them," Finn prompted.

"We do not know," Iseult answered. "Most of them disappeared. The few that remained continued to pick off my clan members over the decades. Now I am all that remains, at least as far as I know."

"Why did you not tell me all of this before?" Finn asked as tears streamed gently down her face.

"I recognized your face from a book the first night I saw you," Iseult explained. "You were special, even among your people. I feared-" he paused. "I feared that you would want to carry out the will of your people once your memory returned. I did not want to speed that process until I'd had the chance to convince you that I want to end the blood-shed, and to keep it from happening again."

"A war between two of the only remaining members of two ancient clans is not much of a war," Finn said as she managed a weak laugh through her tears.

"I believe your people still exist," Iseult offered. "They were not killed by the people of Uí Néid, at the very least, and I believe that the battle in the Blood Forest was the start of the next Faie war. We must stop it before all is lost."

"We will know more when we reach the Archtree," Finn replied. "The answer I want most is what events transpired that led to me becoming a tree."

"Ye two would be surprised at what answers ye really want the most," Àed called back bitterly.

Finn and Iseult rode to catch up with him. "What do you mean?" Finn asked.

Àed spat on the ground. "To know one's truest heart's intent is a very rare thing. Rarer still is the event of one's heart lying in the past. We may believe the past is what matters most to us, but really, it is the present and the future. It is hope that matters most."

A pall of silence fell over the party, as Iseult and Finn both worried about their current hopes obscuring their pasts from them. They rode on like that until the sun set, and they made camp in a forested area, feeling somber and weary.

Finn stared up at the stars from within her bedroll, sandwiched between Àed and Iseult. She let out a deep sigh. Even if she never managed to find answers, there was still hope. She knew her two companions would not abandon her. She would survive.

As she drifted off to sleep, she thought she felt some sort of connection with the earth, almost like the feeling she would get when she still had roots to place into the ground. Perhaps it was because she'd found that people could have roots too, only they were attached to other people instead of the soil.

The night was still and quiet as the three companions slept deeply. Then, a slight shudder could be felt below the earth around the three sleeping forms. Ever so slowly, serpent-like roots forced their way out of the damp soil, searching for their quarry. As they freed themselves, they began to creep across the still form of the Dair Child, crawling up her legs, torso, and finally her face, until all that could be seen was a strand of long, dark-blond hair reaching toward Iseult's sleeping form as if begging to be saved. She should never have gotten so far. Time was running out.

The End

Continue on for a sneak peek at book two!

NOTE FROM THE AUTHOR

I hope you've enjoyed the first installment in the Tree of Ages Series. Reviews are the life-blood of Indie Authors, so please take the time to leave one!

For news and updates, please sign up for my mailing list by visiting:

www.saracroethle.com

GLOSSARY

A

Àed (ay-add)- a conjurer of some renown, also known as "The Mountebank"

Anders (ahn-durs)- a young, archive scholar.

Arthryn (are-thrin)- alleged Alderman of Sormyr. Seen by few.

B

Bannock- unleavened loaf of bread, often sweetened with honey.

Bladdered- drunk

Boobrie- large, colorful, bird-like Faie that lures travelers away from the path.

Branwen (bran-win)- a young, archive scholar.

C

Cavari- prominent clan of the *Dair Leanbh.*

Ceàrdaman (see-air-duh-maun)- The Craftspeople, often referred to as *Travelers.* Believed to be Faie in origin.

À Choille Fala (ah choi-le-uh fall-ah)- The Blood Forest. Either a refuge or prison for the Faie.

Ceilidh (kay-lee)- A festival, often involving dancing and a great deal of whiskey.

D

Dair Leanbh (dare lan-ub)- Oak Child. Proper term for a race of beings with affinity for the earth. Origins unknown.

Dram- a small unit of liquid measure, often referring to whiskey.

Dullahan (doo-la-han)- Headless riders of the Faie. Harbingers of death.

F

Finnur (fin-uh)- member of Clan Cavari.

G

Garenoch (gare-en-och)- small, southern burgh. A well-used travel stop.

Geancanach (gan-can-och)- small, mischievous Faie with craggy skin and bat-like wings. Travel in Packs.

Glen- narrow, secluded valley.

Gray City- See *Sormyr*

Grogoch (grow-gok)- smelly Faie covered in red hair, roughly the size of a child. Impervious to heat and cold.

Gwrtheryn (gweir-thare-in)- Alderman of Garenoch. Deathly afraid of Faie.

H

Haudin (hah-din)- roughly built homes, often seen in areas of lesser wealth.

I

Iseult (ee-sult)- allegedly the last living member of Uí Neíd.

K

Kai- escort of the Gray Lady.

Keiren (kigh-rin)- daughter of the Mountebank. Whereabouts unknown.

L

Liaden (lee-ay-din)- the Gray Lady.

M

Meirleach (myar-lukh)- word in the old tongue meaning *thief.*

Merrows- water dwelling Faie capable of taking the shape of sea creatures. Delight in luring humans to watery deaths.

Midden- garbage.

Migris- one of the Great Cities, and also a large trade port.

Muntjac- small deer.

N

Neeps- turnips.

O

Óengus (on-gus)- a notorious bounty hunter.

P

Pooks- also known as Bucca, small Faie with both goat and human features. Nocturnal.

Port Ainfean (ine-feen)- a medium-sized fishing port along the River Cair, a rumored haven for smugglers.

R

Reiver (ree-vur)- borderland raiders.

S

Sand Road- travel road beginning in Felgram and spanning all the way to Migris.

Scunner- an insult referring to someone strongly disliked.

Sgal (skal)- a strong wind.

Sgain Dubh (skee-an-doo)- a small killing knife, carried by roguish characters.

Slàinte (slawn-cha)- a toast to good health.

Sormyr (sore-meer)- one of the Great Cities, also known as the Gray City.

T

Travelers- see *Ceàrdaman*.

Trow- large Faie resembling trees. Rumored to steal children.

U

Uí Néid (ooh ned)- previously one of the great cities, now nothing more than a ruin.

TREE OF AGES READING ORDER

Tree of Ages

The Melted Sea

The Blood Forest

Queen of Wands

The Oaken Throne

ALSO BY SARA C ROETHLE

The Bitter Ashes Series

Death Cursed

Collide and Seek

Rock, Paper, Shivers

Duck, Duck, Noose

Shoots and Tatters

The Thief's Apprentice Series

Clockwork Alchemist

Clocks and Daggers

Under Clock and Key

The Xoe Meyers Series

Xoe

Accidental Ashes

Broken Beasts

Demon Down

Forgotten Fires

Gone Ghost

Minor Magic

SNEAK PEEK OF BOOK TWO, THE
MELTED SEA

CHAPTER ONE

Finn was bruised, sore, and lying in a ditch. She reached a shaky hand to dab at the blood on her forehead, then listened for signs of pursuit. Her waist-length, light brown hair hung loosely around her, adorned with broken twigs, grass, and dirt. One of the trees blocking her view of the far-off path shifted slightly. The minute movement of the branches would be perceived as wind catching the leaves, but Finn knew better. These *trees* protected her from her captors. . .

She had gone to sleep beside Iseult, the night after they'd left Port Ainfean. She was restless with excitement for the journey ahead, but at the same time was troubled with thoughts on what Gilion had revealed to them. Àed had hoped that his one time friend would have information on who Finn really was. Unfortunately, it was not information that any of them had chosen to accept. Gilion had implied that Finn and Iseult were enemies, or at least they should be. He'd also made it clear that Finn would likely turn on Iseult, once she remembered who and what she was. Yet, Iseult clearly did not believe that Finn would turn against him, else he wouldn't sleep so easily beside her. His black hair, flecked with gray surprising for a younger man, glinted in the moonlight. She almost wanted to reach out and touch it, reassuring herself that this man who'd done so much to protect her was real, but she didn't want to wake him.

She sighed. She would feel better in the morning once Iseult and Àed were awake, and the three of them could have breakfast together. It was that thought alone that allowed her to finally drift off to sleep, and it was the first thought on her mind as she woke gasping for breath.

Leathery appendages entwined around her body, nearly crushing her, but not quite. Soil scratched against the back of her scalp as she struggled to free herself, but it was no use. Suddenly sunlight stung her eyes as whatever entrapped her began to loosen its grip, moving away from her face and neck. Now that she could see, her pattering heart sank. Massive roots were slowly peeling away from her body to return to the earth. They were the same roots that had crushed a man to death before her very eyes. The man had been attempting to kill Kai, but that didn't make the roots any less frightening.

Her eyes searched frantically for Iseult or Àed as the roots retreated, or perhaps even Kai, come to find her after she ran away from him in Port Ainfean. What she hadn't expected was Branwen. At first, Finn was filled with excitement to see her friend alive and well, but that excitement was soon dampened as she took in the blankness in Branwen's honey-colored eyes. The young woman stared down at her apathetically, her tawny red hair hanging matted and dirty down the sides of her angular face. The noonday sun illuminated Branwen's hair so that it looked like fire.

It was only when Branwen turned to look over her shoulder that Finn noticed the creatures gathered around them. Their lower bodies looked just like horses, with fur done in grays and muddy whites, but it was their upper bodies that held Finn's attention. They looked almost human, but with gray, bloodless skin. Gaunt faces were dominated by uptilted, pure red, pupil-less eyes. The creatures appeared to be male, and had an eerie *sameness* to them, down to their lank, silvery hair.

One spoke to Branwen in a language that sounded familiar to Finn, though she didn't understand it. Branwen nodded, then silently helped Finn to her feet and brushed the loose soil from Finn's burgundy skirts. Branwen's deep red cloak was tattered and full of burs, but she didn't seem to notice. She looked like she had been crawling through the underbrush for a week, and it appeared that she'd had very little food in the process, judging by the gauntness of her face and the thinness of her limbs.

"Branwen," Finn whispered, "where are Iseult and Àed?"

Branwen stared at her as the half-man half-horse creatures shifted impatiently. Finn thought that Branwen might not answer, but then she licked her dry, cracked lips and said, "Gone."

Finn inhaled sharply. "What do you mean, *gone?*"

One of the creatures stepped forward and stomped its front hooves inches from Finn's boots. It said something in its guttural language while it gazed down at

Finn with a sneer on its thin lips. A moment later, hands wrapped around Finn's upper arms, lifting her to standing, then all the way off her feet. She didn't resist as she was put upon the back of another one of the creatures, given that her only other choice was to stay dangling in mid-air.

Her skirts hiked up around her legs, she placed her hands against the creature's back to steady herself as the one who had grabbed her let go. She was surprised by the velvety texture of the creature's fur, many times softer than that of a horse. Giving Finn no time to recover, the creatures began to trot in a cohesive unit, jostling her senses, and taking her away from any clues as to how she'd arrived in that place to begin with. She leaned forward and squeezed her legs around the creature's equine back for dear life, not daring to wrap her arms around the humanoid torso.

Panicked, she looked around, hoping for some sign to tell her where she was. The trees here were tall, with broad, star-shaped leaves instead of needles, and the ground was more loamy and green, nothing like the rocky landscape she'd gone to sleep in.

The creature carrying Branwen on its back hurried to catch up to Finn's creature, allowing the two women to ride side by side.

Finn looked over at Branwen silently, afraid to ask her more questions that would garner no real answers. "Where is your brother?" she asked finally. "We left you in his care, but when we returned from the Blood Forest, you were both gone."

Branwen's expression didn't change in the slightest at

the mention of her brother. Instead, she pointed to a structure in the distance.

There was ample moisture and fog in the air, making it difficult for Finn to see the structure clearly, but it looked like it had once been a castle, long since fallen into disrepair. The towers that she could see were partially crumbled, leaving only the lower part of the structure possibly inhabitable. They were several miles off, so she could not distinguish whether or not anyone currently dwelled there.

Finn gulped as her brain rattled from the creature's continued trot. "Is that where we're going?"

"Cavari," Branwen stated.

Finn's thoughts came to a violent halt at the name of her tribe. She had little information on them, and was beginning to strongly suspect that they were the ones who had turned her into a tree, leaving her with few memories, and no explanations. They had also eliminated Iseult's people.

As far as Finn knew, she had aided in the slaughter, at least in the beginning. Then, one hundred years ago, she was left alone in a field as a tree. Could the Cavari be the ones responsible for taking her away from Iseult and Àed? If they had left her as a tree, why would they want her now? Finn shivered. Perhaps they just wanted to root her back in the ground. Weeks ago, she would have accepted such a fate willingly, but now, she was unsure.

"Branwen," Finn whispered, not wanting to draw her captor's attention, though she doubted the horse creatures spoke her language, "I do not think we should go there." She subtly gestured to the castle in the distance.

Branwen glanced at her, then turned to stare straight ahead, dismissing her. Finn searched around for some way to escape, or to at least slow their progress. She wasn't ready to face her people, especially when she didn't know where Iseult and Àed were, or if they were even still alive.

As Finn scanned her surroundings, something caught her eye. It was just the barest hint of movement in the trees. She would have passed it off as nothing, but then she saw it again. The trees along the path they followed were moving in.

Some of the man-horse creatures realized something was amiss, and began barking orders in their strange language. They halted their forward progress and closed in around Finn, though whether they were protecting her, or just preventing her escape was unclear. Whatever they were doing, it obscured Finn's view of the moving trees.

Tension was thick in the air as they waited. Finn's heart thudded in her chest, making it difficult to focus. She sat up as straight as she could, trying to see what was happening. Her panic grew until it felt like she could no longer breathe. The cold air that did find its way in stung her lungs. If she was going to escape, now would be the time, but how?

Her question was answered a moment later as the ground began to tremble. Finn screamed as massive roots shot up from the earth, scattering dirt throughout the air and tossing her equine captors aside like they weighed nothing.

Finn was knocked from her perch to the ground, and would have been trampled by the horse-creature's hooves if one of the roots hadn't darted in to fling her aside. She flew through the air, then hit the ground hard, several feet away. She huddled on the ground for a moment as she tried to regain her breath, then knowing she might soon run out of time, she rolled to the side away from the chaos caused by the roots.

She forced herself to continue rolling, and soon hit a downhill slope. She picked up momentum, hitting painfully against rocks on her way down until she landed in a heap at the bottom of the gully. The trees around her quickly uprooted, then moved on spindly, wooden limbs to replant themselves in front of her, blocking her view of the road. She could hear shouting in the distance, and the thundering of hooves as the man-horse creatures stampeded across the countryside, looking for her. She held a hand to her head, and came away with blood, as a group of the creatures trotted merely twenty feet away from where she was hiding, within the tightly packed group of trees.

Once they'd passed, she quickly returned her hand to her side. It was important to be still. She closed her eyes and gripped her fingers in the damp grass as the shouting continued, and hoof beats thundered all around. The sounds surrounded her for what felt like ages, but eventually they grew distant as the search party deemed the area clear. When the hoof beats could no longer be heard, one of the trees near her bent itself in half, bringing its upper branches toward her face.

The Trow opened its eyes and smiled down at her. It looked much like the Trow she had met in the Blood Forest, with its rough bark and spindly limbs, but she was very far from that place. The Trow's deep green eyes grew concerned when Finn did not return its smile. The jagged crevices in its bark flexed in and out as it took long breaths through its knobby, wooden nose.

"What has happened, Tree Sister?" the Trow inquired kindly in a voice that sounded like bark scraping over rocks.

The other Trow that had helped conceal her all turned curious gazes down to where she still lay.

She shook her head minutely, having no idea how to answer the question. What *had* happened? She'd been stolen away by roots while she slept, but now the same roots had just saved her.

Taking her silence for fear, the Trow comforted, "The Ceinteár are gone now. You're safe."

Finn wiped at the tears streaming down her cheeks as she tried to rise, only to double over in pain. A large rock had jabbed into her ribs on the way down, and it felt like one might be cracked or broken.

"The roots," she began, gritting her teeth against the pain as she forced herself to standing, "they've saved me before, yet they also brought me here. Do you control them?"

The lead Trow seemed confused. "My lady, only one of the Dair can control nature in such a way."

Finn shook her head, spilling her long hair forward over her shoulders as she panted in pain. "I was being taken to the Cavari. Why would my people save me from themselves?"

The Trow looked confused again, until another one stepped forward. This one seemed older than the rest, with large lumps and gray areas mottling its bark. "My lady," it began in a gravelly voice as it gazed down at her, "only one of the Dair could accomplish such a feat. We simply stepped in to shelter you."

"But the roots that brought me to this place . . . " she

trailed off, not understanding why some roots helped, and some hurt.

The Trow shrugged, if the awkward creaking of the bark on its shoulders could be called a shrug. "Perhaps you saved yourself, or perhaps you have friends you've yet to be made aware of. Not all Dair are Cavari."

Finn's head began to spin. She sincerely hoped her skull hadn't suffered any damage. What the Trow said about her saving herself couldn't be correct. She couldn't control anything in nature, especially not without meaning to. Yet the thought of other Dair involving themselves was no more comforting. She knew the Cavari had not been the only tribe involved in the world of man. There were others, at least at one point in time. Whether they were friend or foe, she did not know.

The Trow around Finn waited patiently while she attempted to gather her wits about her, but said wits were nowhere to be found.

~

Kai had been following Finn and the others since they'd departed from Ainfean. At first he'd thought he'd never find them, as there were many tracks leading out of the port town, but sticking to the Sand Road had proven the correct choice. By sleeping little, and taking no time to rest during the day, he'd eventually caught sight of them, only to fall behind before he was spotted in return.

When Finn had left him, Kai had been at first relieved to learn that she had rejoined with Iseult and Àed, but then he'd also learned that they were being followed by a silver haired man. Kai had little doubt that the man in question was Óengus. He'd been curious about Finn back in Baden-mar, which meant he was likely out for the bounty on her head. Óengus was an exceedingly dangerous man, and Kai wouldn't mind being the one to keep Finn from him, if only to prove that he wasn't the man she thought he was. He was sure that once he proved her wrong, he could let her go and move on with his life.

He liked to think that he had rescued her from trouble the first time too, never mind the fact that he was the one that put her in said trouble to begin with, stealing her away from Iseult and Àed in an attempt to gather the same bounty that Óengus was likely after. He sighed as he thought back to the moment she awoke, realizing that he and Anna had betrayed her. Oh, how angry she had been.

Kai could admit to himself now that half the reason he took her was because she intended to branch off with Iseult and Àed the next day, leaving Kai and Anna behind. He wasn't sure why he couldn't just let her go. He was good at letting go. In fact, it was what he did best. Anna wouldn't hear of it though, and after what she had been through in the Blood Forest, he hadn't the heart to tell her no. Plus, it delayed his parting with Finn.

After the initial sighting, he'd continued to follow them, leaving enough distance that they would not catch sight of him. In the evening, they'd made camp, and he'd listened as Iseult and Finn had a rather odd conversation about things out of legend. They'd spoken of the Archtree, and the Faie Queen's shroud, objects straight out of Faiery stories for children. Yet, they'd spoken of them as if they intended to *find* them.

Kai crouched in the darkness as the party's conversation died down, and they eventually crawled into their bedrolls. Finn lay between the two men, who were understandably fearful of losing her again. He waited a while longer, until the night grew still, and the party fell into the gentle rhythms of sleep. Hoping that his movements would not wake anyone, he stood to retreat back to where he'd left his horse, but a sudden movement caught his eye in the darkness. Something serpentine was creeping up near Finn's feet. At first Kai thought *snake*, and was about to rush forward, when countless other *snakes* appeared. They writhed upward in the moonlight, and Kai suddenly realized what they were. *Roots*. Just like the roots that had crushed a man to death in front of Kai while he traveled alone with Finn. He'd speculated that *she* had called those roots forth, but there was no way she had called these. Her small form was perfectly still, deep in the throes of sleep.

He ran forward to save her, pushing aside the memory of the mangled corpse that had been left behind on the previous occasion. He couldn't seem to run fast enough as the roots multiplied and swarmed, fully covering Finn's body, and the bodies of her two companions. Reaching her, he pulled a knife from his belt and hacked away at the vine-like tendrils. The roots coated his hands in their sticky blood as he cut and pulled them away, but the more he removed, the more quickly the roots swarmed. He continued cutting frantically until he reached bottom of the mass to reveal only bare ground. Finn was *gone*.

Panting with exertion, he turned to the other two root-covered mounds, illuminated by the moonlight. With grunts of panic and frustration, he began to chop away at one of them, all the while glancing back at where Finn should have been. Àed gasped for breath as Kai revealed first his head, then his chest. Tears stung at the back of Kai's eyes as Àed struggled free from the rest of the roots, then aided Kai as he freed Iseult. Once Iseult could breathe, Kai fell back, feeling numb and shaken, and let Áed help the other man with the rest of the vines around him. Finn was lost, and it was all Kai's fault. If only he'd been faster. If he hadn't stood gawking when the roots first appeared, he could have saved her.

Once free of his trappings, it didn't take Iseult long to recover. Instantly comprehending Finn's absence, he jumped on Kai like a ravenous beast, knocking him to the ground as he pressed a knife to his throat. Exhausted from his efforts against the roots, Kai barely reacted, not that Iseult had given him much of a chance. Kai felt himself once again in awe of how fast the man could move.

"Where is she?" Iseult growled into his face. His black hair, flecked with gray, tousled from sleep, gave him a wild appearance to mirror the intensity in his grayish green eyes.

"Gone," Kai rasped against the pressure on his throat, "but through no doing of my own." He wouldn't have minded if Iseult had stabbed him right then. He felt little fear at the notion.

Iseult's face crumbled slightly, but his anger was back in the blink of an eye. "Why did you help us?" he asked, his voice barely above a whisper. "Why not simply leave us to die?"

"I'd answer you," Kai managed to grunt, "if I could breathe." He could feel blood welling on his throat as Iseult pressed the finely-honed knife against his skin. Kai was quite sure that he was about to die.

"I should kill you now," Iseult stated coldly, affirming Kai's suspicions.

"Iseult," Àed said calmly, standing back while he brushed the dirt and sap from his ragged clothing, though Kai could make out little else in the darkness. "Let the lad go."

The stinging at his throat made Kai grateful for the interjection. Unfortunately, he was not sure Iseult was going to listen to Àed's advice. More pressure was applied to the blade, to the point where he thought it might cut through more than just skin. The rage in Iseult's eyes spelled the end for Kai.

"*Iseult*," Àed said more firmly. "Finn wouldnae want the lad harmed. I can assure ye of that."

Before Kai could even blink, Iseult was off him, stalking away into the dark trees like an angry predator. Kai had just gathered his wits enough to rise, when Àed's face came into view above him. He offered Kai a hand up, which Kai took appreciatively.

Once he was on his feet, he dabbed at the blood on his throat and looked down at the aged conjurer who'd rescued him. Àed still wore the tattered gray robes that he'd worn when Kai first met him, topped with a burlap cap in even worse shape than the robes. Though his long, silvery hair was matted from sleep, his sky blue eyes were as sharp and clear as ever, looking almost eerily bright in the moonlight.

Those aqua eyes watched Kai steadily. "What did ye see?" he asked suspiciously.

Kai's thoughts raced. He wasn't exactly sure *what* he'd seen. The roots had been just like the ones that killed one of the thugs that attacked him and Finn in the woods, but in that instance, a body had been left behind. No one had been sucked into the earth like Finn.

Kai gestured with both hands to the dismembered roots strewn all about them, oozing dark fluid into the soil where Kai's knife had sliced them. "They covered her like a mass of snakes," he explained. "I did my best to cut them away and free her, but when I reached the bottom, she was gone."

He felt a sudden jolt in his gut at his own words. The roots had taken her, but that didn't mean she was dead. He had suspected that Finn had somehow summoned the roots that killed the thug that day, what seemed like ages ago. She was of the Dair, after all, though he wasn't quite sure what that meant. All he knew for sure was that she wasn't entirely human, and had been trapped in the form of a tree for nearly a century. Still, despite what magic she might possess, he highly doubted that she would summon the roots to steal herself away while she slept. She had been searching for Àed and Iseult, and Kai saw no reason for her to leave them.

Àed muttered under his breath and examined the severed roots. He picked one large chunk up off the ground and held it up to his nose, then dropped it as his lined face crinkled in disgust.

"It's a good thing she's been shining brighter than the sun," Àed said more to himself than to Kai. "She should be easy enough to find."

Hope welled up inside Kai. "So she's alive?"

Àed spat on the ground. "Aye, lad, though what state she's in, I cannae say. I imagine we'll want to be leavin' as soon as Iseult returns."

Kai felt sick again. "We?"

Àed chortled. "Ye've been following us for a reason, and I'm not about to suppose ye've fallen in love with *me*."

Kai's mouth went dry. "I haven't fallen in love with anyone. I followed out of curiosity, nothing more."

"I'd call you a liar," a voice called from out of the darkness, "if I thought you'd take offense."

Kai backed away as a now-calm Iseult approached, but Iseult paid him little mind. Instead he went to stand beside Àed. The two of them peered off into the darkness together, looking odd with the great difference in their heights.

"How far is she?" Iseult asked.

Àed left Iseult's side to untangle their bedrolls from the dead roots. "Far enough, lad. I can sense the direction, but little else. She seems to be on the move."

Iseult finally turned back to Kai. "I imagine you have a horse hidden somewhere around here?"

Kai nodded. He'd left his horse hidden in a copse of trees, fearing the animal would snort or whinny, alerting those he was spying on of his presence. "I'll be out of your sight in no time."

He turned to make his escape, but stopped in his tracks as Iseult said, "I don't think so." Kai turned back around as Iseult continued, "I will not kill you for Finn's sake, but I will not let you run free where you may harm her again. You will travel with us, and perhaps Finn will let me kill you once we find her."

Kai took another step back. "You caught me unawares the first time, but if I choose to leave, I'm not so sure you could stop me."

Àed, who had set to saddling both his and Iseult's

nervous horses, if Àed's small, shaggy mount could be called a horse, chuckled to himself. "Yer just going to follow us anyhow, so ye may as well do as Iseult demands."

Kai's mood soured at that, because it was the truth. He knew he couldn't just let her go. He had to at least know what had happened to her, even if he chose to never see her again after that. Finn thought that he was a bad man. A liar, and a thief. She was right, but it didn't make him want to change her mind any less.

Finn stumbled through the woods, carrying herself in the opposite direction of the ruined castle as quickly as possible. She knew she would need to face her people at some point, but she would do it on *her* terms. She would not let them treat her like an object, something they could stick in the ground, then summon when it suited them.

She shivered as she thought back to the roots *she* had allegedly controlled, though she'd consciously done nothing to call them. The only explanation was that someone else had controlled them, someone who might be watching her, even now.

If the roots were controlled by someone else, she had no idea of their intentions. Even with that distraction, her escape would not have been successful without the help of the Trow, so what was the point? Had whomever summoned the vines known the Trow would step in to aid her? Had the Trow lied when they claimed they didn't know who summoned the roots?

Finn shook her head, unable to believe the Trow had

deceived her. She had given them her thanks before departing, but it didn't seem like enough. Trow had helped her in the Blood Forest too, and once again while she was held prisoner by Anna and Kai.

Finn's thoughts trailed off on that recollection. What she wouldn't give to be back in one of the warm taverns of Port Ainfean with Kai. As quickly as the thought had come to her, she shook it away. It was a product of her cold hands and empty belly, nothing more.

She looked down at the hem of her dirty burgundy dress to her oversized shoes. Neither offered much warmth, and it seemed much colder in this new region, compared to where she had left Iseult and Àed. It didn't help that she had appeared without her bedroll or any provisions. The Trow had helped to conceal her, but they couldn't keep her warm.

Even though every step was painful, her body bruised and sore, she'd had to leave the Trow and their offer of aid behind. She couldn't help regretting the decision. The Trow couldn't provide her with food and warmth, but they at least offered company. Being alone in the woods, with the strange trees and unrecognizable vegetation, she found herself more frightened than she had been at any point in the Blood Forest. She had no way of finding food or water, and the only shelter she'd seen was the ruined castle, which she wanted to stay away from at all costs.

Her fears grew as the sun inched steadily toward the horizon, threatening to leave her alone in the dark. She quickened her pace, though her ribs ached and she felt dizzy with exhaustion.

Eventually, despite her efforts, Finn's fears were realized. Darkness came, and still she walked, panic blossoming inside her. As the last hints of sunshine disappeared, Finn thought she heard an animal growl somewhere to her right. She froze, struggling to see anything within the trees. When no further sounds emanated, she started walking again, repeating in her head that she would be fine, as her breath fogged the chilly night air.

Some time later, panting and drenched in a cold sweat, Finn caught sight of the moon. Its full light swept across the open expanse between the trees. Though the light made Finn's surroundings seem eerie, she was still relieved. The night she'd been taken was a full moon, which meant she hadn't lost much time unconscious. Perhaps only a single night.

She increased her pace, not sure where she was going, but knowing she didn't want to remain in the forest. If the Trow had made it this far, it was likely that other Faie had too. She didn't fancy another encounter with the Grogochs, tiny, rock-like creatures with bat wings, that sung their victims into madness or sleep, and the thought of encountering any of the Travelers, the Ceàrdaman, made her sick.

She stumbled over a rock and had to brace herself against a tree to keep from falling. As she huddled against the rough bark, surrounded by a veil of her long hair, she almost thought she saw a flicker of light, too bright to be caused by the distant moon. It had to be a fire. She straightened and tried to find the light again, but it was gone.

Not willing to let her slim hopes of a warm fire go, she pushed away from the tree and stumbled onward, doing her best to head in the direction of where she'd seen the light. Sounds of wildlife seemed to be all around her, spurring Finn onward. The loud hoot of an owl in a tree directly overhead made her jump. She lost her footing and fell to the ground, then heard a low growl somewhere beside her. Acting purely on instinct, she scrambled to her feet and began to run toward an upward slope. She crested the small hill, and relief flooded through her like lightning. She could see the light again.

Finn couldn't make out much through the trees, but she felt sure that the light emanated from a campfire. It was risky approaching a campground without knowing its occupants, but she found she had little choice. Even if they attacked her, well, she'd surely freeze to death in the woods regardless. The sound of a branch breaking echoed behind her, solidifying her decision as she darted forward.

A few minutes more, and the campsite came clearly into view. As far as she could tell, there was only one figure sitting near, absorbing the fire's warmth. Finn guessed the person was female, or otherwise a slender young man.

She closed the rest of the distance, feeling like she might collapse as soon as she reached the fire. The figure looked up from the light, scanning the darkness.

Finn halted a few feet away from the fire, then collapsed to her knees as her heart caught up with her. As soon as she was able, she lifted her eyes to observe the person still seated on the other side of the campfire.

"You scared me half to death," the woman commented, though she didn't seem frightened in the slightest. In fact, she didn't seem surprised by Finn's sudden appearance at all.

Still, Finn let out a sigh of relief. A single woman was much preferable to a campsite full of Ceàrdaman. "I apologize," Finn panted, forcing herself to her feet to take a few steps closer to the fire. "I'm lost, so I followed the light of your fire."

The woman nodded, shaking her loose, shoulder-length brown hair. She smiled warmly. Finn couldn't tell for sure in the dim light, but she thought the woman's eyes were a deep amber. She wore a heavy traveling cloak, obscuring any other details of her appearance.

The woman lifted her hand and gestured for Finn to move closer. "Come and warm yourself before you catch your death. You're lost, you say? Are you hungry?"

Every muscle in Finn's body relaxed with relief. She was saved, at least for the night. She did as the woman bade her, taking a seat on the opposite side of the fire. The warmth seeped into Finn's bones, which had remained cold and achy despite her exertion. Finn lifted her hands to the flames as the other woman began pawing through her nearby satchel. A moment later, she produced something wrapped in cloth. She tossed it to Finn, who fumbled it with her cold fingers, dropping it into her lap. Laughing softly at her own shaky movements, she retrieved the package and opened it, revealing dried meat, and hard, crumbly cheese.

"I can't thank you enough," Finn said, looking up from what seemed like a feast. "I was worried I wouldn't last the night."

The woman smiled softly as she held her hands up to the fire. "It's nothing. I thought I might go mad soon without anyone to talk to, so really, it is you who is saving me."

Finn chewed on a piece of the meat and smiled. "My name is Branwen," she lied, not knowing if there was still a bounty on her head, or if anyone would have even heard of it in these parts.

"Bedelia," the woman replied happily.

Finn took another bite of the tough meat, and Bedelia handed her a water skin to wash it down.

"Forgive me," Finn said after taking a hearty swig of water, "but you don't seem terribly surprised to see me."

Bedelia smiled again. "I heard you running from aways off. I was just debating whether I should flee when you appeared. You looked frightened, so I guessed you weren't barging into my camp to rob me."

Finn nodded at the explanation, though Bedelia's attitude still seemed slightly off. Regardless, her best chance of survival was to remain where there was warmth and food.

Finn scooted a little closer to the fire, feeling safe for the first time that day.

To be continued...

SPECIAL BONUS SHORT STORY!

A TALE OF TWO THIEVES

A Tale of Two Thieves is the origin story of Anna and Kai.

CHAPTER ONE

Anna

Anna peered down at the man lying on her bedroll near the fire, his body cast in moonlight. No, not quite a man. He couldn't have been more than eighteen, perhaps younger. She'd found him beaten and whipped half to death, left alone in one of the many fields bordering the Gray City. She wasn't sure what had inspired her to drag his limp body further away from the city, into a dense copse of trees where the Gray Guard wouldn't likely find them, especially now that it had grown dark. The sympathy she'd felt for the young man had been out of character for her.

She stood from her seat on a nearby rock, moving to crouch beside him. His hair was a rich chestnut color, trailing down the line of his strong jaw, covered with angry purple bruises. She found herself wondering what color his eyes were, then shook her head. Perhaps he'd incurred too much damage during his beating, and would never open them again.

Sighing, she returned to her original seat. He was clearly of the lower class, likely a farmer, or one of the indentured servants trapped in lifelong debt to the Gray City. That he'd been beaten wasn't terribly telling. Perhaps he'd stolen bread for his family, or tried to escape his state of servitude. He was practically a kid. He shouldn't have been blamed for such things.

A rueful expression crossed her sharp features as she shook her head, tossing her long, dark braid over her shoulder. *She* was barely just a kid. At least it felt that way. She was fast approaching her twentieth year, and still had no place to call her own. No family. No *friends*.

The Gray City hadn't been kind to her either. She hadn't been a farmer like the young man on her bedroll. She'd been worse. One of the poor street youth, skulking around the alleys of the Gray City, begging for crumbs. Once she was old enough she'd turned to a life of thievery. She'd been caught one too many times and could no longer return to the city streets without being recognized by the Gray Guard.

Perhaps it was for the best. She'd always wondered what the cities were like up North. Perhaps she'd leave the South altogether and venture to Migris. There were more sailors up that way. She might be able to find work on one of the ships . . . if she could find someone who'd actually hire a woman to their crew. She'd considered cutting off her long hair many times in an attempt to pass as a man, but her large brown eyes were too feminine, and there was no hiding the curves of her body, even with the taut muscles honed from a life of always running away.

The young man groaned, pulling her out of her thoughts. She hurried to his side, kneeling near his limp arm. His eyes fluttered open. In the dim firelight, she thought they were a pale brown, or maybe hazel.

He slowly lifted his arm toward his face, wincing as he touched the bruises along his cheek and jaw. "Where am I?" he muttered.

"Not far from the Gray City," she explained. "I found you half dead in a field."

With a grunt of pain, he sat up, bringing his knees gingerly to his chest as he curled over them, exhausted. "I have to go back," he moaned. "My family cannot pay their debts without me." He shook his head. "I'm such a fool."

Anna knew she should leave him. Now that she'd ensured he wouldn't die, she needed to be on her way. She'd become accustomed to a life of solitude, and she wasn't about to let this young man change that.

She sighed in spite of herself. "What happened?"

He met her gaze for a moment, then dropped his head. "A mistake, that's what. I was fed up with the Guard and acted without thinking. I refused to work the fields to pay my family's debt. Two of the guards dragged me to the field and beat me. I don't remember anything after that."

Anna pursed her lips in thought, then decided, "If that's the case, you cannot go back. You're lucky they only beat you. Others have been hanged for such insolence."

"I have to go back," he said again. "My family needs me."

"Your family thinks you're dead," she countered, "and it's

359

likely for the best. If you return, they too could suffer as a result of your brash actions."

He sighed heavily, shaking his head. "You're right, I know it, but how can I just leave?" He turned hopeful eyes to her, as if she might possess the answers to all of his problems.

She shook her head. She didn't even possess the answers to her own.

"You can travel with me to the nearest burgh," she offered. "You should be healed enough by then to find work."

He turned his head to peer past the fire, toward the distant lights of the Gray City. "What's the point?" he asked softly. "I have nothing left to live for."

She jabbed his shoulder with her fist.

He whipped his gaze back to her, clearly shocked.

"You have yourself to live for, you fool," she chastised. "Do you think I have anything else to live for? At least you knew the love of a family for a time."

He blinked at her, at a seeming loss for words. "I apologize. I wasn't trying to insult you."

She glared at him. "If you don't want to insult me, then don't be a fool. You're young, and you have an entire life to live. You should not take such a gift for granted."

He stared at her. "I suppose you're right," he said after a moment. "Though I still have no idea what I'll do from here."

She sucked her teeth. Why did she even care? She should have no interest in this young, lost, farm boy. "You'll have three days to figure it out while we travel to the next burgh. Now get some rest."

He watched her for a moment more, then nodded. He laid back down on the bed roll, then curled up on his side, turning his back to her. He was far too trusting of a stranger, but then again, she *had* rescued him. He had no reason to fear her.

Still sucking her teeth in irritation, she returned to her rock. She'd forgotten to ask his name, which irritated her almost as much as the fact that she only had one bedroll, and she'd told him to go to sleep on it.

With a sigh, she spread out her heavy black cloak on the forest floor, then laid down on her back. She stared up at the stars until sleep finally took her, smiling at her final thought before rest. *Despite her irritation, it was nice going to sleep with the sound of someone gently snoring nearby.*

CHAPTER TWO

Kai

Kai's entire body ached. He'd known when he'd refused to work that he would be beaten, or worse, but truly, he hadn't thought the consequences through. At the time it had seemed a good idea. Now the sun was rising on a new day, and he could never return home. He couldn't risk what might happen to his family if he did. They were better off thinking he was dead.

He rolled over in his bedroll, then startled. The woman who'd rescued him the previous night was perched on a rock, staring at him. A bow was leaned against her thigh, and twin daggers rested at her slender hips.

He sat up, rubbing his aching head and coming away with dry flecks of blood.

"What is your name?" the woman questioned, her mood unreadable. For all he knew, she felt the same way about him as she felt about the rock on which she sat, but then, why had she saved him?

"It's Kai," he answered honestly. "Though perhaps I should change it now, just in case any guards from the city decide to search for me."

She tilted her head, trailing her long, nearly black braid over the shoulder of her charcoal vest atop a loose, white blouse. Her black breeches hugged her legs tightly, tucked into knee-high black boots. A black cloak was flung back over her shoulder. What was this woman doing hiding in the woods with a man who was now on the run?

"No need to change it," she said finally. "They won't look for you so long as you don't attempt to return. They'll assume your body was dragged away by small predators."

He shivered at the thought, knowing that would have been his fate had this woman not found him.

"I'm Anna," she continued, rising from her perch. "Make yourself ready and we'll be on our way."

"Do you have a horse?" he questioned without thinking.

She smirked down at him. "No *my lord*, some of us have little choice but to get around on foot."

He blinked up at her, not sure how he'd managed to offend her . . . *again*.

"Prepare yourself," she said again. "Unless you'd rather venture off on your own. It is your choice."

He immediately stood despite his body's protests. He had no food, nor did he know the location of the nearest clean water, and he'd just lost the only people who cared about him in the entire world. He wasn't about to lose the one person who now knew the truth about him, even if she seemed to scowl far more than she smiled.

Kai

Twenty minutes later, now with a meager portion of food in his belly, Kai started along the small trail through the woods with Anna walking a few steps ahead, her pack of supplies slung casually over her shoulder along with her bow and quiver. He watched her cautiously. He wasn't used to people offering aid for no reason. In fact, he wasn't used to people offering aid *at all*. The nearby trees shaded them from the murky sun, birds chattering in their branches. It would have been a nice walk if his body wasn't screaming in agony. He limped along, favoring his right leg, and wincing at a sharp pain in his side with every step. He was quite sure the guard who'd beaten him had broken at least one of his ribs.

"What will you do in the next burgh?" he questioned, wanting to distract himself from his predicament.

Anna glanced back at him as she continued walking. "Resupply, then continue on. I'd hoped to find work on a ship at the coast, but none would take me. Not that they're sailing right now regardless. The men still jump at shapes in the night, though the Faie have all but disappeared from the land. They fear Merrows in the shallows and Sirens in the deeps."

Kai couldn't help his smirk. He'd never seen one of the Faie himself, but he'd heard stories of the Faie War, which had ended roughly seventy years before he'd been born. No one knew why the creatures had vanished, and many lived in fear of them returning.

"So you're a sailor?" he asked.

She snorted, not glancing back at him. "Sometimes. You'll soon learn to do what you must to survive, whether it's sailing, farming, or hiring out your sword."

He glanced at the daggers at either of her hips warily. He'd never handled a sword in his life. "I can farm," he mused, "but I'd likely drown if I sailed or stab myself if I tried my hand at swordplay."

She whirled on him, her dark eyes wide. "You don't even know how to use a sword!"

He blinked at her, stunned, then shrugged. "Why would I? I've spent every day of my life working on the farm to support my family. We could never afford a sword, let alone the time needed to become proficient at wielding it."

She sighed heavily, then turned to continue walking. "You can inquire at farms in the next burgh. You wouldn't last a day on the road on your own."

He scowled at her words, but couldn't exactly argue. Instead, he hurried to her side with a mischievous glint in his eyes. "*Or*," he countered, "*you* could teach me to use a sword."

"You said it yourself," she growled, "swords are expensive, as is the time needed to learn."

Unwilling to give up so easily, his mind raced for something he could offer her, but he had nothing to his name, not even a single coin. "I'd do anything you asked," he blurted. "I've lived my entire life as a slave to the city. I'm used to the work."

She stopped walking, placed her hands on her hips, then looked him up and down. "What makes you think I'd want you? A farmer is of no use to me."

He bit his lip, wracking his brain. "I can do more than

tend crops. A life of farming has made me strong. Since you don't have a horse, I could carry your belongings." He eyed the pack she carried, containing her food, water, and bedroll. "And I've used a bow before," he tapped the top of the weapon slung beside her pack.

She tilted her head in thought. Was she actually considering his desperate plea?

"I'll teach you to handle a dagger once you're healed," she offered. "If you show no promise of skill, you must vow that you will not try to follow me after we reach the burgh. I will not be slowed down."

He nodded eagerly. "Just give me a chance. That's all I ask."

"Fine," she sighed, then immediately turned to continue walking.

He hurried after her, determined to prove himself useful. A sliver of hope had blossomed in his chest. Perhaps there was life after servitude. If he could learn to use various weapons . . . well, he wasn't sure just what he could do with such skills. Anna had hinted at mercenary work, although from what he understood, mercenaries traveled in groups. Anna traveled all alone. He suddenly found himself wondering if she put her weapons to more nefarious purposes. Perhaps she was a thief or assassin. She certainly dressed as he'd imagine a thief or assassin might dress.

As his thoughts spun out of control, his mood darkened. He'd simply have to see what the next few days would bring. Once his wounds were healed, and he'd acquired some skill with a blade, he'd be fully prepared to run the other way.

CHAPTER THREE

Anna

Anna had noticed the footprints in the muddy path over an hour prior. Normally, footprints would be nothing to gawk at, but these were far from the main road, and seemed fresh since the edges were yet to lighten as the moisture in the soil seeped downward. Sometimes hunters used the forest path, or sometimes others not wanting to draw attention to themselves . . . like *her*, but there were too many imprints in the mud to belong to a simple hunting party.

"Why are you staring at the ground?" Kai questioned, tearing her away from her thoughts. "Shouldn't we be keeping an eye on our surroundings in these parts?"

She turned to scowl at him as he walked happily beside her. He tried to smile at her scowl, then winced in pain from the bruises decorating his stubbled jaw.

"Look down," she growled, gesturing to the prints they were both stomping over.

He glanced at the prints, then back to her face. "So?"

She sighed, flicking her gaze around the forest, straining her ears for hints of other voices. When she heard nothing, she replied, "*So*, why would such a large group travel so far from the main road? I'd guess there are at least twenty of them, maybe more. Mostly men, but some women."

He raised his brows at her, then stopped walking to observe the prints more closely. "How can you tell?"

She sighed again and stopped beside him, trying to remember just why she'd agreed to let him travel with her. "Look at the sizes of the prints, and how they overlap," she explained, gesturing down to the prints. "Some are small enough to be women's feet, but they have mostly been obscured, as if they were walking ahead of some of the others."

He nodded, then continued walking. "Well, I don't see how it's any of our business regardless."

Fool, she thought. Out loud she said, "It may become our business when the group of bandits takes us hostage, or *worse*."

"Who said anything about bandits?" he questioned.

Could he really be *this* dense? "Think about where we are," she hissed. She began to say more, then cut herself off. She halted in her tracks.

Kai continued walking, not noticing the voices that had piqued her ears.

She hurried forward and grabbed his arm, then raised a finger to her lips to silence him before he could complain.

He blinked at her, wide-eyed.

She tapped her ear with her free hand, hoping he would understand.

He seemed to listen, then his eyes grew wider.

The voices weren't far ahead. Their owners had likely stopped for a meal on the trail, granting Kai and Anna the chance to catch up to them. Silently, she tugged Kai back a few steps, then off the path and into the trees.

"We'll creep around them," she whispered, standing close enough for him to hear. "We'll keep off the path until we're far ahead, then we'll keep walking through the night. That should place us far enough ahead of them."

"Do we really need to go to all that trouble?" he whispered back.

She scowled. It would be risky, but she needed to teach this boy a lesson. "Follow me," she instructed.

Without waiting to see if he would obey, she crept forward, careful to remain concealed within the shadows of the dense trees. He followed after her, nearly as silent. He might make a good thief if he weren't so naive...not that she had time to train him, and she was better off on her own. She always had been.

The voices grew louder as she continued to creep forward with Kai following close behind. Soon enough, she spotted the first of the men, then another, sitting beside him on a fallen log, eating cured meat and hard bread. She took a few more steps, and more of the men came into view.

Anna tried to keep her breathing even. Her assumption had been correct. These men were bandits, or perhaps hired mercenaries. They wore rough leather armor and weapons at their belts. Not the finely made weapons of the Gray Guard, but the shoddy iron weapons of lowly criminals. She continued silently forward, keeping an eye on the men, then her mouth grew dry as the women came into view.

There were six of them, all weighed down by heavy irons at their wrists. They wore the dresses of simple townsfolk, and all appeared to be under twenty. She hated to think what the men had planned for them. That they were all alive meant they were likely to be sold into servitude, but that didn't mean the mercenaries wouldn't do horrible things to them along the way.

She swallowed the lump in her throat and continued walking. This had nothing to do with her. If she were the one in irons, none of those women would stop to help *her*. She was sure of it.

An arm wrapped around her bicep. She tensed, reaching for her dagger, then relaxed. She had nearly forgotten about Kai. She turned her dark eyes to glare up at him.

He released his hold on her, then gestured silently to the woman, a distressed expression scrunching his face.

Her heart gave a nervous patter, but she shook her head. She turned to continue walking, then flinched as he grabbed her again. She turned, and he once again gestured to the women.

Sighing, she gestured to the armed men. Fifteen of them, if her initial count was correct. Shaking her head, she continued creeping along.

After a moment, Kai followed, though she was quite sure the silent argument was far from over.

Kai

Kai was practically trembling by the time they were well out of sight of the men and their prisoners. He clenched and unclenched his sore fists as Anna finally made her way back to the path. He followed, but every step felt like there was iron weighing down his boots. His entire body ached, he was exhausted, but that was not what held him back. How could they simply leave those women to their fates? They couldn't be any older than his middle sister.

"I know what you're thinking," Anna said as he moved to walk at her side down the path. "But there is nothing that we can do for them. I might be skilled with a blade, but I could not face that many men and survive, and you'd be all but useless."

His face burned at the *useless* comment, because it was true. He'd proven himself useless to his family, and now he was useless to Anna. He was *more* than useless to those poor women back there.

"We could at least alert the Gray Guard," he suggested. "*They* could stop them."

She snorted. "Yes, they're sure to believe a runaway slave and a thief."

"Thief?" he questioned, stopping in his tracks.

Her face grew red, but she didn't take her words back. "I do what I need to survive. The Gray City was never kind to me. I'd think you of all people would understand." She turned and continued walking, hiding her blush.

He hurried to catch up to her. "While I cannot criticize you, I cannot condone you stealing from poor folk struggling just as much as you or I."

She rolled her eyes. "I don't steal from poor folk. What would they have that I'd want? It's not worth the risk for a few measly coins. The money lies in being hired by others to steal the things *they* want. Petty Lords stealing from their rivals. Smugglers stealing from ships and storehouses."

He felt his shoulders relax. Perhaps there was humanity within her yet. He still didn't like the idea of stealing, but really, what might *he* do if he was desperate enough. He was pretty desperate *right now*.

"If you care for the poor folk," he began anew, "then how can you leave those women behind?"

Her eyes darkened as they scanned the path ahead. The path leading them further and further from the women who needed their help. "As I've already explained," she muttered. "There is nothing you nor I could do for them. We would both lose our lives, and the women would still meet their fates. I will not die in vain, not after all I've done to stay alive."

He grabbed her arm to stop her. He knew she was right. He knew it, but he couldn't let it go.

She stopped and peered up at him with her dark, unwavering eyes.

"What if that was you back there?" he questioned, gesturing with his free arm to the path behind them. "What if that was your sister, or someone you cared about deeply? Would you risk your life then?"

Her eyes shot daggers at him, and he knew he'd overstepped.

"I have no one to care about," she said blandly, "and no one cares about me. *That* is why I'm still alive."

He dropped his hand from her arm, shaking his head. "Well I'm going back. I cannot enjoy my freedom while those women have lost theirs."

Her expression didn't alter. "If you go back, you will die."

"So be it," he huffed, then turned to walk back down the path. He had no idea what he was going to do. Perhaps he could silently follow the party and await a good opportunity. This far into the woods, most of the men might sleep easily in the night. With the element of surprise, perhaps he could fell whoever was left awake to watch over the women, then he'd be able to help them escape to hide in the woods.

"In that case," Anna said to his back, "I'm sorry I wasted my time saving you."

He stopped in his tracks, shaking his head as he turned to her. "What is the point of walking forward, when you stand for nothing?"

Some hidden emotion flashed through her eyes, then was gone. She turned and walked away.

He stared after her as she left. If he didn't try, he would always regret not saving the women. Unfortunately, part of him might always regret not saving Anna too.

CHAPTER FOUR

Anna

Such a fool! Anna thought, anger clouding her mind. To throw his life away for *strangers*. He was so young, and she'd offered him a way to survive…She scowled. How could he just throw it in her face like that?

Distant memories pushed their way into her mind as her feet thudded down the shaded path. Growing up on the streets of the Gray City, her teenage friends, screaming for their lives as they were carried away by guards. There was no way to save them, there never was. It was understood that if the guards caught you stealing, no one would come to your rescue.

She stopped walking, lifting a hand to rub her tired eyes. She was still that same girl, powerless against those who would make her a victim. She was fast, smart, *deadly*, yet she was still powerless. Now she couldn't even save Kai. Those mercenaries would skewer him the moment they saw him. His young life would be over.

She turned in her tracks, then shook her head. What was she even thinking? There was nothing she could do for him except die by his side. She would not risk her life now after all she'd survived.

She took another step down the path, back in the direction she'd come. Her instincts screamed at her to run away, but a tiny voice in her head told her to go back. It was a tiny voice she'd learned to ignore long ago. In fact, she'd thought she'd squashed it out altogether, but Kai had somehow awoken it.

She didn't know whether she wanted to thank him, or strangle him

Regardless, the tiny voice cheered her on as she took another heavy step, then picked up her pace down the path toward the mercenaries. The voice echoed in her mind, *What's the point of moving forward, when you stand for nothing?*

As she left the path and crept back into the trees, she became quite sure she'd lost her mind. It was a frightening thought, but just as powerful was the feeling that while she'd lost her mind, perhaps she'd found something else. Something equally important.

Kai

What in the blazes had he been thinking? He was such a fool. He'd crept back into the trees just in time, as the mercenaries had finished their meal to continue on down the path. These men were criminals, trained killers. They'd strike him dead before he could even blink. How had he ever hoped to even stand against one of them?

"You are an absolute fool," a voice whispered beside him, echoing his thoughts.

He whipped his gaze around to find Anna, crouching not three paces away. The corner of his mouth lifted into a crooked smile. "If I'm so foolish," he whispered, "then what are *you* doing here?"

She glared at him. "I spent an entire night rescuing you. I don't like wasting my time."

His grin widened. Anna was only one woman, but she was a trained fighter, at least according to her. His loose plan might actually work with her by his side.

"Whatever you're thinking," she whispered, "*stop*. I'm not going to follow whatever fool plan you have in your mind. If we're going to do this, you will do exactly as I say, exactly when I say it."

He nodded eagerly. "I am at your command."

"Ye gods," she muttered to herself, shaking her head. "How did I end up *here*?"

With the mercenaries now out of sight, they both straightened and walked further from the path. Though Anna's face was set in a scowl, Kai felt hopeful. She might be a thief, but she still had a heart.

Once they were a good distance away from the path, shielded within the dense trees, Anna stopped walking and turned to him. "We'll track them until nightfall," she explained. "It will be easier to strike while most of them are asleep. We can sneak in, pick them off one by one—"

"Wait," he interrupted, his heart lurching into his throat.

"You intend to kill them in their sleep?" He'd never killed anyone before. Perhaps he'd occasionally daydreamed about besting one of the Gray Guard in a duel, but even then, the man would run off in shame. Kai couldn't imagine actually sticking a knife in someone.

Anna raised a dark brow at his horrified expression. "Yes, how else did you plan on rescuing the women? Those men aren't just going to *give* them to us."

"I thought we'd sneak them out," he suggested. "Knock whoever is left awake to guard them unconscious, then lead the girls away."

Anna rolled their eyes. "Two armed foes appear in the night, strangers to these women. What do you think they'll do?"

He sighed. "Scream?"

She smiled cruelly. "You're not as fool-brained as you look, then. The women will scream, and the entire camp of mercenaries will rush in to end us. I'm good with a blade, but I'm not *that* good."

He took a deep breath. There had to be another way. "We'll slip the women a note," he suggested. "We'll tell them to prepare for rescue."

She turned and started walking in the direction the mercenaries had gone. "I take it back, you *are* as fool-brained as you look." He hurried to catch up with her as she continued, "Ignoring the complications of actually getting a note to the women, it would undoubtedly be confiscated by the mercenaries, dashing our plan to bits."

"I just don't want to kill them," he admitted, slowing alongside her as her eyes scanned the trail now far to their right.

She snorted. "Yeah, I got that. What I don't understand is *why?*"

"Because killing is wrong?" he suggested.

She flicked her gaze to him. "These men have doubtlessly killed many innocents," she countered. "They've kidnapped those women to likely be sold into servitude. They have *earned* their deaths."

How could she be so callous? He shook his head. "Well that's not really for us to decide, is it?"

She stopped walking and turned to fully face him, hands on hips. "Do you want my help, or not?"

Did he? He was quite sure working with Anna was the only way he could save those women, but at what cost? Who was he to decide who lived or died?

Reading his expression, she sighed. "I made a mistake coming back. If you somehow survive, seek me out in the next burgh."

She turned to walk away, but he grabbed her sleeve. "Wait," he breathed. "If it's truly the only way, we'll go with your plan."

She gave him a sharp nod, seemingly satisfied.

Despite having a plan, his stomach twisted into knots far more painful than the ache of his bruises. He suspected Anna did not plan to kill all of the men on her own. She'd want him to do his share. The only question was, could he do it? He tried to imagine himself with a blade poised over a sleeping man. Could he puncture flesh and end the man's life?

He wasn't sure. The only thing he was really sure of, was that he didn't have much choice.

CHAPTER FIVE

Kai

Kai grew increasingly nervous as night fell. They'd tracked the mercenaries throughout the day, and had ended up in a small clearing where the men stopped to make camp. The women were forced to sit around a tree with their backs to the trunk, then were bound with heavy ropes.

Kai watched from the concealment of dense shrubs as the night wore on, and the men curled up in their bedrolls one by one. Eventually there were only two men left to stand guard.

"Are you ready?" Anna whispered, creeping up to his side.

He clenched the pommel of the unfamiliar dagger at his belt. He would have preferred to try his hand at Anna's bow, but stealth was of utmost importance. They couldn't risk any of the men screaming before they died. The bow had been left hidden in the brush some distance away, along with her pack.

He shivered. The men would all have to die. If they didn't, the women might suffer an even worse fate. He swallowed the lump in his throat and nodded to Anna.

She watched his face for a moment, then replied, "Good. Don't worry about the two standing guard. I will take care of them. You sneak in from the far end and begin dispatching the men in their beds."

He nodded a little too quickly. He was going to be sick.

"Remember," she added, "just a clean slice to the throat. Silence them before they can scream. We cannot avoid some of them waking up, we can only hope there will be few of them left to fight us." She seemed to think about her words. "If you can, go for the big ones first."

With that, she darted off into the night. He could barely hear her footsteps as she disappeared into the darkness.

His palms slick with sweat, he began to make his way around the clearing. The men's bedrolls were spread out, none sleeping too close to each other. It shouldn't be too difficult to reach the farthest ones without waking any of the others. The difficult part would occur once he reached them.

He couldn't help but feel he was sacrificing a small part of his soul in helping the women. He could only hope they'd be grateful for it.

Anna

Anna took deep, steady breaths, carefully picking her way across the ground so as not to step on any branches or dry leaves. Her daggers rested at her belt, ready to be unsheathed and driven into the nearest throat.

Two men stood guard, one near the women, and one on the other side of the camp, nearest the path. She'd take out that one first, as the one near the women would be tricky. She couldn't risk any of the women screaming while Kai was vulnerable amongst the sleeping men.

She paused near a tree and watched as her primary quarry shifted his weight, constantly flicking his gaze around the forest ahead of him. His bald head reflected the moonlight, showcasing various scars. While he was clearly not new to his trade, he wouldn't expect any threats to come from behind.

She darted behind another tree closer to her quarry. Slowly, she unsheathed her twin daggers, waiting for just the right moment.

The man yawned, stretching his arms over his head, and she leapt, thrusting her right arm over his shoulder seconds before dragging the dagger across his throat.

He made a soft gurgling sound, and she caught his body as it fell to the ground. She let him down gently, careful to not stain herself with the blood welling from his throat, black in the moonlight.

A shiver crept up her spine as she cleaned her dagger on his shirt, then quietly dragged him to the cover of a nearby shrub. She didn't like killing, but she liked these men preying on the weak even less. She'd been weak once, and no one had bothered to save her. These women would not suffer the same fate.

With the dead man as hidden as he was going to get, she turned her attention to the rest of the campsite. Perhaps she should help Kai with the sleeping men, leaving the guard beside the women for last.

Forcing her thoughts away from the corpse she left behind, she crept onward to find Kai.

Kai

Kai knelt before the man sleeping furthest toward the edge of camp. The man's sickly sweet breath permeated his nostrils, making it difficult to breathe. Or perhaps it was just the panic constricting Kai's lungs. He had his dagger ready. He already should have slit the man's throat to move onto the next. He needed to kill as many as possible before one awoke.

He swallowed the lump in his throat and poised his dagger. Sweat dripped down his brow as his hand began to tremble.

He couldn't do it.

He withdrew the dagger and prepared to creep away. He would simply find Anna and tell her they needed a new plan. Perhaps if these men were trying to kill him he would be able to fight back, but to murder someone in their sleep? It just seemed wrong, no matter how deserving the victim might be.

He began to stand, then nearly screamed as his would-be victim's eyes fluttered open. The man stared up at him for a moment, confused, then began shouting. Kai knew he should have silenced him right there, but instead he stumbled backwards.

"You fool!" Anna's voice hissed, as an arm wrapped around his bicep. "Run, now!"

He wanted to obey her, but his feet didn't seem to be working. Roused by the man he should have killed, the mercenaries all climbed from their bedrolls, glancing around. The man who'd started the shouting was now on his feet, advancing toward them while brandishing a small hatchet.

Suddenly he charged, swinging the weapon at Kai as his companions swarmed toward them. Kai would have met his end right there, but Anna darted in, faster than any fighter Kai had ever seen. She deflected the hatchet with one of her blades, expertly flicking the weapon out of the man's hand before slicing her second blade across his throat.

As the man crumpled to the ground, Kai finally found his feet, but it was too late. The men were advancing to surround them, and Anna was already fending off another attacker.

"Run!" she hissed again. "I'll be right behind you!"

This time he was able to listen. He turned on his heel and ran, shutting out the image of the blood pouring from the man's throat. Had he the time, he would have vomited, but he was now too intent on keeping himself alive as the men shouted after him.

He ran and ran into the dark woods. He wasn't sure where Anna was. She said she'd be right behind him, but he couldn't spare the time to look. Instead he charged onward into the night, forcing his legs to carry him faster, though his lungs and bruised ribs screamed out in agony.

He ran until his legs finally gave out, and he collapsed into the dirt. He rolled over, panting and dripping with sweat as he gazed up at the still moon. He could no longer hear the shouts of the men pursuing him, but cold fear still clutched his heart. Where in the blazes was Anna?

CHAPTER SIX

Anna

Anna groaned and lifted a hand to her throbbing head. How had that blasted brute gotten the drop on her? The last thing she remembered was felling another one of the bandits, then something slammed into her skull and knocked her to the ground.

Though she couldn't remember it, something must have hit her in the ribs too. There was a massive weight on her chest. She tried to move, but something rough was pressed against her back.

Her eyes snapped open as full awareness hit her. The weight she felt was a rope looped several times around her chest, pinning her to a tree. The light of dawn was slowly creeping in. She'd been unconscious all night.

She blinked rapidly as her sight went from blurry to clear, then groaned again. She was in a seated position, tied to a tree just a few paces away from where the captured women were tied. One of them was already awake, staring at her with sad blue eyes from beneath matted russet hair.

Her panic increasing, Anna groped at the ropes securing her chest, but could find no knots. It must have been secured on the other side of the tree, the trunk far too wide for her arms to flail anywhere near the knots.

She gritted her teeth and tried to come up with a plan. Kai was most likely dead, so he'd be of little help. There was no way she was getting out of the ropes. Her daggers had been taken away, and . . . she halted her racing thoughts as she shifted her right foot in her boot. *Curses*, they'd taken the dagger there too. The thought of the filthy men thoroughly searching her unconscious body for weapons sent a chill of revulsion down her spine.

She took deep, even breaths, willing herself not to vomit. Back to making a plan. She wasn't getting out of the ropes, but they'd have to untie her when they moved on for the day. Else they'd leave her to either starve or be eaten by wild animals. She found both options preferable to whatever else the men might do to her.

If, however, the men decided to lump her in with the other women and take her with them, she should be able to find a way to escape. Even outnumbered, she could outwit these men with two hands tied behind her back...or shackled with heavy irons.

"Morning, princess," a rough voice said from behind her. "Not so tough without your blades?"

She winced. She'd nearly forgotten about the men she'd killed. She might end up lumped in with the other women, but she'd surely be punished for her crimes along the way.

The man stepped into her line of sight. He was

younger than he sounded, perhaps only just past his twentieth year, though the scars littering his bare, muscled arms told the story of a rough youth. He sneered from beneath grubby, dark bangs, showcasing his numerous missing teeth.

"Who was your friend?" he questioned. "Will he come back for you?"

So he wasn't dead? She smirked. "A casual acquaintance, nothing more." Even if Kai was still alive, he wouldn't likely return for her, but she still saw no benefit to putting the men on their guards.

"You don't seem too sore that he abandoned you," the man observed.

She glared up at him. If he thought she would pour her heart out to him, he was dead wrong. "What do you intend to do with me?" she asked evenly.

He smirked. "You think you're any better than the rest of our fair damsels?" he gestured to the woman tied to the adjacent tree. "You'll all be sold to new masters, though I might take the time to find you a particularly *loving* owner. Some of the men you killed were my friends."

She took deep, even breaths. If she got her hands on a blade, she'd send this foul man right to the grave along with his other *friends*.

"No clever retort?" he asked, then spat in the dirt near her feet. "Fine," he continued. "We're just another day's journey from the drop off point. You'll change your attitude long before then." He gazed lasciviously at the other women. "Isn't that right, ladies?"

The redhead who'd met her gaze before flinched, but the others barely reacted. All Anna could think was *broken, they'd all been broken.* She'd avenge them, if it was the last thing she did.

She smiled sweetly at her captor. "My attitude will only change once I've just cut out your tongue, and you're hanging from a tree by your entrails."

The insult won her a kick in the ribs. Her vision blacked for several seconds.

When it returned, the man had walked away, and the red-haired woman was watching her with a smirk on her lips. Anna returned the smirk with a nod. She knew without asking that when the time came, at least this one girl would be there to help her.

Kai

Think, think, think, Kai repeated in his mind as he trudged through the dense forest. His body was unbelievable tired, and he was starved, but Anna was surely faring far worse. He'd gotten close enough to the camp to see her tied to that tree. He'd been entirely ready to sneak in and save her before that oily, dark-haired man showed up. He'd noted the small axe at the man's hip, and the dagger jutting from his boot, and had known he would stand no chance against him...especially not after the humiliating show he'd put on the night before, running for his life while Anna cut down their foes one by one.

He sighed, kicking his boot into the mucky soil in irritation. Something small and brown came loose from the ground and toppled out of the tall grass. He crouched down and picked up a small mushroom, then took a deep whiff of its porous flesh.

His nose wrinkled at the sweet scent. He'd encountered such mushrooms the previous year. They grew in sticky soil with a high clay content, usually beneath the shade of tall grass or other plants. Because of their tendency to hide, he hadn't noticed the batch growing in their pasture until half of the sheep had eaten them. They'd gone utterly mad, stumbling all over the place and running into fences. Some had even died.

He made to drop the mushroom back into its hiding place, then stopped. *He* might not be able to disarm the men holding Anna captive, but hallucinations accompanied by violent stomach rumblings just might. The only problem was, how would he convince the men to eat the mushrooms?

Leaving that issue for later, he frantically began searching the grass for more growths, plucking them and piling them into the hem of his shirt as he went. He knew he was quite mad for even considering such a plan, but it was the only one he had.

Anna

"We should have killed her for what she did," one of the men nearest Anna grumbled. He was older than the others, yet had fewer scars. As if Anna needed any *more* evidence that he was a coward.

"She's worth more to us alive than dead," the dark-haired man who needed his tongue cut out said.

Each of the two men held on to the ropes binding the women together by their irons. It was difficult enough for Anna to keep her feet as they were jostled about, let alone plan her escape. She'd ended up next to the red-haired woman, but had been granted no opportunity to speak with her. On her other side was a blonde girl, likely still a teenager, whose eyes never left the ground.

The rest of the remaining men walked further ahead or behind, confident the two men would have no trouble herding seven women in irons.

Anna's gaze occasionally flicked the the daggers strapped to the dark-haired man's wrists. If only she'd been placed at the end of the line of women, she could stand a chance of disarming him.

Of course, that was exactly why she'd been placed in the center.

As they trudged onward, her eyes darted about for anything else she might use. There were some small rocks on the dirt trail, and a few branches here and there, but nothing that would do her much good. Her eyes landed on a few oddly round, brown pebbles at they passed them. No, not pebbles, mushrooms. She was not well versed in foraging, and so, did not know their type, but she imagined it was unnatural for them to just be sitting on the side of the trail like that.

She subtly scanned the surrounding woods as the men grumbled amongst themselves, paying little attention to anything other than their tired feet thumping down the path. She nearly gasped at a flash of movement in the low shrubs. She could have sworn she'd seen . . . Kai?

She kept walking, wondering why her eyes were playing tricks on her.

"What are all these mushrooms doing on the path?" one of the men ahead of her asked.

The party stopped walking, giving her a chance to scan the foliage once more, but she did not see the movement again. Yet, what if it had been Kai? Could he actually be planning on rescuing her?

She looked down at the mushrooms as a few of the men knelt to pluck them from the side of the path. Could Kai have placed them there? If so, *why*? She didn't imagine he'd be out to feed the hungry mercenaries.

Suddenly an idea dawned on her. It was far fetched, but she really didn't have anything to lose. She strained against the ropes tethering her to the other women, barely managing to pluck one of the mushrooms from the ground.

A moment later, the dark-haired man swatted it from her grasp.

"What the Horned One's name do you think you're doing?" he growled.

She glared at him. "What in the Horned One's name do you think? You didn't give me any breakfast."

He glanced down at the fallen mushroom as the other men watched on. "How do you know they're safe to eat?"

She rolled her eyes. "I've lived in these woods for a while. I eat them all the time. Another traveler must have gathered them, then dropped them accidentally." So she might be tricking them into eating harmless mushrooms and she'd feel like a fool. If they *weren't* harmless, she'd feel quite clever indeed.

The man watched her, calculating. After a moment, he sneered. "I don't believe you."

Blast it all. Perhaps she'd underestimated his intelligence.

"If you don't want them," the red-haired woman began from her side, "can we have them? My da' used to make a hearty stew from them. The sweet taste reminds me of home."

The dark-haired man shifted his gaze to her, pondering. After a few seconds, he smiled triumphantly. "Gather the mushrooms, lads," he announced. "We'll be havin' a bit more than stale bread tonight!"

The men all laughed and set to gathering the mushrooms sprinkled along the side of the trail. When all of their backs were turned, Anna flashed the red-head a quick smile, which the woman returned, her pale eyes sparkling with excitement. Perhaps she knew more about the mushrooms than Anna, or perhaps she thought Anna knew more about them than her.

Either way, they'd find out that evening.

CHAPTER SEVEN

Anna

Anna grunted as her back was slammed against a tree. One of the men pressed a rope against her chest, then handed the ends to another standing on the other side of the trunk. It would have been the perfect opportunity for her to head-butt the man in front of her, steal his dagger, then stab the other one, but the dark haired man was watching on, his *friends* just behind him, starting a fire. The gathered mushrooms were piled in the dirt next to a large iron pot.

As one man finished tying her ropes, the man who'd unceremoniously slammed against the tree sauntered off toward their nearby supplies, then turned and tossed her a hunk of stale bread, which she barely managed to catch with her shackled hands.

"Eat up," he growled, then ambled off toward the fire.

The other women had once again been tied to a separate tree, too far away for Anna to pinch the red-head as she watched the men preparing the mushrooms a little too eagerly. If they noticed her gaze, they might become suspicious, yet Anna couldn't quite help herself as she too turned her eyes toward the mushrooms, the hunk of stale bread lying forgotten in her shackled hands.

Kai

Had he been wrong? Kai had watched on as all the men partook of their hastily-made mushroom soup, yet they seemed none the worse for it. He'd been *so* sure the mushrooms were poisonous, and had nearly cried out in excitement as he spied Anna tricking the men into gathering them, but now it seemed his luck had run out. Perhaps the heat of the fire had rendered the mushrooms edible. Now the men had full bellies as a reward for their foul deeds.

He touched the knife at his belt. He could always resort to Anna's original plan, killing the men in their sleep…but they'd likely be on their guard, knowing he could still be watching them. Plus, it wasn't like he'd been able to muster the courage before, why would that night be any different?

He pressed his back against the tree concealing him as his mind raced for another option. It would be dark soon, and the time for decisions would come.

"What is that!" one of the mercenaries shouted.

He tensed, had he been spotted?

"I could have sworn I saw a horse," the voice added in disbelief.

"I feel unwell," another groaned.

A grin slowly spread across Kai's face.

Someone in the campsite began retching, as another questioned why the trees were spinning.

It was time to make his move.

Anna

Anna had no time to celebrate her small victory. The dark-haired man stumbled toward her, murder in his eyes.

"What did you do to us?" he hissed as he staggered into her, pressing her more firmly against the tree. His body odor hit her nose, making her gag.

"I did nothing," she said sweetly. "Why, are you unwell?"

She noted his wrist daggers as he placed his hands on either side of her face, but her shackled hands were pinned flat to her body by the weight of him. Perhaps she could grab one with her teeth.

"*Look at me*," he growled. She whipped her gaze away from his left dagger to his face. His pupils were tiny pinpricks, barely noticeable in his deep brown irises. Sweat beaded at his temples despite the cool evening breeze. "*What* did you make us eat?" he demanded.

The other men seemed to be hallucinating behind him. She sensed movement from the women too, but could not focus on them as a hand wrapped around her throat and squeezed.

She sputtered for air as he pressed into her, pinning her arms more securely. She tried to turn her head away, but only managed to scrape the back of her skull against the rough bark of the tree. The corners of her vision began to go gray. How idiotic it would look for her to go to all that effort, only to die like this!

Something thunked down onto the man's head and he fell away. Anna's vision came back in stages to see Kai standing before her, wielding a large rock.

"Took you long enough," she gasped. "Untie me."

He nodded quickly and threw the rock aside, reaching for the dagger at his belt.

"Hey!" one of the men who'd just finished vomiting shouted. "One of the Forest Faie is making off with our girl!"

"Quick!" Anna hissed as he began to saw at the thick ropes binding her.

The men staggered toward them. If Kai could just undo the blasted ropes she could protect them, shackles or no. The mercenaries should not be difficult to defeat in their condition.

"Get 'em!" a female voice shouted.

Just as the ropes released around Anna's chest, the women all jumped up from the tree they'd been bound to, their freshly-cut ropes falling free from their bodies. She noticed a small, sharp object in the red-head's hand before snapping into action.

Leaping away from the tree she'd been tied to and into the fray, she laced her hands together and swung her heavy shackles, smashing into the face of the older man with far too few scars to be a proper mercenary. He fell aside with a wail as the red-haired woman, still in her shackles, threw herself full force at another man staggering into the sudden chaos. He shrieked as he went down, then rolled around on the ground muttering about being attacked by a giant eagle.

The red-haired woman staggered to her feet, then grinned at Anna. "I'm Iona, by the way."

She smirked. "Anna, and this idiot is Kai," she gestured to her friend as he shoved another one of the men aside.

Kai took a second to nod to Iona in greeting, then punched one of the mercenaries in the face, knocking him flat on his back.

Anna grinned. He might not be much of a killer, but he wasn't entirely useless either.

The mercenaries didn't fight for long, and soon enough Anna, Kai, and Iona had them all tied around a tree with the remaining ropes, the shackles now weighing *them* down now that Anna had obtained the key. Most of the men had passed out, or were groaning and muttering nonsense. The other women seemed to have snapped back into reality, having fought their captors and won.

"What should we do with them?" Iona questioned, standing at Anna's side as she peered down at the men.

"I'd say we should kill them," she began, "but *someone* might have a problem with it." She rolled her eyes to Kai, standing on her other side.

He blushed, then cleared his throat. "Yes, I must apologize for last night. I hope I can begin to make up for my cowardice by returning your pack and bow. They're hidden not far off."

Anna smirked, glad to hear her belongings were safe. "No apologies necessary. If you were the one who left the mushrooms on the trail, you saved us all. Perhaps I should have listened to your original plan to begin with."

"My original plan was far less clever," he admitted, though he beamed at her compliment.

"Well," Iona interrupted. "I'm all for leavin' them here to rot. We can report them in the next burgh in case anyone wants to come gather the remains."

Anna was liking Iona more and more. "Let us be off then," she announced, glancing at the other women milling around them. "Hopefully we'll come across a caravan to get everyone back to where they came from."

Iona nodded. "Most of us haven't got too far to go, though a few came all the way from the small villages bordering the marshlands."

"Then let us be off," Anna replied, sparing a final glance to the captured mercenaries. She still wanted to cut out the dark-haired man's tongue, but she'd let it go for Kai's sake.

Really, she should leave Kai at the next burgh with the women. He was beginning to make her go soft.

"I'll kill you!" the dark-haired man suddenly groaned.

She laughed, then turned away. "Not if your stupidity kills you first!" she called out.

Kai, Iona, and the other five women all followed her as she led the way back toward the path. It was a strange feeling indeed, leaving her enemies alive, but one she found she didn't mind. It was always such a pain washing blood from her clothes anyhow.

CHAPTER EIGHT

Kai

They reached the burgh later the following day. With coin stolen from the mercenaries, Anna and Kai had bought themselves a fine meal at the burgh's sole inn, where they now sat. The rest of the coin had gone to the women. They'd all been given enough to get themselves home after they reported the mercenaries to the men in the village.

Kai sighed, poking his fork into another boiled egg. His full cup of tea steamed beside his plate. Speaking with Iona and the other women about the simple, quiet lives they would return to made his heart ache. He missed his family, and though he did not miss the members of the Gray Guard who watched over those in debt to the city, he found he was reluctant to give up quiet mornings on a farm, watching the sun rise amongst golden fields.

Anna ate her meal like a ravenous animal, but he didn't

miss the way she occasionally flicked her gaze to him, waiting for him to announce his intentions.

If he chose to remain with her, to learn the skills of the blade, and perhaps thievery too, his life would change forever. She was cold to him more often than not, but he couldn't forget the way she'd stayed behind to fight the mercenaries, urging him to run away. In the short time since they'd met, Anna had saved his life more than once, and he liked to believe he'd saved hers too, even if he'd been the one to endanger her to begin with. He liked to think it made them friends, though he knew Anna was likely never to admit it.

Still, life with her would at least be interesting, and he'd be his own man for once, indebted to no one.

"Well?" Anna questioned, scraping the last remnants of food from her plate. "Have you made up your mind?"

He took a deep breath. This one decision would likely decide his fate for years to come.

Slowly, a smile crept across his face. "When do we leave? I'd rather like to get started on my new life of adventure."

She grinned, and he found he enjoyed the expression far more than her scowl. "First thing in the morning, but...are you sure? You'll have to get your hands dirty from time to time, and I won't have you looking down on me."

He nodded as the reality of his choice sank in, realizing that he never could have truly considered the alternative. He'd had a taste of adventure. There was no going back. "Well," he began with a wry grin, "*someone* has to keep you from killing everyone."

She snorted, then lifted her hand to call the barmaid over to refill her mug of tea. They finished their meals and relaxed for the rest of the day like nothing had happened, but Kai didn't miss the way Anna smiled whenever she thought he wasn't looking, and he was quite sure she didn't miss him doing the same.

The End

49759973R00226

Made in the USA
Columbia, SC
26 January 2019